HUNTING PARTY

Book One of The Serrano Legacy

Elizabeth Moon

orbit

An *Orbit* Book

First published in Great Britain by Orbit 1999
Reprinted 1999, 2000

Copyright © 1993 by Elizabeth Moon

The moral right of the author has been asserted.

A CIP catalogue record for this book
is available from the British Library.

ISBN 1 85723 881 8

Printed and bound in Great Britain by
Mackays of Chatham PLC, Chatham, Kent

Orbit
A Division of
Little, Brown and Company (UK)
Brettenham House
Lancaster Place
London WC2E 7EN

Elizabeth Moon joined the US Marine Corps in 1968, reaching the rank of 1st Lieutenant during active duty. She has also earned degrees in history and biology, run for public office and been a columnist on her local newspaper. She lives near Austin, Texas, with her husband and their son.

Dedication

In memory of Dorothy Iola Jamerson Norris, 1913-1990, and Lida Sloan Moon, 1911-1992: my mother and my mother-in-law. Two women who proved with their lives, and in their children, that single parents can be good parents, and that "values" are more than campaign slogans. They lived what others preach. And for all the single parents, past and present, whose hard work and good values have been slandered by those who never faced the problems they face.

Acknowledgements

Thanks to those who encouraged this project: Alexis and Laurie, who began the chase by saying "Why *not* fox hunting and spaceships?"; Margaret, who helped retrieve scattered bits after the great computer crash; the several patient friends who read drafts and pointed out logic problems; my husband Richard, who prefers new chapters to hot meals and a neat house; my son Michael, who has finally learned to let me alone until the oven timer buzzes (as long as it's not more than fifteen minutes). The good people at Vic's Grocery — Vic, Martha, John, Debbie, and Penny — whose interest and support keep the absentminded writer from forgetting the milk, bread, and other necessities of life — with special thanks this time to Vic Kysor, Jr., who in a conversation across the meat counter in his father's grocery store created a character and solved a problem for me. Of course the remaining flaws are my fault — even the best helpers can't do it all.

✧ Chapter One

Heris Serrano went from her room in the small but respectable dockside hotel on Rockhouse Station to the berth of her new command convinced that she looked like an idiot. No one laughed aloud, but that only meant the bystanders had chosen to snicker later rather than risk immediate confrontation with an ex-Regular Space Services officer on the beach.

Heris kept her eyes away from any of those who might be contemplating humor, the dockside traffic of the commercial district. Her ears burned; she could feel the glances raking her back. She would not have changed her military posture even if she could have walked any other way; she had been R.S.S. from birth or before, daughter of officers, admirals' granddaughter and niece, a service family for all the generations anyone bothered to count. Even that miserable first year at the Academy had seemed familiar, almost homey: she had heard the stories from parents, uncles, aunts, all her life.

And here she was, tricked out in enough gold braid and color to satisfy a planet-bound admiral from one of the minor principalities, all because of the whims of a rich old woman with more money than sense. They had to be laughing behind her back, those merchanter officers and crewmen who didn't meet her eyes, who went about their business as if purple and scarlet were normal uniform colors, as if two sleeves covered with gold rings didn't look ridiculous, as if the rim of gold and green striped cord around collar, lapels, and cuffs didn't tell everyone that an R.S.S. officer had descended to the level of carting wealthy eccentrics on pleasure jaunts in something far more like a mansion than a spacefaring ship.

Commercial dockside ended abruptly at a scarred gray wall with a lockgate in it. Heris inserted her card; the barred gate slid aside, then closed behind her, leaving her caged between the bars behind and a steel door with a thick window. Another keyslot; this time her card produced a human door-opener, who swung the door aside and held out his hand for her papers. She handed over the neat packet civilian life required. Master's license, certifications in five specialties, Imperial ID, military record (abbreviated; only the unclassified bones), letters of recommendation, and — what mattered most here — Lady Cecelia de Marktos's seal of employment. The human — Station Security or Garond Family, Heris did not know which — ran a handscanner over this last, and replaced the entire pile in its file cover before handing it back to her.

"Welcome to North, Captain Serrano," the man said, with no inflection of sarcasm. "May I be of assistance?"

Her throat closed a moment, remembering the words she would have heard if she had gone through a similar lockgate on the other side of the commercial docks, where sleek gray R.S.S. cruisers nuzzled the Station side by side. Where her gray uniform with its glowing insignia would have received crisp salutes, and the welcome due a comrade in arms. "Welcome to the Fleet," she would have heard, a greeting used anywhere, anytime, they came together away from civilians. But she could not go back there, back where her entire past would wrap around her. She had resigned her commission. She would never hear those words again.

"No, thank you," she said quietly. "I know where the ship is." She would not say its name yet, though it was her new command. . . . She had grown up with ships named for battles, for monsters, for older ships with long histories. She could not yet say she commanded *Sweet Delight*.

North, on all Stations, defined the environs of aristocracy. Wealth and privilege could be found anywhere, in the R.S.S. as well as the commercial docks, but always near something else. Here was nothing but wealth, and its servants. This deck had carpeted walkways, not extruded plastic sheeting; the shops had no signs, only house emblems. Each docking bay had its own lockgate, enclosing two large rooms: one marked "Service Entrance," lined with racks and shelving for provisions delivered, and the other furnished luxuriously as a reception salon for going-away parties. Heris's card in the slot produced another human door-opener, this time a servant in livery, who ushered her into the salon. Heris made her way between overstuffed sofas and chairs covered in lavender plush and piled with pillows in garish colors, between low black tables and pedestals supporting what were probably priceless works of art, though to her eye, they looked like globs of melted space debris after a battle.

The actual docking tube lay unguarded. Heris frowned. Surely even civilians had someone watching the ship's main hatch, even with the security of a lockgate on the dock itself. She paused before stepping over the line that made the legal division between dock and ship. The lavender plush lining of the access tube hid all the vital umbilicals that connected the ship to Station life support. Unsafe, Heris thought, as she had thought on her earlier interview visit. Those lines should be visible. Surely even civilians had regulations to follow.

Underfoot, the lavender plush carpet felt five centimeters thick. A warm breath of air puffed out of the ship itself, a warm breath flavored not with the spice she remembered from the interview, but with the sour stench of the morning after a very large night before. Her nose wrinkled; she could feel her back stiffening. It might be someone else's ship *in principle*, but she did not allow a dirty mess on any ship she commanded — and would not now. She came out of the access tube into a family row; the tube's privacy shield had kept her from hearing it until she stepped across the barrier. Heris took in the situation at a glance. One tall, angular, gray-haired woman with a loud · voice: her employer. Three sulky, overdressed young men that Heris would not have had on her ship, and their obvious girlfriends . . . all rumpled, and one still passed out on a lavender couch that matched the plush carpet and walls. Streaks of vomit stained its smooth velour. As she came through the barrier, the chestnut-haired youth with the ruffled shirt answered a final blast from the older woman with a whined "But, Aunt Cecelia — it's not *fair*."

What was "not fair" was that rich spoiled brats like him hadn't had the nonsense taken out of them in boot camp, Heris thought. She smiled her normal good-morning-bridge smile at her employer and said, "Good morning, milady."

The youths — all but the unconscious snorer on the couch — stared; Heris could feel her ears going hot and ignored them, still smiling at Cecelia Artemisia Veronica Penelope, heiress of more titles than anyone needed, let alone more money. "Ah," said that lady, restored to instant unruffled calm by the appearance of someone to whom it meant something. "Captain Serrano. How nice to have you aboard. Our departure will be delayed, but only briefly" — here she looked at the chestnut-haired youth — "until my nephew is settled. I presume your things are already aboard?"

"Sent ahead, milady," Heris said.

"Good. Then Bates will show you to your quarters." Bates materialized from some angle of corridor and nodded at Heris. Heris wondered if she would be introduced to the nephew now or later; she was sure she could take that pout from his lips if given the chance. But she wouldn't get the chance. She followed Bates — tall, elegant, so much the butler of the screen and stage it was hard to believe him real — down the carpeted passage to her suite. She would rather have gone to the bridge. Not this bridge, but the bridge of the *Rapier* or even a lowly maintenance tug.

Bates stood aside at her door. "If the captain wishes to rekey the locks now . . . ?"

She looked at that impassive face. Did he mean to imply that they had thieves on board? That someone might violate the privacy of her quarters? The *captain's* quarters? She had thought she knew how far down the scale she'd fallen, to become a rich lady's yacht captain, but she had not conceived of needing to lock her quarters. "Thank you," she said, as if it had been her idea. Bates touched a magnetic wand to the lockfaces; she put her hand on each one. After a moment, the doorcall's pleasant anonymous voice said, "Name, please?" and she gave her name; the doorcall chimed once and said, "Welcome home, Captain Serrano." Bates handed her a fat ring of wands.

"These are the rekeying wands for ship's crew and all the operating compartments. They're all coded; you'll find the full architectural schematics loaded on your desk display. The crew will await your arrival on the bridge, at your convenience."

She didn't even know if she could ask Bates to tell the crew when to expect her, or if that was something household staff never did. She had already discovered that the house staff and the ship crew had very little to do with each other.

"I could just pass the word to Mr. Gavin, the engineer," Bates said, almost apologetically. "Since Captain Olin left" — Captain Olin, Heris knew, had been fired — "Lady Cecelia has often asked me to speak to Mr. Gavin."

"Thank you," Heris said. "One hour." She glanced at the room's chronometer, a civilian model which she would replace with the one in her luggage.

"Philip will escort you," Bates said.

She opened her mouth to say it was not necessary — even in this perfumed and padded travesty of a ship she could find the bridge by herself — but instead said, "Thank you" once more. She would not challenge their assumptions yet.

Her master's certificate went into the mounting plaque on the wall; her other papers went into the desk. Her luggage — she had asked that it not be unpacked — cluttered one corner of her office. Beyond that was a smaller room, then the bathroom — her mouth quirked as she forced herself to call it that. And beyond that, her bedroom. A cubage larger than an admiral would have on most ships, and far larger than anyone of her rank ever had, even on a Station. A suite, part of the price being paid to lure a real spacer, a real captain, into this kind of work.

In the hour she had unpacked her few necessary clothes, her books, her reference data cubes, and made sure that the desk display would handle them. The chronometer on the wall now showed Service Standard time as well as ship's time and Station time, and had the familiar overlapping segments of color to delineate four-, six-, and eight-hour watches. She had reviewed the crew bios in the desk display. And she had shrugged away her regrets. It was all over now, all those years of service, all her family's traditions; from now on, she was Heris Serrano, captain of a yacht, and she would make the best of it.

And they wouldn't know what hit them.

Some of them suspected within moments of her arrival on the bridge. Whatever decorator had chosen all the lavender and teal furnishings of the rest of the ship, the bridge remained functional, if almost toylike in its bright, shiny, compactness. The crew had to squeeze in uncomfortably; Heris noticed who squeezed in next to whom, and who wished this were over. They had heard, no doubt. They could see what they could see; she might be wearing purple and scarlet, but she had the look, and knew she had it; all those generations of command came out her eyes.

She met theirs. Blue, gray, brown, black, green, hazel: clear, hazy, worried, frightened, challenging. Mr. Gavin, the engineer — thin, almost wispy, and graying — had announced, "Captain on the bridge" in a voice that squeaked. Navigation First, all too perky, was female, and young, and standing close to Communications First, who had spots and the slightly adenoidal look that Heris had found in the best comm techs on any ship. The moles — environmental techs, so-called everywhere from their need to crawl through pipes — glowered at the back. They must have suspected she'd seen the ship's records already. Moles never believed that strange smells in the air were their fault; they were convinced that other people, careless people, put the wrong things down the wrong pipe and caused the trouble. Gavin's junior engineering techs, distancing themselves from the moles, tried to look squeaky-clean and bright. Heris had read their records; one of them had failed the third-class certificate four times. The other juniors — Navigation's sour-faced paunchy male and Communications' wispy female — were clearly picked up at bargain rates for off-primeshift work.

Heris began, as always on a new ship, with generalities. Let them relax; let them realize she wasn't stupid, crazy, or vicious. Then . . . "Now about emergency drills," she said, when she'd seen the relaxation. "I see you've had no drills since docking here. Why is that, Mr. Gavin?"

"Well, Captain . . . after Captain Olin left, I didn't like to seem — you know — like I was taking liberties above my station."

"I see. And before that, I notice that there had been no drills since the last planetfall. That was Captain Olin's decision, I suppose." From Gavin's expression, that was not the reason, but he went along gratefully.

"Yes, Captain, that would be it. He was the captain, after all." Someone stirred, in the back, but they were so crammed together she couldn't be sure who it was. She would find out. She smiled at them, suddenly happy. It might be only a yacht, but it was a ship, and it was *her* ship.

"We will have drills," she said, and waited a moment for that to sink in. "Emergency drills save lives. I expect all you Firsts to ready your divisions."

"We surely can't have time for a drill before launch!" That was the sour-faced Navigation Second. She stared at him until he blushed and said, "Captain . . . sorry, ma'am."

"It depends," she said, without commenting on his breach of manners. "I know you're all readying for launch, but I would like a word here with the pilot and Nav First."

They edged out of the cramped space; she knew the muttering would start as soon as they cleared the hatch. Ignoring that, she fixed the Navigation First with a firm glance. "Sirkin, isn't it?"

"Yes, Captain." Brisk, bright-eyed . . . Heris hoped she was as good as she looked. "Brigdis Sirkin, Lalos Colony."

"Yes, I saw your file. Impressive qualification exam." Sirkin had topped the list with a perfect score, rare even in R.S.S. trained personnel. The younger woman blushed and grinned. "But what I want to know is whether you plotted the final approach from Dunlin to here." The way she said it could lead either way; she wanted to see Sirkin's reaction.

A deeper blush. "No, Captain, I didn't . . . not entirely, that is."

"Umm. I wondered why someone who'd swept the exam would choose such an inefficient solution. Tell me about it."

"Well . . . ma'am . . . Captain Olin was a good captain, and I'm not saying anything against him, but he liked to . . . to do things a certain way."

Heris glanced at the pilot. Plisson, his tag said; he had been another rich lady's pilot before he came here. "Did you have anything to do with it?" she asked.

The pilot shot Sirkin an angry glance. "She thinks she can shave time to the bone," he said. "It's like she never heard of flux-storms. I guess you could call it efficient, if you're on a warship, but I wasn't hired to kill milady."

"Ah. So you thought Sirkin's original course dangerous, and Captain Olin backed you?"

"Well . . . yes, Captain. And I expect you'll stick with her, being as you're spacefleet trained."

Heris grinned at him; his jaw sagged in surprise. "I don't like getting smeared across space any better than anyone else," she said. "But I've reviewed Sirkin's work only as combined with yours and Captain Olin's. Sirkin, what was your original course here?"

"It's in the NavComp, Captain; shall I direct it to your desktop?"

"If you please. I'll look it over, see if I think you're dangerous or not. Did you ever have any spacefleet time, Plisson?"

"No, Captain." The way he said it, he considered it worse than downside duty. She wasn't sure she wanted a half-hearted first pilot.

"Then I suggest you withdraw your judgment of R.S.S. operations until you see some. War is dangerous enough without adding recklessness to it; I'll expect professional performance from both you and Navigator Sirkin." She turned to go, then turned back, surprising on their faces the expression she had hoped to find. "And by the way, you may expect drills; space is less forgiving than I am of sloppy technique."

Lady Cecelia noticed the shadow in the tube only a moment before her new captain came aboard. She could have wished for less promptness. She would have preferred to finish reaming out her nephew and the residue of his going-away party in the decent privacy afforded by her household staff. Bates knew better than to stick his nose in at a time like this.

But the woman was ex-military, and not very ex- by her carriage and expression. Of course she would not be late; even her hair and toenails probably grew on schedule. Cecelia wanted to throttle the condescension off the dark face that rose serene above the purple and scarlet uniform. No doubt she had no nephews, or if she did they were being lovingly brought up in boot camp somewhere. She probably thought it would be easy to remake Ronnie and his set. Whereas Cecelia had known, from the moment of Ronnie's birth, that he was destined to be a spoiled brat. Charming, bright enough if he bothered, handsome to the point of dangerousness with that thick wavy chestnut hair, those hazel eyes, that remaining dimple — but spoiled rotten by his family and everyone else.

"But it's not *fair*," he whined now. He had expected her to let them all travel with him, all twenty or so of his favorites among his fellow officers and their sweethearts of both sexes. She ignored that, smiled at her new captain, thinking, *Don't you dare laugh at me, you little blot*, and called Bates to take the captain to her quarters. And away she went, impossibly bright-eyed for this hour of the morning (no adolescent partying had disturbed *her* sleep), her trim figure making the girls in the room look like haggard barflies. Which they weren't, really. It was terrible what girls did these days, but these were decent girls, of reasonably nice families. Nothing like hers, or Ronnie's (except Bubbles, the snoring one, and the present cause of dissension), but nice enough.

With a last glance at the captain's retreating form, she turned back to Ronnie. "What is not fair, young man, is that you are intruding on *my* life, taking up space on my yacht, making my staff work harder, and all because you lacked the common sense to keep your mouth shut about things which no gentleman discusses."

Sulky. He had been sulky at one, at two; his parents had doted on his adorable tantrums, his big lower lip. He was sulky now, and she did not dote on the lip or the tongue behind it. "She said I was better. It's not fair that I'm getting sent away, when she's the one who said it. She wanted to be with me —"

"She said it to you, in the confidence of the bedroom." Surely someone had already told him this. Why should she have to explain? "And you don't even know if she *meant* it, or if she says it to everyone."

"Of course she meant it!" Young male pride, stung, flushed his cheeks and drove sulkiness into temper. "I *am* better."

"I won't argue," Cecelia said. "I will only remind you that you may be better in bed with the prince's favorite singer, but you are now on my yacht, by order of your father and the king, and the singer is stuck with the prince." Her pun got through to her a moment before Ronnie caught it, and she shook her finger at him. "Literally and figuratively: you're here, and he's there, and you've gained nothing by blabbing except whatever momentary amusement you shared with your barracks-mates." He chuckled, and the odious George — who had well earned the nickname everyone in society knew — snickered. Cecelia knew the odious George's father fairly well, and dismissed the snicker as an unconscious copy of his father's courtroom manner. She supposed it went over well in the junior mess of the Royal Space Service, where the young sprouts of aristocracy and wealth flaunted their boughten commissions in the intervals of leave and training. "You're the one who talked," she said, ignoring the side glances of her nephew and his crony. "The . . . er . . . lady didn't. Therefore you are in trouble, and you are sent away, and it's my misfortune that I happened to be near enough to serve your father's purpose." He opened his mouth to say something else she was sure she would not want to hear, and she went on, inexorably. "It's better than it could have been, young Ronald, as you will see when you quit feeling sorry for yourself. And I am stretching my generosity to let you bring these" — she waved her hand at the others, — "when it crowds my ship and wastes my time. If it weren't that Bubbles and Buttons were going to Bunny's anyway —"

"Well — in fact they don't want to go —"

"Nonsense. I've already sent word I'm bringing them. A season in the field will do you all immense good." She gave him another lengthy stare. "And I don't want any of you sneaking offship to cause trouble on the Station before we launch. It's bad enough having to wait for your luggage; I shall have your father pay the reset fees for changing the launch schedule. I hope he takes it out of your allowance."

"But that's not —" She held up her hand before "fair" could emerge and decided to drop her own bombshell now.

"And by the way, my new captain is ex-*Regular* Space Service, so don't try any of your tricks with *her*. She could probably tie you all in knots without trying." Cecelia turned on her heel and walked out, satisfied that she had given them something besides her hard-heartedness to think about.

It was too bad, really. She lived on her yacht precisely so as to avoid family complications, just as she had avoided marriage and political service. They could have found some other way to keep Ronnie out of the capital for a year or so. They didn't have to use her, as if she were a handy piece of furniture. But that was Berenice all over again: big sisters existed to be of service to the beauty of the family.

Stores. She would have to check with Bates to be sure they had ordered enough additional food — after last night, she suspected they might need more. Young people did *eat* so, when they ate. She reached her own suite with relief. That miserable decorator Berenice had sent her to insisted on doing the whole ship in lavender and teal, with touches of acid green and cream, but she had not let him in here. Perhaps the young people did prefer lavender plush, but she hated it. Here in her own rooms, she could have it her way. Brighter colors, polished wood, carved chairs piled with pillows.

She paused at her desk. Inlaid wood made a pattern of vines and flowers; until she pressed the central blossom, it could have passed for an antique of Old Earth. The desktop cleared, showing the floorplan of that deck, with ghostly shadows of the others. A cluster of dots showed Ronnie and friends, back in the lounge. A dot in her bedroom; that would be Myrtis, her maid. A dot for the captain, in her quarters; a moving dot that must be Bates, coming back. She touched her finger to that one, and his voice came out of the desk speaker.

"Yes, madam?"

"Have Cook check the quantities Ronnie and his friends consumed last night; they seem to eat quite a lot. . . ."

"Cook has estimated an additional fifteen percent over your orders yesterday, madam, and has the purchase order ready for your stamp."

"Thank you, Bates." She might have known. They were usually two steps ahead of her — but that was their duty. She flicked up the lower service deck on the display, found Cook's dot, and touched it. Cook transferred the purchase order to her desktop, and she looked at it. Even with six additional people aboard, it looked like enough to feed them all three times over. It would serve them right, she thought, if she made them eat survival rations until they got to Bunny's. Certainly it would cost less and take up less room. Cook had pointed out that they'd need to air up two more refrigeration units and set out another full section of 'ponics.

That would start another argument between crewside and staffside. The environmental techs were ship's crew, under the captain's command; Cecelia knew better than to interfere with her captain's crew. But that part of 'ponics devoted to the kitchen came under the heading of "gardening," which meant staff — her staff. Felix, head gardener, and two boys (one female), kept her private solarium in fresh flowers and Cook supplied with fresh vegetables. Felix and the environmental techs always got into some hassle which required her decision — one of the things she had not liked about her former captain was his tendency to let things slide until she had to quell an incipient riot in staff.

She found Felix's icon, touched it, and told him about the 'ponics section. He wanted to use half of it for a new set of exotics he'd bought seedstock for; the pictures of the so-called vegetables didn't impress her. Felix insisted, though, that if he could have seed available when they arrived at Bunny's, he could trade with Bunny's ferocious head gardener for her favorite (and rarest) mushrooms. Cecelia shrugged; Ronnie and his pals could eat the things she didn't like.

"And what you tell the moles, eh?" he said finally, having won his main point. "You got to let them know it's okay, whatever I grow."

"I will tell Captain Serrano, our new captain, that I've approved your use of an additional 'ponics section for fresh produce."

"They bother me, I'll send 'em the halobeets," Felix said. He would, too. He had done it before, when displeased with someone. A genius of his type — but like most such geniuses, a trifle tempery. She put up with him for the luscious fruits and fresh vegetables, the abundant flowers, which so amazed those who came to dinner. . . . No other yacht she knew of was completely self-sufficient in fresh produce.

She looked again for the captain's icon, and found it moving toward the bridge. Best not interrupt her now; she would have had the crew assembled. Cecelia's finger hovered over the control. . . . She could easily listen in on the captain's first briefing . . . but she decided against it. Instead, she routed a message to the captain's desk about the 'ponics, and called up a credit status.

The figures meant little to her; the reality was that she could afford to buy anything for sale on Rockhouse two or three times over. The desktop offered a bright-colored graphic which showed how much more she was spending to transport herself and six young people compared to herself alone. It didn't matter, and Berenice had transferred stock to cover it anyway. She called up Ronnie's status, and pursed her lips. Berenice had put him on the silver family line, and he had already used it. Hardin's Clothiers, Vetris Accessories, Spaulding . . . Cecelia whistled. He had started with two cubes of storage, and at this rate would need another two.

Her desk chimed. "Aunt Cecelia?" came the plaintive voice. "Please — I need to talk to you."

Hardly, she thought. He needed to *listen* to her. "Ah, Ronnie. Very good — I meant to ask you, did you bring your hunting tackle?"

"My . . . uh . . . what?"

"Your riding clothes, your saddles —"

"I — *no!* Of course not. Aunt Cecelia, just because you're crazy enough to ride big stupid animals across rocks and mud —"

"I presumed," said Cecelia, overriding his voice with a surge of glee, "that that was your rather large order at Hardin's and Vetris's and Spaulding's. But since it wasn't, perhaps you'd return some of that foppery, whatever it was, and get yourself some decent riding kit. We are going to Bunny's, as you know, for the season, and since I'm saddled with you, you might as well saddle a horse and learn something useful." She felt good about the pun; puns usually came to her four hours too late, if at all.

The fashion in invective, she was happy to discover, had swung once more from the rough crudities copied from the lower classes to an entertaining polysyllabic baroque style. When Ronnie ran out of breath (which happened more quickly, she noted, with the longer words and phrases), she interrupted again, before he could start another rampage.

"I do not care that you do not like horses, or riding, or that none of your set consider hunting a reasonable or enjoyable pastime. I do not care if you are miserable for the entire year of your exile. You may sulk in your cabin if you like — you will certainly not sulk in mine, or interfere with my pleasure one bit more than I can help. And if you do not order yourself the proper clothes, saddles, and so on, I shall do it for you and charge it to your account." Although it would really make sense to wait until they were at Bunny's — all the really good saddlers came there for the season. But her blood was up. So, it seemed, was his. She could order what she liked, he said angrily, but he was not about to pretend to copy the amusements of a horse-faced old spinster with more money than sense, and he would be damned if she ever found him on a horse chasing some innocent helpless animal across the dripping fields.

"If you think the fox is either innocent or helpless, young Ronald, you are more foolish than I think." She was not sure which of them broke the connection. She did not care. She called her personal assistant at Spaulding's and arranged everything as she wished — of course they knew all his measurements already, and of course they were happy to help a wealthy aunt surprise an almost-as-wealthy nephew. In a final burst of pique, she put the bill on her own account, and not Berenice's. . . . She wanted no questions from the doting mother who had let the brat become so useless.

✦ Chapter Two

Heris led the way into her cabin, wondering if civilians had any concept of shipboard courtesy. Would they know enough to stay on their side of the office? Sirkin did; she stood across the desk as Heris called up the files on the desk display, looking young and earnest.

She looked at the course Sirkin had originally planned. Direct, reasonable flux levels, no abrupt course changes, adequate clearance of the mapped obstacles. It was close to the course she would have selected, although R.S.S. ships could and did shave the clearance margins in the interest of speed.

"And Captain Olin disapproved this course? Why?"

"He said it was too risky. Here —" Sirkin laid her finger on the display, and it enlarged to show finer detail. "He claimed that coming this close to T-77 with a flux of 0.06 was suicidal. I asked him why, and he said he was captain and I'd learn better in time."

"Hmm." Heris leaned over the display. "Did you look up T-77 in the reference library?"

"Yes, ma'am." Heris looked up at the younger woman — then remembered that it might be legitimate civilian usage. The R.S.S. used "sir" for either sex — it meant respect, not recognition of one's chromosome type. Sirkin seemed respectful and attentive. "Baird and Logan said that T-77 is a gravitational anomaly, nothing more. Ciro speculates that it's a burnt-out star. But all the references agree that it's not as dangerous as Gumma's Tangle, and it's perfectly safe to transit that at a flux of 0.2. I *was* being conservative." That had the bite of old resentment. Heris shook her head.

"Captain Olin must have had some reason. Your

relative velocity would have been quite low, there — did you suggest boosting your flux and achieving a higher V?"

"No, ma'am. He said it was dangerous at 0.06; boosting the flux would make it worse —"

"If he meant a flux/mass interaction. That's not the only danger out there." She chewed her lip, thinking. She hadn't been in that area for a long time; she wished she had access to R.S.S. charts and intelligence data.

"But why didn't he say so?" Sirkin had flushed, which made her look even younger. "I could have redone it for a higher flux —"

"He didn't want to go anywhere near T-77," Heris said. "Let's see what else he didn't want to go near." She looked at the rest of Sirkin's course, comparing it to Olin's, and calling up references when needed. Slowly, she felt her way into Olin's logic. "He didn't want to go near any of the low-danger obstacles, did he? Made you go clear around Cumber's Finger, instead of taking that short Wedding Ring hop — and that's a safe hop everyone takes. Made you wander over here — and why?" She looked up, to meet the same confusion in Sirkin's expression. "Did Lady Cecelia have a preferred arrival time? Did she ask him to be here on a certain day?"

Sirkin nodded. "She had wanted to be here eight days before we arrived, for some kind of family party. Olin told her he couldn't make it; it's one reason she wanted a new captain. She said he was too slow."

"You heard her?" Heris let her brows rise.

Sirkin turned red. "Well . . . I overheard it. I mean, Tonni over on the staff side, he told Engineering, and Mr. Gavin told me."

"Staff side . . ." Heris said.

"You know. There's the household staff, with Bates on top, and there's the ship's crew, with the captain — with you — on top. We're not supposed to mix much, but at certain levels we have to. Our moles are always getting into rows with milady's gardeners."

Heris felt she'd fallen into a farce of some kind. Gardeners aboard ship? But she couldn't let this young woman sense her confusion. "When we say 'staff,' we mean non-line officers," she said, as if it had been a confusion of terms.

"Oh." Sirkin clearly had no idea what that meant, and Heris let it pass. Far more important was getting this ship ready to travel. She could ask Sirkin, but she should learn more about the rest of the crew, and inspections would do just that. She looked back at Olin's chosen route and shook her head.

"I wonder . . . it's as if he knew something about these areas not listed in the references." She wondered what. There were always rumors about "robbers' coasts" and "pirate dens" to excuse ships that showed up late or missing cargo. But those were just rumors . . . weren't they? Olin had chosen to skirt more dangerous — according to the references — points more closely; he had shaved past T-89 inside the line she'd have taken with a cruiser. Of course a cruiser massed more. Slow on the first leg of the trip, hanging about for a long time . . . then racing through the middle section, direct and sure . . . then dodging about again at the end. Smuggling came to mind, but she controlled her expression. Later she could figure out what, and with whom, Captain Olin had been smuggling.

"And you're the newest crew member? What made you decide on this job rather than another?"

Sirkin blushed. "Well . . . it was a . . . friend of mine." From the blush and tone of voice, a lover. Heris looked again: blue eyes, brown hair, slender, unremarkable face. Just very young, and very emotional.

"Aboard this ship?" She kept her fingers crossed.

"No, ma'am. She's back at school — a third-year in ship systems maintenance. If I'd signed with a corporate ship, they'd have expected me to stay with them forever." Not really forever, Heris knew, but to the young even the basic five- and ten-year contracts sounded permanent. "When she graduates — she's not exactly at the top of her class — we wanted to be together, same ship or at least same company. . . ."

"So this is a temporary, until she graduates?"

"Yes, ma'am. But I'm not treating it any less seriously."

That in the earnest tone of the very young. Heris allowed herself to smile.

"I should hope not. When are you planning to leave Lady Cecelia?"

"It depends, really. She'll graduate while we're at that fox-hunting place — at Sirialis, I mean." Sirkin's fingers twitched. "Lady Cecelia expects to get back to the Cassian System about six local months after that, and she won't take offplanet work until she hears from me."

You hope, thought Heris. She'd seen more than one juvenile romance collapse when a partner was offplanet for a year or more. "You'll have to keep your mind on your duties," she said. "It's natural to worry about her, but — "

"Oh, I don't worry about her," Sirkin said. "She can take care of herself. And I won't be distracted."

Heris nodded, hoping they hadn't sworn vows of exclusion or anything silly like that. Those were the ones who invariably got an earnest message cube at the next port, with the defaulting lover explaining what happened at excruciating length. In her experience, it always happened to the best of the younglings in her crew. "Good. Now, I plan to have the crew cross-train in other disciplines — would you prefer another bridge assignment, or something more hands-on?"

Sirkin grinned, and Heris was almost afraid she'd say *How fun* — but she didn't. "Anything you wish, Captain. I had two semesters of drive theory and one of maintenance, but I also had a double minor in Communications and computer theory." *Very* bright girl, if she'd topped out in her nav classes and done that as well. Heris approved.

"We'll try you in communications and the more practical side of shipboard computing systems, then. That should keep you busy enough."

"Yes, ma'am."

"That's all, then." With a last respectful nod, Sirkin left. No salute. Heris refused to give in to the wave of nostalgia she felt; she shrugged it away physically and drew a deep steady breath. No more salutes, no more old friends she could call on to find out, for example, what was known about the members of her new crew. She might have that later, as she made friends in the Captains Guild, but not now.

And at the moment, that was her most pressing need: knowledge. According to the ship's record, all the crew but one had been supplied by the same employment agency. A good one: she had chosen to sign with them herself because of their reputation; they supplied crew to major commercial lines and trading corporations. Lady Cecelia was part of an important family; surely they were not sending her their dregs. . . . Yet she had the feeling that at least half these people were below average. She hadn't expected that, not with the wages Lady Cecelia had offered her, and was paying the crew. She should have gotten more for her money. Sirkin was the only really top qualifier, just going by their records — which she didn't. Records only told so much.

She punched up the local office of Usmerdanz, and worked her way up the levels until she found someone she could really talk to. "Captain Serrano . . . yes." The owner of that silky voice had found her reference in the file, she could tell. "We . . . ah . . . placed you with Lady Cecelia —"

"Yes," she said, interrupting. "I notice that Usmerdanz also placed other crew members, and I was wondering if you could give me some details."

"All pertinent details *should* be in the ship files," the voice said, with an edge as if a knife lay under the silk. From their point of view, *she* was the unknown quantity; she had been on their list less than a month, and there would always be questions about someone of her rank who resigned a commission without explanation. "Surely Captain Olin left the files open-keyed. . . ."

"I've accessed the ship files," Heris said. "But I find nothing equivalent to our — to the Space Service's fitness reports. Are periodic evaluations handled by the captain aboard or . . . ?"

"Oh." The knife edge receded behind the silk again. "Well . . . there's no established schedule, not really. In the commercial ships, of course, there's always some sort of corporate policy, but not on private yachts. Usually the captain keeps some sort of reports. You found nothing?"

"Nothing," Heris said. "Just the data that might have been in the original applications. I thought perhaps you —"

"Oh, no." The voice interrupted her this time. "We don't keep track of that sort of thing at all." Far from it, the tone said. After all, one could hardly recommend someone known to have problems on a previous vessel; best not to know. Heris had known Service people with the same attitude. "If there's nothing in the ship files," the voice went on, "then I'm afraid we can't help you. We could supply incomplete data on education, background — but nothing more than that. Sorry . . ."

Before the silken-voiced supervisor could disconnect, Heris asked a quick question. "How do you choose which to recommend to which employers?" A long silence followed.

"How do we *what*?" No silk remained; the voice sounded angry.

"I noticed that only Sirkin — the newest crew member — ranked particularly high in her class, and she's told me she was looking for a short-term job on a yacht for personal reasons. The others generally rank in the middle quartiles. Yet Lady Cecelia's paying top wages; I wondered why you weren't recommending these positions to your most qualified applicants."

"Are you accusing us," the voice said, all steel edge now, "of sending Lady Cecelia unqualified crew members?"

"Not at all," said Heris, although she suspected exactly that. "But you aren't sending her your cream, are you?"

"We sent *you*," the voice replied.

"Exactly," Heris said. "I know I'm not on the top of your list of captains . . . and I shouldn't be." As she had hoped, that admission soothed some of the anger in the voice on the com.

"Well. That's true. I suppose." Heris waited through some audible huffing and muttering, and then the voice went on. "It's like this, Captain Serrano. There's good people — qualified people — who aren't right for every opening. You know what I mean; surely you had people even in the R.S.S. who were good, solid, dependable performers in ordinary circumstances, but you wouldn't want to have them in charge of a cruiser in battle."

"That's true," Heris said, as if she'd never thought of it herself.

"We supply crews to all sorts of people. We tend to hold out our best — our cream, as you said — for the positions where it matters most. It's true that Lady Cecelia is a valued client, and her family is important, but . . . it's not like that yacht is the flagship of Geron Corporation, is it?"

"Not at all."

"She's got a fine ship, relatively new, has it refitted at the right intervals, spares no expense in maintenance, travels safe routes at reasonable speeds. . . . She doesn't need someone who can cope with a twenty-thousand passenger colonial transport, or maneuvering in a convoy of freighters. Other people do. And her requirements dovetail nicely; we suggest for private yachts crew who are stable emotionally, perhaps a little sedate — " Lazy, thought Heris, could be substituted for that euphemism. No initiative. "Obedient, willing to adapt to a variable schedule."

"I see," Heris said, intentionally cheerful. She did see; she did not like what it said about the agency's attitude towards her, or towards her employer. She was sure Lady Cecelia had never been told that her safety was less important than that of a load of frozen embryos or bulk chemicals. She had trusted the agency, and the agency had sent her junk. It had not occurred to Heris before that very rich people could have junk foisted off on them so easily. "Thank you anyway," she said, as if none of that had passed through her mind. "I realize things are different in civilian life; I'll just have to adjust."

"I'm sure you'll do very well," the voice said, once more wrapped in its silken overtones. It wanted to be pleased with her, wanted Lady Cecelia to be pleased with her — wanted everyone to be pleased with everything, for that matter.

Heris herself was not at all pleased by anything at the

moment, but she knew she would adjust, though not the way the agency intended. She would pull this crew up to some decent standard; she would exceed the agency's low expectations and make of Lady Cecelia's yacht a ship any captain could take pride in. Even working with the slack crew she'd been given. She knew Lady Cecelia wanted as speedy a departure as possible, but the delay her nephew caused gave Heris just enough time to interview each member of her crew. Those short, five-minute meetings confirmed her original feeling that most of the crew were past whatever prime they'd had. At least the ship was good: a sound hull, components purchased from all the right places. Regular maintenance at the best refitting docks. *Like the crew*, her instincts muttered. Heris blinked at the screen on her desk, fighting off worry. Surely Lady Cecelia hadn't been cheated on everything.

Departure: their slot in the schedule came late in third shift. Lady Cecelia had already sent word that she preferred to sleep through undockings. Heris could understand that; she did too, on ships she didn't captain. By this time, the ship's own systems were all up and running; by law, a ship must test its own systems for six hours prior to a launch.

Heris arrived on the bridge two hours before undock, having checked all the aired holds herself, and as much of the machinery on which their lives depended as she could. Everywhere she'd looked she'd found gleaming new casings, shiny metal, fresh inspection stickers, their time-bound inks still bright and colorful. It ought to mean everything was all right . . . and the unease she felt must be because this was a civilian ship, tricked out in plush and bright colors, rather than an honest warship.

Her sulky pilot had the helm, his narrow brow furrowed. She put on her own headset and listened in. He was giving voice confirmation to the data already sent by computer: the *Sweet Delight*'s registration, destination, planned route, beacon profiles, insurance coverage. Heris caught his eye, and pointed to herself — she'd take over that tedious chore. The lists of required items came up on her command screen. Why an officer of an outbound vessel had to confirm by voice the closing of each account opened during a Station visit, each time repeating the authorization number of the bank involved, she could not fathom — but so it was, and had been, time out of mind. Even on her own cruiser someone had been required to formally state that each account was paid in full. It could take hours, with a big ship; here it was a minor chore.

"Thank you, *Sweet Delight*," said the Stationmaster's clerk, when she'd finished. "Final mail or deliveries?" Bates had told her that Lady Cecelia had a bag outgoing; the crew's mail had been stacked with it. She sent Sirkin to take it out to the registered Station mail clerk. The furniture and decorations of the outer lobby had already been returned and stowed in one of the holds. When Sirkin returned, the yacht would be sealed from the Station and the final undock sequence would begin.

It seemed to take no time at all, compared to the bigger, more populous ships she was used to. Her own crew closed and locked the outer and inner hatches; the Station's crew did the same on their side of the access tube. The *Sweet Delight*, on her own air now, smelled no different. An hour of final systems checks remained. The crew seemed to be careful, if slow, in working down the last checklists. They didn't skip anything she noticed, although she didn't know all the sequences for this vessel.

"Tug's in position, Captain Serrano," said the pilot. He had been positioning the yacht's "bustle" to protect it from the tug's grapples. Yachts were too small to fit the standard grapple arrangements; they carried special outriggers that gave the tugs a good grip and kept the main hull undamaged. Heris looked at the onboard chronometer: two minutes to their slot. She switched one channel of her com to the tug's frequency.

"Captain Serrano, *Sweet Delight*." There. She'd said it, officially, to another vessel . . . and the stars did not fall.

"Station Tug 34," came the matter-of-fact reply. "Permission to grapple."

"Permission to grapple." Despite the bustle, she was sure she felt the yacht flinch as the tug caught hold. A perfect match of relative motion was rare, even now. Her status lights switched through red, orange, and yellow to green.

"All fast," the tug captain said. "On your signal."

On the other channel of her com, the on-watch Stationmaster waited for her signal. "Captain Serrano of *Sweet Delight*, permission to undock, on your signal. . . ."

"All clear on Station," the voice came back. "Confirm all clear aboard?"

The boards spread emerald before her. "All clear aboard." Fifteen seconds. She, the Stationmaster, and the tug captain all counted together, but the coordinated computers actually broke the yacht's connection with the Station. The tug dragged the yacht — still inert, her drives passive — safely away from the Station and its crowded traffic lanes. Heris used this time to check the accuracy of the yacht's external sensors against Station and tug reports of other traffic. Everything seemed to work as it should. She felt very odd, being towed without even the insystem drive powered up, but civilian vessels routinely launched "cold" and the tug companies preferred it that way. According to them, some idiot was likely to put his finger on the wrong button if he had power.

When they reached their assigned burn sector several hours later, the tug captain called again. "Confirm safe sector Blue Tango 34; permission to release."

"Permission to release grapples," Heris said, with a nod to the pilot and Gavin. The tug retracted its grapples and boosted slowly away. "Mr. Gavin: insystem drive." The pilot, she noticed, was retracting the bustle, and checking with visuals that the lockdown mechanisms secured properly.

"Insystem drive." The yacht's sublight drive lit its own set of boards. "Normal powerup . . ." Heris could see that; she let out the breath she'd been holding. They'd done a powerup as part of the systems check, but that didn't mean it would powerup again as smoothly.

"Engage," she said. The artificial gravity seemed to shiver as the yacht's drive began a determined shove, much stronger than the tug's. Then it adjusted, and the yacht might have been sitting locked onplanet somewhere. "Mr.

Plisson, she's yours." The pilot would have the helm until they made the first jump, and during jump sequences thereafter. Heris called back to the tug: "*Sweet Delight*, confirmed powerup, confirmed engagement, confirmed oncourse."

"Yo, Sweetie —" The tug captain's formality broke down. "Come and see us again sometime. Tug 34 out." Heris seethed, then, at the pilot's amiable response, realized that "Sweetie" was probably this yacht's nickname, not an insult. After all, even Service tug captains called the *Yorktowne* "Yorkie."

So, she thought, here I go. Off to someplace I've never been so my employer can chase foxes over the ground on horseback, and I can spend a month at Hospitality Bay making friends with other captains in the Guild. Somehow the thought did not appeal.

Heris had heard about cruise captains: unlike the captains of scheduled passenger ships, they were expected to hobnob with guests, flattering and charming them. She would not cooperate if that's what Lady Cecelia had in mind. She would make it clear that she was a captain, not an entertainer. She would eat decent spacefaring meals in her own quarters, since the ship offered no separate wardroom for ship's officers.

Cecelia had heard about spacefleet captains from her sisters: cold, mechanical, brutal, insensitive (which meant they had not worshipped at the shrine of her sister Berenice's beauty, she thought). She enjoyed her meals too much to invite a boor to share them.

That first evening of the voyage proper, Heris ate in her cabin, working her way through a stack of maintenance and fitness logs. The crew cook provided a surprisingly tasty meal; she had been prepared for bland reconstituted food, but the crisp greens of her salad had never seen a freeze-dry unit, she was sure. She missed having a proper wardroom for the officers' mess, but the officers on *Sweet Delight*, such as they were, were not likely to become rewarding dinner companions.

At least Lady Cecelia had not stinted on fresh food or on the quality of maintenance. Heris nodded at the screenful of data. Not one back-alley refitter in the lot; if the lady was bent on hiring incompetents, as Heris had begun to suspect, she did so from some other motive than mere economy. The bills would have paid for refitting a larger and more dangerous ship than the yacht, but Heris supposed part of it went into cosmetics, like the decor. Which reminded her; she must explain to Lady Cecelia the need for tearing out that plush covering the umbilicals.

She ignored the gooey dessert for another stalk of mint-flavored celery, slid her tray into the return bin, and called up data from the next refitting. So far — she refused to let herself contemplate all the future days — nothing had gone very wrong. This life might be bearable after all.

"I suppose you want us to dress," Ronnie said. He lay sprawled in the massage lounger, his admittedly handsome body still dripping sweat from his workout on the gym equipment. Cecelia eyed him sourly; she wanted a massage herself, but not on the clammy cushions he would leave behind. When she'd chosen the luxurious zaur-leather upholstery she'd assumed she'd never have to share it. The saleswoman had mentioned the potential problem, and she had shrugged it off. Now she felt aggrieved, as if it were anyone's fault but hers.

"Yes," she said. "I do. And be prompt; good food doesn't improve by sitting."

"Thank you, Lady Cecelia," said Raffaele. She appeared to be George's companion, slight and dark — though not as dark as Captain Serrano. "These young men would never dress if you didn't make them, and we can't if they don't."

"Why not?" She was in no mood to honor custom; she watched the girls share a glance, then Raffaele tipped her head to one side.

"I feel silly, that's all. My red dress, and the boys in skimps?"

Cecelia chuckled in spite of herself. "If you're going to

feel silly just because some lummox doesn't live up to your expectations, you'll have a miserable life. Wear what you want and ignore them."

Another shared glance. One of the girls might have been more tactful, but Ronnie burst out first. "That's what you do — and that's why you never married and live by yourself in a miserable little ship!"

Cecelia stared him down. "That's why I have the money and position I do — independent of any alliance — to do what I want — and that's why I was available to help you when you got yourself into this mess. Or perhaps you don't know that the first suggestion given your father was that you be packed off on an ore-hauler to Versteen?"

"They wouldn't have!" Ronnie looked almost horrified enough.

Cecelia shrugged. "They didn't, but largely because I was available, and could be talked into it. If your mother — well, never mind. But my point is, that if I had been a conventional member of this family, and married to some appropriate spouse, I would hardly have been free to take you on. You persist in regarding this as some kind of lark, but I assure you that most men — grown men, such as your father and his friends — consider your breach of the lady's confidence a disgrace, even apart from its political implications." Ronnie reddened. "Now," she went on. "Go make yourself fit for civilized company at dinner, all of you. That includes you young women. I do not consider the sort of clothes you wear to parties with your own set adequate." She actually had very little idea what kind of clothes they wore to parties with their own set, but had a clear memory of herself at nineteen to twenty-three.

When they had left, Cecelia felt the cushions of the massage lounger and shuddered. Entirely too clammy; she aimed a blow-dryer at it, and decided on a short swim. The pool's privacy screen, a liquid crystal switchable only from within, closed her into a frosted dome, onto which she projected a visual of overhanging forest. She set the pool's sound system, and eased over the edge to the opening bars of Delisande's *Moon Tide*. A choice others would consider trite, but she needed those long rolling phrases, those delicate shadings of strings to ease her tension. The water enfolded her; she let her body and mind merge with water and music, swimming languidly to the music's rhythm, just enough to counter the gentle current.

Just as she felt herself relaxing, the pool's timer beeped, and Myrtis's voice reminded her that it was time to dress.

"Bad words, bad words, bad words." She had gotten away with that in childhood, even before she learned any. Her stomach burned. . . . If it hadn't been for Ronnie and his gang, she could have had dinner held until *she* was ready — and she'd have been ready, because she wouldn't have been interrupted. And her massage lounger wouldn't have been sweaty. She hauled herself out of the pool with a great splash, hit the privacy control without thinking — and only then realized that with guests aboard she would have to be more careful. Luckily they were all off dressing — none of them had straggled back to ask a stupid question. Not that they didn't swim bare, but she had no desire to have them compare her body to their young ones.

She walked into the warmed towelling robe that Myrtis held, and stood still while Myrtis rubbed her hair almost dry. Then she stepped into the warm fleece slippers, took another warmed towel, and headed for her own suite still rubbing at her damp hair. It dried faster these days, being thinner; she hated the blow-dryers and would rather go to dinner a bit damp than use one.

In her cabin, Myrtis had laid out her favorite dinner dress, a rich golden-brown shi-silk accented with ivory lace. Cecelia let herself be dried, oiled, powdered, and helped into the clothes without thinking about it. Myrtis, unlike Aublice, her first maid, had never seen her young body; she treated Cecelia with professional correctness and the mild affection of someone who has worked for the same employer fifteen years and hopes to retire in the same position. Cecelia sat, allowed Myrtis to fluff her short hair, with its odd spatchings of red and gray, and fastened on the elaborate necklace of amber and enamelled copper that made the lace look even more delicate. Those girls might be fifty years younger, but they would know a Marice Limited design when they saw it, and it would have its effect. They would not know it had been designed for her, by the original Marice, or why — but that didn't matter.

The plump roast fowl sent up a fragrance that made Cecelia's stomach subside from its tension. She glanced around the table and nodded to Bates. Service proceeded, a blend of human and robotic. A human handed her breast slices of roast, and the gravy boat, but crumbs vanished without the need of a crumb-brush.

"Do you eat like this all the time, Lady Cecelia?" asked Bubbles. Sober, cured of her hangover, she was reasonably pretty, Cecelia thought, except that her gown looked as if it would burst with her next mouthful. She was not so plump; the gown was that tight. She wore a warm bright green; it showed off her white skin and blonde curls although it clashed with the dark Raffaele's red dress. The other girl, Sarah, wore a blue that would have been plain had it not been silk brocade, a design of fishes: d'Albinian work.

"Yes," said Cecelia. "Why not? Cook is a genius, and I can afford it, so . . ."

"Tell us about your new captain. Why'd you choose a spacefleet officer?"

"Why was she available?" added the odious George. Less handsome than Ronnie, which Cecelia might have approved, but he had the sort of gloss she distrusted, as if he'd been coated with varnish.

"I wasn't satisfied with my former captain's performance," Cecelia said, as if they had a right to ask. She knew she mellowed with good food; it was one reason she made sure to have it. She wasn't going to admit that if Captain Olin had held to her schedule, she'd have been safely distant and unavailable when Ronnie was exiled. Why waste good ammunition? "I wanted more efficiency," she said between bites, making them wait for it. "Better leadership. Before, they were always coming to me complaining about this and that, or getting crossways with staff. I

thought an officer from the Regular Space Service" —
she made the emphasis very distinct — "would know how
to maintain discipline and follow my orders."

"The Regs are crazy for discipline," George said, in the
tone of someone who found that ridiculous. "Remember
when Currier transferred, Ronnie? He didn't last six
weeks. It was all nonsense — it's not as if all that spit and
polish and saluting accomplishes anything."

"I don't know . . ." Buttons, Bunny's middle son, looked
surprisingly like his father as he ran a thumb down the
side of his nose. Gesture, decided Cecelia, and not features; he had his mother's narrow beaky nose and her
caramel-colored hair. "You can't get along with *no* discipline. . . ." And his mother's penchant for taking the other
side of any argument, Cecelia told herself. In the girl, it
had been fun to watch, but as Bunny's wife she had
caused any number of social ruptures by choosing exactly
the wrong moment to point out that not everyone agreed.
The incident of the fish knives still rankled in Cecelia's
memory. She wondered which parent Bubbles took after.

"We're not talking about no discipline." George interrupted as if he had the right, and Buttons shrugged as if
he were used to it. "We're talking about the ridiculous
iron-fisted excuse for discipline in the Regs. I don't mind
fitness tests and qualifying exams — even with modern
techniques, the best family can throw an occasional brain-
less wonder." Cecelia thought that he himself could
furnish proof of that. "But," George went on, in blissful
ignorance of his hostess' opinion, she being too polite to
express it, "I really do not see any reason for archaic forms
of military courtesy that have no relevance to modern
warfare."

This time Buttons shrugged without looking up from
his food. He had the blissful expression most of Cecelia's
guests wore when they first encountered the products of
Cook's genius. George looked around for another source
of conversation, and found the others all engaged in their
meal; with the faintest echo of Buttons's shrug, he too
began to eat.

The rest of the meal passed in relative silence. The

roast fowl had been followed by a salad of fresh diced
vegetables in an iced sauce strongly flavored with parsley:
Cecelia's favorite eccentricity, and one which never failed
to startle guests. It awoke, she contended, the sleepy pal-
ates which the roast had soothed and satisfied. Crisp
rounds of a distant descendant of potato followed, each
centered with a rosette of pureed prawns. The trick,
which no one but her own cook seemed to manage, was
to have the slices of potato boiled slightly before roasting,
so that the outer surfaces were almost crunchy but the inside mealy. The young people, she noted, took additional
servings of potato as they had of the roast fowl. Finally,
Bates brought in tiny flaky pastries stuffed with finely
diced fruit in chocolate and cinnamon sauce. One each,
although Cecelia knew that a few would be waiting for
her later, safely hidden from the young people.

Satiety slowed them down, she noticed, nibbling her
own pastry with deliberate care. They looked as if they
wanted to throw themselves back in deep chairs and
lounge. *Not in my dining room*, she thought, and
smiled. The elegant but uncomfortable chairs that
Berenice's designer had foisted on her had their
purpose after all.

Cecelia neither knew nor cared about the current
social fashions of the young. In her young days, the great
families had revived (or continued) the custom of a separate withdrawal of each sex with itself for a time after
dinner, the women moving to one room and the men to
another. She had resented it, and in her own yacht
ignored it; either she invited guests (all of them) to continue their discussion in the lounge, or she excused
herself and let them do what they would.

Tonight, with a good meal behind her, she felt mellow
enough to grant them more of her time. Perhaps well fed,
with hangovers behind them, they would be amusing; at
least she might hear some interesting gossip, since none
of them seemed to have the slightest reticence. "Let's
move to the lounge," she said, rising. The young people
stood, as they ought, but Ronnie frowned.

"If it's all the same to you, Aunt Cece, I'd rather watch

a show. We brought our own cubes." The dark girl, Raffaele, opened her mouth as if to protest, but then shut it.

"Very well." Cecelia could hear the ice in her own voice. Snub her, would they? On her own yacht? She would not stoop to equal their discourtesy, but she would not forget it, either. Buttons again tried to intervene.

"Wait, Ronnie . . . we really should —"

"Never mind," Cecelia said, with a flip of her hand. The quick temper that she'd always blamed on her red hair slipped control. "I'm sure you're quite right; you would only be bored talking with an old lady." She turned on her heel and stalked out, leaving them to find their own way. At least she didn't have to spend more time in that disgusting lavender and teal lounge the designer had left her. She toyed with the idea of having the yacht redone, and charging it to her sister, but the quick humor that always followed her quick temper reminded her how ridiculous that would be. Like the time she and Berenice had quarrelled, only to discover that her brothers had taped the row for the amusement of an entire gang of little boys. A snort escaped her, and she shook her head. This time she was justified in her anger; she wasn't ready to laugh.

Myrtis, recognizing storm signals, had her favorite music playing and stood ready to remove her jewels. Cecelia smiled at her in the mirror as the deft fingers unhooked the necklace. "The young people prefer to watch entertainment cubes," she said. "I'll be reading late, I expect." What she really wanted to do was hook up the system and take a long, strenuous ride, but that would mean another swim to cool off, and she suspected the young people would keep late hours. When Myrtis handed her the brocade robe, she slipped it on and went back to her study. Here, with the door closed, and the evening lights on in the solarium, she could lie back in her favorite chair and watch the nightlife. Two fan-lizards twined around a fern-frond, their erectile fans quivering and shimmering with delicate colors. At the sculpted water fountain, two fine-boned miniature horses dipped their heads to drink. They were not, of course, real horses; other small species had gone into their bioengineering specs. But in the dusky light, they looked real, or magical, depending on her mood.

Something flickered along the shadowy floor of the tiny forest, and a sere-owl swooped. Then it stood, talons clubbed on its prey, and stared at her with silver eyes. Not really *at* her, of course; it saw the window's farside illusion, a net of silvery strands that even an owl would not dare. The little horses had thrown up their heads, muzzles dripping, when the action began; they had shied, but returned to the water as the owl began to feed. Kass and Vikka, Cecelia thought. Her favorite of the little mares, and her yearling. In daytime lighting, the mare was honey-gold dappled with brown on top, with a white belly and striped mane of dark and cream. It was as close as Cecelia had ever found in the miniatures to her performance horse. . . . Most breeders of the tiny animals liked the exotic colors the non-equine species introduced.

When the mare led the young one back into the undergrowth, Cecelia sighed and blanked the window. Now she had the view that in all her memory made her happiest: her study at Orchard Hall, with the window overlooking the stableyard. Across the yard, the open top doors of a dozen stalls, and the horses looking out eagerly for morning feed. If she wanted, she could set the view into motion, in a long loop that covered the entire day's activities. She could include sounds, and even the smell (although Myrtis would sniff, afterwards, and spray everything with mint). But she could not walk out the door over there, the one with the comfortable old-fashioned handle, and step into her former life. She shrugged, angry at herself for indulging even this much self-pity, and called up a new view, a seascape out a lighthouse window. She added the audible and olfactory inputs, and made herself breathe deeply of the salt-tang in the air. She had told Myrtis she would read late: she would read. And not a cube, but a real book, which enforced concentration far better. She allowed herself the indulgence of choosing an old favorite, *The Family of Dialan Seluun*, a wickedly witty attack on the pomposity of noble families four generations past.

"Her sweet young breast roused against the foe, Marilisa noted that it had not hands nor tentacles with which to wield the appropriate weaponry. . . ." As always, it made her laugh. Knowing it was coming, it still made her laugh. By the end of the first chapter, she had finally quit grumbling inside about Ronnie and his friends. She could always hide out in her cabin reading; they would think she was sulking miserably and never know that her sides ached from laughing.

✦ Chapter Three

Heris had had no idea a yacht could be this complicated. It was so small, after all, with so few people aboard
. . . but rich civilians did nothing efficiently. As she
worked her way through the manuals, the schematics, the
overlays, she wished she'd had weeks aboard before the
first voyage. Hours were not enough. She wrinkled her
nose at the desk screen, muttering. The owner's quarters
separate from the household staff's quarters, and both
separate from crew quarters. Four complete and separate
hydroponics systems: crew support, household support,
food, and flowers. *Flowers?* She pushed that aside, to
consider later. Ship's crew, *her* people, were responsible
for all life support, but not for the household food and
flowers. Ship's crew maintained all the physical plant, the
wiring, the com connections; in one of the few duties that
did overlap, the household kitchen supplied the crew.
Not madam's own cook, of course, but her assistants.

Eventually she went in search of further enlightenment,
and chose the most senior employee aboard: Bates. She had
stayed out of his path, which seemed to be what he expected,
but no captain could command without knowledge.

"Who does this in a planetside house?" asked Heris.
Bates folded his lip under. She waited him out. He might
be a butler, but she was a captain.

"It . . . varies," he said finally. "More than it used to;
more than it should, some say. Originally, household staff
did it all, unless a wall fell in or something. Then as
houses became more technically oriented — plumbing
inside, gas laid on, electricity —" Heris had never considered that having indoor plumbing meant someone was

technically oriented. "Then," Bates went on, "owners had to resort to outside expertise. Calling in the plumber or the electrician when something went wrong. Some found staff members who could do it, but most of those trades thought themselves too good to be in service. . . ."

"So . . . usually . . . it's outsiders?"

"Mostly, except in the really big households. Where we're going, of course, the staff does it all, but they've a whole planet of homes to care for."

"The whole *planet* is one household?"

"Yes — I thought you understood. Lord Thornbuckle's estate *is* the planet."

She had known it, in an intellectual way, but she had not ever dealt with its implications. Of course the super-rich owned whole planets . . . but not as pleasure-grounds. She had thought of them as owning the land, perhaps — but never as owning everything on the planet — the infrastructure, the houses, the staff to manage it. But it wasn't that impossible, she reminded herself. The R.S.S. owned several planets as well: one for resources, and one for a training base. This would be like a large military installation. At once her first frantic concerns — where do they buy groceries? Where do they educate the kids? — vanished.

"So Lord . . . er . . . Thornbuckle has all the support staff on hand already," she said. "Technicians, moles, all the rest?"

"Yes, Captain. In the off-season, the planet's population is less than two hundred thousand; in the main season, he'll have at least two thousand guests — which means, of course, another ten to twenty thousand of their ships' crews, and ships' staff all rummocking about the Stations or off at Hospitality Bay."

Hospitality Bay sounded like the sort of place Fleet marines went to gamble, wench, and pillage. From Bates's explanation, it was designed as a low-cost recreational base for ships' crews and off-duty house staff . . . in other words, a place to gamble, wench, and pillage. Most of the wealthy guests who arrived in their own yachts left them docked "blind" at one of the Stations (which one depended on the guests' rank). It had proved cheaper and more pleasant, Bates said, for the crews and staff to vacation planetside than to enlarge the Stations enough to hold and entertain idle servants. A largish island, complete with a variety of accommodations, automated service, recreational facilities, and the chance to meet crew and staff from the other yachts. Clubs, bars, entertainment booths, and halls — everything the vacationing staff might want.

"No riots?" asked Heris, remembering the Fleet marines. "No . . ." What would they call shore patrol? "No — security officers?"

"The militia," said Bates, wrinkling his nose in distaste. "Of course there are always those who take advantage, and someone must keep order. It's understood that the usual . . . er . . . structure of command does not apply. I am not held responsible, let's say, if an under-gardener from this ship gets into trouble. Milady would consider that, afterwards, and might say something to me, but not the militia. We each have our own places, you see."

Enlisted bars, NCO bars, and officer bars, Heris thought. She called up a list of the branches of the captains guild, and found one listed for Hospitality Bay. . . . so she, too, would be expected to sit out the hunting season entertaining herself with other captains from yachts. Why was that so much worse than spending leave with other Fleet officers? She knew the answer, but pushed it away. She'd joined the Captains Guild; that was all she could do for now. Someday she would belong again . . . or she wouldn't. She'd live with it either way.

"I suppose," she said, looking at Bates carefully, "that if anything . . . arises . . . on the household side that I need to know about, you will inform me?"

"Yes, Captain Serrano." He smiled at her, evidently pleased. She could not imagine why.

"This is *very* different from the Regular Space Service," she said, to see what his reaction would be.

"Yes, it is, Captain." His smile broadened. "It's even different from most civilian households. Lady Cecelia likes to do things her own way."

That, Heris had figured out from the lavender plush. Perhaps servants like Bates took pleasure in their employers' eccentricities, but she didn't. Yet.

"I must warn you," she said, "that I'm planning to run emergency drills just as I would aboard a warship. It's a matter of safety, you understand. Do the . . . er . . . staff have training sessions aboard?"

"Not normally, no, although we do have assigned places and duties for various emergencies. Captain Olin never found it necessary." A faint air of distaste, whether for Captain Olin or her proposal, she couldn't tell.

"Captain Olin, I'm afraid, had eccentricities unsuited to the master of a spacefaring vessel," Heris said, and then realized how odd that sounded. Eccentricities implied activities engaged in with objects obtained from catalogs with names like *Stirrings* and *Imaginations*. The only person she'd ever known thrown out of the Service for "eccentricities" had insisted on sharing his delight in electrical and plumbing lines with those not so inclined. She had sat on the court martial, and remembered suddenly that he'd also liked having his mouth packed full of feathers. Captain Olin's eccentricities, she was sure, had been ethical and not sensual.

Bates no longer smiled. "And these drills will be . . . unscheduled?"

"Yes. I'm sorry; I realize it's inconvenient, but one never knows when a real emergency will occur, and drills must be a surprise. That way we can find out what didn't work, and prepare for it." She paused. "However, if you would like to arrange training first, I'll delay the drills. At the least, every member of staff should have an emergency station where he or she will be safe and out of the way of crew members with assignments. Ideally, staff would help with things like verifying that emergency hatches have locked, that ventilation systems are working according to specs, and so on."

"What about Lady Cecelia and her guests?"

"They too must have emergency stations where they will be safe. They need to practice evacuation drills just like anyone else. If something should happen — unlikely as that is — we must know where they are to rescue them."

"I see." Bates looked surprisingly grim, as if he had never thought about the dangers inherent in space travel before. "Are there standard ways to do this?"

Heris stared at him, then recovered herself. "You — haven't had any instruction, ever?"

He looked unhappy, but determined. "No, Captain Serrano. To my knowledge, none of Lady Cecelia's captains have ever had drills that involved the staff, owner, or guests."

Heris managed not to sigh aloud, but inwardly she fumed at the incompetence of those captains. Did they have no professional pride at all? "I'd better speak to her, then, hadn't I?" she said gently. "If she doesn't realize the importance of these drills, she might make it very inconvenient for you. And after that, if you have any time . . . perhaps we could work together to decide on the best staff response."

He relaxed, and smiled, and seemed perfectly agreeable. Heris took the list of staff positions, and their listed specialties, and went back to her side of the ship, carefully not muttering.

The yacht's database included, as law required, the complete text of the standard manuals of emergency procedures for crew and passengers. At this point, Heris considered the staff and guests equally passengers. She decided to print out a hard copy — it would be impressively thick, with the Transport Code seal on the cover, and perhaps that would convince Lady Cecelia that it wasn't her own peculiarity.

The last access date for that file was — she stared, though she felt she should not have been surprised — the date the yacht left the builder's. All those years . . . her stomach clenched, as she thought of the past possibilities. No, she could not expect Lady Cecelia, or her woefully ignorant staff, to go through disaster drills until they'd had some instruction. She wondered what the correct procedure was — if there was a corect procedure — for informing a wealthy yacht owner that her ship was, and had been, unsafe for years.

The hard copy thunked into the bin, and she picked it out. The Transport Code seal looked less impressive than she'd expected, but the thing was thick enough. She looked into it, wincing at the bureaucratic prose. It was as bad as Fleet directives. Everything unimportant specified in intricate detail, with requirements to document that it was done, and the important things buried in multisyllabic generality. How far above the deck warning signs must be, and how high the letters, and what color, but — she stopped suddenly. Warning signs? What warning signs?

She flipped to the back sections, headed REQUIRED ITEMS OF COMPLIANCE, and PENALTIES FOR NON-COMPLIANCE. Despite the current inspection stickers, the *Sweet Delight* was out of compliance on at least fifty items — on the first page alone. And the penalties, if subsequent inspection discovered those discrepancies . . . made an astonishing figure. For one thing, a hard copy of that manual — and the ship's own customized emergency procedures manual — were supposed to be available to passengers. She knew no such hard copy existed.

"I knew," she muttered, "that that stupid purple plush shouldn't be there."

"Captain?" Heris looked around guiltily. Gavin stood near the door, looking apologetic. "I did ask," he said, "but you didn't seem to hear."

"I'm sorry, Mr. Gavin," she said, focussing again. "What is it?"

"It's about those crew evaluations you wanted," he said. "We never had anything like that when Captain Olin was here. . . . I'm not exactly sure what you want. . . ."

Your head on a platter, Heris felt like saying, but in fact he wasn't the worst of them. "Mr. Gavin, I need to know how you feel each crew member is doing: do they know their jobs, are they doing their jobs?"

He looked as if he would be sulky if he had the courage. "They've always pleased Lady Cecelia before," he said. "If she don't have any complaint . . ."

"Mr. Gavin, Lady Cecelia is hardly qualified to judge the skills of a navigator or engineer, is she? That's my job, but since I'm new, I'm asking you to help. That is your job."

"But . . . well, you know, Captain, they all have to know I'm doing this."

"They do?"

"An' I don't like saying things that, you know . . . an' someone new like Sirkin, it's different. But these others . . . we been together a long time, and I don't want to hurt anyone's feelings, not that there's anything they've done wrong, but you said to rank them. . . ."

Heris allowed herself to glare at him. "Mr. Gavin, you are an officer of this ship; you were second in command to Captain Olin, as you are to me. It is your duty to consider the ship's welfare first and friendship second. No one need have hurt feelings to be ranked second. . . . There is no disgrace in it, as long as the overall performance is satisfactory. Now, if you don't feel equal to the requirements of your position —"

"It's not that," he said.

"Very well. Then I'll expect to find your evaluations on my desk within forty-eight hours. It is unfortunate that Captain Olin did not carry out regular evaluations, so that you and the rest would realize how necessary they are, but since he did not, you will simply have to cope."

"Yes, Captain." But he did not move away, and simply stood there looking glum.

"Do you have another problem?" Heris asked after a long pause.

"Well . . . it's about those emergency drills you mentioned. I need to know when you're planning one so that I can have things ready."

Heris barely restrained herself from pounding her head on her desk. "Mr. Gavin, the whole point of an emergency drill is that it is *not* scheduled. Emergencies aren't scheduled. Do you expect the universe to let you know when it plans to put a rock through the hull?"

"Well . . . no. But that's not the same thing —"

"It *is* the same thing, if drills are to mean anything. If you knew when something was about to go wrong, of course you'd be prepared. So would I. So would everyone. Didn't you see the report on the *Flower of Sanity* while we were in dock?" Gavin nodded. "Well — remember how the reports said that the crew's training in emergency procedures was what let them save all those passengers? Even though it happened when most of the crew was off-shift? I'm sure those passengers — and even the crew — didn't like unscheduled emergency drills, but that's how they learned to cope with unscheduled emergencies."

"I can see that, but — but that was a big ship, a commercial ship. This is only a little yacht. It can't be that —"

Heris interrupted again. "An electrical fire just broke out in the number seventeen box: what is still functioning in this compartment — the captain's office?"

He stared, eyes wide. "Well — I'd have to ask Finnie — but I think —"

"There's no time to think, Mr. Gavin. There's only time to react. Box seventeen supplies the blowers for alternate compartments on this passage, overhead lights for the compartments whose blowers are controlled by box eighteen, and the electrical outlets in the heads — the bathrooms — in all compartments on this passage. And since four boxes are clustered with box seventeen, an electrical fire in that is likely to knock out sixteen, eighteen, and nineteen as well. That means all the blowers in the crew quarters, all the overhead lights, wall sockets, passage lights, and com terminals, since all the compartment desktops take their power from box twenty. It's dark in here, Mr. Gavin, and there's a fire somewhere aboard — do you know if the door will unlock?

"No . . . no, I didn't . . . I don't . . ."

"And that's why we have emergency drills, Mr. Gavin. To find out, before we find that we're locked in dark, airless boxes while a fire rages somewhere." Before he could say more — and anything he said now would enrage her — she thrust the hard copy of the manual at him. "Here; start learning this. I'll make additional hard copies, and I'll expect you and your section chiefs to have marked necessary modifications within forty-eight hours." He was too stunned to react; he took the manual and backed out.

Heris watched the door slide closed behind him, and then shook her head. It was much, much worse than she'd thought, to be the captain of a rich lady's yacht.

Lady Cecelia had never thought of herself as an old lady. Age had nothing to do with it, nor the number of rejuvenation treatments. As long as she could ride to hounds, as long as she could go where she wanted, and do what she wanted, and cope with whatever life put on her plate, she was not old. True, she didn't compete in some fields where once she had been at the top, but that she thought of as outgrowing old interests — as developing new ones — as a natural shift from one thing to another. Old people were those who had quit changing, quit growing. Some people quit growing at twenty, most by forty or fifty, and became old within a decade. They would live another thirty to fifty years — longer with rejuv — but they lived those years as old people. Others — her own grandmother Serafina for one — seemed to stay lively and interesting until the last year or so before their deaths.

Staying away from the family kept her from feeling old, too. Nothing like children growing up and turning into difficult adults to make you feel your age. Particularly if they thought you were an old lady, and treated you as one. She did not look at herself as she dressed in her soft velour exercise suit; she did not want to be reminded of her age. If they were in the gym, she'd throw them out. It was her turn.

But the gym was empty, silent, scented with her favorite aromatics. They had not been here; the cushions of the lounger had dried. Cecelia locked the doors and set up her simulator. She would ride this morning, no matter what anyone said.

An hour later, refreshed after a pleasant but demanding ride over a training field, she stowed the simulator and pocketed the cube. This was not a group she wanted riding over her shoulder, so to speak. She didn't want to hear whatever they might say. She looked at the gym's status board, and saw that they were all still in the guest suites. Fine. She stripped, showered, and let herself into the pool enclosure, blanking the canopy and turning the waterstream up a little. The pool's surface heaved, then steadied, as the current increased. She swam against it vigorously, then climbed out, toweled dry, and wrapped herself in her heated robe. Another check of the board; they were moving now. She grabbed her exercise suit and headed for her own suite; she should be safe.

They did not meet at breakfast. Cecelia ate in her own suite, as she often did anyway, and she paid no attention to the young people. She had her own daily routine — checking with Cook, listening to Bates's report, going over whatever her captain chose to tell her about the ship status. With Olin, that had often been a single bare statement that the ship was proceeding according to plan. She wondered about Serrano. The first day's report had been two pages long, most of it incomprehensible detail about why she'd chosen to move something from one storage hold to another . . . as if Cecelia cared. As long as staff knew, and could find, whatever she wanted, she herself didn't want to worry about something as technical as "center of mass" and "potential resonance interference."

This morning, it was one page, headed with "Emergency Drills." Cecelia blinked. Why should that concern her? The crew would have emergency drills, she assumed, but yachts, unlike liners, did not have to inconvenience their passengers. She read on, already resisting the idea. This Captain Serrano must think she was still a military commander. Her house staff to be given emergency assignments? She and her guests expected to learn and follow emergency procedures? How absurd! She remembered the fire drills, long ago when she had attended the Sorgery School, and how they had all known the drills were useless. If a fire ever did start, it would not wait around for people to get out of bed, find their assigned partner, and "walk down the stairs quietly, without talking, and without pushing or running."

Captain Serrano's reasoning, when she got that far, made somewhat more sense. She had not really thought about the things that could go wrong, barring late meals or illness in a crew member. The vulnerability of a small yacht wandering through interstellar space hadn't occurred to her; everyone she knew traveled in space, and the rare disappearances and accidents were no more frightening than accidents groundside. Sometimes trains and aircraft and limousines crashed; sometimes yachts disappeared. For a moment she almost felt it, the fragility of the ship, the immensity of the universe, but she pushed that away. It was like thinking about the fragility of her skull and the size of a horse and the fence it was approaching. . . . If you thought about it, you'd sit in a padded cocoon forever, and that was ridiculous.

Still . . . perhaps some emergency drills might be a good idea. Not this many, and certainly not without adequate warning (what if she were in the swimming pool?) but some. She called Bates.

"Yes, madam. Captain Serrano has already spoken to me about this matter — she considers it important to your welfare. She would like to help me give your staff instruction, although that would take time —"

"Before these emergency drills?"

"Yes, madam."

"I suppose . . . it's something that should have been done before, though none of the others complained."

"Captain Serrano seems very competent, madam." Which meant that Bates approved. Damn. She had better agree, so it could be her idea, because when Bates approved of something, it happened, owner or no owner. She had wished more than once that he was her captain. He had a talent for command.

"Very well, then. You and the captain see to it, but if she gives you too much trouble, Bates, feel free to let me know."

"I don't think she will, madam. She's not like the others." Whatever that meant. Cecelia didn't ask. She asked how the young people were doing, with no real interest, and Bates reported that they had appeared to enjoy breakfast, and were now viewing old entertainment cubes in the lounge. Cecelia felt an unreasonable irritation that they were happy. They were her guests; they ought to be concerned about her. She went into her garden to play with the miniature equids. . . . They would always come for sugar.

Ronnie watched Raffaele covertly, and wondered if she had heard about the opera singer. He hadn't really noticed before, thinking of her as George's girl, but she had a lovely line of jaw and throat when she lifted her head. Slender without weakness, she seemed hardly aware of her grace. . . . She was chuckling over something Buttons had said. Bubbles, beside him, waved a hand in front of his face.

"Wake up, sweet — you're staring right through Raffa, and it could make me jealous." Bubbles exuded sensuality of a very studied sort, from silver nails to tumbled blonde curls, from the deep-plunging neckline of her clinging jersey to the cutouts on the long black tights. Next to the opera singer, he had always thought of Bubbles as the sexiest girl he knew, but at the moment he was finding her tiresome. She had been singing along with the lyrics from the cube, and the opera singer had spoiled him. Now he could hear the breathiness and the slight errors of pitch.

"Sorry," he said. "I was wondering what we're going to do all that time at your father's. Surely not fox hunting."

"It's not that bad," Buttons said, looking up. "I rather like it, sometimes. If we jiggle the weather-sats, so it's not as cold and wet —"

"Father will find out," Bubbles said. "He likes authenticity."

"I don't see how you can have authenticity when the foxes aren't even foxes," Sarah put in. "Didn't I read somewhere that they're actually reverse-gengineered from cat genes?" Ronnie doubted her interest in bioengineering; she and Buttons had signed the second-level prenuptials, and this was her first official visit to his family. She would be trying to make points.

"A chimaera," Buttons said, settling into the lecturing tone that made him less than popular in the regiment. Stuffy, in fact, because he couldn't just answer a question: he had to explain all the juice out of it. "Nobody bothered to save Old-Earth red fox genes, so what Dad's people did was go from descriptions, and use what seemed to work.

Luckily Hagworth had already done jackals from dogs, and two of the fox species that got publicity. . . . The real problem was getting the color and the bushy tail with a white tip. Our neo-foxes are part kit fox, part jackal, a bit of cat, and raccoon, for the tail."

"I didn't know anyone had saved raccoon genes; I thought they were too common."

"Only to give an outcross for the red panda," Buttons said. Ronnie would not have expected him to know, but after all his father was an enthusiast on many forms of hunting and preservation. Buttons went on to discuss the genetic possibilities at length. Ronnie let his mind drift . . . to the opera singer, in whose bed he had learned about things that before had been only rumors . . . to the prince, whose jealousy he had been glad to arouse . . . to that night in the mess when he had boasted . . . somehow it didn't seem quite as clever now as it had then. Perhaps Aunt Cecelia was right, and he had been a cad. No. The prince should have been a better sport.

He reached up and stroked Bubbles's arm, wondering if anything would come of it. He could not think of anything to say, though, and after a few seconds, she withdrew the arm and stretched herself on the couch across from him. The same couch where she had been so unfortunately sick. . . . He wondered if she remembered. She looked healthy enough now, though her expression of mild sulkiness fit his mood as well as hers.

"I suppose we should get into shape," George said. "Your aunt has that handy little riding-thing. An hour a day, and none of us would have to worry about saddle sores."

"Her simulator?" Ronnie asked. "Do what you like, George, but I have no intention of bouncing around on a mechanical horse. It's bad enough to contemplate bouncing around on a real one. Do you know she had the gall to order me riding attire?"

"Well, you'll need it." Buttons had settled into a pose the male equivalent of Bubbles's sprawl; together they took up both of the couches. Ronnie wondered why he'd thought exile would be more fun with these people than alone. They were looking at him as if he were responsible for entertaining them, when none of it was his fault. Buttons went on. "First of all, my father's head instructor will check you out, before you're assigned your mounts —"

"And he's a terror," Bubbles said. "So far as I know, there's not a military unit in the known universe that still uses horses, but he acts like a cartoon drill instructor. You'll spend at least two hours trotting before he decides what to give you."

"I'd like to see him test Aunt Cecelia," Ronnie said.

"Not her," Buttons said, grinning. "She's an old guest, and he's more likely to ask her to test the horses. 'Pick what you like, milady, not that there's anything here worth your time,' is what he'll tell her."

"Is she really that good?"

Buttons stared at him, eyes wide. "You haven't ever seen her ride?"

"No. The family doesn't think much of her hobby." His father had said that, often enough, and he'd heard his mother talking to his other aunts about "poor dear Cecelia, what a shame she wasted her life on horses."

"It was hardly a hobby, Ron. . . . The woman won the All-Union individual cross-country championship five times, and ranked in the top five for fifteen years." Buttons turned to Bubbles. "Remember when we were just learning to ride, and old Abel was yelling at us, and she stopped him?"

"She got me over my first jump," Bubbles said, sitting upright now. She looked less like a fluffhead than usual. Could she possibly *enjoy* hunting? Ronnie had a brief unpleasant view of himself married to a fox-hunting wife. No. It would not do. "I'd forgotten . . . that was that old gray pony, the one that seemed to like dumping us. She didn't yell at me, just talked me through it."

"Yes, and then she got on one of the good horses and showed us what we were supposed to be doing. Abel fairly purred."

Ronnie felt a knot in his head tightening. It wasn't fair that they knew more about his aunt than he did. That they admired his aunt for things he hadn't known about, and that his family hadn't respected. Things were not going the way he'd planned. He'd expected his friends to rally around him, support him, do what *he* wanted . . . and here they were swapping stories of his old maiden aunt.

"Does everyone hunt together?" he asked Buttons. If he couldn't avoid the topic of horses, at least he could get the conversation away from his aunt. "How many horses does your father have, anyway?"

"To answer your first question, no. There are three hunts out of the main house, where we'll be. Each has its own territory. We'll each be assigned to one of them, depending on riding ability. As for horses . . . many thousands, I suppose, altogether. The main house stables will hold five hundred, though we won't use that many. Hunters, hacks, young horses in training." Ronnie tried to imagine five hundred horses in the same place, and failed. The Academy had had ten, for the training of its young officers, and he had no idea what a "hack" was. He was not about to ask.

"We don't hunt every day," Bubbles put in. "Some people do, but most ride out on alternate days. Particularly in the lower hunts, where they're not as good and get really stiff."

"I'll get really stiff," Raffa and Sarah said together, like a chorus.

"Isn't there anything else but hunting?" Ronnie asked, hoping he didn't sound as desperate as he felt.

"There are other kinds of hunting," Buttons said. "Not all of it's on horseback. You can shoot grouse and pheasant, that sort of thing. It's the wrong season for fishing in the nearby streams. Indoors — well, the things my father assumes were normal indoor sports of the time: billiards, cards, amateur theatricals."

"Oh . . . dear." Worse then he'd imagined. Worse than his mother had imagined, he was sure. Traveling with a wealthy aunt on her private yacht had seemed like a good idea when his mother mentioned it. Perhaps he'd have been better off going to some dull assignment in an out-of-the-way base. At least it wouldn't have had fox hunting, and his work might have kept him busy part of the time.

"There are other places on the planet," Bubbles said. "But we can't possibly get away more than once. We should save that for when you're really desperate. Poor Ronnie."

He wanted to snarl at her. Poor Ronnie, indeed. He needed real sympathy, not the mocking look Bubbles had given him. He needed them to understand that it wasn't his fault — none of it. "I'm not desperate," he said firmly. "For all you know, I may take to hunting as easily as any other sport. I may be leaping over fences and dashing along at a run —"

"Gallop," put in Bubbles.

"Whatever. I mean, I'm naturally athletic, perfectly fit: how hard can it be?" He tried to say it with complete confidence; Bubbles, Buttons, and Raffaele burst into laughter. Raffaele? What did she know about riding? He tried to hide his irritation, and forced himself to laugh with them.

"Better try your aunt's simulator," Buttons said, still chuckling. "You may find a few muscles that aren't quite perfectly fit." Then he sobered. "You should do well, Ronnie, really. You're right: you are a natural athlete; it's quite possible that after a few lessons you'll be up to riding in the field. But it's not like anything else."

Ronnie forced himself to smile, and wondered if he could hide in his stateroom all day and night, watching entertainment cubes, until they got to Buttons's home planet. Probably not. He was going to have to think of something they could do . . . something fun, something to reestablish his leadership of the group. Something mischievous, perhaps. Play a harmless practical joke on the old lady, or the crew.

"You may be right," he said, without meaning it. "I'll see what you look like on the simulator first, and then . . . we'll see."

"We ought to see about some swimming, I think," Raffaele said. "C'mon, girls. Let's go play in the water." Before he quite knew how it happened, the girls had vanished, and his two bosom friends were watching him, bright-eyed.

"Come on," said George. "Tell us more about that opera singer. Is it true they have specially developed muscles?"

✧ Chapter Four

"I didn't ask you if it was 'going fine,' " Heris said. "I asked you what the sulfur extraction rate was. Do you know, or not?" With each day, her unease about the yacht's basic fabric and systems had grown. Getting answers from the crew had turned out to be harder than she expected.

The moles looked at one another before Timmons answered. "Well . . . pretty much, Cap'n. It's below nom at the moment, but it usually runs that way 'cause that dauber wants a sulf-rich sludge for his veggie plots."

It took Heris a moment to translate civtech slang and decide this meant Lady Cecelia's gardener wanted more sulfur in the first-pass sludge. In the meantime, they still had not answered as she thought they should. She let the steel edge her voice. "Below nom is not what I'm looking for. What, precisely, is the *number* you have for sulfur clearance?" Again, the sidelong look from one mole to another. This time it was Kliegan who answered.

"It's . . . ah . . . zero point three. Of first-sig nom, that is —"

"Which is . . . ?" prompted Heris; she could feel temper edging higher.

"Well, the *book* says one point eight, but this system's never worked any better'n one point six, just under first-sig. Mostly we run about two sigs below, say about point seven or so. System's underutilized, so it's not that important. It's rated for a population of fifty, and we don't have that many aboard."

Heris closed her eyes briefly, running over the relevant equations in her head. Sulfur clearance was only one of the major cycles, but critical to the ship's welfare because errors could not only make people sick, but degrade many ship components as well. Delicate com equipment didn't like active sulfur radicals in the ship's atmosphere. She added ship's crew, house staff, and owner's family. "In case you haven't noticed," she said briskly, "we now have fifty-one humans and a long voyage ahead of us. I presume you flushed the tanks and re-inoculated them while we were in port —?" But the hangdog looks told her they hadn't. "And the last logged maintenance by offship personnel was this — Diklos and Sons, Baklin Station?"

"That's right, ma'am," Timmons said. "They couldn't have done such a good job, fancypants as they are, 'cause the system never did pick up the points, but Captain Olin said never mind —"

"Oh, he did?" Heris struggled to keep her thoughts off her face. First his demand for an odd, inconvenient course that did not meet the owner's needs, and now a tolerance for malfunctioning environmental equipment — something no sane captain would have. Failing to order the tanks flushed and recharged at Rockhouse might have been spite — revenge for being fired — but until then he had risked his own life as well. What could have made the risk worth it? "We'd better see how bad it is," she said briskly. "Suit up and we'll go take a look —"

"You, Captain?" asked Iklind. He almost never spoke, she'd discovered, letting chatty Timmons say anything necessary. But now he looked worried.

Heris let her brows rise. It had worked on other ships; it should work here. "Did you think I wouldn't want to check for myself?"

"Well, it's not that, Captain . . . only . . . these things can smell pretty bad." Pretty bad was an entirely inadequate description of a malfunctioning sulfur loop, and she was sure more than the sulfur scrubbers were in trouble. Once the pH had gone sour, many of the enzymes in other loops worked erratically, as the chemistry fluctuated.

"That's why we'll be suited," she said. When they didn't move she said. "Five minutes, in the number four access bay."

"Complete suits?" asked Timmons. "They're awfully hot —"

"You prefer to risk the consequences?" Heris asked. "With a system you know is malfunctioning?"

"Ah . . . it's just stinks," Timmons said. When she glared at him, he said, "All right, Captain. Suits." But as he left, she heard him mutter, "Damn lot of nonsense. Can't be enough reaction in that loop to give us mor'n a headache at worst."

Quickly, Heris gave Gavin his orders for the next hour: which compartments to seal, which backup crew to have ready, suited, in case of trouble. Then into her own suit — the cost of which had come from the advance on her contract, and which she never begrudged. Whatever else on this gilded cesspool of a yacht did or did not work as designed, her own personal self-contained suit would . . . or her family would enjoy the large sum which Xeniks guaranteed if any of its suits failed. She wasn't worried — only twice in the past fifty years had Xeniks had to pay out.

When she was still a corridor away from the access bay, the alarm went off. For an instant she thought something had gone wrong on the bridge, but then she realized what it must be. One of those fools hadn't waited for her.

"Captain!" Gavin bleated in her ear. She thumbed down the volume of the suit comunit.

"What is it?" she asked. "I'm at E-7, right now." Ahead of her, a gray contamination barrier flapped down from the overhead and snicked tight, its central access closed.

"Computer says dangerous chemical — sulfur something — and the motion sensor said someone was there, but isn't moving. But they're in suits —"

"Get those backups down here," Heris said, mentally cursing civilians in general and the ship's former captain in particular. "Make sure they have their helmets locked on. I'm going in." Despite her faith in Xeniks's legendary suits, she shivered a moment. The gas in there was deadlier than many military weapons, but so familiar throughout human history that people just did not respect it. She wriggled through the access iris, which lengthened into a tube and sealed itself behind her. The suit's own chemical sensors flicked to life, giving the readout she expected: hydrogen sulfide, here in less than life-threatening concentration.

Heris hurried, even though she knew it would almost certainly be too late. Around the corner, she came upon Timmons, who had suited up but not locked on his helmet. Presumably he'd planned to do so when he got to the access bay itself. He lay sprawled on the floor, one arm outstretched towards Iklind, slumped against the open access, wearing no protective gear at all.

She went to Timmons first, locking his helmet in place and turning his oxygen supply to full with the external override. Her suit had all the necessary drugs for standard industrial inhalation accidents — but she'd never used it, nor was she a medic. She'd have to rely on the backup team. Iklind wasn't breathing at all, and no wonder — the hydrogen sulfide concentration in here had peaked at over 1,000 ppm, according to the monitor above the open access hatch. Inside, someone — presumably Iklind — had cracked the seal on a sludge tank. It was brimful, far above the safety line. A black line of filth drooled over its lip.

Heris picked up the wrench on the floor, closed the cover, and tightened the seal, then closed the hatch. Now the monitor indicated the concentration was below 200 ppm, still dangerous but not instantly lethal. They were lucky, she thought, that the agitator hadn't been on in the sludge tank (and why not?) or the concentration could have been a log or so higher.

A shadow moved at the corner of her vision. The backup team — that would be the number two engineering officer and the off-shift senior mole — came around the corner and stopped. Even through their helmets their eyes showed wide and staring.

"Come *on*," Heris said. "Get Timmons to the medbox — he might have a chance." It seemed to her they moved too slowly, but they did wrestle Timmons back up the corridor towards the contamination barrier. Heris called the bridge. "Iklind's dead," she said. "Hydrogen sulfide — apparently he opened the sludge tank without any protective gear —" Gavin started to say something, and she overrode him. "We have three problems here — Timmons first: is that medical AI capable of handling inhalation injuries? Second: we've got to clear up the rest of the contamination, and the system is too overloaded to resorb it unless you can come up with a cargo section full of reactant. And third, of course, is Iklind. We need medical and legal evaluation; I will take that up with Lady Cecelia. Oh — and another thing — we're not going to continue in this unsafe condition. I want Sirkin to plot a course to the nearest major repair facility, preferably on the way to our destination."

"The medbox . . . I don't know, Captain," Gavin said. "It's not — you know — meant for major problems."

Heris managed not to snap at him. "At least you can tell it the problem. All I know is it's a cellular poison, and there's some kind of antidote. Now: send someone down with a recorder, so that I can document Iklind's position and the monitor readings. Then we can bring his body out." Even as she said this, she realized she was straining the crew's resources.

"Milady," said Heris, "we have several problems."

Just what I need, thought Cecelia. Problems with the ship. Now she'll start whining about how different this is from the military. She nodded, trying for a cool distancing expression. That and a straight back usually dissuaded complainers.

"We've had a death among the crew, environmental technician Iklind."

"What! A heart attack? A stroke?" Despite her determination not to react, she felt her heart lurch in her chest, and her voice came out shrill and harsh.

"No, Lady Cecelia." Heris had tried to think of a nonthreatening way to tell her employer — considering how old the woman was — but had not come up with anything better than the bald truth. "He died of hydrogen sulfide poisoning, the result of opening a sludge tank without protective gear. In addition, another crewman is suffering severe inhalation injury from the same source."

"But all we have is a medbox!" Cecelia felt as if she had

just fallen off at a gallop. A crewman dead, and another sick . . . was this what came of hiring an ex-military captain? She tried to remember the specifics of the medical unit.

"It's a standard industrial pollutant," Heris said. "The unit has the right medications and the right software to treat him — I checked that, of course, before coming to you."

"Oh — I —" Cecelia realized she'd slumped, and straightened again.

"I'm very sorry to have given you this shock. Perhaps I should call someone?"

Cecelia recognized someone giving her time to pull herself together, and was caught between resentment and gratitude. "I've never lost a crew member before," she said. "Not since I've owned the *Sweet Delight*." She struggled with the mix of emotions, and tried to think clearly. "Poison gas from the sludge tank, you said? Has someone put something in it?"

Heris recognized the attempt for what it was, and masked her amusement that anyone — even a rich old lady — could travel in space and not know the most common and deadly of the environmental by-products. "No, milady. Sludge generates several toxic gases, which are normally converted into harmless chemicals used in your 'ponics sections, when the environmental system is functioning smoothly. This isn't sabotage, just a mishap. . . . Iklind apparently decided to open the tank without proper protective gear, and Timmons tried to rescue him, but hadn't sealed his own helmet."

"Then who saved Timmons?" asked Cecelia.

"I did," Heris said. Cecelia's eyes widened, but she didn't say anything. "I had told them I would inspect the system, and they were to meet me — properly suited — at the access bay. Instead —" She shrugged. "I don't know why Iklind didn't wear his suit, or why Timmons didn't wear his helmet . . . but I will find out."

"Very well, Captain." That was clearly dismissive. "I . . . will expect to hear more from you tomorrow."

"That's not quite all," said Heris carefully.

This time the gaze was direct and challenging. "What? Is something else wrong?"

"I realize," Heris said, "that you just had this vessel redecorated, and it must have been expensive . . ."

"My sister did that," Cecelia said. "What of it?"

"Well . . . your main environmental system is over-loaded; that's why I was going to inspect the system: it was not functioning to specifications. Your former captain did not have the system purged and recharged at the correct intervals —"

"He must have! I remember the bills for it." Cecelia called up her accounting software and nodded when the figures came up. "There it is: Diklos and Sons, Refitting General, Baklin Station."

"Sorry, milady," said Heris. "You got the bill, but the work wasn't done. I could see that from the sludge tank Iklind had opened, and since then I've had the other moles — environmental techs — check the filter and cul-ture chambers. It's a mess. The sulfur cycle's in trouble, and that impacts your nitrogen uptake in hydroponics. It isn't presently dangerous, but it will require some caution until we reach a refitting station. My recommendation would be to do that as soon as possible. By choosing a dif-ferent set of jump points, we can be at your chosen destination only one day after your request."

Cecelia glared. "You didn't find this out before we left."

"No, milady, I didn't." Cecelia waited for the excuse that she herself had rushed their departure, but it didn't come. Her captain had no expression at all, and after a moment went on. "Initially I accepted the log showing that the purge and recharge had been done, and the fresh inspection stickers; you are quite right that I should not have done that. Logs have been faked before, even in the Regular Space Service." A tight smile, which did not reach the captain's eyes. Cecelia wondered if she ever really smiled. "But I noticed an anomaly in the datas-tream two days ago, and began tracking it down. Your moles — sorry, ma'am, your environmental technicians — claimed it was your gardeners' fault. But the plain fact is, the work wasn't done. I believe it will be possible to document that, and get a refund from Diklos and Sons; your reputation should help."

"Ah . . . yes." Cecelia felt off balance; she had been ready for evasions and excuses, and her captain's forthright acceptance of blame surprised her.

"I realize, milady, that one reason you changed captains is that your former one could not keep to your schedule. But in this instance, I feel that your safety requires an emergency repair of the system."

"I thought," Cecelia said pettishly, "that I had specified an environmental system far larger than I'd ever need, just in case something went wrong."

"Yes, milady, you did. But with your present guests and their personal servants, that limit has been exceeded — and with the degradation of performance of the system, and the lack of refitting capabilities at Lord Thornbuckle's, it would be most unwise to proceed without repair."

"And that will take —?"

"Six days to the nearest refitting facility, I'd trust; two days docked; and with a reasonable course and drive performance, we should be, as I said, just one day late at your destination."

"I suppose that's better than the eight days late I had before — which landed me with young Ronnie, because I wasn't there to argue hard enough and loud enough." Cecelia shrugged and said, "Oh, very well. Do what you think best; you're the captain." But her captain didn't leave, merely stood there. "What else?" she asked.

"I strongly recommend some restrictions in the next six days. At present we have no shipwide emergency, but I would prefer to prevent one."

"But it's only six days —" Cecelia began, then stopped. "You're really worried." To her surprise, her captain smiled slightly.

"Yes, and I cannot justify it by the data alone. But although I've been on this ship only a short time, there's a *feel* of something wrong —"

"Intuition in a Fleet officer?"

"Just so. Intuition I have learned not to ignore. I am

instituting quite severe restrictions in crew activities, and strongly recommend them for your staff and guests as well."

"Such as?"

Her captain ticked them off on her fingers. "A change in diet to minimize sulfur and nitrogen loading of the system — for six days, the loss of muscle mass or conditioning from a low-protein diet should not cause any distress, and if you have someone with special needs, that can of course be accommodated. Restrictions in water use, to include the exercise pool since that water is cycled through the same systems, and organic compounds inevitably end up in it. The . . . er . . . gardens will need to be handled as part of the regular environmental system as well. . . ."

"The gardeners will love that —!" She thought of her pet equids with a pang. They would have to go — perhaps she could flash-freeze them, but it was always chancy. And the beautiful flowers, the fresh fruits and vegetables — they would have to restock or eat preserved food all the way to Bunny's.

"Sorry, milady, but the environmental tech's excuse for letting the system go outside nominal is that your gardeners had requested a particularly high sulfur effluent for some special crop."

"I see. So we're to arrive at some shipyard hungry, thirsty, dirty, and bored —"

"But healthy and alive. Yes."

Cecelia's heart sank. She could imagine what Ronnie and his friends were going to say about this. It had been bad enough already. For a moment, she was tempted to let go in one of the towering rages of her youth — but she was beyond that now. She had no energy for that kind of explosion. "Very well," she said again. "If you will enter the specifications, I will inform staff and the others."

"Thank you, milady." Her captain's face looked as if it might be intending an apology, but she did not then apologize. She gave a curious stiff nod, and went out quickly. Cecelia blew a long, disgusted breath and called Cook. She might as well get on with it.

❖   ❖   ❖

Takomin Roads occupied a location that made it ideal for refitting deep-space vessels and little else; not even the most ship-fevered spacer would choose for recreation the bleak cold planet the Station circled. Farther insystem Merice offered sweet shallow oceans, and Golmerrung spectacular peaks and glaciers . . . but Takomin Roads offered reasonable proximity to four mapped jump nodes, one of them apparently bound to the planet. Heris had stopped there with a battle group once, and been impressed by the size of the fixtures and the quality of the crews.

The *Sweet Delight* had communications equipment only just inferior to that of the cruiser Heris had left. She could pop a message just as they left FTL flight, and it would arrive well before them, given the necessary deceleration of the yacht. Mr. Gavin, still gray around the gills from her lecture and Iklind's death, and the very close shave with Timmons, presented her with his estimate of the work to be done, down to the specifications for every component fastener. She took that estimate to the moles themselves, and when they would have initialled it without discussion she insisted on going over every item with them.

"I'm sure Mr. Gavin is right," the junior kept saying, with nervous glances at the other. She had hardly met Ries before the emergency.

"I'm not." Heris was past worrying about Gavin's reputation with the moles; she was far more concerned with getting the yacht safely to refitting, and back out as quickly as possible.

"I guess you want us to look up this stuff in the manual. . . ." said the senior mole, Kliegan.

"I want you to do your jobs," Heris said. "If you are not sure, of course you must look up the specs."

"Well, I do, but . . ."

"Then is this correct, or not? Don't hedge about, mister." She wondered, not for the first time, how Lady Cecelia had survived so many years with incompetents manning her yacht. Did rich people not even know the

difference? She supposed not. A shiny surface would satisfy them, even if it covered decay.

"Yes," he said, after a moment. She nodded; she would
hold him to it. At the end of this voyage, she would suggest to Lady Cecelia — no, she would insist — that she
replace the least competent of the crew. In fact, with Iklind dead, perhaps they could find someone competent at
Takomin Roads.

The refitting specifications all went into the message
capsule, along with Lady Cecelia's credit authorization.
By the time the *Sweet Delight* had come within a light-
hour of the Takomin Roads, the refitters had had time to
ready their equipment, unpack the necessary parts, and
shift their workload to accommodate a rush job.

Or so they should have, Heris thought. The first message she received began by explaining how impossible it
would be to do the work at all, and the next (a day later)
argued that it could be done, but not within the time limit
she had specified. Heris took none of these to Lady
Cecelia; refitting was her responsibility and she knew already that a yacht owner, like an admiral, doesn't want to
hear about problems that can be solved at a lower level.
Besides, arguing with refitting had been a normal part of
her duties as a cruiser captain. Those who didn't argue
went to the bottom of the stack and got leftover parts.

She fired back her own messages as fast as the uncooperative ones came in, pointing out Lady Cecelia's holdings
in the companies whose ships formed a large part of
Velarsin & Co, Ltd.'s work. Alienating a major share-
holder could have a negative impact on future contracts.
. . . she ignored, as beneath her notice, the long list of
other work that would run overtime if Lady Cecelia's
were done. The refitters capitulated, finally, in the last
message received a half-hour before docking, when a Station tug already had a firm grip on the *Sweet Delight*'s
bustle. Heris watched the docking critically; she had no
real confidence in their pilot, and luckily no need for it —
the Station's AI had no glitches as it eased them to Berth
78.

"I hope you're satisfied!" growled the bulky man in a

dark gray shipsuit uniform when she called Velarsin & Co. "Shifted a dozen jobs for you, we have. Gonna lose a bonus on one of 'em."

"I shall be satisfied when our work is complete, correct, and prompt," said Heris.

He snorted, half anger and half respect, just like every Fleet Yard superintendent she'd ever known. "I have your specs," he said. "They're as foul as you claim your bilges are."

"I'm not surprised." Heris smiled at him. "We had nonconformance at the last maintenance, before I took this ship; it's my guess it hasn't met the original specs in years. When will your crew board?"

"They're waiting at your access," he said. "And me with 'em. I want to meet the captain of a private yacht that can bend the rules upstairs."

"Fine," said Heris. "I'll be there in five minutes. I have to inform the owner."

The owner, when Heris called her, sounded stiff and resentful. "I still do not understand, Captain Serrano, why we could not have stayed aboard. Surely, with the umbilicals to Station Environmental, we don't need to worry about contamination aboard. . . ."

She had explained before; she explained again, patiently but firmly. "Milady, even the best refitting crews cannot access the system without an occasional leak. It will stink — and worse than that, you might be exposed to hydrogen sulfide or other toxic contaminants. It is safest to seal the crew, staff, and owner's space — the vents themselves — which means no circulation at all. All the working crew will be in protective gear, as I will be while I supervise. It takes only one good lungful of sewer gas, milady, to kill you." She did not need to say more; Lady Cecelia gave a delicate shudder. And she had already arranged for the appropriate law enforcement division to take over Iklind's body, along with the meager evidence. "The crew is waiting, milady, and the sooner they start —"

"Very well." It was crisp and unfriendly, but not an argument. "And where are we staying?" The real problem, Heris thought, was that Lady Cecelia had never been here before and wasn't sure of accommodations. As well, those brats were probably whining and dragging their feet.

"You, milady, have a suite at the Selenor, where the shipping line executives stay. There's limited space, and I had to book the young people into a different hostelry on another level. I realize that's inconvenient —"

This time a trace of warmth in her employer's voice. "I can survive that. Meet me for dinner, then; I'll want a report. Twenty hundred, local time." Six hours; they'd just have started, really. Heris had counted on supervising them closely all through the first shift. But she could come report, and return quickly. She would not have to stay for a meal, she was sure.

"Of course, milady. I'll be at the maintenance access as you leave; please have Bates call when the staff has cleared the ship."

"Very well."

Heris gave her crew a stern look. "Mr. Gavin, you and Environmental will suit and observe the first shift. The rest of you are booked into transient crew quarters less than fifteen minutes from here; I expect you all to stay available. We'll have at least two crew aboard the ship at all times, and you'll rotate." A stir, no more; they knew better than to protest by now. "Have you confirmed Station air supply to every compartment?" she asked Gavin.

"To all but the owner's quarters, ma'am," he said. "I was going to do that as soon as milady left the ship; computer says it's fine, but . . ."

"Do that, then, while I go meet the refitters. Lady Cecelia is debarking now."

She followed the crew off the ship, and met the crew chief of the refitters in the maintenance access. He and his workers already wore pressure suits to protect themselves from contamination and carried helmets tucked under their arms. By the sudden flicker of his eyelids, she saw that he recognized her origins.

"I'm Captain Serrano," she said. "And you're . . ."

"Kev Brynear," he said, a slow smile lighting his heavy face. "'Scuse my asking, but you're ex-Regs, aren't you?"

"That's right," said Heris. She wondered if he'd ask more, but he merely nodded.

"Guess that's why you managed to put fear into management. They don't hear command voice real often. Well, Captain, let's see what you've got." He wasted no time asking for details she'd already sent, but ordered his crew into helmets, and nodded sharply to Heris. She suited up, locked her own helmet on, and led him into the ship.

"Let's start from the bottom up," he said over the suit radio. She could hear his voice, but not the clear words, through the helmets; it formed an irritating echo. "Worst first, and then we can give you an estimate."

Heris had always hated suit drill, and even after the suit had saved her life she still disliked it; she hated being closed in with her own breath sounds and the hissing of the air supply. She had two hours of air in her own rebreathing tanks, and the exterior connector allowed her to plug into Station air in any compartment with a vent, but she *felt* smothered.

In the lowest environmental level, her own moles were already suited; they managed to look sheepish even in suits, as well they ought.

"Mr. Brynear," she said to her moles. "He's in charge of this overhaul."

"And here are my shift supervisors," Brynear said. "Herak Santana, first shift; Allie Santana, second shift, and Miko Aldovar on third. Any time I'm not here, one of them will be; I expect to be here most of the time, but I may have to goose inventory control if you people are in as bad shape as you said."

The shift supervisors, in bicolored orange and silver suits, stood out from the orange-suited crew, but nonetheless had name and position stenciled on front and back of both suit and helmet. By local time, it was now second shift; the first shift supervisor waved to Brynear, who nodded, and then left. The second shift supervisor's voice came over the radio.

"Captain, would you have your crew secure compartments."

"Certainly." This command she could give herself, direct to the computer; the compartment hatches slid shut. Status lights changed, and they all moved to connect their

suits to the compartment's exterior air supply vent. From
now on they would have to take care not to tangle each
other's umbilicals. "Confirm external air . . ." she said, and
waited for each response before nodding to Brynear.

Brynear pointed to one of the ship's moles. "Let's take a
look at the scrubber that's looking worst on the computer."

Inside the first protective shell, streaks of black slime
marked the joints of the inner cover, and corrosion had
frozen the bolts. Heris noticed that the gas sensors had
gone red, instantly. One of the refitting techs grunted.
"Who'd you say was supposed to have done the refit? And
how far back?"

"Never mind, Tare," Brynear said. He moved over to
look; when he tapped the scrubber with a wrench, more
black goo oozed out. The readouts on the scrubber shell
were all offscale. "That's the owner's problem; ours is fix-
ing this mess. And I can tell right off we're going to need
more equipment. You were right, Captain, this is an
emergency refit if ever I saw one." His orders to his crew
were, Heris heard with relief, as decisive as she'd have
heard in a Fleet dock, and his explanation to her assumed
that she would understand the technicalities.

"We're going to have to vacuum your entire system —
and this Yard charges for hazardous storage. On the other
hand, if it's this thick it may generate enough methane to
pay part of your storage fee. And we've got a repair job in,
a big Overhull tanker, that's going to need a whopping
inoculation of its hydroponics. . . . I might be able to do a
deal with them."

"Safety first, then speed," Heris said. "Money counts,
but only third."

"Fine. We suck everything out, sort it, clean and repair,
and put back your basic inoculum. . . . How about the living quarters — did you have much contamination up
there?"

"No, probably because of the oversized filters; I kept
thinking I smelled it the last day or so, but the sensors
didn't react."

"Then we'll try a wet flush there — saves time — but
the bottom end is going to be a bitch."

"Estimate?"

"Full crews — and it'll depend on whether we replace units or rebuild them —"

"Replace 'em," Heris said. "Anything you can."

"Forty-six hours," he said. "And that's spending your owner's money flat out. Can't be done in less than forty-two, if everything goes right, and it won't. Might be a little longer. . . ."

"Do your best," Heris said.

She had not expected real speed from a civilian refitting firm, but when Brynear's crews moved into high gear, she realized that they made their profit from speed. By mid-shift, four great hoses were draining the muck from *Sweet Delight* into the Yard storage tanks. Half the damaged scrubbers were out; Brynear, she noticed, was meticulous about giving credit for those which could be rebuilt. She and Brynear had documented the condition of scrubbers, chambers, and pipes; Lady Cecelia should have no trouble making a claim on Diklos & Sons. Or for that matter a case against Captain Olin.

In the second half of the shift, new components stacked up on the access bay: scrubbers, environmental chambers, parts, controls. Brynear and Heris inspected them together, helmets off.

"We don't have enough to give you a matched set," he said. "You'll get thirteen Shnairsin and Lee 4872's, same as original equipment, and seven Plekhsov 8821's. Personally I prefer the Plekhsovs — we use 'em a lot as replacements and I think they're tougher — but I'd give you a matched set if I could. The performance specs are identical . . . here." Heris looked at the printout and passed it to her moles.

"That's good enough," she said. "What about environmental chambers? And the runs?"

"You'll have to have new chambers — every single culture either overgrew or was contaminated by one that did. Again, we have Shnairsin and Lee, but I recommend Tikman. They've come out with a lining that really is better — we've had about five years' experience with it."

"Go with the Tikman," Heris said. The Regs had seven years' experience with the new polymer lining; she hadn't realized it was available on the civilian market. "The runs?"

He frowned. "That depends on whether you want to put up with a little pitting. We can cut out the worst, and patch — we have good pipefitters, and I guarantee you won't have turbulence problems at the joints. Or we can pull them all and restring the runs. Pitting . . . it's not dangerous, once we cut out the really bad patches, but you'd want to replace it within a year or two. It'd get you where you're going, safe enough. Restringing all the runs will really squeeze the time I gave you."

"So would finding all the bad places, and being sure of them," Heris said. He nodded. "I want a safe ship, Mr. Brynear; I'll take my owner's heat if you run a little over. But . . ."

"It better be worth it — I understand that. I tell you, Captain, I'm really shocked at Diklos. They used to be good. I'd have trusted 'em with my own ship, if I couldn't get here."

"Mistakes happen," Heris said, somewhat grimly. "But not on my ship, not again. Now, if you have the hard copy estimates, I'll go see Lady Cecelia."

✧ Chapter Five

Even in the garish purple uniform, Heris felt more comfortable on the dockside, with honest ribbed deck-plates and not plush carpet beneath her feet. Everyone here worked on ships, and in that way everyone here was one of her kind, someone she understood. After a walk long enough to make her legs ache, she came out of Velarsin & Co., Ltd.'s docks and into the commercial sectors. She was glad she'd thought to have her luggage taken ahead, with her employer's. Here, sleek transport tubes marked one side of the walkway; fronting the other were shops, hotels, and eating places. None of the great logos bannered here, but often locals were as good. Heris stopped to consult a map display, and decided to take a tram the rest of the way to Lady Cecelia's hotel. As usual, the good hotels were as far as possible from the rumble and clatter of hard work.

She walked through a narrow door, with only the engraved plate with *Selenor* in slightly archaic script to indicate the identity, into a lobby that reached the stars. After one flinching look, she realized it only seemed to. The geometry of this Station allowed those with inside exposure to use the entire interior well as a private display. Those tiny lights were on the far side . . . except for the interior transports, sliding along maglines.

Meanwhile, the concierge was already smiling at her. "You must be Captain Serrano. . . . Lady Cecelia gave us your description."

"Yes —"

"And your room is ready, Captain. In the mauve tower,

2314, adjoining hers. Lady Cecelia said she didn't know when you might be in, but she supposed you'd like something to eat at once."

"How very thoughtful." She was hungry, now that she thought of it, but she needed to see her employer first.

"She said to tell you she would be resting, but — oh, wait. The light's changed. She's up again. I'll let her know you're on your way, shall I?"

"Yes, thank you."

The mauve tower droptubes were scented with a warm flowery fragrance that made Heris think of summer on one of the planets with native grasslands. She emerged into a small lobby splashed with soft color, and felt like a large purple blot. Lady Cecelia's suite unfolded its entrance for her, and a gust of pine fragrance overlay the summer grasslands. Heris felt its carefully engineered stimulants flicking her cortex, and resented it.

"Ah . . . Captain Serrano. And how is the *Sweet Delight*?" Lady Cecelia was not giving a millimeter. She wore a formal dinner gown, cream-colored and drapey, with her graying hair swept up to a peak by a jade clip. Behind her Heris could see a table set for two. Heris wondered who her guest would be. The entire sitting room of the suite seemed to be lined with mauve plush, on which cream-colored furniture floated like clouds in an evening sky.

"Missing a lot of essential equipment," Heris said. "I've authorized replacement rather than repair, since that is quicker and Diklos should reimburse you. They're keeping a complete record of the damage for legal use."

"Ah. And will we be out of here in forty-eight hours?"

"Very likely, but I cannot guarantee that. Sixty is the outside limit." Heris looked around. "If you'll excuse me, milady, I'd like to clean up and eat something before I go back to the ship."

Lady Cecelia's brows raised. "Go back? Surely you're going to rest. . . . I intended you to eat dinner with me. Don't you remember?" Heris had forgotten, but she couldn't say that. Besides, the ship mattered more.

"Considering what happened last time she was in for work —"

"Nonsense. You need sleep the same as anyone else. At least, have dinner here. . . . go freshen up, get out of that uniform, and relax awhile." Heris wondered if she had correctly interpreted the tone of *that uniform*.

"Umm . . . milady . . . you would prefer that I not wear your uniform here?"

Lady Cecelia's lips pinched; she sighed. "I would prefer that my sister Berenice had not tried to compensate me for Ronnie by insisting that I use her decorator. I would prefer I had had the wit to refuse, but I was already rattled by the change in schedule, by Ronnie, by his friends —"

Mental gears whirled. "You don't . . . ah . . . *like* all that lavender plush?"

"Of course not!" Lady Cecelia glared at her. "Do I look like the kind of silly old woman who would?" That was unanswerable; Heris kept her face blank. Lady Cecelia shook her head and emitted a snort that might have been anger or laughter, either one. "All right. You don't know me; you couldn't tell. But I don't like it, and I'm having it out as soon as I decently can. Your uniform — that's another thing Berenice insisted on. Captain Olin had always worn black, and Berenice thought it was dull and old-fashioned."

"Surely," Heris said carefully, "there's something between black and loud purple with scarlet and teal trim?"

Lady Cecelia snorted again, this time with obvious humor. "You don't know the worst: Berenice wanted me to approve cream with purple and teal trim. She told me the gaudier it was, the more a new captain would be impressed. The purple was the darkest thing offered."

"Ah. Then you wouldn't mind if I . . . modified this a bit?"

"Be my guest." Lady Cecelia scowled again. "Although I don't suppose you can arrange a complete redecoration while we're here?"

Heris grinned, surprising herself as much as her employer. "To be honest, milady, I've wanted to get that lavender plush off the access tube bulkheads — for safety reasons, I assure you — since I first came aboard."

"Safety reasons?" Now Lady Cecelia grinned, more

relaxed than Heris had yet seen her. "What a marvelous idea! Is it true?"

"Oh, yes. There's a lot hidden on your ship that shouldn't be — it's pretty, but it's hard to see trouble in the early stages. We certainly don't have time here for a complete redecoration, but a little *un*decorating won't slow things down."

"Well. Good. Now, about dinner . . ."

"Let me change into something comfortable. Ten minutes?"

Heris returned to her employer's suite in her own off-duty clothes — the first time she'd worn them since leaving the Service. Since Lady Cecelia was wearing a formal dinner gown, she put on her own, and had the satisfaction of seeing her employer truly surprised.

"My dear! I had no idea you looked like that!" Then Lady Cecelia blushed. "I'm sorry. That was unforgivable."

"Not really, although it was your uniform that made me look the other way." Heris knew very well what the close-fitting jet-beaded bodice did for her; the flared black skirt swirled around her ankles as she came to the table. She would never have the advantage of Cecelia's height, but she had learned to use color and line to compensate. "Oh — one last bit of business before dinner . . . what about the inquest on Iklind?"

"Not a problem." Lady Cecelia slipped into her seat and picked up her napkin. "With the documentation you supplied, and the medical evidence from Timmons, this will be treated as an obvious accident."

Heris sat down; she knew she shouldn't continue the subject at table, but questions cluttered her mind. "I wish —"

"Not now," Lady Cecelia interrupted her. "We can discuss this later, if you wish, though I would prefer to wait until tomorrow, local time. By then forensics should have confirmed the cause of death, and I'll know more."

Heris blinked. She had not realized that Lady Cecelia would be dealing with the legal problems of Iklind's death while she worked on the ship; she had thought she would have to do it all herself.

Dinner arrived, with a cluster of attendants. Heris found herself staring at a tiny wedge of something decorated with a sprig of green.

"Lassaferan snailfish fin," Lady Cecelia commented. "The garnish is frilled zillik. We grew that aboard, before — at one time."

Heris tasted the snailfish fin, which had been dipped in a mustardy sauce; it had an odd but winsome flavor, perfectly complemented by the zillik. She had eaten at places that served this sort of food, usually while on a political assignment, but the Service favored less quixotic cuisine. One rarely had time to spend hours at the table. She hoped she would not have to spend hours at dinner now — with the relaxation induced by comfortable clothes, she had begun to realize how tired she was.

Next came a hot soup, its brilliant reds and golds contrasting with the pallid snailfish fin. Fish and vegetables, flavors well-blended, with enough spice to make her eyes water . . . "Sikander chowder," Lady Cecelia said, smiling. "Good when you're tired. I used to have this a lot when I was competing." Heris wondered what she'd competed at, but didn't ask; she could have eaten two bowls of the chowder, and twice as many of the crisp rolls served alongside it.

"This is delicious," she said, as she finished the chowder.

"I thought you'd like that," Lady Cecelia said. "I'm going to try their roast chicken and rice, but if you want more chowder just say so."

Courtesy and appetite argued, and courtesy won; Heris let the waiter remove her soup plate and accepted the roast chicken — slices of breast meat, marinated and grilled after roasting, formed the wings of a swan; its body was a mound of spiced rice. The graceful head and neck had been artfully formed of curled spicegrass. She took a cautious bite of the rice — ginger? mustard? coriander? — and devoured it with almost indecent haste. She had been hungrier than she knew. . . . The slices of chicken disappeared, then the spicegrass.

The next course seemed out of sequence to Heris, but

she realized that Lady Cecelia could set her own standards. Still, the platter of fruit, 'ponics-grown melons and berries, didn't suit her at the moment. She nibbled a jade-green slice of melon, to be polite. Lady Cecelia, too, seemed as ready to talk as eat. She began with a question about the literature studied at the Academy — one of her great-nephews had said no one there read Siilvaas — was that true? Heris recognized this opening, and added to her reply (yes, they read Siilvaas, but only the famous trilogy) a comment about a more contemporary writer. For a few minutes they discussed Kerlskvan's recent work, feeling out each other's knowledge. Lady Cecelia had not read the first novel; Heris had not read the third most recent.

The cheeses came in; the fruit remained. Heris sliced a wafer of orange Jebbilah cheese, and floated a comment about visual arts. Lady Cecelia waved that away. "As for me," she said, "I like pictures of horses. The more accurate it is, the better. Aside from that I know nothing about the visual arts, and don't want to. I was made to study it when I was a girl, but since then — no." She smiled to take the sting out of that. "Now, let me ask you: what do you know about horses?"

"Nothing," Heris said, "except that we had to have riding lessons in the Academy. Officers must be able to sit a horse properly for ceremonial occasions: that's what they said." In her voice was much the same contempt her employer had expressed for visual arts. Anyone who could prefer a horse picture, good or bad, to one of Gorgini's explosive paintings . . .

"You don't like them?" Lady Cecelia asked.

"What — horses? Frankly, milady, to a spacer they're simply large, dirty, smelly animals with an appalling effect on the environmental system. I remember one time having to inspect a commercial hauler which was taking horses somewhere — why, I can't imagine — and it was a mess. I don't blame the animals, of course. They evolved on a planet, and on something the size of a planet there's enough space for them. But in the hold of a starship? No."

"Did you like riding them?" asked Lady Cecelia. She had a mild, vague expression which didn't suit her.

Heris shrugged. "It wasn't as bad as some of the other things we had to learn. I did fairly well, in fact. But it's so useless — when would anyone need to ride a horse anywhere?"

"Only on uncivilized planets where it rains without permission," Lady Cecelia said. Heris was sure she detected an edge to her voice, but the expression stayed mild. Belatedly, she remembered that the reason her employer so wanted to be on time was for the start of the "fox-hunting season" which had something to do with horses.

"Of course," she said, "many people do enjoy them. Recreationally."

"Yes." This time the edge was unmistakeable. "Many people do. I, for one. Did your lessons at the Academy ever include riding them in the open — across country?"

"No — we had all our lessons in an enclosed ring."

"So you have no experience of real riding?"

Heris wondered why riding in a ring was not real. The horse had been large and had smelled like a horse. The sore muscles she got from riding had been real enough. But from her employer's face, this was not going to be a popular question. "I haven't ridden anywhere but in those lessons, no," she said cautiously.

"Ah. Then I suggest a wager." This with a bright-eyed glance that made Heris suddenly nervous.

"A wager?"

"Yes. If the refitters are finished, and we clear this station forty-eight hours after we arrived — no, fifty hours, for you will need a little time, I'm sure, to ready for departure — then you win, and I will submit to be lectured by you on visual arts for ten hours. If, however, we are delayed, you lose, and will owe me ten hours, which I shall use in teaching you to ride — really ride — on my simulator."

"An interesting wager," Heris said, nibbling her cheese. "But that assumes that I want to bore you with ten hours of visual arts, which I don't — I'm an admirer of some artists' work, but no expert. What I wish you knew more about was your own ship. Suppose, if I win, you spend ten hours with me learning how to tell if your refitters did a good job?"

"You are that confident that we will be out in fifty hours?"

"I am confident that, either way, we will both learn something worthwhile," said Heris. Lady Cecelia flushed.

"You're mocking me — you don't think riding is worthwhile!"

"No, milady. I am not mocking you, which would be both rude and foolish. You think it is important; I have not, up until now, but perhaps I'm wrong. If I lose, you have the chance to convince me. And I'm very sure that you would have been spared expense and inconvenience both had you known more about the workings of your yacht. Did you always take the horse a . . ." She struggled for the word, then remembered it. "A groom brought you, and get on and ride away? We were taught to inspect the . . . the tack . . . for ourselves, to look at the animal's feet —"

"Hooves," put in Lady Cecelia, cooler now.

"Hooves, and see if it had any problems."

"I see your point," Lady Cecelia said. "No, certainly I did not take my grooms' word for everything." The quick color had gone from her cheeks, and she seemed to have recovered her earlier good humor. "Very well, then: if you win, I will study my yacht's particulars, and if I win, you will study horsemanship. Is it agreed?"

"Certainly." Heris reached across and shook her employer's hand. How hard could it be, after all? The simulator wasn't a real horse; it couldn't step on her, or bite her, or run away with her.

Whatever else she might have said was interrupted by a chime; Lady Cecelia touched the table's control pad and the concierge's voice announced that her nephew and his friends were on their way up.

"No — I don't want to see them!" Lady Cecelia said. Heris noticed the quick flow and ebb of color to her face.

"I'm sorry, milady; they're already in the tube."

"Blast it!" Lady Cecelia half rose from her chair, and the attendants scurried to help her. She waved them away, reseated herself, and glanced at Heris. "I apologize, Captain, for the past moment and the coming hour. I'll get rid of them as soon as I can."

"Aunt Cecelia, it's unforgivable!" That was Ronnie, first in the door when it opened. "That disgusting captain of yours put us in a cheap place as far from here as you can imagine; they don't even have a — " He stopped abruptly as Heris turned to face him. She was delighted to see how far his jaw dropped before he got it back under control.

"It's the captain," said George unnecessarily. The two young women looked ashamed of themselves and their companions; the blonde one opened her mouth and shut it; the dark one spoke up in a soft voice.

"That's a lovely dress, Captain Serrano." Heris noted that Ronnie gave her a disgusted look, so she smiled at the young woman . . . Raffaele, she thought her name was.

"Thank you," she said sweetly. "I'm glad you appreciate it."

"You might want to know," Lady Cecelia said, in stiff voice, "that *I* approved your assignment to that hotel. If you want to blame someone, blame me. Captain Serrano has been far too busy saving our lives to spare any energy to make your lives miserable."

Ronnie was a strange color two shades darker than bright pink.

"What is unforgivable," Lady Cecelia went on, "is your rude intrusion into my dinner and private conversation, and your insulting my captain. You will apologize to Captain Serrano, now — or you can find your own way home and take whatever punishment you get, which I am sure you richly deserve."

"Here, now —" began George, but Lady Cecelia quelled him with a glance. Ronnie looked from one to the other, and gave a minute shrug.

"I'm sorry, Aunt Cecelia . . . and Captain Serrano. It was not — I didn't mean to be rude — I just —"

"Wanted your own way. I know. And that is an entirely inadequate apology. You called Captain Serrano 'disgusting'; you will retract that." Heris had not realized that any civilian could sound so much like a flag officer. Suddenly it was easy to imagine Lady Cecelia in full dress uniform with braid up to her shoulders.

Ronnie's flush darkened and his lip curled; the glance he shot Heris was unchastened and furious. "I'm sorry, Captain Serrano," he said between his teeth, "that I referred to you as 'disgusting.' It was ungentlemanly." Heris nodded, dismissing it. She would say nothing that might make things worse between aunt and nephew.

"You may go now," Lady Cecelia said. She picked up her glass and sipped; Heris doubted if she knew whether she had water or wine in it. The girls turned to go at once; George backed up a step, but Ronnie looked as if he were inclined to argue. "Now," Lady Cecelia said. "And don't roam too far from your hotel unless you carry a comunit. I will give you only one hour's notice to reboard, and it would not hurt my feelings to leave you here."

Ronnie gave a stiff bow, turned on his heel and almost pushed the others out of the suite. When the entrance refolded itself, Lady Cecelia shook her head. "I'm truly sorry," she said. "Ronnie suffers from . . . from being the oldest boy in his family, the first grandchild in our branch, and his parents' pride. He was spoiled before he was born, I daresay, if there's a way to indulge an embryo in the tank. The mess he's in now —" She spread her hands. "Sorry. It's not fair to bore you with this."

Heris smiled, and sipped. Water, for her, while the refitting was going on; she could afford not the slightest haze between her and reality. "Lady Cecelia, nothing that concerns you bores me. Surprises me, perhaps, but don't fear that I'm bored. If you wish to discuss it —"

"I suppose you think you could straighten him out." Lady Cecelia looked grumpy now, in the aftermath of the argument.

Heris shrugged. "It's not my job, straightening out your nephew — unless you request it. And then — I don't know. When I've had someone of his social class to deal with, it's because he or she volunteered; I had leverage based on their own motivation."

"You must despise us," Lady Cecelia said.

"Why? Because you have a bratty nephew? I've seen admirals' children with the same problem."

"Really. I thought military children were born saluting

the obstetrician and clicked their heels as soon as they stood up." Although the tone was wry, there was an undertone of real curiosity. Heris laughed.

"Their parents wish! No, milady, we're born squally brats the same as everyone else, and have to be civilized the same way. Your nephew seems to me the logical result of privilege — but no worse than others."

"Thank God for that." Lady Cecelia looked down. "I'd been imagining you all this time turning up your nose at me for having such a nephew." Heris hoped her face didn't reveal that she had thought that, and shook her head.

"Milady, as you said, I've been too busy to give much thought to your nephew. Your crew, now . . ." Was this the time to bring up those problems? No. She smiled and went on. "If you want to talk about your nephew, feel free. I'm listening."

"He got in trouble," Lady Cecelia said, with no more preamble. Heris listened to the story of the prince's singer and the rest with outward calm and inward satisfaction. About what she expected from that sort of young man. She hadn't realized he was in the Royal Aero-Space Service — and wondered why he'd been foisted off on his aunt, when his colonel should have been able to handle the situation. She asked.

"Because my sweet sister wouldn't allow it," Lady Cecelia said grimly. "He certainly could have been posted to . . . say . . . Xingsan, where his regiment has a work depot, for a year. Or someplace where he'd actually do useful work. But Berenice interceded, and got him a year's sabbatical — a sabbatical, in the military — on the promise that he would not show his face in the capital."

"Mmm," said Heris, considering just how Cecelia's sister could have that much influence with the Crown. Her train of thought came out before she censored it. "Does . . . uh . . . Ronnie look much like his father?"

Lady Cecelia snorted. "Yes, but that doesn't answer your real question. Ronnie's an R.E. — " At Heris's blank look she explained. "A Registered Embryo, surely you have them?"

"I've heard of them." It cost more than a year's salary to have an R.E., and what you were paying for was not technology but insurance. In this instance it also meant that Ronnie had not resulted from a casual liaison.

"Anyway," Lady Cecelia went on, "my sister Berenice decided that I should take Ronnie on. She never has approved of the way I live, and I was there, handy."

"Because Captain Olin ran late," Heris said.

"Yes. Normally I'm at the capital only for the family business meeting — in and out as fast as possible. This year I missed the meeting — which meant my proxy voted my shares, and *not* as I would have wished — and arrived just in time for Ronnie's disgrace. These are not unconnected; it was apparently in celebrating his first opportunity to vote his own shares at the meeting that he overindulged, and came to brag about the singer."

"So — your sister had your yacht redecorated —"

"And she is paying for Ronnie's expenses. Up to a point. I'm supposed to be grateful." Lady Cecelia made a face; Heris wondered what had caused the bad feeling in her family in the first place. She waited in attentive silence, in case Lady Cecelia wanted to say more, but the older woman turned to ask the attendants to bring the sweet. Heris was glad to see the last of the fruit and cheese, but not really interested in the sweet. She wanted a few hours' sleep.

"If you'll excuse me," she began. "I really need to check with the refitting crew aboard, and my watch officer."

"Oh — certainly. Go ahead." Lady Cecelia's expression was carefully neutral. Did she think Heris was disgusted with her? Heris felt a surge of sympathy for the older woman. She grinned.

"I have a wager to win, remember?"

That got the open smile she hoped for, and Lady Cecelia raised her glass in salute. "We shall see," she said. "I have the feeling you'll make an excellent horsewoman."

Heris laughed. "As the luck falls, and my ability to push the refitters succeeds. See you later."

❖   ❖   ❖

Lady Cecelia watched her captain leave the room, and wondered what the woman really thought. Clearly she had more qualifications than shipboard skills alone: she was well read, she wore good clothes, she knew what to do with the array of eating utensils common to fine dining, and she had surprising tact. On the face of it, she would have made a far more compatible sister than Berenice. She let herself imagine the two of them riding side by side across the training fields . . . relaxing together over dinner. No. This woman never relaxed, not really, while she . . . Lady Cecelia allowed herself a relaxed sigh. Her captain might snatch a few hours' sleep, but would doubtless dream of wiring diagrams and structural steel. She herself would follow this excellent dinner with a relaxing stroll in the hotel's excellent garden, and then sleep as long as she liked in her luxurious bed with all its inventive amenities.

The stroll and the engineered scents in the garden eased the last of the tension her nephew's rudeness had put in her shoulders, and she slipped into the warmed, perfumed bed contentedly. She could hear Myrtis checking all the room's controls, murmured that she'd like it a bit cooler, and was asleep before the cooler draft had time to reach her cheek.

Morning brought complications, as she'd expected. This was not the first time one of her employees had died, just the first on her yacht, and by far the most violent. She had already contacted the legal firm recommended by her family's own solicitors; the bright-eyed young man in formal black had been waiting downstairs by the concierge's desk when she emerged from her bedroom and called for breakfast. She looked at the local time, and whistled. Mid-morning of mainshift, and he had time to wait on her? She checked her captain's whereabouts while he was on the way up, and found, as she expected, that Serrano was back at work on the yacht.

He was talking almost before he got into the room. "Now, Lady Cecelia, I'm sure you're simply devastated by this, but let me assure you that our firm is experienced —"

She stopped him with a gesture. "Wait. I'm going to eat breakfast, and you're welcome to join me. But no business until afterwards, though in fact I'm not devastated, and if you weren't experienced, you wouldn't have been recommended." That stopped him, though he fidgeted all through breakfast, refusing to eat. Finally his nervous twitches got to her, and she gave up on the diced crustaceans in a puree of mixed tubers. . . . It was mediocre anyway, too heavily flavored with dill and some local spice that burnt her tongue without offering a taste worth the pain. She finished with a large pastry, and a silver bowl of some red jam — quite flavorful — and nodded to him. "Go on, now; what's the damage?"

"Your crewman . . . that was killed . . ." He seemed stunned that she wasn't falling apart. What did he think, that older women never saw death?

"Environmental technician Nils Iklind," Lady Cecelia recited. "He disobeyed the captain's orders to wear his protective suit, opened a badly overfull sludge tank, and died of hydrogen sulfide poisoning. You have seen the data cubes?"

"Yes, ma'am . . . Lady Cecelia. Our senior partners reviewed them, and feel that you have a very strong case for accidental death."

"So what is the problem?"

"Well . . ." The young man fidgeted some more, and Lady Cecelia began to compose the memo she would send to the family solicitors explaining why this firm was *not* suitable. "It's the union, ma'am. They think it's the captain's fault for sending him into a dangerous area — for inadequate supervision in allowing him to enter the area without his suit on. Particularly since your other crewman also did not have his suit properly on, and says that all the captain did was tell them to meet there, suited up."

Cecelia sniffed. "And how was the captain to know that he would open the hatch before she got there? Why didn't he wait?"

"That's not the point. They're inclined to argue that the captain should have been there to enforce the order to suit up. Or at least another officer. On larger vessels, of course, there would be a supervisor. Technically, Iklind held a supervisory rating, but he hadn't been acting in that capacity. And the maintenance logs and emergency drills —"

"That was Captain Olin's misconduct; Captain Serrano told me she had begun training crew and reestablishing the correct procedures."

"But she hadn't completed that process yet, and that's what the union is arguing. I'll need to interview the captain —"

"She's aboard the ship, overseeing the refitting. You'd have to suit up." A chime sounded; when she looked, the comunit flashed discreetly. "Excuse me a moment."

"It might be the office for me," he said, but Cecelia waved him to silence as she pressed the button to her ear.

"Sorry to bother you," Captain Serrano said, "but we have a new problem that may help solve an old one."

"What's that?" Cecelia asked. The young man across from her looked as if he were trying to grow his ears longer; it gave him a very odd expression.

"Mr. Brynear has found . . . items . . . in one of the scrubbers. It might explain why Iklind risked going in unsuited, and it might explain why Captain Olin connived at a fake maintenance procedure." Her captain said no more; Cecelia hoped it was because she assumed her employer's innocence and intelligence both.

"Ummm. You would prefer to discuss this someplace else?"

"I would, but it is clearly a matter for law enforcement. Mr. Brynear has documented the discovery." Which meant law enforcement had already been summoned. What, she wondered, could Captain Olin have been up to? Smuggling? But what? She realized she had no idea how large a "scrubber" was, or what would fit into it. But she couldn't ask over an unsecured com line.

"It seems I have a good chance to win our wager," Cecelia said. "Where shall I meet you? I have legal advice with me."

"We could all come there, or you could come to the refitters. . . . your counsel should know. . . . "

"We'll come." She felt she had to have some refuge from

conflict; she would meet trouble elsewhere. In a few brief phrases she explained the little she understood to the young man, who gulped and asked permission to call back to his office. "While I change," she said, and headed for the bedroom and Myrtis. What did one wear when one's crewman had died of an accident that might be related to smuggling, and the goods — whatever they were — had been found aboard one's yacht? What could convey innocence, outrage, and the determination to be a good citizen? She had never been skilled at this sort of thing. . . . Berenice would have known instantly which scarf or pin, which pair of shoes, would give the right impression. Cecelia opted for formal and dark, with a hat, which hid the unruly lock of hair that wanted to stand straight up from her head.

When she emerged, the young man explained that a senior partner would meet her at the refitter's . . . he would escort her there, and hand over the case papers. Cecelia smiled at him, and raged inwardly. They should have sent a senior partner in the first place . . . no doubt they were billing the family at the senior partner's rate.

✧ Chapter Six

"Ah . . . Lady Cecelia?" The gray-haired man flicked a glance at the younger one that made him hand over his briefcomp and then leave.

"Yes, and you're —?"

"Ser Granzia, and you're quite right that we should not have sent a junior partner." He offered his arm; she took it. "We should have known that you would not call in legal help for a minor problem, and the . . . individual who made that decision has been so informed."

"Ah. I had wondered." Cecelia let herself be guided into the front office of the refitters. A respectful secretary murmured that Mr. Desin and Chief Brynear were waiting for them in the conference room. Ser Granzia, it seemed, knew the way; his guidance was subtle but unmistakable. Cecelia noticed that the flat gray tweed carpet of the front office gave way to a flat utilitarian surface dully reflecting the overhead lights. On either side, small offices stood open, cluttered with terminals, parts, schematics. She didn't recognize any of it. Around a corner, carpet reappeared, this time a rich green, much softer. Double doors at the end of the corridor led into a spacious conference room with a wide window to the same sort of view her hotel suite provided. Four people waited there, a tall man in conventional business attire, a shorter one in a rumpled coverall, a nondescript person no doubt representing law and order, and Captain Serrano. On the wide polished table that Cecelia recognized as brasilwood lay a small packet, something lumpy encased in a bag or sack.

"The owner, I presume?" said the tall man. "I'm Eniso

Desin, madam. And this is Chief Brynear, the individual
in charge of your refitting, and Mr. Files, the local investi-
gator for CenCom."

"Lady Cecelia de Marktos a Bellinveau," said Ser
Granzia. Cecelia had not heard herself introduced formally for some time; now she remembered why she
disliked it so. It sounded silly. "Of the Aranlake Sept, fides
de Barraclough." It could also go on another five lines or
so, if she didn't stop him. The complete formality gave
the genetic makeup, political affiliations, and social standing of the male and female lines for six generations . . .
but was usually reserved for those assumed to be ignorant
of it, and in need of awe.

"And yes, I'm the owner," she said, when Granzia
paused for breath.

"The ship's registry," Files said, "lists you as Lady
Cecelia Marktos. I presume that's equivalent?"

"Yes," Cecelia said. "The registry doesn't have room on
the owner's line for all of it. I asked, and they said it would
be adequate."

"And you are the same Lady Cecelia to whom the yacht
designated SY-00021-38-HOX was originally registered?"

"Yes, of course I am." Who else, her tone said.

His gaze flicked from her to Captain Serrano and back.
"Then I regret to inform you that your vessel has apparently
been involved in illegal activities of a criminal nature."
Cecelia wondered what illegal activities of a non-criminal
nature would be, but didn't ask. "How long has this . . .
Captain Serrano . . . been your commanding officer?"

"Since I left the Court. I dismissed my former captain
for incompetence and refusal to follow my orders, and
Captain Serrano had just resigned from the Regular
Space Service. She had signed with the employment
agency I use and they recommended her highly."

"And that agency is?"

"I don't see what this has to do with anything," Cecelia
said, beginning to feel grumpy. Whatever was going on,
she was sure Captain Serrano hadn't been involved. The
woman might be a stiff-necked military prig, but she
wasn't any kind of a criminal. "Perhaps you would be kind

enough to explain just what sort of illegal activity you are talking about."

"Do you know what that is?" Files pointed to the packet on the table.

"No." She felt her brows rising, as much irritation as ignorance. She didn't like people playing games with her. "I suppose you are going to explain?"

"In good time, madam. You're sure you've never seen it before?"

"I told you —" she began in an exasperated voice; Ser Granzia intervened.

"Excuse me, but if you are contemplating criminal charges against Lady Cecelia, or her captain, you surely remember that you must inform them."

"I know that," Files said. "But if the lady had nothing to do with it, her answer might help —"

"I think she will answer no further questions until you have explained, to my satisfaction, what you think it is." Ser Granzia's voice, mellow and lush though it was, contained no hint of yielding.

"We believe it to be smuggled goods. It has not yet been subjected to forensic examination, but just glancing at it my guess is proprietary data." From Files's expression, he hoped she wouldn't understand.

"You mean — trade secrets? Something an — an industrial spy might have made off with?"

"Possibly. Because proprietary data is secret —"

"Are secret," Cecelia murmured. She might not know much about industry, but she knew data was a plural noun. Files grimaced.

"Whatever you say, madam. Are secret — anyway, theft is not reported. It may not be known. It's not like jewels in a vault."

"Could it be military?" That from Heris Serrano. Cecelia looked at her captain who looked back with dark, inscrutable eyes.

"Possibly," Files said. "Forensics will tell us." Clearly he had no intention of sharing his turf with anyone. "Then, if it is —"

"Fleet should know." Not even a ridiculous purple

uniform could make Heris Serrano look unimportant. Cecelia tried to imagine her former captain in the same garb, and realized that he'd have looked like a purple blimp straining at its tether. This woman, in his black, would have looked dangerous. "Fleet forensics could assist."

"I'll be the judge of that," Files said. Ser Granzia stirred at Cecelia's side; Files shot him a glance. "Did you have *legal* advice, Ser Granzia?"

"That if it is possibly a military secret, the captain is correct: some representative should be present when it is examined in any detail. Otherwise we may all find ourselves compromised. You remember, no doubt, the decision of Army versus Stillinbagh?"

"Very well." Files looked angry. "I will inform the local military attaché."

"Perhaps," Ser Granzia said, "we could wait while you did so?"

Cecelia wondered if she was imagining the threat in his tone. Files flushed, asked for a comlink, and spoke into it. He set it back down with care, as if he really wanted to throw it through the wall, and said the attaché would be along shortly. Cecelia was in no mood to wait for more information. "Captain Serrano," she began, bypassing Files, "can you tell me how this was found?"

Her captain smiled, as if glad to be asked the question. "Yes — you remember that I authorized Velarsin and Co. to exchange all damaged units from the environmental system, rather then repairing them in place?"

"Of course," Cecelia said.

"That was for reasons of both time and safety. You may recall that I also had Mr. Brynear document the condition of those components, to back up your damage claim on Diklos and Sons." When Cecelia nodded, she went on. "Some components could be repaired, and we were to get a refund on those. In the process of examining the components removed, Mr. Brynear's technicians found items secreted in several. Most suggestively, in the scrubber which we were going to examine when Iklind was killed because he didn't have his suit on."

Cecelia felt only confusion. "What does that have to do with it?" Before Serrano could answer, Cecelia realized. "Oh — he *knew* something was there? Something you'd find?"

"We can't know, Lady Cecelia." Heris glanced at Files, who clearly wished she wouldn't explain more, but she went on. "There's a chain of occurrences that makes me suspicious of Iklind and possibly others formerly or presently in the crew. The system flush and recharge that Diklos and Sons didn't do. The curiously inefficient course your former captain set on the way to Court, which made you late. Iklind's apparent haste to get to that scrubber before I did — at the cost of his own life."

"You think he was smuggling something. Iklind and . . . and Captain Olin?" First came anger: how *dared* he? And then fear . . . how had she not known what was happening on her ship? How were the smuggled items transferred, if they were? Would Olin have opened the ship to boarders?

"It's possible, madam," said Files, with a sharp glance at Heris. "Ship's crews have been known to do so, without an owner's knowledge. Of course, sometimes the owner is also involved."

"Surely you jest." That was all she could say. The impertinence of the man!

"Are you suggesting the Lady Cecelia was involved in any putative illegal act?" asked Ser Granzia. "Remember —"

"I remember the Sihil-Tomaso ruling, Ser Granzia," said Files. "I made no accusation; I merely answered what seemed to be Lady Cecelia's question." His smile was more of a smirk, she decided. He went on. "Now: procedurally, we must impound the evidence, which includes the location in which it was found; I'm afraid your ship is that location —" Cecelia could hardly believe her ears. Was everything against her?

"Not so, Mr. Files." Her captain's crisp voice interrupted Files. "The scrubbers were not in the ship when the items were found. They had already been removed. All environmental system components are dockside; what's in the *Sweet Delight* is new and empty."

"But that's where they *were*," Files said. "On that ship

with the contraband in them. There may be more, hidden somewhere else. It doesn't matter where the scrubbers were when the evidence was actually found —"

"On the contrary." Ser Granzia's honey-smooth voice had an edge to it now. "According to the rules of evidence in a list of rulings going back to Essex versus Jovian Mining Ltd, impoundment of the container does not include impoundment of the vessel in which that container was transported, if the discovery occurred while the container was not aboard."

"But we *know* the contraband was aboard," Files said, more loudly.

"But it doesn't matter, Mr. Files." Ser Granzia did not raise his voice, but Cecelia saw the other man wilt. "The rulings are all clear, and all in favor of my client. I will be glad to get a local ruling, of course, but I'm sure it will uphold my client's position. Now — shall we contact Fleet? I believe it is better for us to do this together."

Files looked angry, but nodded; Ser Granzia turned to Eniso Desin, the senior partner of Velarsin and Co. "May we use your equipment?"

"Of course, Ser Granzia. But I am afraid that we cannot give Lady Cecelia full credit for the reparable elements of the system until they are released from official custody. . . . I am sorry, but —"

"I quite understand," Ser Granzia said. "Indeed, it would be unfair, and my client will be satisfied if you keep account of what was impounded; if it should be released, and still worth repair, perhaps you will bid on it?"

"Oh, certainly," Desin said. "Mr. Brynear assures me that at least sixty percent of the components would be worth working on."

"Excellent." Cecelia wondered if she, too, should say something, but Ser Granzia rolled on. "Now — it seems to me, Mr. Files, that the discovery of items secreted in the scrubber suggests a motive for Iklind to attempt removal at risk of his life. In fact, it strongly suggests his complicity in some illegal activity, and Captain Serrano's innocence. I would suggest that a search warrant, limited to Iklind's personal items and storage spaces, might prove fruitful."

"But —!" Cecelia got that much out before his hand clamped on her wrist.

"It need not," he went on, "inconvenience Lady Cecelia or interfere with her schedule, provided that you act in a timely manner."

"Right." Files seemed sapped of energy. Cecelia wondered if Ser Granzia's voice had a hypnotic overlay. "I'll — get that done as soon as we've contacted the military."

Before she knew how it happened, Cecelia found herself sitting across a table from Heris Serrano in Desin's private office, with a tray of hot pastries and a variety of drinks before her. Ser Granzia was still in conference with Mr. Files and Desin; Desin's assistant had brought the refreshments and now left them alone. Cecelia watched her captain pour herself a cup of something hot from a fluted pot. The woman had a quality Cecelia had not yet defined, but found attractive. She never fidgeted, never seemed divided against herself. Yet she did not seem insensitive . . . someone who had read and enjoyed Siilvaas could not be insensitive.

"You may win our wager, milady," she said now. She offered the steaming cup to Cecelia, who shook her head. She wanted something cold, and chose a bottle of fruit juice from an ice bucket.

"Circumstances have changed," Cecelia said. "Perhaps I should withdraw?"

"No — a wager's a wager." Serrano's short black hair actually moved when she shook her head; Cecelia had begun to wonder if it was a wig. "I shall look forward to my lessons on your mechanical horse." She had an engaging grin, Cecelia decided, which made her look years younger.

"Ummm. I still think the interruption of officialdom makes it unfair: suppose I exchange honors and let you teach me more about my ship? I'm now convinced my own ignorance is both inconvenient and culpable."

The dark eyes measured her; Cecelia felt suddenly as if she had become a novice rider, facing a stern judge in her first event. Why had a woman with such a gift of command given up her commission? Cecelia could not believe it was anything dishonorable . . . not with those eyes. A mistake? A quarrel? She had not seemed quarrelsome so far, even when confronted with Ronnie's rudeness.

"If it is your pleasure," Serrano said. "Then I will be very glad to show you over your ship. But I cannot consider it as your obligation under our wager unless I actually win . . . and despite the best your legal firm can do, I expect we will be late leaving."

Cecelia snorted. "I'm beginning to think this year's season is jinxed. Here I was invited for the opening day — planned to be early for once, planned to attend the first ball, even. Then Olin got me to Court late, and I had young Ronnie foisted on me, and now this. If I'm not careful I'll break a leg or something and miss hunting altogether."

"How long does it last? If it's more than a few days, we should be there for some of it."

The ignorance surprised her again, but she reminded herself that even among her class, not everyone knew much about fox hunting. "The season is just that," she said gently. "A whole season — in this case, a planetary quartile. Ideally, fox hunting is done when it is cool enough so that the horses don't overheat in the long chase, damp enough for hounds to pick up the scent."

"Then —"

"Oh, we'll arrive before it's over, if something else doesn't happen. But it's the opening — the first day — that excitement —" Cecelia stared out the window at the view without seeing it. "You can't understand; you haven't been there. I love it anyway, wet days and dry; I'm one of the last to leave. It's just different, that's all."

"Did you ever do any sailing?" Serrano asked.

"Sailing? You mean on water?" When Serrano nodded, Cecelia went on. "Yes, a little. Bunny has lodges on island groups; I remember sailing little boats, hardly more than floatboards, one afternoon. Why?"

"Because what you describe for hunting reminds me of racing season at my grandparents' place on Lowein. There again there's a season, a weather pattern, that fits the sport, and on the first day all the boats, from the little sailboards up to square-riggers, parade along the coast. Everyone wants to be there."

Cecelia recognized the note of longing. "Did you race sailboats?"

Serrano smiled. "A cousin and I did, before we went in the Academy — it was a Rix-class, which wouldn't mean anything to you, any more than horse terms do to me. And I crewed on a larger yacht one summer."

"And will you do that when you retire? Go back there and sail?"

Serrano's face seemed to close into an impenetrable shell. "No, milady. Lowein is where Fleet officers retire. . . . I wouldn't fit in there, and I've no desire to embarrass my family."

"I hardly think you'd embarrass anyone," Cecelia said. "Is it such a disgrace to captain my yacht?" She was surprised herself at how angry she felt at that thought.

"No — not at all." The voice carried no conviction, though. "Nothing to do with that — this — at all." Serrano managed a forced smile. "Never mind — my retirement plans are far away, and we have a present problem: how to get you to your hunt on time. I'll check with Sirkin, and see if we can't cut some corners."

"With your concern for my safety?" That was meant as a joke, but came out sharper than she had intended.

"Yes — with due concern for your safety." Serrano was serious again. "There's another matter, milady. It's about your crew."

"What — do you think they're all smugglers?" Again, a lightness she couldn't sustain. Cecelia shook her head. "I'm sorry: I am trying to be funny and it's not working."

"No wonder," Serrano said. "You have had your schedule disrupted; you have lost a crewman through a dangerous accident; you have nearly been accused of smuggling; and you had to spend several days of uncomfortable travel under emergency restrictions. Frankly, I think you're holding up surprisingly well."

"You do?"

"Yes. Nonetheless, I must bother you about the crew." Serrano paused to sip from her cup and take a bite of pastry. Cecelia noticed again the dark smudges under her eyes — had she slept enough? Or was it worry? She picked up a pastry herself, and tried it. Leathery, compared to those her own cook turned out. "You hired your crew from one employment agency," Serrano said. "Who recommended that agency to you?"

"I hired you from the same agency," Cecelia said. "What difference does that make?"

"It's a bit of embarrassment, but . . . they don't send you their best. They admitted that to me, when I asked them to forward some information on the crew."

"But — but I'm a *Bellinveau!*" Cecelia's voice rose. "Surely they wouldn't —"

"What they said," Serrano broke in, "was that you did not need the level of expertise that a large ship did. Their top people go to big shipping and passenger lines, where they have a chance to move up —"

"I pay very high salaries," Cecelia said. "That ought to mean something, if my name doesn't." She didn't like being interrupted, and she didn't like the implication that her ship was unimportant compared to a commercial liner.

"It means you get greedy incompetents." Serrano stared her down; Cecelia felt again the power of that dark gaze. Then her face relaxed and she grinned. "Except me, of course. I wasn't so much greedy as desperate to get a civilian job. But they did not recommend me for a commercial ship because of my background — the big corporations like to train their own people their own way, and find a military background a hindrance. You've got a very good navigator in Sirkin — she topped her exams, and I'm very satisfied with her work." Cecelia had the feeling that "very satisfied" from Captain Serrano would have been a dozen flowery adjectives from someone else. "But the others, milady, looked on your yacht as a cushy berth where they would be well paid for doing little, and your previous captains seem to have concurred."

"But everything seemed to run smoothly," Cecelia said, trying to remember if she'd ever noticed anything. Not really. As long as she arrived where she wanted to, when she wanted to, she had assumed the ship was fine. It

certainly cost enough. "And I had the regular maintenance and inspections — I don't know what more I could
have done." Even as she said it, she realized how she'd
feel if someone said that about a stable in which they
boarded their horses. She had had contempt for owners
who didn't know, who didn't seem to care, about the details of stable management. Apparently she had made the
same error with her own ship.

Serrano did not seem surprised, but didn't dwell on
the point. "You paid for them, you mean. You had to trust
your crew, because you didn't know yourself what to look
for. And I think that for some years you had honest, if less
than superb, crew members who did their duties fairly
well. A good captain would have been enough, to provide
the initiative and discipline for crew who were competent
but uninspired. But in Massimir Olin, you did not have a
good captain. I don't know with any certainty, but I suspect that he was looking for exactly such a ship, a small
but fast vessel belonging to someone with no knowledge
of ships or space, a vessel whose owner might be
expected to visit places closed to commercial trade. You
let him choose replacement crew, of course, and when
old Titinka had that heart attack, he hired Iklind — from
the same agency as the rest."

"But it's quite reputable," Cecelia said. Her mind
whirled. She had never thought of herself — independent to the point of eccentricity and with no romantic
susceptibilities — as anyone's natural prey. The image of
herself as a fat sheep which a wolf might stalk seemed
both ridiculous and disgusting. "It's the top agency in its
field." Implicit in that was the assumption that no Bellinveau would use less.

"It is reputable," said Serrano. "But no agency is
immune from penetration. Where there is blood, the
blood-suckers gather: where there is wealth . . ."

"I know the saying," Cecelia said. "But I never
expected it to apply to me — I'm old, unattached and in-
tend to remain that way, my money will revert to the
family when I die —"

"You are free transportation for your crew," Serrano

said. "You pay well enough that they know you must have more — you have everything done by top firms. But I think for Olin it was the places you could go without comment — the places he wanted to go, which you could take him to."

Cecelia thought about that, and set it aside. What Olin's motives had been did not concern her now. "You had a point to make about the crew?" she asked. Serrano's twinkle rewarded her for coming back to that point.

"Yes, I did. I had intended to suggest some replacements of the least effective after your season of hunting; considering what's happened, I think you have both cause and justification for making some changes now. Assuming you don't want to start with me."

"Don't be silly!" Cecelia said. "I don't blame you for any of this."

Serrano shrugged. "You might well have. Good captains don't let such accidents happen. Anyway, you need a replacement for Iklind. I'm seriously concerned about the entire environmental department, and would suggest you also drop the new juniors, retaining only the survivor of the accident. Mr. Gavin I believe to be honest, though totally devoid of initiative, and I think he can be salvaged by some good training. Your pilot . . . actually, besides his manner, I have no complaint of his performance. But he strongly defended Olin's choice of course, in the face of a possible course that would have had you on your schedule. I suspect his complicity. We could do without a pilot; I am licensed for that duty, a separate qualification, and the expense of this refitting would explain your dropping him entirely."

"But can we find good crew out here?" Cecelia asked.

"Yes — in fact I've asked Mr. Brynear about that already. As this is a major repair facility, there are always crews coming through. Someone is sick, and stays behind; someone is unhappy and jumps ship — not that we want that sort. Velarsin and Co., and other firms, hire these temporaries, and their work records here give us something to go on. Also there are people who start in refitting who want to work aboard a ship; if they've taken their exams, and we interview their supervisors, we can find some good ones. But it's up to you, milady."

Exactly what she didn't want, on her ship. She wanted it to function perfectly without her having to make any decisions at all. Just transportation . . . but of course, there were people who looked at horses as just transportation, and she knew what she thought of *them*. "I've always left it up to my captains," Cecelia said slowly. "Are you asking me to interview with you, or —"

"If you wish; it might be helpful to you to understand what I would look for in applicants. But what I meant is that I would not dismiss your employees without gross negligence on their part. You had some input, I assume, in the size of crew when you started out?"

"Well . . . to be honest . . . I took the advice of the employment agency even then. Told them what I had bought, and asked them to arrange a crew." She could see by her captain's expression that this was not the right thing to have done. She shook her head. "I was a fool, wasn't I? Just like people I've known who've gone broke with racing stables. It just never occurred to me that the same things could happen here, in a simple little yacht." Serrano's expression did not change, but her eyes softened.

"You had other things to think about, I'm sure. Why don't you come along to some of the interviews, at least, and begin to pick up some of the terms? It will impress applicants, and it won't bother me."

"Fine. I will." She would learn every screw and bolt on her ship, the way she had once learned the anatomy of horses and every piece of leather and metal on her tack. How could she have left herself unguarded like this?

"And don't be hard on yourself," Serrano said. Cecelia blinked. Was the woman a mind reader as well? "Remember, I still don't know anything about horses."

"Welcome aboard, milady," Heris said. Eight hours late, they would be, undocking, but she felt happy anyway. Better a good job than a fast sloppy one. She had inspected the replacements with Mr. Brynear six hours before, and knew the new system was up to spec. Her

new environmental team knew what they were doing,
and Timmons was rapidly learning; he wanted to keep his
job. The disgruntled pilot had complained bitterly about
being dumped in the middle of nowhere; Lady Cecelia
had finally paid his passage to one of the inner worlds of
the system, even though her legal advisor said it wasn't
necessary. Lady Cecelia had told her gleefully about the
stormy battle going on between Diklos & Sons, the insurance company, and her lawyers; she thought she would
get her money back, at the least, and she had convinced
the union that Iklind's death was probably due to the bad
work done by Diklos . . . so now Diklos had the union on
their backs as well. Lady Cecelia's staff had boarded an
hour ago. Heris had given Bates the staff emergency
directives, and he'd taken them without comment. . . .
They would soon begin emergency drills, proper drills,
and this would be a proper ship.

"Thank you, Captain Serrano." Lady Cecelia and her
maid came aboard serenely, as if nothing had happened;
Heris saw her eyes flicker at the change in uniform. Heris
had squeezed in a visit to a good tailor, and while it was
still purple, it lacked the scarlet, teal, and cream trim and
about half its gold braid. The docking access tube still had
a thick carpet, but the walls were properly bare for inspection, conduits and tubing color-coded in accordance
with Transportation Department directives.

Behind Lady Cecelia, her nephew and his friends
straggled in. Heris watched them with contempt behind
her motionless features. Rich, spoiled brats, she thought.
A waste of talent, if they have any; a waste of the genetic
material and wealth it took to rear them this far. She gave
a crisp "Welcome aboard," and then walked past them out
the tube to the dockside. Bates was waiting in the passage
to see to anything more they needed. She would have
avoided the greeting altogether except that she wanted to
say a last few words to Brynear.

"I hear you had a wager with your owner," he said,
grinning at her. "She making you pay up?"

"She'd have let me off, considering the circumstances,"
Heris said, grinning back. She liked his sort of toughness,

his competence. He reminded her of the best she'd known, a memory she didn't want right now. She pushed it out of her mind. "But the forfeit's to learn more about what fascinates her — horses, of all things! — and if I'm to be a good captain for her, I need to understand her."

"If it weren't rude and nosy, I'd ask you a question," Brynear said.

"It is, and I won't answer it," Heris said, with an edge. Then she softened. "I know what you'd ask, and I'm not ready to talk about it. Just wanted to thank you for a good job done well in a hurry. I'm glad we were able to argue our way past your schedule — and sorry to disrupt it."

"You can disrupt my schedule any time," Brynear said. "As I would have made clear, if you weren't leaving so soon."

"You can repair my ship anytime," Heris said, smiling. He was attractive, but not that attractive. Yet. The other memories were still too clear. "As I did make clear — but I wish we didn't have to leave now. Thanks."

"You're welcome, Captain." He threw her a civilian's version of a salute and turned away. Heris went back to the ship and thoroughly enjoyed showing her crew that she was as good as the former pilot at undock and tug maneuvers.

"You shouldn't have insulted the captain to her face," Raffa said severely. They were two days out of refitting, two days of cool courtesy between Cecelia and the young people. Ronnie pouted, but she did not relent. "Don't put out your lip at me," she said. "It was wrong, and you know it."

"I didn't know she was there. I didn't know Aunt Cecelia had approved it. It's too bad, really. I never asked to come along on this ridiculous cruise; it was all my mother's idea."

"You'd rather be supervising a loading team at Scavell or Xingsan?" asked Buttons. "Come on, now, Ronnie . . . this isn't bad. I admit, I wasn't planning to be home for the season this year — no more than Bubbles — but it's not as if visiting my father were a hardship."

"That's not what I meant," Ronnie said. He looked

around for sympathy, and found expressions that told him he was boring, and boring was one thing they would not accept.

"Why don't we swim?" asked Bubbles. "Now that we can use the pool again, a nice swim would be fun." She stretched her long, elegant arms, and wriggled in a way that suggested something other than swimming.

The others agreed; Ronnie knew he should swallow his sulks and go with them, but the sulks were too embedded. "Go ahead," he said, when they turned to look back at him. "I'm going to try Beggarman one more time." That was the computer game they'd been playing until it palled . . . and Ronnie never had gotten above the eighth level.

He had no real intention of playing Beggarman. . . . He wanted to regain the ground he felt he'd lost with the captain. A private apology should do it; he had charmed his way past fiercer dragons than this. No woman of her age could be immune to boyish charm. He showered, put on a fresh jumpsuit, and looked at himself in the mirror. He slicked his hair: innocence? No. It looked as if he were trying for innocence. He tousled it: mischievous waif? Yes. That should do it. He waited until the others had logged into the pool enclosure. Then he strolled down the curving passage, slipped through the hatch between crew and staff areas, and found his way to the bridge. It wasn't that hard; he had memorized the ship plan on his deskcomp.

The bridge did not meet his expectations. He had envisioned something like the bridge of the training cruiser. . . . Aside from that, and the small craft he'd piloted, he'd never been aboard a ship. He stared at the small room crowded with screens and control boards, the watch seats crammed in side by side, the command bench hardly an arm's length from any of them. Something was going on. . . . He sensed the tension, heard it in the low voices that reported values he did not understand. He had expected to find silence, even boredom; he had expected to be a welcome break in a monotonous shift. But no one seemed to notice him. Captain Serrano uttered a series of numbers as if they were important. . . .

But how could they be, out here in the middle of nowhere? It must be one of her stupid drills or something.

With all the confidence of youth and privilege, Ronnie strolled into the crowded space.

"Excuse me, but when you've got a moment, Captain, I'd like to speak to you." He spoke with the forthright but courteous tone of someone with a perfect right to be where he was, doing what he was. He expected a prompt response.

He did not expect the smart crack of an open hand across his face; it sent him reeling into the back of someone's chair. He grabbed for a support, and found a handy rail along the bulkhead. His cheek hurt; his mouth burned. Anger raged along his bones, but he was still too shocked to move. Serrano's voice continued, low and even, with one number after another. Someone repeated them, and he saw hands flicker across control boards. Just as he got his breath back, he felt the gut-deep wrench he knew from his one training voyage: the yacht was flicking in and out of a series of jump points.

Anger drained away; fear flooded him now. Jump transitions . . . they'd been near *jump transitions*, and if he'd interfered they might all have been killed. The quick remorse he was never too proud to feel swept over him. He gulped back the apology he wanted to make — he should wait, he should be sure it was safe.

Then Captain Serrano turned to him, anger on her dark face. "Don't you *ever* come on my bridge again, mister," she said. Ronnie's eyes slid around the room; no one looked at him. "Go on — get out."

"But I — I came to say something."

"I don't want to hear it. Get off the bridge."

"But I want to apologize —"

She took a step toward him and he realized that he was afraid of her — afraid of a woman a head shorter — in a way he had not feared anyone since childhood. She took another step, and his hand fell away from the rail; he backed up. "You can apologize to my crew for nearly getting us all killed," she said. "And then you can go away and not come back."

"I'm — I'm sorry," said Ronnie, with a gulp. It was not working the way he'd planned. "I — I really am." She came yet another step closer, and he backed up; she reached out and he flinched . . . but she touched a button on the bulkhead, and a hatch slid closed four inches from his nose. BRIDGE ACCESS: PRESS FOR PERMISSION appeared on a lightboard above it. Ronnie stood there long enough to realize that his cheek still hurt, and she wasn't going to let him back in. Then he got really angry.

"It wasn't my fault," he told George later. No one else had seemed to notice, but George had asked about the mark on his face. "I mean, it was, in a way, but I didn't mean to interrupt during a jump transition. She didn't have to take it that way. Damned military arrogance. She *hit* me — the owner's *family* — all she had to do was explain. Just you wait — I'll get even with her."

"Are you sure that's a good idea?" But George's eyes had lit up. He loved intrigue, especially vengeance. George had engineered some of their best escapades in school, including the ripely dead rat appearing on the service platter at a banquet for school governors.

"Of course," Ronnie said. "She has other duties; we have nothing to do between here and Bunny's place but get bored and crabby with each other." He felt much better, now that he'd decided. "First thing is, we'll get into the computer and find out more about her."

"You could always give a little kick to one of her drills," George said.

"Exactly." Ronnie grinned. Much better. A good attack beats defense every time; he'd read that someplace.

✦ Chapter Seven

Heris could have believed the *Sweet Delight* knew it smelled sweeter — or perhaps it responded to the change in the attitude of its crew. Without the sour-faced pilot, and the inept moles, with the addition of two eager, hard-working newcomers, crew alliances shifted and solidified around a new axis. A healthier one, to Heris's mind. They were not yet what she would call sharp, but they were trying, now. No one complained about the emergency drills. No one slouched around with the listless expression that had so worried her before. Perhaps it was only fear of losing their jobs, but she hoped it was something better.

It had been unfortunate that she'd hit the owner's nephew. She knew that; she knew it was her fault from start to finish. She had let them leave the hatch to the bridge open. . . . On such a small ship, with a small crew, where the owner never ventured into the working compartments, it had seemed safe. She had not noticed when he came, and when he startled her she had silenced him in a way that might have been hazardous — would have been, with some people. She was ashamed of herself, even though they'd made it through a fairly tricky set of transition points safely.

She called Cecelia as soon as they were through, and explained. "It was my fault for not securing the bridge —"

"Never mind. He's been insufferable this whole trip; his mother spoiled him rotten."

"But I should have —"

Cecelia interrupted her again. "It's not a problem, I assure you. If you want to feel chastened, schedule your first riding lesson today."

Heris had to laugh at that. "All right. Two hours from now?"

"I'll be there. Regular gymsuit will do for now."

Heris finished the necessary documentation of jump point transition, completed a few more minor chores, and left the bridge to Mr. Gavin.

"This," said Cecelia cheerfully, "is your practice mount." Heris had expected something like a metal or plastic horse shape on some kind of spring arrangement, but the complicated machine in front of her looked nothing at all like a real horse. Except for the saddle — a traditional leather saddle — on a cylindrical section that might have been plastic, it could have been an industrial robot of some sort, with its jointed appendages, power cable connectors, sockets, and dangling wires with ominous little clips. Heris had seen something vaguely like it in one of the wilder bars on Durango. . . . Only that had been, she thought, a mechanical bucking bull.

The jointed extension in the front, Cecelia explained, acted as the horse's neck and head, allowing the rider to use real reins. At the moment, the real reins were looped neatly from a hook on one side. "There are sensors in the head," Cecelia said, "which record how much rein pressure you're using, and feed back to the software. Yank the reins, and this thing will respond very much like a real horse. You'll also get an audible tone, to let you know when your rein pressure is uneven." The VR helmet rose from a cantilevered extension behind the saddle. "It's set now at beginner level," Cecelia said. "I'll control pace and direction; you'll just feel the gaits at first." She stood near a waist-high control panel, which Heris noted had several sockets for plug-in modules as well as the usual array of touchplates.

Heris stared at the thing. She had not enjoyed the obligatory riding lessons at the Academy that much, and this looked like the perfect apparatus for making someone look stupid and clumsy. But a bet was a bet, and she owed Cecelia ten hours. The sooner she mounted, the sooner it would be over.

"You don't have to use the VR helmet at first," Cecelia said. "Why not just get on and off a few times, and let me start it walking?"

"Fine." Heris tried to remember just how mounting went. Left foot in the stirrup, but her hands . . . ? On the real horse they'd been taught to grip the reins and put a hand on the neck in front of the saddle; here that would have meant on a pair of gray cylinders like slim pipes. She put both hands on the front of the saddle and hauled herself upward. The machine lurched sideways, with a faint hiss of hydraulics, and she slipped back to the deck.

"Sorry," Cecelia said, trying to hide a grin. "I wasn't ready to correct for that kind of mount. You need to be closer, and push off more strongly with your right leg. Straight up, then swing your leg over. If you hang off the side of a real horse like that, it's likely to unbalance, reach out a leg, and step on you."

Heris tried again, this time successfully. She felt around with her right foot until she got the stirrup on. Cecelia came over and moved her feet slightly. "Weight on the balls of your feet, for now. We're going to start with a simple all-around seat. And no reins for now, until you've got the seat right. Just clasp your wrists in front of you. Let me connect the other sensors. . . ." This meant clipping a dozen dangling wires to Heris's clothing; she felt she was being restrained by gnats. Cecelia retreated to the control column and touched something. The machine lurched; Heris wondered if she was about to be thrown off, but it settled down to a rhythmic roll and pitch. Her body remembered that it felt quite a bit like riding a real horse.

"It's — strange," she said. She might have to take riding lessons, but she didn't have to refrain from comment.

"It's expensive," Cecelia said. "Most riding sims are limited to three gaits, one speed at each gait, and all you can do is go in a circle or straight. This one can keep me in shape." Heris did not say what she thought this time: keeping one old woman in shape hardly suggested that the simulator had great powers. She didn't have to refrain from comment, but she didn't have to be rude, either.

"Let me try the helmet now," she said instead. If her

face was covered by that mass of instrumentation, no sudden expression could give her away.

"Go ahead," Cecelia said. "I think you'll be surprised."

The helmet had all the usual attachments and adjustments; Heris got it on as the sim kept up its movement. As her eyes adapted to the new visual field, she saw in front of her a horse's neck swinging slightly up and down, with two ears . . . and reins lying on that neck, and a long line from the horse's head to someone standing in the center of a white-railed ring. "It doesn't look like you," she said. "Who's the brown-haired man with his arm in a sling?"

"Sorry." Cecelia's voice in the helmet sounded masculine for a moment, then changed. "Someone I used to train with — is that better?" Now it was Cecelia, but a younger Cecelia — her hair flaming red-gold, her tall body dressed in sweater and riding breeches. She looked vibrant and happy and far more attractive than Heris had imagined her.

"Yes — it really does look like a horse." Of course, the simulator for a cruiser really did look like a cruiser, and the simulator for a Station tug really did look like a Station tug. That's what simulators were supposed to do, but maybe Cecelia didn't know that.

"Like *any* horse," Cecelia said, and into the helmet appeared a dizzying array of horse necks and ears: black, brown, white, gray, short, long, thick, thin, with and without manes. Heris blinked.

"I can see that." But after all, how hard could it be to change colors and lengths of neck? It wasn't like going from, say, the bridge of a flagship like *Descant* to the bridge of a tug, or a shuttle. All horses were basically alike, large smelly four-legged mammals that would carry you around if you had no better transportation. The visual settled back to the original neck and ears — light brownish yellow.

"Now — you're going to reverse." Heris expected to halt and back up, but reverse in this case meant making an egg-shaped turn and beginning to circle in the opposite direction, once more facing forward. Different terminology: she filed it away. Next time she would be properly braced for the turn, rather than the halt.

By the end of that first hour, she had walked virtual circles in both directions, halted, reversed, and even done enough trotting to make her thighs ache. She remembered this from her Academy days. There, too, they had walked and trotted back and forth until their legs hurt. It seemed pointless, but harmless, and it might even be good exercise. When she lifted off the helmet, Cecelia smiled up at her.

"And did you find it as bad as you expected?"

"No . . . but is that all there is?"

Cecelia's grin might have warned her, she thought later. "Not at all — I go faster."

"You . . . race?"

"Not racing. Eventing. Do you know what that is?"

Heris racked her memory, and came up with nothing. Event — had to be a sporting event of some kind, she presumed. But what?

"Would you like to see?" Cecelia asked.

"Yes. Of course." Anything her employer cared about that much ought to be important to her.

She had not expected anything like the cube Cecelia showed her, and came up from it breathless. "You — did *that*? That was you on that yellow horse?"

"Chestnut. Yes. That was my last championship ride."

"But those . . . those — obstacles? — were so big. And the horse was running so fast."

Cecelia grinned at her, clearly delighted at her surprise. "I thought you didn't understand. That's what's different about this simulator. You can do all that on it . . . well, all but falling in the actual water, or getting stepped on by the actual horse."

"You mean I could learn to do that — to jump over things like that?"

"Probably not, but you could come close." Cecelia extracted the first cube and fed in another. "This is what fox hunting is like — in fact, this is a cube I made three years ago."

"You made —?"

"Well, I used to be under contract with Yohsi Sports. They'd mount the sim-cam in my helmet, and I wore the wires as well. . . ."

Heris felt that she'd fallen into another layer of mystery. What, she wondered, was "wearing the wires" and what did it have to do with a sports network? But she was tired of asking questions that must sound stupid, so she simply nodded. This time the cube was not *of* Cecelia riding, but from the rider's viewpoint. . . . She saw the green grass blur between the horse's ears, saw a stone wall approaching far too fast . . . and then it was left behind, and another appeared. Little brown and black and white things were running ahead, yelping, and other horses and riders were all around.

"Those are the foxes you're chasing?" she asked finally, as field and wall followed wall and field, apparently without end. There were variations, as some fields were grassy and others muddy, and some walls were taller or had ditches on one side, but it seemed fairly monotonous. Not nearly as interesting as the varied challenges of the cross-country. Cecelia choked, then laughed until she was breathless.

"Those are *hounds*! The fox is ahead of the dogs; the dogs find the scent and trail the fox, and the horses follow the hounds." Then she quit laughing. "I'm sorry. It's not fair, if you've never been exposed to it, but I thought everyone knew about foxes and hounds."

"No," Heris said, between gritted teeth. Some of us, she wanted to say, had better things to do with our time. Some of us were off fighting wars so that people like you could bounce around making entertainment cubes for each other. But that was not entirely fair and she knew it. It probably did take skill to ride like that, although what the use of that skill was, once you'd gained it, she still could not figure out.

"Here." Cecelia handed her yet another cube. "This is the text of an old book on the subject, and since it's one of the few left, you might want to look at it. Bunny's designed his entire hunt around it, even though we know that it predates the twentieth century, Old Earth, and things must have changed afterwards."

Heris looked at the cube file labelled "Surtees" with suspicion. Apparently she would be expected to watch it on her own time. Historical nonsense about horses struck her as even more useless than current nonsense about horses.

"And to be fair, I think it's time I schedule my first lesson in shipboard knowledge, or whatever you want to call it. Do you have time for a student later today?"

Cecelia was, after all, her employer, and she was making an effort to share an enthusiasm. Heris thought of all the things she'd rather do, but nodded. "Of course. When would you like to start?"

"Well . . . after lunch?"

"Fine." Food always came first. But then, it should.

"You could eat with me," Cecelia said, "and give me a head start. I don't even know what you want me to learn."

Meals with the owner. Heris started to grumble internally, then remembered that she'd already had meals with the owner . . . and it hadn't been that bad. "Thank you," she said. "I am at your service."

Heris had no equivalent of the riding simulator to help Cecelia, but she used the next best: the computer's three-dimensional visuals.

"This is a very nice hull," she said. Always start with the positive. "You've got a fair balance of capacity and speed —"

"But my captains always said it was a slow old barge, compared to other ships," Cecelia said. "A luxury yacht can't be expected to compete —"

"You and I both know your former captains had other reasons," Heris said. "It may be a luxury yacht, but we use a very similar hull for —" She stopped herself in time from saying for what, exactly, and managed to finish. "For missions that require a fair turn of speed. And you've got the right power ratio for it; whoever designed this adaptation chose well. Now — let me highlight each system in color, and you can begin to learn how it works."

Cecelia, Heris found, was an apt pupil. She had a surprising ability to grasp 3-D structures, and spotted several features Heris had meant to mention before she could bring them up.

"Yes — you do have waste space there; that's a design compromise, but it's not a bad one. Look at the alternatives. If you ran the coolant this way — see — you get this undesirable cluster of conduits here —"

"Oh . . . and that's supposed to be at a constant temperature —"

"Yes. Now, let's add the electricals."

They both lost track of time, and Cecelia's deskunit finally beeped with a reminder about dinner. She looked surprised. "I didn't — this isn't really dull at all. I could learn this."

"So you could. I'm glad I didn't bore you." Heris stood, and stretched. She would need a hot bath, to get the kinks out this time. "I'll be going — I've got some crew business to take care of."

"Well . . . thank you. Tomorrow, then?"

"I'll look forward to it," Heris said, hoping that could be taken for both sessions, though she was not in fact looking forward to more riding. But fair was fair, and Cecelia was as diligent a pupil as she could wish.

After a few days, Heris found herself enjoying the riding instruction more than she'd expected. The soreness wore off; she had good natural balance, and a lot of experience with simulators. It was less monotonous than the usual exercise apparatus in the crew gym, or swimming against the current in the pool. And she could not have asked for a more attentive owner. Cecelia had her own way of thinking about the various systems, relating them more often to equestrian matters than Heris thought necessary, but if she could understand better that way, why not? At least she was learning, paying attention . . . and in the future that might save her life.

Still, Heris had not forgotten the need for emergency drills. She herself gave a training session to the house staff, and a separate one to Cecelia. Cecelia suggested letting Bates hand out the assignments to the young people, and Heris agreed. She had managed to avoid young Ronnie successfully so far.

That first unannounced shipwide drill would have made a good comedy cube, Heris thought later. She had entered the

specs into the main computer the night before, using an
event function that kept the time from her as well. It should
have been simple: a single small fire, in one of the fire-prone
areas. But very little went as planned. The alarm went off at
0400, ship's time. Heris, fairly sure what it was, nonetheless
responded as she would to any emergency. Those crew
members she thought of as the best arrived at their
emergency stations within the time limit; the others straggled
in late, in one case three minutes late. ("I was in the head,"
mumbled the guilty party. "Havin' a bit of a problem, I was.")

Cecelia logged in within the limit, as did Bates and the
cook (who, spotting the faked "fire," promptly put an
upturned garbage container on it: the right decision.)
Four of the young people sauntered in to their assigned
stations late (but flustered) and two did not appear at all.

"They have to be somewhere," Cecelia said, when
Heris told her.

"Oh, they are. They're in the number five storage bay,
ignoring the whole thing."

"But they can't — who is it?"

"Ronnie and George," Heris said, having no more
patience with them. "Since you gave them their assignments, via Bates —"

"I'll be glad to ream them out, but are you sure they
heard the alarm in there?"

"All compartments have a bell. No, they're hiding out,
for purposes of their own. One thing I could do is put a
scare into them. They think this is just a stupid drill . . .
but they don't know what the supposed emergency is. If I
dump power in there . . . take off the AG, or lose a little
pressure . . ."

"Do it," Cecelia said. Red patches marred her cheeks
again. Heris thought to herself that one of the advantages
of darker skin was that blushes didn't show. Much. "Do
you have sensors in there?"

"Oh, yes." Heris called up the compartment specs.
"You have a pretty fair internal security system, probably
to let your staff monitor offship loading . . . see?" There
were Ronnie and George, looking stubborn, hunched
over a hard copy of something. She did not wait to hear

what they were saying, but her fingers flicked over the screen controls. The young men suddenly stopped talking, and stared at each other.

"She wouldn't!" George said in a tinny voice.

"Why's he sound like that?"

"Air pressure," Heris said. "Their ears just popped, I'll bet." Her fingers moved again, and both of them looked pale and ill at ease. "You'd better go," Heris said to Cecelia. "You want to be properly angry and upset, and you don't want to know what happened to them . . . not until they tell you. I won't hurt them."

"I know that," Cecelia said, but she left reluctantly.

"If you get into the computer, then you can pull drills on *her*," George said. "She won't know —" He lounged against a burlap sack marked "Fertile seeds: contains mercury: do not use for food."

"Neither will we," Ronnie said. "I don't want to be up all night every night."

"You don't have to be. That's the beauty of it. You just set them up, but cut our bells out of it."

"She'll know who did it," Ronnie said. "I still think I should start with the internal monitors. She's spending a lot of time with Aunt Cecelia now; she's bound to say something I can use." They had a hard copy of the communications board specs, left in an unsecured file from one of Cecelia's training sessions. Getting into the secured files would be harder. Ronnie had the feeling that Captain damn-her-backbone Serrano would not leave *her* files unsecured.

"Yes, but what can she do? You're the owner's nephew — she can hardly throw you out in the void."

"Maybe." Ronnie stared at the specs, trying to remember all that stuff he had had in class. This little squiggle was supposed to mean something about the way that channel and this other channel interacted . . . wasn't it? He put his thumb firmly on the line that came from Cecelia's sitting room, and a finger on the one that came from the gym. He really needed a tap in both. If only Skunkcat had been along. . . . Scatty was the best for this sort of thing.

"Here's the captain's direct line to the bridge," George said, trying to be helpful. George had good ideas, but always managed to get the wrong slant on them. Ronnie did not want to interfere with the captain's communication to the bridge; he wanted them to know how ineffectual she was going to be once he figured out how to sabotage her.

Suddenly his ears popped, then popped again. He saw from George's face that the same unsettling shudder was going through his stomach, too. George said something; he paid no attention. Lower air pressure . . . shifts in the artificial gravity . . . could it have been a *real* emergency? He was suddenly sweaty, and as suddenly cold, the sweat drying on him. No. It had taken too long. That bitch of a captain was doing something to him, doing it on purpose.

"Out!" he said, across the middle of something George was trying to say. "Before the pressure locks engage."

But they had. He could not wrestle the hatch open against the safety locks; he *would* not call for help. His stomach protested, as another shift of AG squashed him, then released . . . and the air pressure dropped again, to another painful pop of his ears.

George looked green. "I . . . I'm going to —"

"Not in variable G — hold it, George." There was nothing to use for a spew-bag. Every storage container in there — bags, boxes, tubes — had a lock-down seal on it. A surge of AG crushed him to the deck, then let up slowly. Air pressure returned; his ears popped just as many times on the way back to ship normal. His stomach tried to crawl out his mouth; George looked as bad as he felt, but had managed not to spew. He swallowed the vile taste in his mouth and rolled over onto his back. He had a sudden pounding headache.

Something banged on the closed hatch. "Anyone inside?"

George croaked, and the hatch opened. A crewman, someone Ronnie did not recognize, in full emergency gear. "My — you weren't in here for the drill, were you?" Without awaiting the obvious answer, the man went on, "It's not anyone's assigned station — you're lucky I found you. We're doing a pressure check on all compartments —"

"Just get us out of here," Ronnie said, staggering to his feet. "That miserable captain —"

"Wasn't her fault," the crewman said, as if surprised at his words. "It's a computer-generated emergency; they all are, you know. Didn't you get your handouts?"

"Yes," George said. "We got our handouts. Thank you. Just let me pass, please." He shoved past and shambled down the passage to the nearest toilet, where Ronnie could hear him being very thoroughly sick.

Ronnie himself hoped to sneak back to his own stateroom, but in the lounge he found a very angry Aunt Cecelia. She said all the things he expected, and didn't want to hear, and he managed not to listen. She had said them all before, and so had others, and it was not really his fault anyway. It was that captain. That arrogant, stiff-necked, conniving bitch of a captain, and he was going to get even with her. If Aunt Cecelia didn't want to see his face for two days, that was fine. He could eat in his room; he would be *glad* to eat in his room. All the more time to figure out how to do what he was going to do. Still, an attempt at patching things up never hurt. He did his best at a contrite apology, but she turned away, ignoring him. Ignoring *him*. No one ignored him.

By the time he reappeared in the dining room, several days later, to all appearances chastened and determined to be a good boy, Ronnie had figured it out. At least the beginning of it. It had been easy, using the specs he had, to get a tap into his aunt's sitting room. And into the gym. He hadn't yet dared try the captain's cabin, but he was hearing a lot as it was. That fool captain actually *liked* his ridiculous aunt, he'd discovered. Enjoyed the riding lessons, enjoyed explaining to Cecelia how her ship worked, enjoyed the relaxed conversations in the evenings, when they explored each others' backgrounds.

A lot of it bored him silly: talk about books he'd never read, and art he'd never seen, and music he avoided. (Opera! He had liked the opera singer's body, and the competition with the prince, but not the music she sang onstage. It was hard to believe even someone like his aunt actually *liked* all that screeching.) No juicy gossip, no political arguments — it was almost like hearing an educational tape, the way they discussed the topics and deferred courteously to each other.

Other bits, though, fascinated him. His aunt's analysis of the workings of the family businesses. . . . His own father hadn't made it that clear. Captain Serrano's version of her resignation from the Fleet, which his aunt teased out of her with surprising delicacy. . . . He had never imagined that someone in the Regular Space Services would dare to disobey an order; they were all such stiff-necked prigs. It didn't make sense; she should have known she would lose her ship, one way or the other. He could almost feel guilty listening — he would not have expected to hear that woman so upset, or for that reason — but he loved the sense of power it gave him. She could be shaken from her calm, controlled persona; she was not invincible. He would start with something simple, he decided. Something that might be an accident, that would be hard to trace back to him.

Heris used the reins when she rode now, and the soft tones in her earphones let her know how she managed the tension, even before the simulator responded by swinging one way or the other. If the tones matched, the rein tension was equal; a higher tone meant more tension. She had discovered, as Cecelia gradually enabled the simulator's sensors, just how sluggish that first "mount" had been. Cecelia had shown her a cube of herself at that first lesson, and she was ready to laugh at the novice who couldn't even keep her position for a single circuit. On *this* program, that novice would have been bucked off already. Heris listened to Cecelia's voice, coaching her in the next maneuver, and tried to respond. The brown neck and ears in front of her changed position; she felt the movement in her seat and the lessening tension of the reins in her hand. The simulator lunged; this time Heris was ready, and controlled that with a leg and hand . . . and . . . they were cantering. She liked cantering. Circling. Straight. Circling again. Today she would "jump" for the first time; she was eager, sure she was ready.

A small white fence appeared ahead of her. "Keep your legs on him," Cecelia's voice reminded her. She squeezed, and the fence moved toward her faster. Then the horse's back rose beneath her, and fell again, and she grabbed — and got a handful of metal tubing. The illusion went blank; the simulator beneath her was once more an inert hunk of metal and plastic.

"Not bad," Cecelia said. "You grabbed for the right thing, at least. I had one student who reached for the helmet. And you didn't fall all the way off."

Heris blinked and took a deep breath. "Umm. A real horse wouldn't stop and let me get my breath, would it?"

"No. You can grab for mane like that and stay on, usually, but you were pretty high out of the saddle. I think you need more time in the two-point. Let's go."

The rest of that session, and the next, Heris spent practicing the position she should have taken over the jump. Then she put on the helmet to find the ring full of jumps. "Nothing big," Cecelia said cheerfully. "But if you see more than one, you can't get fixated on it. Now — pick up a trot."

She came out of that lesson a convert to riding. "It's like a boat," she tried to tell Cecelia. "Bouncing over the waves, only in a boat you're *in* it, and this way you're *surrounding* it. Not really like sailing, more like white-water kayaking." Cecelia looked blank. "You never did any?"

"No, just the little bit of sailing I told you about."

"But it's the same thing." Heris ran her hands through her hair, not caring if it stood up in peaks. "You're swooping along between obstacles, only they're rocks making standing waves, not fences."

"If you say so. I always thought of it as music, myself. A choral or orchestral work, where if everything goes well it sounds lovely, and if you get out of time you crash."

"Anyway," Heris said, "I like it. I don't want to quit when my ten hours are up — that is, if you'll let me —"

Cecelia chuckled wickedly. "Your ten hours were up *last* session. Do you think I'd let a potential convert quit before she got hooked? I thought you'd come around. Just wait until you can jump a real course — small, but a real one."

"And you — don't tell me you don't like knowing more about your ship," Heris said.

"That's true." Cecelia rubbed her nose. "I know you think I'm crazy to liken it to stable management, but that's how it makes sense to me."

"Whatever works," Heris said. She would have said more, but Ronnie and the other young people came into the gym.

"Is the pool available, Aunt Cecelia?" He asked politely enough, but his expression showed what he thought of two older women exercising. He did not look at Heris at all.

"Yes — for about an hour," Cecelia said. "But you ought to get in some riding time, Ronnie."

"I'll get enough riding at Bunny's," Ronnie said. It was not quite sulky. "We'll leave you the practice time. . . . Are you enjoying yourself, Captain?"

It was the first time he'd actually spoken to her since the incident on the bridge. His expression was so carefully neutral it could have been either courtesy or insult. "Yes, I am," she said, pleasantly. "Lady Cecelia is an excellent teacher."

"I'm sure." He would have been very handsome, Heris thought, if he'd learned to limit that curl of lip to moments of passion. His voice sharpened. "It's too bad you'll have to let your newfound expertise wither in Hospitality Bay . . . although I understand they have donkey rides along the beach."

Heris would not have answered so childish an insult, but Cecelia did. "On the contrary, Ronnie, I'm taking Captain Serrano with me; she's going to be quite adequate by the time we arrive." Her cheeks flamed; her hair seemed to stand on end. Heris blinked; that was the first she'd heard of this plan.

"You're taking — her — but she — she's just a —" Ronnie looked from one to the other, then to his friends.

"If you'll excuse me, Lady Cecelia," said Heris, giving

her employer a covert twinkle, "I have urgent business on the bridge — remember?"

"Oh. Yes, of course." Cecelia dismissed her with a wave, and turned back to her nephew; Heris used the gym's other entrance. It was not all a fake, though she had no desire to watch aunt and nephew sparring — she had in fact scheduled another emergency drill for the crew only, and needed to change. She and the crew would all be wearing full sensor attachments, so that she could analyze the drill in detail later on. She had allowed herself fifteen minutes, originally, but Ronnie's interruption had cost her a couple.

In her cabin, she ripped off her sweaty riding clothes, spent a minute in the 'fresher, and dressed in her uniform with practiced speed. Anyone who couldn't bathe and dress for inspection in eleven minutes would never have survived Academy training. She picked up the sensor patches and placed them on head, shoulders, hands, chest and back of waist, and feet. The recording command unit slipped into her pocket. Three minutes. She picked up the last of her personal emergency gear with one eye on the chronometer's readout. Breather-mask, detox, command wand for hatchlocks, command wands for systems controls . . . the little plastic or foil packets that she had learned to use so long ago, that never left her except in the 'fresher, where she kept them stuck to a wall in their waterproof pouch.

Now. She left her quarters and moved without haste toward the bridge, turning on the recording command unit. Sometime in the next two minutes, something would go wrong — without triggering any alarm on the family side, unless the lockout patch failed. Her skin felt tight. Riding an electronic virtual horse was good exercise, but this was the real thrill: waiting for trouble you knew was coming.

Whatever it was, the crew had just noticed something wrong on the displays when she came onto the bridge at precisely the hour she had set.

"Don't know what that is —" the ranking mole said. "But we'd better find out; cut it off the circulation —"

"Captain on the bridge," said Holloway, with evident relief. "Captain, there's something in environmental —"

Inadequate, even so soon; she switched the command screen to environmental and almost grinned. Pure happenstance, but she'd seen something like this before. She didn't say that; she said, "Isolate that compartment." The mole's hands flickered across his console.

"Captain — the fan blower's stuck on."

Not *quite* the same problem. She hoped it was mostly virtual; the actual compound stank abominably, and would penetrate any porous material. The mole had the sense to cut out the electrical line supplying the blower. Heris said, "Good job," and then the blower cut back in. Something prickled the back of her neck as she watched Gavin override the mole's commands and cut power to the entire section. Having the fan blower stuck on was within the parameters she'd given the computer. Having it come back on after its normal electrical connection was cut pushed the parameters as she remembered them. Had she been imprecise? Could she have forgotten to close a command line somewhere in the problem set? The fan stopped. She listened to Gavin give reasonable orders for clearing the contaminant, based on its presumed identity. Then — and she was not surprised — the fan came back on. Gavin turned to her with an expression between disgust and worry.

"I've got it," she said. From her console, her command set blocked the computer's own, briefly, as she isolated and locked out all executing logic loaded in the past seventy-two hours. That would undo some things that would have to be redone, but it should safely contain the problem. And that second startup took it well beyond the parameters she'd set; someone had interfered. Interfered with her ship, on her drill. . . . Rage filled her, along with the exultation that conflict always brought. This was an enemy she could fight. She knew exactly whom to blame for this one, and he had been ordered off her bridge only sixty-three hours before.

The fan had stopped for good, this time, and she went on with the drill, noting that the crew had responded well even to this more complicated problem.

The question was whether to tell Cecelia. She liked Cecelia, she'd decided, and it wasn't her fault that she had a bratty nephew or even that she'd been stuck with him for this trip. If she could contain Ronnie without bothering Cecelia . . . but on the other hand, she was the owner, and the owner had a right to know what was going on. If it had been an admiral's nephew, she'd have known what to do (not that any admiral's nephew would have gotten so far with mischief still unchecked).

But the first thing to do was find out how he did it, and when.

"Sirkin, you're cross-training in computer systems. I want you to crawl through every trickle in the past . . . oh . . . sixty hours or so, and identify every input." Sirkin blinked, but did not look daunted. The young, Heris thought to herself, believed in miracles.

"Anything in particular, Captain?"

"I entered a problem set for the drill yesterday. What just happened was not within parameters. . . . Someone skunked them. I want to know when, from what terminal, and the details of the hook. Can do?"

"Yes — I think so." Sirkin scowled, in concentration not anger. "Was it that — that young idiot who got himself caught in the storage compartment?"

Heris glanced around; the entire crew was listening. "It might have been," she said. "But when you find out, suppose you tell me, not the whole world."

"Yes, ma'am."

Ronnie threw himself back in the heavily padded teal chair in his stateroom and stretched luxuriously. George, in the purple chair, looked ready to burst with curiosity.

"So?"

"So . . ." Ronnie tried to preserve the façade of cool sophistication, but the expression on George's face made him laugh. "All right. I did it, and did it right. You should have seen them, trying to turn off a fan that wouldn't turn off."

"A fan." George was not impressed, and since he'd been decanted looking cool and contained, he could do that look better than Ronnie. The only thing, Ronnie maintained, which he did better.

"Let me explain," Ronnie said, taking a superior tone. That came easily. "The little captain had scheduled another emergency drill, this one for the crew alone. I'd already put my hook into the system — remember? — and had a line out for just this sort of thing. I reeled it in and rewrote it — actually, all I had to do was put a loop in it — and sent it on its way."

"So the fan kept turning back on," George said. "And they couldn't stop it. . . ." A slow grin spread across his face. "How unlike you — it's so gentle. . . ."

"Well," Ronnie said, examining his fingernails, "except for the stink bomb."

"Stink bomb?"

"Didn't I mention? The little captain had put three scenarios in the computer; it would generate one of them, using her parameters. I sort of . . . mixed two. One was a contamination drill . . . and it wasn't that hard to change a canister which would have released colored smoke for one releasing stinks." Ronnie smirked, satisfied with the look on George's face as well as his own brilliance. "The little captain was most upset."

"When she figures it out . . ." George went from gleeful to worried in that phrase.

"She'll never figure it out. She'll think it's her own problem set — even if she calls it up, she'll see that loop. Everyone makes mistakes that way sometimes."

"But that canister?"

"George, I am not stupid. I spent an entire day repainting the drill canisters so they have the wrong color codes. *All* of them. She'll assume it's something left over from the previous captain — like that great mysterious whatever that held us up at Takomin Roads. That's the first thing I did, right after we decided to scrag her. She can look for prints or whatever as much as she likes: she picked that canister up herself, and put it where it went off." Ronnie stretched again. Sometimes he could hardly believe himself just how brilliant he was. "Besides — she thinks I'm a callow foolish youth — that's what Aunt

Cecelia keeps telling her — and she won't believe a spoiled young idiot — my dear aunt's favorite terms — could fish in her stream and catch anything." As George continued to look doubtful, Ronnie leaned forward and tried earnestness. If George got nervy, his next intervention would be much harder. "We're safe, I promise you. She can't twig. She can't possibly twig, and if she even thinks of it, Aunt Cecelia's blather will unconvince her."

✧ Chapter Eight

"We have a slight problem," Heris said to Cecelia. It had not been easy to spirit her employer away along paths she knew were safe, but she managed. They were now in the 'ponics section reserved for fancy gardening. Cecelia had banished the gardeners.

"Again?" But Cecelia said it with a smile.

"Your nephew," Heris said. "I can deal with him, but he may come running to you, if I do. Or I can try to ignore him out of existence, but he may cause the crew some inconvenience."

"Somehow when you say 'inconvenience,' what I hear is much worse." Cecelia looked down her nose as if she were wearing spectacles and had to peer over them. She reminded Heris of one of the portraits of her ancestress.

"Well . . . I can probably keep it to inconvenience." Heris reached out to feel the furry leaf of a plant she didn't recognize. It had odd lavender flowers, and it gave off a sharp fragrance as she touched it.

"I hope you're not allergic to that," Cecelia said. "It makes some people itch for days."

"Sorry." Heris looked at her fingers, which did not seem to be turning any odd color or itching.

"It's got an edible tuber, quite a nice flavor." Cecelia looked at the row of plants as if blessing them with her gaze. "I hope Bunny will trade for this cultivar; that's why we're growing it now. We had to replant, of course, after the . . . mmm . . . problem."

Heris had not considered what, besides convenience, might have been sacrificed. "Did you lose all the garden crops?" she asked. "I thought they'd be unharmed." She also wondered what this had to do with Ronnie, and hoped it meant Cecelia was thinking on two levels at once.

"We lost some . . ." Cecelia's voice trailed away; she was staring at another row of plants, these covered with little yellow fruits. "I don't know what they're thinking of; half those are overripe. And they're not fertile; there's no sense wasting them. . . ." She picked one, sampled it, and picked another for Heris. "You're asking about Ronnie. I've told you before — I'm sick of that boy. If he's done something that deserves response, do what you will, short of permanent injury. I do have to answer to Berenice and his father later; it would be awkward to admit that I sanctioned his death. But aside from that —" She made a chopping motion at her own neck.

Heris ate the yellow fruit, a relative of the tomato, she thought, and watched Cecelia's face. "You're not really happy about that," she observed. "What else?"

"Oh . . . I think what makes me so furious is that he's not all bad. He may seem it to you —"

"Not really," Heris said. "Remember, I told you before that I've seen a lot of young officers, including very wild ones. For that matter, I *was* a wild one."

"You?" That deflected her a moment.

"What — you really thought I was born at attention, with my infant fist on my forehead?" It was so close to what Cecelia had thought, that the expression crossed her face, and Heris laughed, not unkindly. "You should have seen me at sixteen . . . and will you try to tell me you were completely tame?"

"At sixteen? I spent all my time with horses," Cecelia said. Then she blushed, extensively, and Heris waited. "Of course, there was that one young man —"

"Aha!"

"But it didn't interfere with my riding — nothing did — and nothing came of it either." Heris couldn't tell from the tone whether Cecelia was glad or sad about that. "But Ronnie —" Cecelia came back to the point, as she always did, eventually. "He's got brains, and I don't really doubt his courage. He's just spoiled, and it's such a waste —"

"It always is," Heris said. "What he needs is what neither of us can give him — a chance to find out that his own foolishness can get him in permanent trouble, and only his own abilities can give him the life he really wants. At his age, such tests tend to be dangerous — even fatal."

"But you think you can do something?"

"I think I can convince him to play no more tricks on me. That won't help overall, most likely; he'll blame me, or you, and not his own idiocy."

"It's that crowd he hangs around with," Cecelia said. "Yes, his mother spoiled him, but so are they all spoiled."

Heris did not argue; her own opinion was that the influence went both ways. Ronnie was as bad for the others as they were for him. But it wasn't her nephew, and she didn't have any remnant guilt feelings. She suspected Cecelia did. Cecelia had commented more than once on the family's attempts to make her perform in ways they thought important; some of that must have stuck, even if it didn't change her behavior.

Cecelia ate another of the yellow fruits. Heris hadn't liked the first one well enough to pick another; she watched Cecelia poke about, prodding one plant and sniffing another. Finally she turned back to Heris. "All right. Do what you can; I won't expect miracles. And I won't sympathize if he comes crying to me."

"I don't think he will," Heris said. "He has, as you said, some virtues."

"Do you want to tell me what you're planning to do, or do you think I'll let something slip?"

"No — you wouldn't, I'm sure. But my methods are, as before, not entirely amiable."

"Go on, then. I won't ask. Just see that you're on time for your lesson — today you get higher jumps and more of them."

Heris looked at her. "That's one I hadn't thought of . . . don't use the simulator until I've had a chance to check it, will you?"

"Ronnie wouldn't touch it — he's being tiresome about horses."

"No — not for himself or even you — but to get at me.

I'll be on time — in fact, I'll be early, and I'll make sure it hasn't been tampered with."

Ronnie had never believed in premonition; he had known himself far too mature and sophisticated for any such superstitions. Thus the results of his first touch of the keyboard, after George left, came as a complete surprise. He had thought of another glorious lark, something harmless to baffle the little captain even further. She liked to go riding on Aunt Cecelia's simulator . . . well . . . what if it turned out to be under his control, and not Cecelia's? He had in mind a mad gallop across enormous fences that would surely have her squealing for mercy — and to Cecelia it could still appear that nothing was wrong and the captain's nerve had broken. He held out for some little time, letting himself imagine all the ramifications: his aunt's scorn of those who couldn't ride well, the captain's fear and then embarrassment, the confusion of both. They would never figure it out, he was sure.

Then he reached for the console. He would just take a preparatory stroll around his battlements, so to speak, making sure that all his hooks were in place. . . . His fingers flicked through the sequence that should have laid all open before him, and the screen blanked.

As anyone who has just entered a fatal command, he first thought it was a simple, reparable error. He reentered the sequence, muttering at himself for carelessness. Something clicked firmly, across his stateroom. It sounded like the door, but when he called, no one answered. Imagination. The screen was still blank. He thumbed Recall, and the screen stayed blank. Odd. Even if he'd hit the wrong sequence, the screen should have showed something. He hit every key on the board, in order, and the screen stayed blank. He felt hot suddenly. Surely not. Surely he hadn't done something as stupid as *that* — there were ways to wipe yourself out of a net, but his sequence had been far from any of the ones he knew.

He stared at the screen, and worry began to nibble on the edge of his concentration. He didn't have to enter the commands here, of course — shifting control to the console in George's or Buttons's suite would do — but he hated to admit he'd been such a fool, whatever it was he'd done. But the screen stayed blank, not so much as a flicker, and he didn't want to lose his good idea. The captain would have her riding lesson not that many hours later, and he wanted to be sure he got the patches in first.

With a final grunt of annoyance, he shut off his screen and went to the door. It didn't open. He yanked hard at the recessed pull, and broke a fingernail; the door didn't move at all. He thumped it with his fist, muttering, with the same effect as thumping a very large boulder: his fist hurt, and the door did not move.

He had flicked the controls of the com to George's cabin when the realization first came. . . . This could not be an accident. The com was dead; no amount of shaking the unit or poking the controls made any sound whatever come out of the speakers. He flung himself at the terminal console again, determined to break through. The screen came on when he pressed the switch, but it responded to nothing he did. No text, no images, no . . . nothing.

"Dammit!" He followed that with a string of everything he knew, and finished, some minutes later, with "It isn't *fair*!"

From the corner of his eye, he saw the screen flicker. Only then did it occur to him that while he might be cut off from the outside, the outside might very well be watching him. He came closer.

ALL'S FAIR IN LOVE AND WAR. The screen's script even seemed to have a nasty expression. DON'T MESS WITH MY SHIP. The meaning was clear enough, though he was in no mood to give in. But the messages stayed, two clear lines, and again nothing he did changed them. Ronnie turned away, furious, and kicked the bulkhead between his room and his private bath. With a *whoosh*, the toilet flushed, and flushed again, and flushed again, three loud and unmistakable raspberries.

"You can't do this to me!" he yelled at the ceiling. "This is *my* aunt's yacht!"

The shower came on; the automatic doors that should

have enclosed it had not budged, and he had to wrestle them into place. A dense steam filled his bathroom. He saw with horror that the drain hadn't opened; water rose rapidly, then trickled out between the doors. He yanked towels from the racks, from the cupboards, and threw them at the overflow. . . . If it got into the bedroom, it would stain the carpet. . . . His *mother*, not just Aunt Cecelia, would be furious if he stained new carpet. When every towel was soaked, the drain opened, as if it had eyes to see, the shower stopped, and the water drained peacefully away.

The wet towels squished under his feet; his shoes were soaked, and his trousers to the knees. Ronnie felt the onslaught of a large headache, and glared at the mess. He wrung out the towels into the shower enclosure — better than walking on the wet mess — and hung as many as he could from the racks. The floor was slick; it could be dangerous. He grubbed into the back of the cupboard and found the cleaning equipment he had never used. A sponge — dry, for a wonder — a long-handled brush, a short-handled brush, and two bottles of cleaning solution, one blue and one green. The sponge eventually soaked up most of the damp on the floor, though it still felt clammy.

He had only thought he'd been angry before. Now he experienced the full range of anger . . . anger he had not even suspected he could feel. He was so angry that for once in his life he did not strike out at walls or doors or furniture. Instead, he went back to the terminal and sat before it. As he had expected, the screen had another message line now:

YOU ARE CONFINED TO QUARTERS. YOU WILL RECEIVE ADEQUATE RATIONS.

He wasn't hungry; he didn't care about any blankety-blank rations. . . . He filled in all the blanks he usually did not allow himself to fill, forgetting none of the expressions he'd ever heard. But he did so silently. He was not going to give her the satisfaction.

How had she done it? How had she figured it out? She wasn't that smart; she had to be nearly as old as Aunt

Cecelia. He fumed, silently, staring at the screen. Suddenly it cleared, and after a moment of blankness, reappeared in almost normal configuration. Almost, because the usual communications icon had been replaced by a black diamond.

Gingerly, as if the screen could bite him, he touched the service icon. A menu appeared: food, linens, clothing, air temperature, water, medical assistance. He thought it had had a few more items the last time he'd noticed it . . . but he hadn't paid much attention. The servants were usually hovering; he hadn't needed to call them. Now he touched linens. The screen blanked and displayed a flashing blue message: NOT IN SERVICE.

"What d'you mean, not in service!" he growled. In the bathroom, the toilet burped: warning. He pressed his lips together, amazed that he could be even angrier than a moment before. He was stuck with wet towels . . . what a *petty* revenge. That captain must come from a very ill-bred family. When he did revenge, he did it with style. He poked the board again; it returned him to the service menu. He thought of trying every single choice, but decided against it. It would only make him angrier to know that the others didn't work either.

He backed out of the service menu and looked at the main screen. Innocent, bland, it looked back. No communications, and missing functions on other icons, he didn't doubt. What else could he try? Information? He almost snarled at the little blue question mark, but controlled himself and put a finger on it.

The screen blanked and gave him a solid ten seconds of GOOD CHOICE before turning up the information menu. He had never tried this one before, since he'd never thought a ship as small as his aunt's could hold serious surprises. Now, he found a choice of items he was sure had not been his aunt's idea.

1. WHAT DID I DO WRONG?
2. WHAT CAN I DO NOW?
3. WHAT ARE YOU GOING TO DO?
4. WHAT DO THE OTHERS KNOW ABOUT ALL THIS?

It looked like someone's bad idea of a strategy game.

He was going to have nothing to do with it. . . . It had to be a trap . . . but after sitting there for a long time he realized he was tired, stiff, and hungry. Food had been promised, though it hadn't arrived . . . and he did wonder just how much the little captain knew.

He pressed the first choice. In a cheerful electronic voice, the monitor said, "Good choice." Ronnie jumped. He'd hated the more vocal teaching computers he'd happened across. This one had a particularly chirpy intonation. The screen blanked, then filled with a list which he supposed represented his errors. It was not framed in terms his Aunt Cecelia would use; what hurt particularly was the assumption that he and the captain shared a frame of reference . . . the military. In just the way that his instructors had dissected unfortunate actions of the past, she dissected his action against her. Without, it seemed, the least rancor. That hurt, too. She didn't think of him as a rich spoiled brat — but as an incompetent junior officer, one of many. He did not like being one of many.

He was chagrined to learn that his hooks had been found and rebaited, so to speak; she had the entire conversation with George (it was played back for him) and from his own speech samples had produced com messages to the others telling them he felt like some time alone.

"Of course," the computer voice said brightly, "they think you're in here plotting more mischief against the captain and crew."

"But when am I —" He stopped when he heard the water start to run in the bathroom again. Evidently, he was not meant to do any talking.

"If you have questions," the voice said, "you may choose them from the menu when they appear." As if that captain would know what questions he wanted to ask. But after another paragraph of careful explanation of his faults, he found a list of questions. He chose the one about the canisters, because he really couldn't understand why repainting them had been so bad. They were just disaster-drill fakes anyway. What did it matter if one of them turned out to have red smoke, blue smoke, or a bad smell?

His comunit chimed. Ronnie leaped for it. This time the voice that came out was the captain's.

"You asked about the canisters," she said. "Do you know the chemical compounds in each?"

"You — no." He had caught his first angry response in mid-leap.

"Then you are not aware that some of the compounds are toxic, and some are flammable?"

"They are?" He could not have concealed his surprise if he'd tried. They were for *drills* — the label said so — and things used in drills were harmless, weren't they?

She had a human chuckle, which he didn't want to admit was pleasant. "Tell you what — I'll put the contents up on your screen in detail. Did you have any system in mind when you repainted those canisters, or did you do it at random?"

"Well . . ." Ronnie tried to remember. "Mostly I did them the color of the ones in the next box. That way I always knew which ones I'd done. There were a few, though, that were loose, and I just made 'em all orange with a brown stripe. Most of those were blue and . . . and two green stripes, but one was white and gray."

"Then you switched the box labels?"

"Yeah . . . how'd you know I'd repainted them?" He had been so careful; he could not believe she'd noticed.

"How do you think I knew which storage bay you were in with George?" she asked. He had no idea. He'd assumed she'd messed with all the storage bays. "Think about it," she said. The com went dead. He didn't even bother to try calling out again.

The screen had changed; now it was full of chemical formulas and reaction characteristics. Ronnie fought his way through it. He was actually supposed to know most of this; he remembered having seen it in class. But he had never had a good reason to put it together. He caught himself muttering aloud, and gave the bathroom a nervous look, but the toilet didn't burp. " . . . oxidizes the metallic powder and . . . gosh!" The stuff would really burn. *Really* burn. "I could have built a damn bomb!" he said, almost gleeful for a moment. Silence mocked him.

He didn't need a warning roar from the plumbing or a smart remark from the computer to point out that setting off a bomb on a spaceship in deep space was not an intelligent thing to do, and setting one off without even knowing it was, if possible, stupider.

He felt cold, almost as cold as he'd felt when he realized he'd intruded on the bridge during jump transition. If the captain had picked another canister — the gray and white one he'd painted orange and red, rather than the blue and gray he'd painted black and green — it could have been a real emergency. A real disaster. A real — another look at the screen to confirm it — end of the whole trip. For everyone.

"I'm sorry," he said to the silent cabin. "I didn't mean to cause any real trouble."

Instead of an answer, the screen changed yet again, to show a transcript of what he'd said to George, every word. It looked worse, far worse, in glowing script on the screen. It looked as if he had indeed wanted to cause trouble — to harrass and humiliate the captain, to frighten and divide the crew. "I didn't mean it that way," he said, but he knew he had meant it that way, back when he thought it was safe to mean it that way.

The food, when it came, was bland and boring.

Heris climbed off the simulator after a vigorous ride across country on a large black hunter; every time she took the helmet off, the simulator startled her with its metal and plastic parts. Cecelia nodded at her.

"Very good indeed. You'll certainly qualify for one of the mid-level hunts. Depending on who's here, you might even be with me for a run or two."

"Are you sure you want to drag me along?" Heris asked. "I know it's not —"

"It's not common, but it's not unheard of, and anyway I do as I like. It's one of the perks. Bunny won't mind, as long as you can ride decently and don't cause trouble, which you won't. I'll enjoy having you to talk with — there are few enough single women, and I'm past the point where the men want to talk to me."

Heris was not sure she liked the assumption that she herself was also past that point . . . but it was true, she wasn't on the prowl. She wasn't over losing her other ship yet — though she could now think of it as "the other ship" and not the only one — and she would have to get her crew — and certain members of it — out of her mind before she could respond to advances. If anyone made them.

"What's the matter?" Cecelia asked. "Don't you want to go? Would you rather hang around Hospitality Bay with the other captains?"

"No!" She said it more forcefully than she meant to. "I'm sorry — the thought of those other captains has haunted me all along. I hate that. And yes, I would love to see what an estate set up for fox hunting looks like. It's just — I didn't want you to think you had to do it, because you said it in front of Ronnie."

"Nonsense. I said it because I wanted to; Ronnie's opinion is unimportant." Cecelia looked hard at her captain. "And by the way, how is that young man?"

"Perfectly healthy." That was true, if incomplete. He wasn't even that bored, because she had him doing the work he should have done in his basic classes. Math, chemistry, biochemistry, ship systems, military history, tactics. . . . When he kept his mind on it, all his plumbing worked and his food arrived regularly, and the lights worked. When he threw a tantrum — and he hadn't thrown one in the last several days, was he learning? — he found himself dealing with other problems, and the work still to do afterwards. "He may be rejoining you shortly, if you've no objection."

"What have you done, chained him in the 'ponics to dig potatoes?" Then she held up her hands. "No, don't tell me — I don't want to know. But I shall be fascinated to see what happens."

"So shall I," said Heris. She had found him more interesting than she'd expected, in the rare moments she tutored him over the com herself. He had a supple, energetic intelligence that would have rewarded good initial training. It was a shame that no one had ever made him

work before. He could have been good enough for the
Regular Space Service.

Ronnie reappeared at breakfast one morning, smiling
pleasantly. Cecelia, at Heris's suggestion, had begun
breakfasting with the young people some days before.
This way, Heris had said, the collusion would be margin-
ally less evident. She noticed that Ronnie was clean,
dressed neatly, and showed no visible bruises — of which
she approved — and the sulky expression she disliked no
longer marred his face.

"Well?" George said. "Tell all."

"All of what?" Ronnie looked over the toast rack and
chose whole wheat with raisins.

"You said you were up to something." George looked
at the others for support, but they weren't playing up.
"You said you were —"

Ronnie looked at him, a bland good-humored look.
"I've said many things, George, which aren't breakfast
conversation. And I'm hungry." He smiled at Cecelia.
"Excuse me, Aunt Cecelia — could I have some of that
curry?"

Cecelia smiled back. Whatever had happened, she
wasn't going to interfere with it. "Certainly. I hope you
haven't been ill. . . ."

"Not at all." He engaged himself with the curry, and
the variety of other edibles that Cecelia considered
appropriate to breakfast with company. George opened
and shut his mouth twice, then shrugged and went on
eating omelet. Buttons, never very forthcoming in the
morning, finished nibbling toast, excused himself, and
went away; the three young women, after glancing several
times from Ronnie to his aunt and back, also left. Cecelia
ate her usual large breakfast, trying to ignore all the signals they were trying to pass so obviously. Finally only
George and Ronnie were left, Ronnie eating steadily, as if
to make up for many lost meals, and George in spurts,
eyeing Ronnie. Cecelia struggled not to laugh. It was,
after all, ridiculous. There was George, trying to protect
Ronnie (too little and too late) from whatever horrors an

elderly aunt could inflict on him. Finally she decided to intervene, before Ronnie burst himself overeating, or George had a stroke.

"I am not planning to harm him, you know," she said to George. George turned bright red and nearly choked on a muffin.

"She's quite right," Ronnie said, in the same pleasant tone he'd used so far. "It's safe to leave us alone."

"But — but you said —"

"It's all right," Ronnie said. "Really it is. I can tell you're not hungry — why not go play something with the others? I'll be along shortly."

George, still red and coughing, managed to say that he hadn't meant to interfere and Ronnie would know where to find him. Then, with a nod to Cecelia, he got out of the room as gracelessly as Cecelia had ever seen him move.

"You are all right. . . ." Cecelia said. Ronnie's clear hazel eyes gazed into hers, a look that combined all the charm and mischief she had seen in him since birth.

"I'm fine," he repeated. "Why shouldn't I be?"

"Well . . ." Cecelia pleated her napkin, a gesture that she knew conveyed feminine indecision to the men in her family. "You were fairly cross about my new captain, and when I wasn't sure your message to me was . . . was quite true, about studying for exams, and I pressured George —"

Ronnie flushed, but managed a smile. "Did he break down and tell you I had planned some mischief? I'm sure he did. Well — so I had, but I — I changed my mind. And I did study for exams, but if I tell George that —"

"Ah. I see." Into Cecelia's mind came the faint glimmer of what Heris must have done. How she had done it still remained a mystery. But she understood this much of the psychology of the younger set. "You don't want George to know you changed your mind, or that you studied — you must have been awfully bored, Ronnie, to decide to study." She hoped her voice didn't tremble with repressed laughter on that . . . or would he think it was a senile tremor?

"It was the only thing I could do in that room without — without letting George know —" That was undoubtedly the truth, Cecelia thought. What a jewel of a captain. What a marvel. She felt like grabbing Heris and dancing her along the passages . . . and at the imagined look on Heris's face she could hardly contain her laughter. Ronnie, she saw, was looking at her with some suspicion.

"My dear, please, I'm just glad you're not sick, and that you didn't do something awful that Captain Serrano would have had to complain to me about, and that you thought better of it and made good use of your time. I have to admit I find the need to placate George amusing . . . but then I'm old, and no longer worry about the opinions of friends. When I was your age, their opinions mattered much more."

"Even you? I thought you never cared about anyone." The tone was more respectful than the words.

"I didn't care about some members of the family — and I'm not bragging about it. But I had friends — others who shared the same interests — and it mattered a great deal to me what they thought. So I will conceal from George your careful study of whatever it was you studied, and pretend to know nothing — which is in fact just what I do know."

"Thank you, Aunt Cecelia," he said. Something in his eyes made her think he was not entirely chastened, but overly polite was easier to live with than whining complaint. "I suppose," he went on, "I should ask you to let me try your simulator." His tone, again, was almost too bland, but she chose not to notice.

"Of course. Some of your friends — Bunny's children, and Raffaele — have been using it; I made up a schedule so that we don't interfere with each other."

"And the captain," he went on. She noticed the tension in his jaw which he probably thought he'd concealed. "Is she coming along well?"

"Oh, yes," Cecelia said. "It's too bad she didn't start earlier; she'd have been competitive in the open circuit. As it is, she'll be a reasonable member of the field once she's had some real experience." She smiled at the look on his face, mingled of mistrust and envy. "You'd be good too, I'm sure, if you spent the time on it she has. You're the right build."

"But I'm not horse-struck," Ronnie said. "Just as well; Mother would say you'd contaminated me."

"Well, make a try at it. You might like it better than you think. The family brought you up to think it was ridiculous, and all because my parents wanted me to marry someone for a commercial alliance, and I wanted to ride professionally. Whether I was right or wrong doesn't affect the nature of the sport."

"All right." He held up his hands, as if in defense, and Cecelia realized her voice had risen. That old quarrel with her parents and her uncles could still make her angry. If they had not been so ridiculously prejudiced, she would not have been that defiant: she would have quit in another year or so, certainly after losing Buccinator, and married someone. If not Pierce-Konstantin, someone reasonable. But they had tried to have her barred from competition, when she was leading for a yearly award; she had rebelled completely.

It occurred to her that she had more in common with Ronnie than she'd imagined.

Most major space stations followed one of three basic, utilitarian designs: the wheel, the cylinder, and the zeez-angle for situations requiring specific rotational effects. When Heris called up the specs for Sirialis, which all her passengers called "Bunny's planet," she felt she'd taken another giant step into irrationality. A blunt-ended castle tumbling slowly in zero-gravity? This time she didn't ponder it alone; she called her employer, and sent along a visual of the Station where Cecelia had said they would dock.

"Is there an explanation, or do I just assume civilian-aristocratic insanity?" she asked.

"Insanity isn't a bad guess," Cecelia admitted. From the tone, she was neither surprised nor insulted by Heris's reaction. "There's been a certain — oh — eccentricity — in that family for some generations. Some of us think that's why they got so rich so fast; they've got monetary instincts where the rest of us keep our common sense. This Station, though — let me see if I can explain it."

"No one," Heris said, watching on her own screen the

display of crenellations, towers, stairs, arches, and cloisters, rotating but somehow not making sense, *"no one could explain this."* Her eye tried to follow the progression of one staircase up to a square tower, which was suddenly not where it should have been. . . . The staircase had to be going *down*. Someone, she thought, must have made an error in the display.

"It began with Bunny's great-great-uncle Pirdich," Cecelia went on, ignoring the comment. "They'd just managed to recover the worst the original colonists had done, and the lords of the Grande Caravan had been teasing them about how impossible it was. He wanted to make a statement."

"That Station is a statement?"

"Of sorts, yes. He decided that having overcome what everyone said was an impossible problem in reclamation, he would celebrate it by building an impossible space station. Bunny's family's been overfond of the early modern period of Old Earth all along; this Station is built to look like a design by an artist of that period. I don't know the name; visual arts is not my thing. It is strange, isn't it? And if you think it's impossible, wait until you see the internal configuration and the fountain in the central plaza. Everything in it is taken from the work of the same person, and it's all delightfully skewed."

Delightfully was not the word Heris would have picked. In her experience, design problems in space stations caused everyone grief, especially captains of ships docking there. Creativity should be subordinate to efficiency. "Are all three stations like this one?" she asked. If not, maybe she could talk Cecelia into docking somewhere other than the prestigious but clearly impractical Home Station.

"Of course not. Once they had one unique impossible station, they wanted each one different. Here —" From Cecelia's desktop to Heris's the new visuals flashed: one like a stylized pinecone, in silver and scarlet, and one that looked like a worse mistake than the others, as if someone had dropped a pile of construction material onto a plate with a glob of sticky in the middle. "I think that's the worst,"

Cecelia said. "It's a Dzanian design, very neo-neo-neo, and the fault of Bunny's aunt Zirip, who married a Dzanian, and insisted that her family's fondness for Old Earth was pathological. You can't take anything very big into it, because the parts that stick out are nonfunctional; the docking bays are all nestled among them. There's only one berth for a decent-sized ship, and that's where they do cargo transfer. Zirip thought it was cute, she told me once, because it made for intimate spaces. But Zirip is also the one who converted the closet in her room into her bed and study, and used the room itself for a dance studio. Up until then, I'd thought the oddness in that family rode the Y chromosome."

Heris pitied the captains of cargo vessels loading and unloading there, but supposed they got used to it. "And the . . . er . . . pinecone?"

"Symbolic. So they told me. I've been there once, on a family shuttle; the docking facilities are lovely, but I got very tired of green and brown and the same aromatics all the time. It has the most capacity, and most guest yachts will dock there." At the end, that had the smug tone of someone who knew she was docking at a more prestigious slot; Heris sighed. She knew what that meant — no hope of talking Cecelia into using another station.

Instead, she looked again at the information for inbound ships. It might look like a peculiar sort of castle in the air, but it had modern, well-designed docking bays. The guidance beacons, the communications and computer links, the lists of standard and on-request equipment and connectors: all perfectly normal, exactly what they'd had at Takomin Roads. She wondered who in the family had had the sense to design the practical part.

"What sort of facilities does it have for off-duty crew?" Heris asked. She knew this was going to cause an explosion, and it did.

"What do you mean, off-duty crew? The crew goes to Hospitality Bay, as I explained earlier." Cecelia sounded annoyed.

"Milady." That formality should get her attention. Cecelia was susceptible, Heris had discovered, to very severe courtesy. "You have an entirely new set of environmental components, and the run here from Takomin Roads was just long enough to break them in — not long enough for this crew to be what I consider well trained. I want a standing watch aboard —"

"The Stationmaster won't like it; everyone sends their crews down to Hospitality Bay, and the ships are secured. What do you think, that rustlers or smugglers or something will come aboard?"

Heris didn't answer that, although she thought that leaving a ship uncrewed at a private station made it very easy for smugglers to do what they'd already done to *Sweet Delight*. She waited. Cecelia was not stupid; she would think of that herself in a few minutes. After a silence, Cecelia's voice came back, unsubdued but no longer angry.

"I see. You do think exactly that. And someone did put whatever it was in my scrubbers." It had now become "my" scrubbers, Heris noted with amusement. At least she knew what scrubbers were. Cecelia went on. "Did you ever find out what that was?"

"No," Heris answered. "And I doubt we will, unless it comes to court. My point is that we need a standing watch aboard; if you authorize it, the Stationmaster will agree."

"But what about the expense? And the crew expects their vacation at Hospitality Bay — won't they be angry?"

"Look — what if a pipe breaks while you're planetside, and floods dirty goo all over this carpet? You don't like the lavender plush any more than I do, but imagine the mess. Imagine what your sister would say. As for the crew, that's my problem; if they're angry, they'll be angry with me. Time they earned what you pay them."

"You're determined, aren't you?" That with a slightly catty edge.

"Where your safety and the integrity of this ship are concerned, yes," Heris said.

The Stationmaster required all the weight of Cecelia's patronage to change his mind. "It is not the usual procedure at all," he said. "We have that procedure for a reason; we can't have idle ships' crews roaming about the Station getting into trouble."

"They won't be," Heris said. "They'll be busy learning the new systems recently installed on this ship. During their shipboard rotation, they will have very little time to roam about — and if you insist, I can confine them to the ship, although I would prefer to allow them a moderate amount of time off. Lady Cecelia expressly requested that the crew be thoroughly trained — there had been incidents —" She didn't specify, and he didn't ask.

"Yes, but — we really don't have facilities . . ."

"Six individuals at a time aboard," Heris said. "No more than three offship —"

"Only three?" the Stationmaster said. Heris smiled to herself. She had won.

"Yes. They'll be standing round-the-clock watches, and they have a lot of work to do; I would prefer, because of that, to let them get their meals on the Station, rather than also detail a cook —"

"Oh . . . I see. Lady Cecelia's credit line?"

"Of course: the ship's account, with a limit —" She had to put a limit, or both the Station vendors and the crew would be likely to cheat.

"I would suggest thirty a day per person," the Stationmaster said. She haggled him down to twenty; she had already called up the vendor ads and knew her people could eat well on fifteen.

Next she had to tell the crew. She did not expect much trouble, and they listened in respectful silence, although she noticed some sideways glances. The new members, who had never been to Hospitality Bay, were glad enough to rotate in and out. Those who were accustomed to idling away a planetary quartile on full pay might have complained, but remembered the departure of the pilot. Heris hoped some of them would decide to quit; she knew she could do better. When she called for volunteers for the first rotation, Sirkin and the newest crew members got their hands up first — exactly what she'd expected. She had planned shorter, more frequent rotations (over the protests of both Cecelia and the Stationmaster) on the grounds that unused skills quickly deteriorated. In fact, there were crew members she didn't want to leave in the ship too long.

By the time they docked — without incident: the peculiar looking Station turned out to be well designed where it mattered — Heris had the roster settled, and enough work planned to keep the standing watch alert. She had scattered her new and most trusted crew among each rotation . . . and hoped that would keep any remaining smuggler-agents from doing whatever they might otherwise do. Then it was time to pack her own kit, and prepare to accompany Lady Cecelia's entourage to the planet.

"You were right," Heris said to her employer, as she came out of the droptube into the central area of the Station. "I don't believe it." The ornamental object in the middle had as many eye-teasing impossibilities as the Station itself, and in addition offered the appearance of a stream of water flowing merrily uphill. That alone wouldn't have been upsetting: everyone had seen inverse fountains or ridden inverse scare rides, since the invention of small artifical gravity generators. But this one flowed uphill without a substrate, burbling from one visible guide channel to another through the empty air. "It's a holo, right?"

"No — it's real, in its own way. You can put your hand into it and find out." Cecelia looked entirely too pleased with herself. Heris argued with her mind, and her stomach, and did not put her hand into the water. She was not going to ask how the illusion had been accomplished. Cecelia grinned. "I can tell you won't ask, so I'll give you a hint: Spirlin membrane."

Heris was very glad she hadn't put her hand in; it could have been embarrassing. Spirlin membranes, suspended in water, increased surface tension dramatically. They were also highly adherent to human skin, which often reacted with the Spirlin chemistry by fluorescing for days after the contact.

"I . . . see." Heris looked around. This area of the Station seemed to consist of gardens designed to the same weird standards as the Station itself and the fountain. Steps, low walls, terraces with seating arrangements that argued visually with each other — that seemed determined to flow from angular to curved, and back to angular, or, in some cases, to suggest by forced perspective the incorrect size or distance. Planters suspended at unnerving angles, all full of strange plants pruned to look like something else. When she looked up, Heris found herself staring into the canopy of another garden, looking down onto the heads of people walking along — she swayed, disoriented for a moment. Cecelia grabbed her arm.

"That one *is* a holo. I should have warned you — sorry. Almost no one looks up."

After that, Heris had no idea what kind of shuttle they would find in the bay . . . but although it was more luxurious than commercial or military models, it looked much the same on the outside, and brought them to the surface safely. Lady Cecelia's party had it to themselves; Lady Cecelia and Heris in the forward compartment, the young people in the main compartment, and Lady Cecelia's maid and a few other servants in the aft section. Once well down in the atmosphere, the cabin steward served a full dinner; by the time they landed, shortly before sunset, Heris had almost reconciled herself to being a passenger.

✧ Chapter Nine

"We hoped you'd be here for the first day, Lady Cecelia," said the gnarled little man at the entrance to the stable block. They had walked down from the Main House — which Heris had barely seen the night before, after the drive from the shuttle-port — to a set of buildings that looked as large as the house. Pale yellow stone, trimmed with gray stone around windows and doors; a wide, high arch with metal gates folded back . . .

"Things happen," said Cecelia. "Here — I want you to know Heris Serrano, my guest this year. She's a novice at hunting, but she's developing a decent seat."

"Pleased, mum," the man said. Heris felt herself under inspection of some sort, though she wasn't sure what he was looking for. Apparently she passed, for his thin mouth widened to a smile. "Go on in — he'll be waitin' for you."

"Now you'll see," said Cecelia as they came out of the arched entrance into a wide bricked walk that lay between the rows of stalls and a low-fenced dirt enclosure. Beyond was another archway, across which Heris saw a horse and rider move at a trot in yet another enclosure.

"Lady Cecelia!" It was clear from the rearrangement of wrinkles that this man's face seldom found such a smile. Lean, tanned, upright, brisk — this had to be the "Neil" who supervised all the training and the assignment of riders. "About time — I've held back two good prospects for you." He glanced at Heris, and dismissed her, waving for someone to bring a horse forward. Cecelia interrupted him.

"First — meet Heris Serrano. She's my guest this year, and I've been giving her preliminary instruction on the simulator —"

He looked at Heris again, this time with attention, and then back at Cecelia. "With full programming?"

"What I use myself. She's a novice, but she's solid as far as she goes. She's taking meter jumps now, but it's only sim; she needs practice before she goes out in the field. . . ."

"And you don't want me to treat her like a boneheaded kid who thinks he can ride because he once stuck on a horse at a gallop, is that it? Did you think I couldn't recognize maturity?"

"No — but I want her to have a good experience. And I want you to supervise, not one of your assistants, unless you've got better than last time."

"No . . . they go away when they get too good." His eyes measured Heris again. "Of course . . . size doesn't matter, and all that, but I'd think to start her on something reasonable. Sixteen?"

"Fine."

"She has to show me in the ring that she has the basics, but I'll shift her to the outside course right away."

"Thanks, Neil."

"No problem." He was still staring at Heris as if she had sprouted scales, then he nodded sharply and called "Bring me the bay mare in seventeen; size sixteen saddle, and the eggbutt snaffle." To Heris he said, "If Lady Cecelia says you're a promising novice, I'll believe it, and that mare will give you the chance to show it. Honest, can jump, but not fast enough for the field. If you suit, you can use her here until you qualify." Then, to Cecelia, "Now watch this."

A thin girl led up a horse that looked enormous to Heris; it was a brown so dark it looked black except in clear sun. Cecelia nodded. "Is that what you got with the Buccinator sperm?"

"Yep. Off the Cullross mares. Two of 'em; the other's a liver chestnut. This one's five, and before you say anything I know I didn't show him to you last year. . . . Milord said not to, because it's a surprise. Want to try him?"

Heris could see the flush on Cecelia's cheek, the delight and eagerness that made her almost girlish.

"Of course. . . ." She was up in a flash, rising lightly to the hand that gave her a leg up. Heris had, by this time, seen her employer on many horses in the training cubes; she thought she knew how that long, lanky body, almost too stiff at times on the ground, would look astride. Cecelia looked better — as if she and the horse had fused into one.

"Here, sir." That was someone else, with a smaller brown horse for Heris. The man nodded at her, and she mounted without waiting for assistance.

"Come on, the both of you," he said. "You'll need to warm up inside anyway."

Heris, on her first live horse since her time in the Academy, found that coordinating the movement of legs and hands while the horse actually walked — walked toward something — was harder than she expected. She liked the higher viewpoint, but wanted to spend it looking around, not steering. Ahead of her, on the dark horse, Cecelia seemed to be having no problems. Heris lined up behind her and hoped her horse would follow calmly while she tried to remember all the lessons.

The inner training area, a walled oblong, offered fewer distractions. They walked to the right; Neil moved to the center, watching. Heris began to relax, letting her body discover the difference between the simulation and reality. It still felt strange. This was not a mechanical device, or an electronic image: this was an animal, a live thing, that smelled like an animal and felt (when she dared touch the neck) like an animal. The horse blew, a long slobbering breath, and Heris felt that in her legs.

Simulations work, she told herself. They're effective training tools; you learned to pilot a ship off simulators; of course you can ride this animal. The animal was slowing down, she realized, because she wasn't giving enough signal with her legs. The simulation tended to keep a pace more easily; Cecelia had mentioned that some horses required more leg pressure. Heris increased it, and the horse's head came up (just like the VR image!) and it walked faster. Mare. The man had said mare, and mares were females . . . so *she* walked faster.

"Reverse," Neil said. Almost before she thought, Heris had shortened one rein, shifted her legs slightly and the mare was turning smoothly to reverse directions. It worked. Of course it had worked in the simulator, but it worked on a real horse, too. She felt better. Maybe everything would work on the real horse. She looked over at Cecelia, across the circle. Her employer did not look anywhere near her actual age on that horse; she could have been Heris's age or even younger.

"Pick up a nice trot, now," Neil said.

Trotting felt completely different from the simulator. She was off balance at first, and she sensed Neil's disapproval. It took her an entire circuit of the ring to figure out what was wrong; her ship-trained sense of balance had worked on the simulator because it wasn't going anywhere relative to the ship — but the horse was going somewhere on the ground. If she leaned forward a bit more — she experimented — suddenly the movement felt right. Cecelia was right — it could feel like dancing.

With that experience to draw on, she was prepared for the difference in the feel of the canter, and compensated within a few bounds. The rush of cold air on her face was exhilarating; she didn't want to stop.

"She'll do," Neil said to Cecelia. Then, to Heris, "All right, Captain — back to a walk now, and bring 'er in to the center. You can watch Lady Cecelia." Heris slowed, remembering to brace her back, and guided the mare to near Neil. Cecelia's horse was walking again. Heris tried to notice the things she'd been taught to notice, but what struck her most was the horse's size. Even from up here, it looked big. When Heris had settled the mare in a halt, Cecelia nudged her mount to a trot. She hadn't waited for Neil's signal, Heris noticed. Watching the big horse trot, she wondered why Cecelia hadn't overtaken her. It moved so much faster. . . . Cecelia slowed it again; its neck arched and its steps shortened. Then it stretched, then compressed again. Heris was fascinated.

"Let's try you both on a few fences," Neil said. He led the way out of that ring into another, where four small jumps were set up. "You first," he said to Heris. "Just pick up a trot and take the little white one."

Heris collected the mare, pushed her into a trot, and

approached the first jump. It seemed to stay in place while she moved, while the simulator had given the illusion of the jump shifting toward her. Even as she thought this, the mare rose to the jump, and Heris leaned into it. It felt the same, though. She turned the mare around, awaiting orders.

"Now try these two," Neil said. That, too, went smoothly; she felt steady and safe, but she knew the jumps were small. At Neil's command, she trotted over all four, then cantered over a pair — an in-and-out, he called it. He yelled, and several husky youths appeared and moved the jumps around. Again she jumped, first at a trot, and then a canter; first one way, then the other, as the fence crew changed distances and heights. Neil said nothing about her performance until it was over, when he called her to him. "Lady Cecelia's right," he said. "You're a solid novice. We'll see later what you do in the open. Walk 'er in circles down there —" He pointed to the far end of the enclosure.

Now it was Lady Cecelia's turn. The big dark horse poured over the jumps at a trot, hardly seeming to lift itself. The jumps were raised, the distances changed. Cecelia had explained the reasons, but even the simulator had not made it clear to Heris just what these changes demanded from a live animal. She watched the dark horse arch, lifting its knees high, as the jumps came up; she watched it compress and lengthen as the jumps were placed closer together or farther apart. And Cecelia, whom she had once considered a rich old eccentric . . . Cecelia flowed with the horse, a part of it.

When they were through, they walked back up to the house together. Cecelia had told Neil she would come back later to ride the other horse. "Now I want to be sure Heris is settled," she said. "She needs to meet a few people, learn where things are."

"Of course," Neil said. "But give me a call just before you come down."

Now Heris looked around her, more at ease than before. Like the house itself, all the surrounding buildings were either built of stone or faced with it. Most had stone or tile roofs as well. It looked remarkably like the cube of Old Earth Europe.

"I suppose it's like the old parts of the Academy," she said, turning to watch someone ride along a narrow cobbled street lined with stone buildings. "Nostalgia or something . . ."

"And economy, here," Cecelia said. "You have to remember when this was settled — a bare two centuries ago. Bunny's ancestors had money, yes, but it was far cheaper to import workers to build with local stone, than to import an entire factory to create conventional materials. I suspect that the first ones simply copied designs from old books — and then it began to look Old Earthish, and if someone teased them . . . well, that would have done it. They'd have insisted it was intentional." She walked around a circular tub planted with brilliant red flowers. "Of course it had all the usual comforts from the beginning; they didn't start out to build historical reproductions."

"But what about the horses? Have they always had horses here?"

"Probably. Colonial worlds usually have horses; they're cheap local transportation, self-replacing. Horse-based agriculture, too. Have you visited many worlds in the early stages of settlement?"

"No, not on the surface. Except for leave, I've spent my time in ships or offices."

"Mmm. Well, most import draft animals. Which ones depends in part on the world itself, and in part on the settlers. The dominant draft animal can be equine, bovine, or camelid."

"Camels?" asked Heris. She was not sure she knew what a camel looked like.

"And llamas," Cecelia said. "Have you ever seen camels?"

"No." This time she didn't explain.

"I haven't either, except in illustrations. One early Old-Earth breed of horse was used in the same culture that also had camels. Ugly beasts, with humped backs. It was said that they could be ridden, but I don't see how." Heris didn't even want to think how. Tomorrow morning, she would be hunting again. She was sure Heris would graduate into a hunt soon, and perhaps into the greens in a week or so, but for now all she wanted to think about was tomorrow morning.

If it wasn't Opening Day, with its farcical reproductions of ancient ceremonies via Surtees and Kipling, it was a hunting dawn. Cecelia put her head out the window and breathed deeply. Yes. Cool enough, crisp and dry, and she would have a new mount today. A Buccinator son. Sometimes the gods rewarded you for virtues unknown.

Bunny's staff served impeccable, lavish hunt breakfasts — and she enjoyed food — but today she hardly noticed either the traditional dishes or the taste. The green hunt, composed of the most experienced and best riders, talked little at breakfast this early in the season. Later, perhaps. Now they all wanted but one thing — the horses, the cold air, the speed, the chase. They recognized this in each other; glance met glance over the clattering silverware.

Outside, with the low sun gilding the stones, Cecelia walked down to the stable block as happy as she had felt since leaving competition. This is what life was about: a hot breakfast comfortable in one's stomach, and the prospect of a good horse to ride over open country until the day ended. In her saddlebag was her personal choice for a lunch snack — on this, Bunny made no attempt to enforce the more foolish tradition: if you wanted a thermpak of shrimp-in-sweet-sauce, you could have it. Cecelia favored a hot turkey sandwich, pickles and cheese, and hot coffee.

Buccinator's son, powerful and alert, stood waiting, held by a groom. She mounted, picked up her reins, nodded to the groom, and set off at a walk to quarter the yard. Then out the great stone arch to the front of the Main House, where Bunny and the huntsmen would have brought the pack by now. Hooves rang on the stones, riders began to talk, once mounted, in the quiet tones of those who expect to be listened to.

She came around the side of the house. . . . There, in the sunlight, were the hounds, sterns wagging as they

swirled in controlled chaos around the hunt staff in scarlet. Bunny grinned as she rode up to him. "You like him,
do you?"

"You stinker — you might have let me see him last
year."

"He wasn't ready. But you're first to take him into the
field; he's been schooled but never hunted."

"You are most generous." And he was. To let a guest
take a green horse into the field — with the green hunt,
over the most demanding country — she was not sure she
would have done it, had it been her horse and her country.

"He couldn't be in better hands," Bunny said. "One
concession — we're going to start with the Long Tor foxes
today." Which meant less woods riding, more in the open,
but the fences were stone walls, unforgiving of mistakes,
and in the open they'd be riding faster.

"Sounds like fun," Cecelia said. Other riders came up
then, paying their respects to the master, and she circled
away.

The Long Tor foxes cooperated by leading a long, cir-
cuitous chase across the open slopes, in and out of
difficult ravines, back up and around almost to their
beginning. The Buccinator son proved himself, maturing
at every wall and ditch, the scope and speed of Buccinator bloodlines keeping him out of trouble and well up.
Cecelia didn't push him. There was no reason to race;
everyone knew how she could ride, and everyone knew
the horse was green. Far more important to give him a
good day's work, and the confidence to go on another
time. They rode back in a golden afternoon, the young
horse still with power to spare, and Neil gave her a
thumbs-up when she came through the arch.

"Cool and quiet, and not a mark on him . . . and you're
happy with him?"

"He's all you promised. Never shirked, never tried to
turn away from anything. He'd have gone faster if I'd
asked — actually, I had to hold him back at first."

"Good. That's what I hoped for. He should be ready

day after tomorrow; you can have old Gossip tomorrow, if you want."

"Give him two days off," Cecelia said. "It's his first season. Flat work tomorrow, and the day after I'll come do a little schooling on him when I get back from the hunt —"

"You think you'll have the energy?"

Cecelia gave him a mock glare. He was always trying to suggest she was too old, but they both knew it was a joke. "I could school three horses now, as you well know — shall I prove it?"

"No . . . just give Gossip a run tomorrow. I let Cal have him for Opening Day, and he bucked over the first ten fences, Cal said. Your friend Captain Serrano's doing well; I'm going to put her in the blues, for her first run."

Cecelia came back to the house thoroughly satisfied. Now if Heris and young Ronnie would only realize how much fun this was.

Heris had spent several hours riding to Neil's exacting standard, on the flat and over the fences of the outside course. His announcement that she would ride in the blues was, she knew, a reward, though she would just as soon have had something more tangible and immediate. She came back to the house stiff but not really sore, ready for a hot bath, but the house itself fascinated her.

The big stone building was huge, an institution rather than a dwelling place. It had four levels aboveground and one below, and an astounding number of rooms, corridors, staircases, arches, ramps, lifts, balconies, and other architectural bits for which Heris had no name. On the ground floor were rooms devoted to reading, sitting, talking, dancing, dining, lunching, breakfasting, and playing games of chance or billiards. High ceilings and large rooms made Heris think of an overdecorated flight deck on her cruiser. Most of the guest rooms were on the second floor, along with another library and a "withdrawing room" for women, which overlooked a rose garden. The third floor, Cecelia said, had both guest rooms and family suites, while the fourth was (traditionally) the servants' quarters.

Heris had a bedroom the size of her entire suite on the

yacht, with a bathroom almost as large as the bedroom. Two windows opened to the east, with a view across a lower roof to scattered buildings on green fields beyond. A white vase filled with fragrant roses stood on the black polished bureau; a deskcomp stood beside it. The bathroom amazed her even more. As big as most rooms, it had every luxury fixture she'd heard of, and two she hadn't. She eyed the nozzles with suspicion and left them alone. She bathed, relaxed for a time in swirling hot water, and dried her hair, half amused at herself for taking so long. It was a very unmilitary situation.

The same dress she had worn that first night at Takomin Roads would do, Cecelia had said, for dinner. She added a simple but elegant silver necklace, then made her way through the maze of corridors to the main stair, and descended its graceful curves. Voices rose towards her; she felt as shy as she had the first night on a new ship, coming to the wardroom.

Cecelia waited at the foot of the stairs, her short hair lifted into a graceful wave of silver and auburn. She wore the amber necklace Heris had admired, and a long, beaded tunic in bronze and ochre over a flowing copper-colored skirt. It was hard to believe she was an old woman, and had spent all day on a horse. She smiled.

"I thought you might like a few introductions."

"Thank you," Heris said. She had tried to form no expectations, but she was surprised. All the men in traditional black and white, all the women in long gowns, looked more like athletes than wealthy layabouts. Yet the surroundings, and the clothes, and the jewelry, were straight out of caricature. She managed not to stare as a dark-haired beauty undulated by in a rustle of silvery silk, its folds seemingly held to her by affection alone.

"That's the Contessa," Cecelia said. Her eyes twinkled. "That's what she likes to be called, rather. It's all a sort of game . . . being a character out of history, or rather out of a story about history. They've read all the fiction of the period, and they take parts. Not formally, in the evenings, but one is expected to recognize a good version of a familiar character."

"Books . . . like the Surtees and Kipling you loaned me?"

"That's a beginning. You'll have to look into Bunny's library. Come along — you need to meet him."

Heris tried to suppress her curiosity in the presence of her host, Lord Thornbuckle. Was he, too, taking a character to portray? Was that long, foolish face his by nature or by design? He murmured a greeting to her, a longer and warmer one to Lady Cecelia, along with his regrets that she had not made the Opening Day.

"We had some delays," Cecelia said.

"So I understand from the children," he said. "How nice of you to have brought them along. Sorry — let's talk after dinner —" And he turned to greet someone else, with a faint shrug that made clear to Heris he'd rather talk to Cecelia.

"And you must meet Miranda," Cecelia said. "His wife, Buttons and Bubbles's mother, though it's hard to believe. She takes rejuv like kittens take cream."

And in fact Heris would not have suspected the sweet-faced blonde to be old enough to have children Bubbles's age . . . let alone older ones. Miranda murmured polite nothings to them, and introduced them to a Colonel Barksly, who eyed Heris warily before wandering off to get something to drink — or so he said. Heris suspected he would go straight to a comp and start looking her up in some index of officers somewhere. She wished him luck. Miranda confided to Cecelia that they were having trouble again with "that Consuela woman" and Cecelia made appropriate sympathetic noises before excusing herself to "introduce Captain Serrano around a bit."

Heris had never been fond of the predinner social hour anyway, and this one seemed to last forever. She felt out of place in these tall, cold rooms with their consciously ancient decorations, surrounded by people whose gowns had cost more than her Fleet salary. But just as she thought how much she would prefer a snack in her room, a sweet-toned bell rang and someone (she couldn't see who) announced dinner. A flurry of movement; she found herself provided with a dinner partner (and felt fortunate to have read the Kipling) and soon sat at the long, polished table beneath the pseudobaronial banners.

Her partner, it seemed, was one of Bunny's distant cousins, and "desperately keen to hunt." Heris had no trouble with the conversation. The cousin wanted only a listener for his tale of the Opening Day hunt, today's hunt, the performance of his horse, the beauty of the weather, the cunning of the fox, and the inept handling of the hounds by the new huntsman.

"— wouldn't pay him any mind at all, and worse all day. Bunny should never have let Cockran retire."

"Nonsense!" huffed a husky man from across the table. "Cockran hasn't been well the last two seasons, and he's due for rejuv. Bunny had no choice. Besides, Drew wasn't that bad. That couple of pups gave him trouble, but the good old 'uns stayed true. And that last run —"

"Well, but you weren't up where you could see the cast in that wood —"

The food that came and went through all this was ample and hearty, not nearly as elegant as the meals Cecelia had served her, but more filling. Heris wondered if Bunny's household adhered to the custom of women leaving the table early, or to the more modern format where the heavy drinkers dispersed to one room, and those preferring stimulants to another. The latter, she found; she went into the "coffee-room" with some relief, for the long-winded cousin had chosen to drown his bruises in brandy.

"You're ex-military aren't you?" asked someone at her elbow. The colonel she'd been introduced to earlier, in fact. Barksly, that was his name. Heris repressed a sigh. Two bores in one evening? But the colonel's brown eyes twinkled at her. "You deserve a medal for that — Laurence Boniface has rarely had such a patient listener; most of the ladies gather their conversational reins at the beginning and try to make a race of it."

"The food was too good," Heris said demurely. He laughed.

"And I thought it was recognition of a hopeless cause. Tell me, though: royals, regulars, or ground forces?" He was not one to give up an inquiry.

"Regulars." She would make it short and firm; would he take the hint?

"Ah," he said. She could almost hear the gears twitching in his brain. "I met an Admiral Serrano once, at an embassy do on Seychartin."

"If he was two meters tall, with a scar from his left ear across his cheek, that was my uncle Sabado. If she was my height, with lots of braids, it was my aunt Vida." Actually there had been eight Admiral Serranos in the past fifteen years, but only two that she knew of had served on Seychartin while holding that rank.

"Your aunt, then. There's a strong family resemblance."

"So I've been told," said Heris. She braced herself for more questions; she knew he was asking them in his mind. But his next words left the questions untouched.

"It's unusual for Regular Fleet officers to have riding as a hobby," he said.

"Lady Cecelia would convert anyone," Heris said, relieved. Maybe she was safe, now, although this sort of colonel had a habit of making oblique attacks later in an acquaintance. "We had a wager, which she won; the forfeit was that I would take instruction from her. In the process, I discovered an interest."

"Ah," he said, this time in a different tone. "Do you know, years ago when I was a small boy, I happened to see her ride, one of her professional events. It was cold and wet, I remember, a nasty blowing mizzling rain that went right through whatever you wore. I had been bored, even though I rather liked horses, because I couldn't see over the grownups. I would see the top of someone's cap flash by, and that was it. People would groan or cheer, and I didn't know why. My feet were cold; my neck was wet; I'd have gone home if I could. Then everyone was saying 'Here she comes!' and someone — I never even knew the man — set me up on his shoulders, and out of the murk came this huge horse with a red-headed woman on it, and they jumped something that looked to my child's eyes to be four meters high and every bit that wide. Of course it wasn't, but I was impressed anyway. For a whole term I wanted to be an event rider."

"Were you ever?" asked Heris. She found she really cared; he had a gift for storytelling that Bunny's poor cousin utterly lacked.

"Oh, no. I was too young to be faithful to dreams; the next thing I wanted to do was play a very rough ball game popular at our school, and since it was available and good horses were not, I learned to play that, and liked it. Real riding came later, and by then I knew I wanted a career in the military or possibly security forces."

"I wish I'd seen her," Heris said. "She's shown me the cubes, of course, but now that I've ridden a real horse I can imagine that the effect is very different if you're actually there, seeing it."

"Magnificent," he said, smiling. "But do you have your hunt assignment yet?"

"Blue," said Heris. "Day after tomorrow, Neil said; tomorrow I'm to have another session over fences."

"Good for you. If he's scheduled you into the blue, you're doing well. Let me introduce you to some of the other blue hunt members." He led her to a cluster of people who were all talking about the day's chase. Heris wondered which hunt he rode with. Cecelia had explained the system, but it still seemed odd. . . . For one thing, she didn't understand why the hunt levels didn't have names taken from the books, instead of colors. If they were all so interested in reproducing history . . .

"Ah," said a tall lanky blond man. "Captain Serrano, Lady Cecelia's new friend — we've heard about you." Heris had no chance to wonder what he meant, for he went on. "Neil's bragging to everyone — of course, she's his pet example of what we should all aspire to, and now as a teacher as well as rider. Is it really true that you had never mounted a live horse until today?"

Heris allowed herself a slow smile. "Not at all. But it's true I had ridden little, many years ago, and hadn't been on a horse since I was . . . oh . . . perhaps twenty-three."

"You'd never jumped?"

"No."

"I told you, Stef, Lady Cecelia's simulator is legendary." That was a red-haired woman about Heris's height, who wore a gown of mossy green with wide sleeves. . . . Heris realized why, when she saw the wrist brace.

"It must be." Stef, the tall man, shook his head. "Maybe it would help me. It took me five seasons to work up from the red hunt to the blue, and I've been stuck in blue for ten." Others chuckled; the red-haired woman turned to Heris.

"Tell me — did you find real horses easy after the simulator?"

"Not exactly easy, but much easier than I would have without it. And after the second ride, it was almost the same, a continuation of the same training."

Cecelia appeared at her shoulder. "I hate to break this up, but you've got that early lesson, and I'm off with the greens at dawn — and there's a message from the Station." She smiled at the group around Heris, and they smiled in a way that let Heris know how much clout Cecelia had. She was almost tempted to refuse the suggestion just to see them react, but that would be cheap, so she said good night and followed Cecelia upstairs.

"Message?" she asked on the way.

"Nothing much — the ones you left aboard —"

"The standing watch," Heris murmured.

"Whatever. Letting you know that the others arrived safely in Hospitality Bay, and that the new equipment is functioning correctly so far. Did you ask for regular reports?"

"Of course," Heris said. "If they didn't report, how would I know whether things are going well?"

"Oh. I'd assume they were — but before you even remind me, if it were a stable and not a ship I would be the way you are. When I was off competing, I spent incredible sums checking back with the home yard to see if they'd remembered things — and they always had."

"Because you checked," Heris said. "I'll call back up — anything else?"

"Well . . . yes. I hope you won't be offended —"

"I won't." Although she wasn't entirely sure. On her home ground — and she treated Lord Thornbuckle's planet as her home ground — Cecelia had some of the very habits Heris had feared when she first hired on with a rich old lady.

"Some of them are terrible gossips," Cecelia said, speaking softly. "It's not just that they'll repeat what you said. . . . They'll embellish it. It'll be worse because you're here as my guest; they've chewed my past to tasteless mush already, and you're something new. I know you can deal with it, but don't be surprised if you hear that we're lovers or something."

"Lovers!" Heris nearly choked. "Us?"

"Predictable gossip," Cecelia said. Her cheeks were very pink.

"I'm sorry." Heris realized that her reaction could be construed as unflattering. "It's just — I mean —"

"We aren't. I know. But since I never married, they've been trying all the theories about why not, one after another until the end and back again. That crowd that rides the blue hunt is the worst — Stef, in particular, would rather talk than ride, as you can tell when you see him mounted."

"You know," Heris said, as they mounted another flight of stairs, "I wouldn't talk about you — or Ronnie."

"I know. It's not that. I just — I want you to enjoy this, Heris. Not as my captain, but as my guest. And it occurred to me that you might not have their sort of gossip in the military."

"Oh, don't we!" Heris chuckled. "Same both places, I expect. Some wouldn't touch it, but others can't wait to guess who's in bed with whom, using what chemicals or gadgets. Don't worry; I can be dense when it suits me."

"Good." Cecelia took a few more steps, then stopped to face Heris. "If you pay attention in the blue hunt, you'll probably be up in green very soon. They're looking for several things — how solid you are over fences, how done the horse comes back, and whether you interfere in the field."

"Do you want me in the green hunt?" Heris asked. It had become clear how much respect the greens had, but not whether Cecelia wanted competition.

"Of course I do! Heavens, girl, I wouldn't have brought you if I'd thought you'd be stuck in a lower hunt the whole season. It wouldn't have been fair to you, or a much fun for me. Go on, now, and get your rest. I'll be interested in hearing about your day."

That last visit to the tailor had taken out the sligh wrinkle in the back of her jacket. . . . Heris looked at her self in the mirror with a mixture of amusement and pride Amusement, because the clothing proper to foxhuntin still struck her as ludicrous: why wear light-colored tight breeches when you were going to gallop big dirty animals through the mud? And pride, because at over forty she still had the condition to look sixteen or so in those same tight pants, white shirt, and dark jacket.

Despite the training, and Cecelia's assurance that she was ready, Heris found the chaos in the blue hunt's meeting area tingling along her nerves. She looked for Neil but saw only the second level of help. Of course, Neil would be with the green hunt. Surely he'd chosen the mounts, though. . . . She eyed the big red — chestnut, she reminded herself — gelding being led towards her with some concern.

"Tiger II," said the groom, a thickset woman even darker than Heris. "Need a leg?"

"In a moment." Heris went through the drill Cecelia had taught her, checking the bridle and girth herself, then accepted a leg and swung into the saddle. She hoped the beast's name did not reflect his temperament.

"He pulls, sometimes," the groom said. "But he'll answer a sharp check. Keep him back, and calm, and he'll go all day. Get in a fight with him, and you'll wish you hadn't."

Great. She had a problem horse for her first hunt, her first performance in front of everyone. She looked down at the groom, expecting to see sly satisfaction, but the woman's smile was friendly. "Don't worry," the woman said. "He's not a bad 'un for a first time out; he can jump anything, and will — the only thing is don't let him go too strong till he's worked himself down a bit."

"Thank you," Heris said. "Any other advice?"

This time the woman's face creased in a broad grin.

"Well — I wouldn't let him slow down in water . . . he likes to roll. If you come to a stream, get him over in a hurry."

The horse snorted and shook his head; Heris firmed her grip on the reins. "I'll be careful," she said. The groom stepped back. Heris looked around and saw that about half the riders were up. She had room to walk the red horse — Tiger — in a small circle, and did so, first one way then the other. As the minutes passed, she calmed down. It was just another horse, and they were going out to ride over just another field. She had told herself that same lie in other situations, and it always helped. So did "tonight this will be over."

✧ Chapter Ten

The hounds led the way, their long tails — Heris couldn't make herself call such a biologic ornament a stern; ships had sterns — whipping back and forth or carried high, eager. She got only a glimpse of them before the rest of the field passed out the gate and blocked her view. She intended to make sure Tiger understood who was in charge while they were still at a walk.

As they came around the end of the stable wing, Heris could see both the other hunts moving away to the east and west. The beginners (so Cecelia had called them), would hunt the flat, open country to the east, where the fences were lower and the pseudofoxes lived in brushy thickets. The green hunt had the western hills, with long open slopes and timber at the top and bottom. And they, the blue hunt, had a mixed country, rather like lumpy potatoes in a kettle. Little hills with little creeks between them, little patches of woods and others of brush, odd-shaped fields bordered with stone walls or ditches or both.

Verisimilitude, Cecelia had explained, influenced only some of Lord Thornbuckle's eccentricities. That rather lumpy country had been the first colony settlement on this world, bought out by one of the present owner's ancestors. They had tried to make a quick profit out of open-pit mining to pay off their initial investment, then botched the mid-level terraforming that was supposed to convert the area into something their heirs could live on and from. Instead, they went broke, and left behind ugly pit mines, irregular heaps of spoil, ponds and wandering streams fouled with acid and heavy metals. Now, some hundreds of years later, the area was still unsafe for use in any food chain humans would use, but it could support hardy plants, animals with a tolerance for heavy metals and acid water, and recreation. Wool and leather and sport were its crops.

Tiger yanked on the bit, and Heris brought her mind firmly back to the immediate moment. Someone had trotted past — she found it hard to recognize, in the plain black coats and hats, the people she had met at dinner the night before — and the red horse wanted to follow. She refused, and met his attempt to sidle out from behind the horse in front with a firm leg. He tested her in the next few minutes, as they rode to cover, with a curvet here, and a pretense at a shy there; she was reminded of certain troublemakers she had known, and had no problem keeping him under control.

"Ah — Captain Serrano!" The grinning man next to her was the tall lanky blond Cecelia had said liked talk better than riding. He was on a horse which looked like a stuffed caricature of the animal Neil had shown Cecelia: large, dark brown, but this time coarse and bulgy instead of powerful and sleek. And he rode sloppily; even Heris could tell that. "Lovely morning, isn't it? Are you ready for Tiger? Did they tell you?"

"That he pulls, yes, and to keep him out of the water." Heris glanced around. They were near the tail of the group, and she could tell from the tension in the reins that Tiger wasn't happy about it.

"You don't have to stay back here," the man said. Stef, his name was. "Mid-field's enough; just keep him away from the leaders."

"I'm fine," Heris said. "I like to watch the others." Cecelia had told her to stay well back, even this far back, and she trusted Cecelia's advice more than someone who sat his horse like a jellied custard.

"Come *on*, Stef!" someone called from ahead, and he shrugged and kicked his horse into a trot. Heris anticipated Tiger's attempt to lunge forward, and rehearsed for the hundredth time what Cecelia had told her, and what she had read.

The hounds would be turned loose to find the smell —
the scent — of one of the pseudofoxes, and then they
would "give tongue." Now that Heris had heard them,
from a distance, she agreed that "barked" was inadequate.
With the hounds following the scent, the field would follow — cautiously — because pseudofoxes, like their Old
Earth predecessors, were tricky beasts. More than once
they'd popped into view in the midst or even rear of the
field, causing a wild confusion of horses and hounds and
usually getting clean away. One had to give the pack time
to work the scent, to untangle the maze the prey left, and
push the fox into the open. Only when the fox was sighted
did things move faster — eventually very fast.

They came to a scrubby wood bordered on one side by
a tangle of two-meter brush. Riders gathered in a clump;
the few who spoke did so quietly, and most checked
girths and stirrup leathers, and kept quiet. Heris put a leg
forward cautiously and found that Tiger's girth could
come up another notch, just as the groom had said. She
drew in a long breath of cold, moist morning air, on which
the smell of horse and dog and wet clay hung suspended
in a fundamental cleanliness utterly unlike ship's air. Planets felt so spacious; there always seemed to be room,
somewhere beyond — although she knew very well they
were as tightly limited as any ship, just larger. Somewhere
ahead and to the left, she heard the noise of the pack, the
busy feet pattering on leaves and twigs, the coarse, eager
panting, an occasional muffled yelp. Something small and
gray and bouncy — not a pseudofox, but something it
probably ate — shot into the clearing and two horses
shied away from it. Tiger threw up his head, but Heris
held him firmly and the little animal scuttered through
the field without causing any real damage. Another animal — Heris got a good look at this one, and it was a
small, black, tree-climber with a bushy tail — clung to a
nearby tree and made angry chattering noises at them,
flipping its tail as punctuation.

Heris had just begun to wonder if anything would happen when one of the hounds gave a sobbing moan, and
another joined in. She had lost track of their movements;

they now sounded ahead and to the right, and she could hear crackling in the brush. Around her, the riders gathered up reins, and edged into position. Some began moving, at a walk, in the direction of the noise. Then a horn blew a signal she didn't know, and everyone set off after it.

For a long time they seemed to move at a walk or slow trot, making their way through the woods and through a lane in the brush beyond it. Tiger tossed his head a lot, but otherwise gave Heris no trouble. At the end of the brush a low stone wall offered the first chance to test jumping skills in the field. Heris, at the end of the field, had to wait a long time while others scrambled over, some with difficulty. By the time it was her turn, stones lay tumbled at the foot, and the wall was scarcely a half-meter high. Tiger bounced over it with contempt, ears flat, and kicked up on the far side. Only those who had had refusals and turned aside to wait were behind her now. She could see the backs of the first riders rising as their horses leaped an obstacle across the field she'd just jumped into.

Tiger fought the bit all the way across the field, took off late for the rail fence on its far side, and whacked it with his forelegs. Heris had no trouble staying on, but she could tell her shoulders would hurt if he was this stubborn all day long. The fence seemed to have settled him, though, for he followed the field along a track through sparse trees without trying to race ahead. Heris couldn't see exactly where they were headed next, but she felt more confidence in her ability to survive this odd ritual.

Tiger's strong trot brought the field back to her, as most of the riders chose to squeeze through a gate at the end of the track rather than jump another, higher wall. Some of those who had tried the jump hadn't made it; Heris saw one woman climbing back onto her horse, and a man stalking a loose horse which was slyly moving off just too fast to be caught. Beyond the gate, they faced a sluggish stream, well-muddied by recent crossings, and a steep slope across it up one of the small irregular hills. Remembering the groom's advice, Heris took a firm contact, and gave Tiger a smart tap in the ribs. With a snort, he plunged into the water, and lurched up the far bank. Heris couldn't remember if she was supposed to avoid trotting up hill or down (someone had said something about it, she thought) so she walked sedately up, trusting that she could see where everyone was from the top. Tiger's ears were no longer back; apparently he'd given up the fight.

She had imagined a hill like an overturned bowl, with a definite top, from which she could see all sides. As soon as the slope flattened, she realized her mistake. She might as well have assumed that being at the top of a loading platform or the flight deck of her carrier would let her see everything going on below. From the irregular and unlevel top of the hill, the downward slopes were mostly invisible. Some fell off steeply, and others were hidden in clumps of trees or brush. She looked around for a clue. The ground had plenty of hoofprints, but she was no tracker to know which were recent. Far off in the distance, tiny horses stretched across the slope of another hill — but that couldn't be the hunt she was following, it was too far away. A fresh breeze made just enough noise in the nearest trees to cover the sound of the hounds . . . although she hadn't heard it for some time, she realized. She'd just been following the tail-end riders.

She felt stupid, and bored, and suddenly very irritated with Lady Cecelia. Surely this was not what riding to hounds was supposed to be like, dawdling along at the end of a group of people who fell off and got lost. How could they call it hunting? Only those in the front of the group were actually hunting, and they were just following the hounds, who were chasing a fake fox, an artificial animal designed to be quarry. The whole thing was a fake — a pretense of historical accuracy, modified for modern convenience.

A quiver beneath her reminded her that she wasn't standing on a machine, or a fake animal, but riding a real, living animal with its own initiative. Tiger's ears were forward, pricked, and he stamped the ground with a forehoof. She looked in the direction of his gaze. The little horses had disappeared into a wood, too far away still, she was sure . . . but Tiger didn't think so.

She muttered a curse that was thoroughly untraditional on the hunting field, being born of things you could do with weapons found only on spaceships, and nudged Tiger into motion. "You like to hunt, they told me," she said to the horse's ears. One of them flicked back, as if he understood. "Find the damned hunt, then." Tiger picked up a trot, and as the downhill slope steepened, he lunged into a gallop. Heris had just time to think she shouldn't have let him do that. Then they were in the trees, and she was too busy keeping her head off limbs to worry about it.

Out of the woods, into a field bounded by more woods: Tiger took the fence from trees to grass in an easy bound, crossed the field in five strides, and rolled over the wall at the far side into a track Heris had not noticed until they were in it. No trees . . . a long curving ride up and around the shoulder of another hill, through an open gate, down across a grassy field. Tiger, wiser than she, skirted the rock-edged sinkhole in the middle and made for a gap he evidently knew well. A downward rocky slope, where even Tiger slowed to a walk, and Heris got her breath back as they slithered through some spicy-smelling trees towards another creek. That had been fun, if scary: she began to think that whether it counted as hunting or not, it was more fun to ride fast than slow.

By this time Heris had no idea where they were, but the horse's ears still pricked forward. He minced across the little creek and into the woods on the far side. Suddenly Heris heard the hounds again, and from this distance had to admit they sounded almost like horns themselves. They were ahead through the woods, moving left to right. . . . She gathered herself just in time, as Tiger sprang upward, dodging through trees with no regard at all for her legs. She could steer him, she found, and even moderate his speed; she pulled him to a solid canter rather than a headlong gallop.

The belling of hounds rang out nearer; at the top of the wood, they came out of the trees to find the hounds strung out on that hill's bald top, with the field close behind them and the fox in view before. Heris managed to swing Tiger around behind the front runners, though he fought her. Then they were in with others, galloping over short grass toward what looked like a pile of rocks. The leaders swerved around it, and poured over a wall just ahead of Heris. Tiger rose to the wall, and she got a quick glimpse of where they were going — the hounds, the streak of red-brown that must be the fox, the huntsman in red — before they were into the next field, this one draped across the shoulder of its hill like a shawl. Tiger flattened beneath her, passing a gray horse and a black, and jumping the briars and stones that separated that field from another.

"Well ridden!" came from behind her, but she had no attention to spare. His earlier exertions hadn't tired the red horse, and he was pulling her arms out. The leaders were nearer now, as Tiger thundered on, lunging against the reins, and his next jump put him even with the first of the field. Heris knew she should be holding him back . . . but excitement sang the last remnants of doubt out of her bones. She had not felt this exultation since — she pushed that away. Now — this horse, this field, this next jump — was all that mattered. All in a clump they raced, angling across the field after the hounds, to jump a sharp ditch. . . . Someone fell there, but Tiger had carried her over safely.

Ahead was another rockpile, to which the fox sped, and into which it vanished. The hounds swarmed over it, clamoring, but they were not diggers and the fox had found a safe lair. Heris got Tiger slowed, then circled him until he walked; he was wet and breathing hard, but clearly not exhausted. Nor was she; she hoped they'd find another fox and do it again. She could have laughed at her earlier mood: boring? This? No. It was all Cecelia had promised.

The huntsmen set to work to call the hounds back and get them in order. Meanwhile the rest of the blue hunt rode up. Some she had met, and some she hadn't, all now willing to speak to her and tell her how well she'd done.

"I didn't really," she said to the third or fourth person who came up to her. "I got lost, then the horse seemed to hear something —"

"But that's wonderful," the woman said. She had one wrist in a brace, and Heris realized it was the same one she'd seen at dinner. "That's what you're supposed to do, and you actually caught up. Most people, once they're lost, spend the whole day wandering around without a clue, or give up and go home."

"Which hill were you on?" one of the men asked. Heris looked around, but had no idea. The jumbled landscape looked as confused to her as a star chart probably would to these people.

"It was near the beginning," she said slowly. "There was a track through woods, then a creek, then a lot of tracks straight up the hill. . . ."

"The Goosegg? You got here in time for the final run from Goosegg?" Now they seemed even more impressed. Heris wondered why. She thought of asking but shrugged instead.

"Tiger did it," she said. It was true, anyway: he had known where to go, and he'd taken her there without any serious bruises. They liked that, she could see; Cecelia had told her that horse people expect riders to praise horses and take the blame themselves for errors.

For a time, nothing much happened; the hounds stood panting, tongues hanging out; some of them flopped down and rolled. Riders stretched, or took a swallow from flasks in the saddlebag. A few dismounted, and disappeared discreetly behind the rockpile. Horses stood hipshot, or walked slowly around as their riders talked or drank. A few stragglers appeared, one by one, on lathered mounts, but perhaps a third of the field had disappeared. Heris wondered if they were going to look for another fox — it was still morning, by the sun.

When the hunt moved again, it was both calmer and more businesslike than the morning's first action. Heris felt the difference as a sense of purpose, as if a ship's crew steadied to some task. First the huntsman took the hounds down the field, toward a patch of woods near a stream — this one, Heris noted from the hillside, widened to a pond at one point. Riders rechecked girths and stirrups; those who had dismounted got up again, and those who had been chatting stopped. Someone Heris didn't yet know put to her eye a most untraditional military-issue eyepiece; Heris wished she herself had had the wit to get one; that lucky soul would be seeing whatever she looked at in plenty of magnification and perfect lighting. She could see fleas on the fox's coat, if a fox came out.

Then the hounds found another trail. At the first peel of the horn, Tiger trembled; Heris steadied him, but didn't hold him back to the rear of the group this time. Steadily, without haste, the field moved toward the call at a brisk trot. This time no one in front of Heris had a refusal at the low wall and ditch . . . nor did she . . . and they trotted on through the woods, lured by the hound song and the horn. Behind her, the bulk of the field stretched out.

Out of the woods: she could see the scarlet coats ahead, the hounds now fifty meters in the lead across a field. Tiger wasn't pulling as badly, but her sentiments were with him, now; she would like to have charged at the next field as fast as he would go. It had become more than the physical delight of riding over fences at speed; it was a hunt, and she wanted to be part of it. Now she could admit it to herself — she had not felt this completely alive, this exultant, since she'd commanded her own ship in combat. And that had been tempered with grief and worry, knowing that she risked her crew, people who trusted her. Here, she risked only herself; she had no responsibility for the others. No wonder people liked hunting . . . but she had no more time to think about it, and that, too, became part of the pleasure.

That run, her first full run, remained a confusion in her mind, when she tried to tell Cecelia about it. Field and wood and field succeeded each other too rapidly; she had to concentrate on riding, on steering Tiger around trees and readying herself for the fences, walls, ditches, banks that came at her every time she thought she'd caught her breath. It felt as if they'd been riding all day — a lifetime — when she heard the hounds' voices change, heard the huntsman yell at them, and realized that they'd caught the fox, out in the middle of a vast open bowl between the hills, with a little stinking marsh off to one side. This time

Tiger was willing to stop; she sat there panting and hoping she would not disgrace herself by slithering off his back to lie in a heap on the ground.

Breath and awareness came back to her even as the rest of the field came up. "You *can* ride," said the woman with the wrist brace, again beside her. "Don't tell me it's all that horse; I've ridden him myself."

In the hunting frenzy of Lord Thornbuckle's establishment, Ronnie saw his companions change. Buttons, who had been growing perceptibly stuffier over the last year, became a proper son of the household, and took over the red hunt without complaint. He seemed almost a parody of his father, despite the difference in looks. Sarah simply vanished; when they asked, Buttons looked down his nose and muttered something about wedding preparations. Ronnie wished he had such a handy excuse. The others had to undergo evaluation by the head trainer — a humiliating experience, Ronnie thought. Raffaele rode better than he'd expected; though the trainer complained about her form, she never fell off, and was passed to the blue hunt after only a week's review. He and George and Bubbles, though, were stuck with two daily lessons.

Ronnie hated the lessons; they spent nearly all the time at a walk or trot, with a sharp-voiced junior trainer nagging them about things Ronnie was sure didn't really matter. The trainer wasn't nearly as hard on Bubbles; he figured that was favoritism toward a family member. Afterwards, on the way back to the house to swim or play chipball, Bubbles would critique his lesson again, in detail. When he finally burst loose and told her she had to be as bad, or she wouldn't still be having lessons too, she slugged him in the arm.

"I could ride to hounds any day of the week, you idiot. I'm babysitting you two. It wouldn't be fair to make you stay in lessons by yourselves, Dad said." She glared at both of them. "You ought to be grateful, but I don't suppose you are."

Ronnie wasn't. That only made it worse, and his arm really hurt. He hadn't asked for this. She was supposed to be his girlfriend, and she'd been acting as if he were a nuisance.

The crisp, clear weather of the first few days ended with a cold front, clouds, and drizzle. It made no difference what the weather was — lessons and hunts went out on schedule. Ronnie hated the cold trickle down the back of his neck, the horrid dankness of wet boots, and he didn't want to get used to it. Tradition be damned; why couldn't they wear proper weather-sensing clothing like the Royal Service did on maneuvers?

At dinner each day, the Main House crowd seemed to divide naturally along hunt lines. The greens, his Aunt Cecelia quite prominent among them, had their favorite rooms and corners, and so did the blues. The reds condescended subtly to those not yet assigned, but knew their place compared to the other hunts. Bubbles left them, pointedly showing off, Ronnie thought, her ability to mingle with ease as well as her white shoulders. The only young women among the unassigned were too young for him, and too gawky — a pair of earnest cousins so obviously overawed by their surroundings that they blushed if anyone came near. Bubbles had introduced them as "Nikki and Snookie; they used to come a lot back when I was a kid" and then walked off.

When Captain Serrano showed up with a foxtail one evening ("Not the tail, stupid, the brush!" Bubbles hissed) after her first hunt with the blues, Ronnie was disgusted. He had spent five hours that day riding three different horses in boring circles, trotting over boring little fences in a boring ring. He'd been told he might be allowed on the outside course in a couple of days, if he concentrated. And she — twenty years older, if a day — had been allowed to skip the red hunt altogether, go into the blues, and had had a good first hunt. It wasn't fair. For the first time since his lessons on the ship, he thought of revenge, but he resisted. It wasn't worth it.

His only solace in these trying days was Raffaele, of all people. George dragged her away from a group of blues one night, and gave a humorous account of their day's lessons. Ronnie felt humiliated — he didn't fall off that

often, and George didn't mention any of his own mistakes
— but Raffaele's glance at him was sympathetic. After
that she came of her own accord every evening, for a few
minutes at least. She asked once where Bubbles was, and
Ronnie shrugged. She asked no more, but he noticed that
she talked to both of them, not just George. And when
George was taken up by a group of older men who knew
his father, Raffaele kept coming, chatting quietly with
Ronnie in a way he found more and more soothing.

By the time he finally got his pass to hunt with the reds
(two days before George, a minor triumph which by then
he didn't enjoy), he expected no pleasure. The morning
dawned murky and cold with vague clots of mist hiding
the low places; Ronnie felt stiff before he even got to the
stables. Buttons, spruce and cheerful, grinned at him as
he stumped into the yard where the hunt gathered.

"Good for you!" he said, too loudly for Ronnie's taste.
"I knew you'd beat George out of the lesson pit. It's a
good day for scent, anyway." He wore the red coat and
insignia of the M.F.H. of the reds, and looked as if he'd
been born in it.

"Oh . . . George will be along soon enough," said Ronnie vaguely, looking around. "Where's Bubbles?"

Buttons laughed. "Taking a vacation. She's riding with
the blues today. We decided George could survive without a family member for one lesson."

This reminder of his situation did not help. Ronnie
grunted, and looked around again. A groom waved to
him, and he went over to get on the dark, heavy animal
that was his for the day. "Thumper," he was told, "is good,
solid, reliable, and not too fast. Bring him home safe."
Ronnie noticed nothing was said about *his* safety.

They rode out into the cold murk. Thumper seemed to
think his place was the back of the field; Ronnie kicked
vigorously and got him up to the middle. "Eager, aren't
you?" asked someone sarcastically. Ronnie ignored him.
They all milled around in a wet meadow while the hounds
cast about for a scent. No one spoke to Ronnie, and he
knew they were all eyeing him. His neck felt hot. When
the hounds began to speak, he urged Thumper in that

direction, but the others were faster. He trotted along
near the back of the group, getting well spattered with
mud the other horses kicked up. Thumper slowed, and
Ronnie couldn't blame him. It must be worse for the
horse, he thought, getting mud in his face and not just on
his legs.

After awhile, the horses ahead of him sped off at a
canter. Ronnie followed. Now the mud flew higher; he
could see it spattering the ground ahead of him. A hedge
appeared from the murk, and Thumper lifted to it. On
the far side, a ditch gaped; Thumper stretched, and Ronnie clung, slipping a bit at the rough landing. But he
regained his seat and urged Thumper on through a flat
field after the others. He wished someone had seen — it
was a larger jump than he'd ever taken in a lesson.

After some minutes of this he was breathless and sore. It
was much harder than the lessons, even the ones on the
outside course. He couldn't tell what kind of obstacle was
coming. There never seemed time to plan an approach, to
get himself ready for the jump. Thumper had a rough,
lumbering stride, and while he jumped safely, never hitting
anything, he took off with a lurch and landed hard each time.
He was doing better than some (he had seen riders sprawled
on the wet ground, loose horses, people remounting) but he
couldn't get Thumper to catch up with the field.

Far ahead, the horn rang out again. Thumper knew that
signal, and churned ahead faster. Now they passed
stragglers, riders whose strained faces showed that they
found this as tiring as Ronnie did. He wondered why they
bothered. . . . Were there that many bossy aunts in the
universe? He saw a rail fence coming up, and braced
himself. . . . They were over safely, but another loomed up.
With a curse, Ronnie grabbed mane, and survived that one
too. Thumper plunged on, into the rear of the slowing field.
. . . The dogs had caught the fox, though Ronnie couldn't see
it. He pulled on the reins, and Thumper slowed to a walk,
then stood, sides heaving. No one seemed to notice them
now; the red-coated hunt staff in the center were doing
something, and then everyone laughed and cheered.

The crowd spread out, as the riders walked their horses

slowly around. "Made it, did you?" asked someone Ronnie had seen in the red hunt group at dinner. "Must have been pretty far back. Too bad you weren't up. You might've had a chance at the brush, being as it's your first day."

"Well, I made it," Ronnie said. He meant to say it blithely, but it came out sounding disgruntled. The man rode off with a shrug. Thumper heaved a great sigh, and shook his head a little. Ronnie noticed others getting flasks out of their saddlebags. He started to reach for his, and remembered that he'd forgotten to bring it. It seemed suddenly darker, and the first cold drops of the day's rain splashed his hot neck.

By nightfall, he had ridden too many hours, fallen off twice (both times some helpful stranger caught Thumper and brought him back) and was wet to the skin with both sweat and rain. His throat felt raw, his nose was running, and his knees and ankles felt as if he'd played the finals of some dismal professional sport involving large angry men pounding each other to mush. He managed to stay on Thumper until he guided him through the gates of the yard, and then slithered off, staggering as he landed.

"Do you need assistance?" asked the groom, with a quick glance at him. She was already pampering Thumper, he noticed.

"I had a fall," he said, through gritted teeth. "But nothing's broken."

"Good day, then," she said, leading the horse away. "If nothing broke."

He stumped up to the house, hoping to make it to a hot bath without meeting anyone, but of course there was George, dapper and witty, with Raffaele on his arm.

"What did you fall into, the pigpen?" asked George. Ronnie was glad to note that Raffaele did not smirk. She was dry and clean and lovely, but she did not smirk.

"Just a muddy ditch," Ronnie said. He hoped it sounded casual, the way he'd heard others speak lightly of problems in the field.

"I haven't fallen off in a week," George said. "Even though it really rained hard during my second lesson today."

"It's different out there." Ronnie shot a glance at Raffaele. She wasn't even smiling; she looked as if she knew that his shoulder and hip hurt, and was sorry.

"I'll bet Bubbles and Raffa didn't fall," George went on. "Did you?"

Raffa turned an enchanting shade of pink; Ronnie had never thought how lovely a blush could look against dark hair. "Almost," she said. "My horse stumbled on landing over a big drop, and I was right up on her neck. . . ."

"But you didn't fall," George brayed. "Now if that had been Ronnie, he'd have gone splat, right?"

"Excuse me," said Ronnie, trying for coolness and achieving only the very tone of wounded dignity he least wanted. "I'd like to take a bath before dinner."

"I should hope so," George said. "You certainly need one."

Ronnie fumed his way to his room. Bad enough to have to spend a wet cold day riding a clumsy horse over mud and rock. Bad enough to fall off and be bruised from head to heel. But to meet the impossibly dapper George on the way back — to be twitted about his muddy state — that was too much. People that thought this was fun must be completely insane . . . except maybe Raffa, because after all women were different.

He simply could not spend the entire winter at this ridiculous sport. He had to get away, somehow, and do something where he didn't feel a complete fool.

✧ Chapter Eleven

"I'm not sure this is a good idea," Ronnie said.

"Do you really want to spend another day bouncing around on that horse?" asked George. Of course he didn't; that was the point. It had been bad enough before George got into the hunt, and worse afterwards. But sneaking off like this? George went on, "You look ridiculous —"

"I do *not*." Ronnie glared at his friend. George had not fallen off in his first time in the field, and it had gone to his head. He seemed to think a successful maiden appearance made up for later runaways, buckings off, and an inability to keep up with the field on a slow day. "I ride better than you —"

"And not nearly so well as your aged aunt or that demon captain of hers. Honestly, I had no idea the Regs went in for horse riding; I thought they spent all their time polishing weapons and doing drills."

Ronnie snorted. "They do love drills, don't they? At least down here Captain Serrano can't interrupt our sleep."

"No. That's the purview of your aunt, waking us up before daylight to gobble a disgusting breakfast and clamber onto great clumsy, smelly animals. . . ."

Ronnie felt a perverse desire to insist that it wasn't that bad, but Bubbles had already started laughing.

"And you did look so funny, lamb, when you were stuck in that hedge, all red-faced and blubbering." She patted him on the shoulder as she clambered past him. He could see by the dome-light that Raffa was trying to smother her giggles and shush Bubbles.

"Fine." Ronnie slid the canopy forward; the others

were still giggling and stowing their supplies in the lockers. He was beginning to wish he hadn't agreed to this, but how could he back out now? He called up the preflight checklist on the display and started down it. The computer would have done everything, of course, but he was not as careless as his aunt thought.

"Come on, Ron," George said. "Get this thing off the ground."

"Preflight," Ronnie said. George should know that — or was he so involved with Bubbles that he'd lost the rest of his wits? George heaved a dramatic sigh, which Ronnie ignored. He worked his way down the rest of the preflight list in silence; as usual, everything seemed to be in order. Ronnie inserted the cube and checked the readout: it had accepted his course programming, and calculated fuel consumption based on satellite weather information. "Refuel once," he said. "Anyone care if it's Bandon or Calloo?"

A ragged chorus, which sounded louder for Bandon; Ronnie entered that with the touchpad, cast a glance back to make sure all the loose items were stowed, and pressed the green button. The engines caught, and the computer took over the final preflight power checks. At least he knew what the readouts meant, though he could not, from this point on, override the computer's decisions. Not much like a Royal trainer; these civilian models would fly themselves, given the chance. He laid his hands lightly on the yoke anyway, and punched for manual takeoff. He felt the yoke quiver, and the computer displayed his options. If he stayed within these margins, he could have control — and within those, he could control one axis. For a moment it amused him — for a human to be allowed to fly the machine, he had to fly *like* a machine.

It would be practice, and he had always enjoyed flying. He flicked his fingers over the yoke studs — power, directional focus, attitude — and the computer agreed that he knew what he was doing. He didn't know if the others noticed, but he had manual control until he chose to relinquish it, when the craft was at 5,000 meters and on course to Bandon.

"It's dark outside," Raffaele commented as the craft leveled. "There's nothing but —" She peered back. "Nothing but the House lights. . . ."

"We had to leave before daylight," George pointed out. "Or Ronnie's aunt would have stopped us."

Ronnie tried to see past the reflections on the canopy. Nothing but darkness. . . . He flicked off the interior lights, and looked harder. Nothing ahead but darkness, nothing to either side but darkness. He'd never seen anything quite so black in his life.

"It'll be dawn soon," he said. "And the computer doesn't need daylight." As it came out of his mouth he realized that they knew that — he was comforting himself. Darkness hid his blush. Behind him, ostentatious yawns indicated that the others would pretend to sleep. Someone turned on one of the tiny reading lights, a soft glow in the rear of the cabin; Ronnie left the main cabin lights off.

He found that he kept looking to the right, hoping to see some glimmer of dawn. Just when he had given up hope, and convinced himself that he would have to endure flying down a black drainpipe forever, a sullen glow lit the horizon, more feeling than color. Soon he was sure of it; a dim redness blotched with black — clouds, he realized — and then a curious fuzzy quality to the outside. Still dark, still impenetrable, but somehow seeming larger than it had. As the light strengthened, he saw the sea beneath, oddly brighter than the sky. Away toward sunrise it stretched, and the clouds hung over it in dark columns, their tops flushed pink now with the coming light.

Ronnie had never flown along a coast at sunrise; he had not imagined the impossible combinations of green and blue and purple, the piles of pink and gold, which clouds and sea and sunrise make. He looked down on the dark land slowly coming out of the dark haze of night, the shoreline edged with ruffles of colorless surf that would soon be silver and blue. His quick memory for maps told him they were almost a third of the way to Bandon; the computer would soon change their course away from sunrise, across the narrowing belt of land and out across the ocean to that cluster of islands. He hoped it would not change before he could see the sun lift out of the sea.

"There's nothing down there at all," Raffaele said, in a voice that began sleepy and ended worried. "Where are we?"

"This is the Bottleneck," Bubbles said, yawning. "Gorgeous morning, especially since I don't have to climb on a horse. Don't worry, Raffa, we can't get lost. The computer on this thing has a direct line to the navsats. If we went down, someone would be there in no time."

"But somebody must live somewhere," Raffa grumbled.

"On up the coast a bit there's a settlement of wildlife biologists," Bubbles said. "They're to keep the stuff we don't want out of the Hunt grounds."

The sun came up and glittered on the surf just as he had imagined, and a few minutes later the computer swung them left, away from the coast, and across the forested Bottleneck. Bubbles served breakfast, pastries and fruit and hot coffee she'd filched from the kitchen before they left. Ronnie stretched, enjoying the comfort of baggy trousers, loose shirt, and low, soft-sided boots after the confines of hunting attire. By the time they'd eaten, they'd crossed the other coast and were headed across a blue wrinkled ocean toward the islands. Ronnie had nothing to do, so he turned his seat around and listened to the girls speculate on when Bunny would send someone after them.

"I hope it's not Aunt Cece," Ronnie said.

"He wouldn't send her; she's a guest," Bubbles said airily. "It'll probably be some boring mid-level administrator."

"We could just *tell* your father," Raffa said. "Once we get there, that is."

Bubbles wrinkled her nose. "You don't know how he is. He'll lecture me. I'll get mad. We'll argue. And then I'll have to make up, or he will, and that takes time I could be enjoying with you."

Ronnie put the landing system on automatic when he thought they were in range of Bandon. It would contact the field, and bring them in without his intervention, though he hoped the computer would allow him a "manual" landing. When the com beeped, and the field-authorization light turned red, he assumed that the field wanted a voice-contact; it seemed a reasonable way to keep out unwanted guests. "Any special code words?" he asked Bubbles. She shook her head.

"No — just give the flitter number. It's on the family list."

"Bandon field," Ronnie said. "Permission to land and refuel, number 002413."

"Permission denied." The flat, almost metallic voice conveyed no interest in negotiation. Ronnie stared at the computer display. He had never heard of a civilian field refusing permission to land and refuel.

He repeated his original call, and added that they were low on fuel.

"Permission denied," the voice said again.

"Override that," Bubbles said from behind him. "Put in 'Landsman 78342' and see what happens. That's Father's personal code."

Ronnie poked at the screen, and hit the orange override button, but the voice repeated the same statement with the same mechanical lack of expression.

"Can we make Calloo from here?" asked George.

"Just barely," Ronnie said, with a glance at the fuel readout. "And I don't see why we should. This is Bunny's flitter, and Bubbles just gave us the internal authorization number. If it won't accept it, something's wrong."

"We don't want to land if something's wrong," George said. Then, "What could be wrong? What's on this island, anyway?" He turned to Bubbles.

She frowned thoughtfully. "Well . . . the landing field, maintenance station, and the family's lodge — no resident staff, though —"

"There's a lodge here, too?" Ronnie asked. "Then why did you tell me to program for Whitewings?"

"We wanted to be out of everyone's reach. This is too close — it's the first place they'd look."

Ronnie looked out the canopy. Heavily wooded islands

lay scattered in odd shapes across the sea. Bandon, the computer readout told him, was a half hour ahead. He could see its distinctive shape beyond the nearest island. Calloo, the northernmost of the chain, lay far to their right. "We ought to find out what's wrong," he said. "We'll go on to Bandon and take a look." They could still make Calloo, he thought, if they had to, and if they found out something important, Bunny might forgive their disappearance. With the vague notion that he was being careful, Ronnie let the flitter drop lower and skimmed just above the forest, following the contours with care, then made a low approach across the sea between that island and Bandon, edging past a smaller island not quite in his path between them. He did not look outside, concentrating instead on his instruments. If he dipped too low, the flitter's automatic safety overrides would lower the plenum and convert it to an airboat. That could be most embarrassing.

George saw the danger first. "Look out!" he yelled. Ronnie looked back at him, wondering what kind of game they were playing back there; Raffa yelped, peering out the starboard side. Then he saw it, just before it struck, an odd shape trailing a line of orange smoke. The flitter jerked itself out of his control, bouncing up and sideways, and a good half of the readouts went red; something snarled angrily in its power section, a sound that spiralled up into a painful whine and then stopped abruptly.

Ronnie grabbed the controls back, felt the ominous mushiness, and went into the emergency landing sequence he had never expected to use once past his piloting exam. Would they make it to land? The airspeed readout, like all in that bank, was dead; the white beach and green trees ahead moved nearer too slowly. Behind him, no one spoke. George clambered forward, disturbing the flitter's precarious balance, and dropped into the other forward seat.

"I think it was a signal rocket," he said calmly, as if continuing a casual conversation. "All that red smoke . . ."

"She's nose-heavy," Ronnie grunted. "And the hydraulics are shot. Use that big foot on the floor, not your mouth."

Whatever George did made no difference; the flitter sank towards the waves. "Brace up, you girls," George said to the back seats; Raffa was the one who said, "Brace up yourself, Gee — we're trying to get the raft out."

Ronnie tried once more to pull the nose up, but the flitter shivered all over like a nervous dog. *Flitters don't stall*, he remembered being told, *but they crash all the same*. It occurred to him that even if they made it to land, he might simply crash head-on into the lush forest. Could he maneuver at all? *Altitude, then maneuver*, he remembered. But he had no altitude. He tried; the flitter slewed sideways, but answered sluggishly. He could parallel the coastline and those trees. . . .

"George — there — those people —" Ronnie did not look; he had to keep the flitter in the air as long as he could. George leaned to see, then grunted, as if it were a marvel.

"Damn near naked," he said. "But armed. . . . I think that's the launcher he hit us with."

Ronnie put all his strength into willing the flitter not to crash into a lump of trees nearer shore than the rest.

They were down, and not dead — at the moment, that was all he cared about. His hands ached; his ears rang; his whole body hurt. But they were alive, and out of the flitter — which now looked far too small to have held so many people and so much fear. Bubbles and Raffa, with far more gumption than he would have expected, had unloaded everything useful from the flitter. The survival raft and all its provisions, the scuffed but whole duffles.

"Never pays to buy cheap luggage," George said, in the tone that had won him the nickname "Odious," as he brushed the sand off his and hoisted it to his shoulder. "Come on, now, Ronnie — give the girls a hand, can't you?"

Ronnie glared at him. He looked, the odious George, as he always did — fresh, creased, polished to a high gloss. Not a hair of his dark head ruffled, not a smudge. He looked like that on horseback, and even when he fell off he never looked rumpled or dirty. He looked like that on mornings after, and on hot afternoons on parade. It was unfair, and his brother officers had done all sorts of things to ruin that polish — but nothing worked. "Dip the odious George in shit," some senior cadet had said their first year, "and not only wouldn't it stink, it'd take a shine."

Now, on the sandy beach after a flitter wreck, Ronnie thought he knew what *he* looked like. He said nothing, but picked up two of the remaining duffles, staggered a bit, then dropped them.

"What now?" asked George.

"The beacon," Ronnie said, clambering onto the flitter. He wished he could remember how he'd gotten out of it. "We need to signal for a pickup, unless you plan to swim back to the mainland."

"You gave it to me," Bubbles said. She looked worried. "You don't remember?"

He didn't remember. He crouched on the flitter's canopy, suddenly aware that he was not functioning in some important way. He looked around, blinking. The sea, the sand, the trees: he remembered that. They'd crashed the flitter, and whoever owned it would be furious. Who had crashed the flitter? They weren't designed to crash easily and he and George were both good pilots. He looked at the flitter itself, at the large hole in the engine section, the scorchmarks black on the outer skin. "What happened?" he said, knowing it was a stupid question, though it was all that occurred to him.

"Damnation!" George's voice, closer. "He's concussed; he doesn't know what's happened or — c'mon, ladies, we've got to get him away from here."

He heard Raffa ask why, and Bubbles remind George that injured people shouldn't be moved until medical personnel arrived, but someone stronger than Raffa or Bubbles pulled him off the flitter and slung him over a muscular shoulder. That completed his collapse; he spewed the breakfast he'd eaten down George's legs and knew nothing more for a time he could not measure.

Ronnie awoke lying on his back with the sun prying his eyelids apart and someone beating his head with a collection of spoons. At least that's what it felt like. He had no desire to move, though he would have appreciated quiet, darkness, and a cool wet cloth on his forehead. A sympathetic murmur would have been nice too. Instead the only voices he recognized sounded angry and frightened.

"If my father knew —" That had to be Bubbles, pulling off her best daughter-of-greatness act.

"And what makes you think he doesn't?" asked a man's voice, in a tone that meant Bubbles was making no impression at all. Or the wrong one.

An instant's pause, then, "What do you mean, he knows?"

Laughter with no humor in it, the kind of thing Ronnie had heard only a few times in his life; it frightened him then, and now.

"I don't suppose he knows his daughter's involved, no." The man's voice had some familiar tone that Ronnie felt he should know but could not quite recognize. "But something like this, as big as it is, on his favorite resort world: how could he not know?"

"Something like *what*?" That was Raffaele, Ronnie thought. A girl who believed that the facts would explain themselves.

Another man's voice, this one quite different. "Oh, I 'spect you know, little lady." Every hair on Ronnie's body rose at that "little lady." He wanted to leap up and knock that voice into the sea, but he could not move. "It's a hunter's paradise, isn't it? And your dad, or maybe it's her dad, is a famous sportsman, isn't he? And the whole point of sport is you give the prey a chance, eh? Isn't it? That makes it a challenge, see?"

The reiterated questions struck Ronnie as false, theatrical, like something from a storycube. Certain dialects did that, he thought.

"Manhunting," the first voice said. "As you very well know, since you came here for that purpose." Ronnie tried to process that: manhunting? Manhunts were for escaped criminals, or lost children.

"But it can go two ways, see?" the second voice interrupted. "Hunting predators it can always go two ways, and men are the most dangerous. There was a story once —"

"Everyone knows the story, Sid; be quiet." The command in that first voice finally made the connection for Ronnie. It sounded like Captain Serrano. It sounded like Captain Serrano the time she had ordered him off her bridge, or the time he had overheard her talking to Aunt Cece about battle. He struggled to open his eyes and found himself blinking up at a dark unsmiling face. "Well," the man said. "And what have we here, young man? Who are you?"

"Ronald Vertigern Boniface Lucien Carruthers," he heard himself say, as if in one of the practice sessions in the squad. "Royal Aero-space Stellar Service." He looked around, now that he could see, and there was the odious George, looking remarkably tidy with a gag stuffed in his mouth and an angry expression on the rest of his face. Bubbles looked almost as angry; he wondered if she was going to come out of her usual wild-blonde disguise for the occasion. And Raffa —whom he hoped would someday be *his* Raffaele — had no expression at all. He had never seen her like that, and he hoped he never would again.

The dark face above his did not smile. "Royal ASS, eh? And you probably think that means something here."

Ronnie had heard that version of his service's initials before; he ignored it now, as beneath the notice of a wounded officer. "And you?" he asked, as he wondered which of his limbs still worked. "I have not the honor —"

A snort of contempt, and a growl from others he had not yet noticed. "That's the truth, little boy soldier — you have not the honor indeed. You don't know what honor *is*."

From a little distance, he heard another mirthless chuckle. "Little peep plonks down in a flitter and bumps his poor little head, pukes out his guts, and thinks he has a right to say the H-word. . . ."

"Shut up, Kev. We don't have time for your nonsense any more than *his*." A jerk of the head indicated George. The dark eyes contemplated Ronnie. "But you — you're going to give us the truth, Mister Ronald Vertigern Boniface Lucien Carruthers of the Royal Assholes. You didn't learn to fly with that bunch of old ladies, boy: who are you really from?" Hard hands grabbed his ears and shook his head. He had thought it hurt before; now he knew it had merely been uncomfortable. He felt his eyes water, and hated the man for that. His stomach roiled, and he choked back another wave of nausea.

"I told you," Bubbles said, before he could get any words out. "We're from the Main Lodge; we wanted to get away from the fox hunting —"

"And try other game?" suggested another voice he could not see.

"And just play around," Ronnie said. At the moment he didn't care if he did die; his head might as well have a real axe in it as whatever was causing what he felt. He knew his voice sounded weak and querulous; he *felt* weak and querulous. "My aunt Cece — you wouldn't know her — and that demon captain of hers wanted me to spend all day every day on a horse chasing some miserable little furry thing over fields of cold mud and fences designed to make horses fall down and dump their riders." He took a breath; no one interrupted. "And we got tired of it," he said, closing his eyes against the bright glare of the forest canopy. "We wanted to rest. We wanted to have fun. I asked Bubbles if there wasn't some place on this miserable dirtball that wasn't cold and muddy and full of horses, and she said let's go to the islands."

"Oblo?" The first voice seemed to be addressing someone else; Ronnie gave himself up to contemplation of his headache and the mystery of his stubbornly unhelpful arms and legs. He finally thought he felt something weighing him down, or tying him down, or something of that sort. External, not internal — he was sure he was wiggling his toes. For some reason, the discovery that he probably didn't have a broken neck did not make him feel better.

"No weapons — not with them or on the flitter, 'cept a cateye. That's standard survival gear on flitters, most worlds." Oblo, if that was the speaker, had the same businesslike tone as the first voice. "Food and minor medical supplies in stuff they'd pulled out to take with them. All the IDs check out, as far as we can know without

accessing a link. Flitter ID was still in the active comp, no
sweat getting it out; it's Lord Thornbuckle's all right."

"And the beacon?" asked the first voice.

"Back aboard, sir, same's you said. Tough to make it
look like it hadn't ever been out, though. On the other
hand, maybe they'll accept all that cracked casing as why
it doesn't work. Did my best."

"I'm sure you did, Oblo."

Ronnie opened his eyes again, to find the dark face he
remembered looking across him to someone else. "Why'd
you put the beacon *back*?" he asked. "That's stupid — we
need rescue here."

"You may need rescue," the dark man said, "but we
don't need hunters tracking us by that thing."

"You . . . shot us." He was sure of it, though he saw no
weapon that could have served.

"Yep. Thought you were the hunters, and we had a
chance to drop you in the water. Not a bad job of work,
the way you got that flitter to land." The dark man
hawked and spat juicily. "Wasted all the work on you,
looks like now, and we've still got them to deal with. And'f
they know about you, we've got even more trouble, if
that's possible."

"Oh." Ronnie could not think of anything to say, and
looked at George — but George, gagged, could not argue
for him.

"I'm sure my father doesn't know," Bubbles said, into
the brief silence. Her blonde hair looked straggly, coming
out of whatever she'd done to keep it in tousled curls. She
raked it back with both hands, hooking it behind her ears,
and started in again. "This is our special place, the kids'
place — even if he did something so horrible, he wouldn't
do it here."

"Kids' place?"

"We camped here, every summer until I was fifteen or
so. Some of the younger cousins still do." Ronnie let her
voice lull him back to sleep; he didn't like being awake
any more.

When he awoke again, the first thing he heard was

George's voice. *Poor idiots* he thought lazily. *You should have left him gagged.* Then he realized what he'd thought, and woke up the rest of the way, ashamed of himself. He was no longer tied (if he had been tied; he found his memory wobbly on that and other points) and when he tried to sit up, someone's arm came behind him, lifting his shoulders. Even under the forest canopy, he could tell that some hours had passed; the bits of sun poking through came at a different angle. Someone had cleaned his face; he couldn't smell the vomit anymore, and was grateful. Without a word, a brown hand came from behind him and offered a flask of water. He took it and drank.

They were all there: Bubbles, Raffa, and George, and the faces he remembered from that nightmarish time when he'd been flat on his back. Now, right side up, he recognized the hostile expressions as exhaustion, fear, uncertainty. He saw only eight or nine, but noises in the thick undergrowth suggested at least as many more.

"The point is, Petris," George was saying, "that Ronnie and I are both commissioned officers of the Royal . . ." His voice trailed away as the snickers began, and he turned red.

"Son," the dark man said, "the point really is that we know how to fight a war and you don't. You'd get us killed; you damn near got yourself and your girls killed. I don't care how many glittery stripes and pretty decorations you've got on your dress uniform, nor how bright your boots shine; you don't know one useful thing about staying alive in this mess, and I do."

George looked around for support, and caught Ronnie's eye. "Good — you're awake now. Tell him — we're officers; we should be in charge."

In charge? In charge of what? The dark man — Petris? — had said something about a manhunt, but he didn't want to hunt anyone. He wanted to wait until he could think straight, and then fly back to the mainland. His mind gave a little jerk, like a toy train jumping to another track. *They* were being hunted, that was it, the men on the island. They were trying to fight back, to hunt the hunters. And George thought he and Ronnie should organize that? Ridiculous. Ronnie shrugged. "He's right, George. We're worse than the girls — they at least know what they don't know. We keep thinking we do know." He hardly knew what he was saying, over a dull pounding in his head, but that made the best sense he could. "You're — Petris, sir? I agree with you."

The dark man gave Ronnie the first friendly look he'd had. "Maybe that knock on the head put your brain right side up after all. Oblo, give this lad a ration bar." The same dark hand that had passed him the water flask held out a greasy, gritty bar that Ronnie recognized as part of the flitter's emergency supplies. He took it and nibbled the end. His body craved the salt/sweet flavor.

"Ronnie, you can't let that — that *person* ignore your seniority."

Ronnie grinned, and his head hardly hurt at all. "I'm not letting *him* ignore my seniority; *I'm* ignoring it. Remember what old Top Jenkins said about tooty young cadets?"

"We aren't cadets any more." George was still bristling; for the first time, Ronnie saw his father in him, the court-room bully. "We're *officers*."

"We're prisoners, if you want to be precise," Ronnie said. "Come on, George . . . look at it this way. It's an adventure." Petris scowled, but George finally grinned. Ronnie tried to explain to Petris. "It's a saying we have. . . . We started in boarding school together . . . and George would think these things up, or Buttons would, or Dill, and the rest of us would say how crazy it was, and how much trouble we'd get in, and whoever began it would say, 'It's an adventure.'"

George chuckled. "I remember who started it — Arthur whatsisname, remember? Had that streak of pale blue hair he claimed he'd inherited? Got us into some frightful row, and when we were called up said, 'Look at it this way, boys — it's an adventure.' And we all went in sniggering like fools and got twice as much punishment as usual."

"I can see why," Petris said, with emphasis that stopped the chuckle in Ronnie's throat. "This is not an adventure. This is a war. The difference is that between whatever punishment you got, and death. Go in sniggering, as you put it, here — play the fool here — and you will be dead. Not charmingly, tidily, prettily dead, either." His gaze encompassed George, who still looked entirely too dapper for the circumstances.

"I know that," George said irritably.

"Then act like it." Petris turned back to Ronnie. "And you, young man, if you're finally getting sense, get enough to live through this and grow up." He glanced sideways at the girls, but said nothing to them directly. Did he think women were nonentities? He must not have known Captain Heris.

He didn't realize he'd said the name aloud until the other man reacted.

"Captain who?" Petris looked dangerous again. Ronnie choked down the rest of the ration bar.

"Serrano. Heris Serrano. She's ex-Regular Space Service, like you."

"So that's where she ended up." A feral gleam lightened his dark eye. Ronnie was startled; it was the first personal emotion he'd seen Petris exhibit. Petris grinned; it was not a nice grin. "She did have a comedown, after all."

"A comedown?"

"To play captain of a rich lady's yacht. Serves her right."

"What for?" asked George. Ronnie was glad; he too wanted to know, but he had already been chewed out for asking too many questions.

Petris glared at him. "None o' your —"

"Tell them," Oblo said. "Why not? You don't want to protect her."

Petris shook his head. "No. That's right enough. But do you think these Royal-ass punks can understand it?"

"Might learn something," Oblo said. Ronnie felt a tension between the two men, not quite conflict, and wondered what it could be.

"All right." Petris wiped his mouth with his hand, and settled back, looking past them. "It started with the Cavinatto campaign, which is too new to have been in your studies, so don't argue with me about it. Scuttlebutt says it was Admiral Lepescu who thought up the lousy plan; from what I know of him I wouldn't doubt it. If our captain had followed his orders, most of us would've died, and it wouldn't have accomplished a damn thing. It was a stupid plan, and a stupid order."

"But —" George began; Petris glared him down.

"Do you want the gag again? Then be quiet. I know what you think — officers that refuse orders are traitors and should be shot — right?"

George nodded and shrugged at the same time, trying not to offend. Ronnie almost laughed aloud — but not when he saw Petris's face.

"That's what the rules say," Petris went on. "No matter how stupid, how bloody, or how unnecessary, officers obey their seniors and enlisted obey officers. Mostly they do, and mostly it works, because when you're not in combat, a stupid order won't kill you. Usually. But then there's combat. You expect to die someday — it's not a safe profession, after all —" Behind Petris, the others chuckled, but he ignored them. "But what you hope for is that your death will mean something — you'll be expended, as the saying is, in some action that accomplishes something more than just turning you into a bloody mess." He was silent after that so long that George stirred and opened his mouth; Ronnie waved at him, hoping he would keep quiet. Finally Petris looked at both of them and started speaking again.

"It's not that anyone doubted Serrano's courage, you know. She'd been in action before; she had a couple of decorations you don't get for just sitting by a console and pushing the right buttons. No — what she did, refusing a stupid order that would kill a lot of people without accomplishing any objective, that was damn brave, and we all knew it. She was risking her career, maybe her life. When it was over, and she faced the inquiry on it, she didn't try to spread the blame — she took it just the way you'd expect — would have expected — from knowing her before. I'd been with her on three different ships; I knew — I thought I knew — what she was. She was facing a court-martial, dishonorable discharge, maybe prison time or execution, if she couldn't prove that Admiral Lepescu's order was not only stupid but illegal. I was scared for her; I knew she had friends in high places, but not that high, and it's damned hard to prove an admiral is giving bad orders just because he likes to see bloodshed."

He paused again, and drank two long swallows from his flask. "That was the Serrano I thought I knew — the woman who would risk that." His voice slowed, pronouncing every word as if it hurt his mouth. "Not the woman who would take the chance to resign her commission before the court and lay the blame on her crew. Leave *us* to face court-martial, and conviction, and *this* — this sentence." His wave included the place, the people, the situation. "She didn't come to our trial; she didn't offer any testimony, any written support, nothing. She dumped us, the very crew she'd supposedly risked her career to save. It didn't make sense, unless her decision to avoid that engagement really was cowardice, or she saw it as a way to leave the Service. . . ."

Ronnie said nothing. He remembered his first sight of Captain Serrano, the rigidity with which she had held herself, like someone in great pain who will not admit it. He remembered the reaming out she'd given him, that time on the bridge, and what he'd heard her say to his aunt . . . scathing, both times, and he'd sworn to get his vengeance someday. She had held him captive, forced his attention, "tamed" him, as she'd put it. He had had to watch her take to riding, and hunting, as if she were born to it, while he loathed every hour on horseback; he had had to hear his aunt's praise of her captain's ability, and her scorn of him. That, too, he had sworn to avenge. Now was his chance, and it required nothing of him but silence.

He met George's eyes. . . . He had told George, he remembered, what Serrano had said about her past. He had been angry, and he had eavesdropped without shame, and shared the gossip without shame. Now he felt the shame; he could feel his ears burning.

"It wasn't that," he heard himself saying. Petris looked at him, brows raised. "She didn't know," he said.

"How do you know?" asked Oblo, before Petris could.

"I — I heard her talking to my aunt," Ronnie said. He dared not look at Raffa; she would be ashamed of him. "They told her — I suppose that admiral you mentioned — that if she stood trial, the crew would be tried with her, but if she resigned, no action would be taken against her subordinates."

Petris snorted. "Likely! Of course she'd make up a good story for later; she wouldn't want to admit she'd sold us —"

"I'm not sure," Oblo said. "It could be. Think, Petris: which is more like *our* Serrano?"

"She's not *my* Serrano!" Petris said furiously. For a moment, Ronnie thought he might attack Oblo. "Dammit, man — she could have —"

"Could have been tricked, same as us." Oblo, Ronnie realized, had never wanted to believe Serrano guilty of treachery. He turned to Ronnie. "Of course, lad, she's your aunt's captain — you'd like her and defend her, I daresay. . . ."

"Like her!" That was George, unable to keep quiet any longer. "That — that puffed-up, arrogant, autocratic, bossy — ! No one could like her. Do you know what she did to Ronnie? To Ronnie — on his own aunt's ship? Slapped him in the *face!* Ordered him off the bridge, as if he were any stupid civilian! And me — she told me I was nothing but a popinjay, a pretty face with not the sense to find my left foot —"

"George," said Ronnie, trying not to laugh. "George, never mind —"

"No, Ronnie." George looked as regal as he could, which was almost funnier. "I've had enough of this. Captain Serrano may have been your aunt's choice, but she was not mine. All those ridiculous emergency drills — I've never seen such a thing on a proper yacht. All that fussing about centers of mass, and alternative navigation computer checks, and whatnot. I'm not a bit surprised that woman got herself in trouble somewhere; she's obsessed with rules and regulations. That sort always go bonkers sometime. She drove you — the least mischievous of our set — to eavesdrop on her conversations with your aunt —"

"Enough," said Petris, and George stopped abruptly.

"Let's hear, and briefly, from you, Ronnie. What precisely did you hear, and under what circumstances?"

Ronnie gathered his wits again. "Well . . . she had chewed me out, and waked us up three lateshifts running for drills. I wanted to get back at her —" Put that way, it sounded pretty childish; he realized now it had been. "So I patched into the audio in my aunt's study." He didn't think he needed to tell Petris about the stink bomb, or its consequences. "She and my aunt talked a lot — mostly about books or music or art, sometimes about the ship or riding. But my aunt wanted to know about her time in the Service, why she resigned. I could tell the captain didn't want to answer, but my aunt can be . . . persuasive. So that's what she said, what I told you before. She was offered a chance to resign her commission rather than face a court-martial, and was promised that if she resigned no action would be taken against any of her crew. Otherwise, she was told, her crew would also be charged, and it was more than likely they'd all be condemned. She . . . cried, Petris. I don't think she cries often."

The man's face was closed, tight as a fist; Ronnie wondered what he was thinking. Oblo spoke first.

"That's *our* Serrano, Petris. She didn't know. She did it for us — they probably wouldn't let her come back and explain —"

"Yes," Ronnie put in. "She said that — she had to resign, right then, in that office, and not return to the ship. She said that was the worst of it, that someone might think she'd abandoned her crew, but at least they'd be safe."

"That . . . miserable excuse for an admiral . . ." Petris breathed. Ronnie sensed anger too deep for any common expletives, even in one so accomplished. "He *might* have done that. He might think it was funny."

"Nah," said Sid. Ronnie recognized the nasty voice that had raised the hairs on his arms earlier. "I don't believe that. It's the captain, like you told me at first. Why'd she resign if she wasn't up to something, eh? Stands to reason she has friends to cover for her."

"You weren't in her crew," Oblo said. "You got no right

to judge." He looked at Ronnie. "You are telling the truth." It was not so much a statement, as a threat.

Ronnie swallowed before he could answer. "I overheard what I told you — and I told George. I hated her; I hoped to find some way to get back at her. But . . ." His voice trailed away.

"But you couldn't quite let us believe the lie, eh?" said Petris. He smiled, the first genuine friendly smile Ronnie had seen on his face. "Well, son, for a Royal ASS peep, you've got surprising ethics." He sighed, and stretched. "And what would you want to bet," he asked the others, "that Admiral Lepescu planned to let her know later what he'd done? When it was too late; when it would drive her to something he could use. . . ."

"Does he know she's here?" Ronnie asked, surprising himself. "Could he have known who hired her, where she was going?"

"Lepescu? He could know which fork she ate with, if he wanted to."

✧ Chapter Twelve

Heris came out of the shower toweling her hair, to find Cecelia sitting upright in the desk chair, already dressed for the day's hunt.

"I didn't know I was late," Heris said. Her own clothes lay spread on the bed; she had come from the shower bare, as usual, and shrugged when she realized it was too late for modesty. She hoped anger would not make her blush; Cecelia had no right to invade her room.

"You're not," Cecelia said. "I can't find Ronnie. Or George. Or their girlfriends." Then her voice sharpened. "That's a — a scar —"

Heris looked down at the old pale line of it, and shrugged again. "It's old," she said. And then, realizing why Cecelia was so shocked, explained. "No regen tanks aboard light cruisers. If you get cut or burned, you scar." She pulled on her socks, then her riding pants, and grinned at Cecelia. "We consider them decorative."

"Barbaric," said Cecelia.

"True," Heris said. "But necessary. Would you have quit competitive riding if you'd had to live with the scars of your falls?"

"Well . . . of course not. Lots of people did, in the old days. But it's not necessary now, and —"

"Neither is fox hunting," Heris said, buttoning her shirt and tucking in the long tails. "Very few things are really necessary, when you come down to it. You — me — the horses — all the rituals. If you just wanted to exterminate these pseudofoxes, you'd spread a gene-tailored virus and that'd be it. If you just wanted to ride horses across fences, you could design a much safer way to do it — and not involve canids."

"Hounds."

"Whatever." Heris leaned over and pulled on her boots; they had broken in enough to make this easier and she no longer felt her legs were being reshaped as the boots came up. She peered into the mirror and tied the cravat correctly, slicked down her hair, and reached for her jacket. "Ready? I'm starved."

"You didn't hear me," Cecelia said, not moving. "I can't find Ronnie and the others."

"I heard you, but I don't understand your concern. Perhaps they started early — no, I admit that's not likely. Perhaps they're already at breakfast, or not yet up from an orgy in someone else's room —"

"No. I checked."

Heris opened her mouth to say that in a large, complicated building with dozens of bedrooms, near other buildings with dozens of bedrooms, four young people who wanted to sleep in could surely find a place beyond an aunt's sight. Then she saw the tension along Cecelia's jaw. "You're worried, aren't you?"

"Yes. They didn't hunt yesterday; they were supposed to be out with the third pack, and Susannah mentioned she hadn't seen them. The day before, you remember, Ronnie missed a lesson."

"But —"

"I found Buttons, and asked him. He turned red and said Ronnie, George, and the girls had gone picnicking day before yesterday. He didn't know about yesterday, or said he didn't. And there's more." When Cecelia didn't go on, Heris sat on the bench at the foot of her bed. She knew that kind of tension; it would do no good to pressure her. "There's a flitter missing," Cecelia said finally. "I had to . . . to bribe Bunny's staff, to find that out. Apparently Bubbles is something of a tease; it's not the first time she's taken out her father's personal flitter, and the staff doesn't like her to get into trouble. They cover for her, with the spare. So Bunny doesn't know a thing. . . ."

"And they've been gone a day . . . two days? Maybe three?"

"Yes. According to the log — they do keep one, just to be sure Bubbles doesn't get hurt — they left well before dawn day before yesterday. Filed a flight plan for some island lodge called Whitewings. I've never been there, but I've got the map." She handed Heris the data cube; Heris fitted it into the room's display. "The problem is, they aren't at Whitewings, either. It's a casual lodge — no resident staff, although it's fully equipped. There's a satellite beacon on the flitter, of course, and there's been a steady signal here —" Cecelia pointed to an island much nearer than Whitewings. "No distress call, and it's at another lodge. Michaels, who's the flitter-chief, thinks Bubbles just changed her mind and decided to hide out on another island in case I followed the trail this far."

"She'd know about the beacon, though —"

"She'd think I wouldn't."

"Ah." Heris stared at the display. "What's on this other island?"

"Bandon? It's another lodge, more a family place, although it's got a large landing field. Michaels says the family goes there every spring, at least once. When the children were younger, they used to camp on one of the smaller islands, while the adults stayed on Bandon. He says it's lovely: forested islands, clear water, reefs. Imported cetaceans, some of the small ones that Michaels said play with humans. Bubbles has always liked it better than anyplace on the planet, he says. Whitewings is colder, usually stormier."

"That makes sense. So you think they're all sunning themselves, swimming lazily —?"

"No. I can't say why. But I think they're in trouble. And I can't imagine what. This is a safe world; there's nothing on the islands to hurt them — I asked Michaels. Their com links are unbreakable; if they needed help, they'd ask for it. They can't be in any real trouble — not all four of them. But —"

"Tell Bunny," Heris said. When Cecelia's expression changed, she realized she'd used his nickname for the

first time. He had always been Lord Thornbuckle to her.
She started to apologize, but Cecelia was already talking.

"I don't want to do that. Not yet. He's upset right now
with that anti-blood-sports person who got herself invited
under an alias. He's not at his best."

"But if his daughter — no, never mind. What do you
want me to do?"

"I'm not sure. I don't suppose there's any way the
Sweet Delight could tell —?"

Heris smacked her forehead with the flat of her hand.
Stupid! She'd nearly turned into a dirtsider, all the time
she'd spent traveling at the speed of horseflesh. "Of
course," she said. Then — "But can I get a closed channel, a secure channel, from the house?"

"Yes, with my authorization. We'd best do it from my
room."

Cecelia's room, Heris noted, had even more windows
on the morning side of the house — no wonder she woke
so early — and was half again as large as her own. The
deskcomp looked the same, however, and Cecelia soon
had what she considered a secure line to the station. She
handed the headset to Heris.

"Captain Serrano; a secure line to the officer on deck,
Sweet Delight."

"At once, Captain." She thought that was probably the
Stationmaster himself, but no visual came up. When the
screen lit, it was to show the familiar bridge, warped a bit
by the wide-angle lens, and Nav First Sirkin.

"Captain Serrano," the younger woman said. She
looked only slightly surprised.

"I'd like a scan report from . . . oh . . . say . . . fifty-five
hours back. Did you log a flitter flight from the Main
Lodge, this location, to an island group to the west?"

A broad grin answered her. "Yes, ma'am. That was my
shift, and I remember it. Let me bring up the log and
scan." The log display came online, a narrow stripe along
the side of the screen, with time and date displayed in
both Standard and Planetary Local. The log entry, terse
and correct, noted the size of craft, the course, and the
recognition code of the flitter beacon. The scan proper, a

maze of graphics and numbers, matched the log except in one particular.

"They signalled," Heris said, her finger on the scan. "They called a fixed station — probably the landing field at Bandon. And something responded —"

"Michaels says it's an automatic loop. There's no one at the field unless family's expected."

"Hmmm. And what's this?" Heris pointed to a squiggle she knew Cecelia could not interpret, and spoke to her Nav First. "Did you log the other traffic?"

"Yes — although since it didn't have a satellite locater signal, I assumed they were just maintenance flights or something."

"Or *something*," said Heris. She felt an unreasoning surge of glee and grinned at Cecelia. "Good instincts: something is definitely going on out there."

"Smugglers, I suppose," Cecelia said with refined distaste. "I never saw a world without some of it. Probably off-duty crews."

"No," the Nav First interrupted. "At least some of them are Space Service. Regular, Captain, like yourself." Heris winced at the pronoun; centuries after overzealous English teachers had tried to stomp out misuse of *me*, the reflexive overcorrection lingered as a class distinction. But that was unimportant now.

"How do you know?" she asked. The younger woman flushed.

"Well, I was sort of . . . listening in to see how good that new scan technology was —"

"And you picked up Fleet traffic?" If she had, Heris would report it, small thanks though she'd get for it.

"No, ma'am. It was a private shuttle from a charter yacht docked at Station Three. Someone groundside asked if Admiral Lepescu was aboard, and the shuttle said yes."

Heris felt as if someone had transplanted icewater into her arteries. She started to ask more, but Cecelia interrupted, with a hand on her arm.

"I want to go after them."

"Why?" Heris's mind had clamped onto the admiral's

name; she could not think why Cecelia would want to follow him.

"To bring them back. Before Bunny finds out."

The youngsters. Ronnie and all. Not Lepescu. Heris struggled to keep her mind on the original problem. They had gone off illicitly, and had not signalled, and their craft's locator beacon still functioned. And Cecelia wanted to bring them back. That ought to be simple enough. She forced herself to look closely at all the details Sirkin had displayed. One caught her eye at once.

"Sirkin — that flitter locator beacon — it's not on Bandon."

"No, Captain; there's a whole group of islands, and it's on the one just north of Bandon."

Heris turned to Cecelia. "But the family lodge is on Bandon proper, surely — with the landing field?"

"I think so." Cecelia's face contracted in a thoughtful frown. "I don't really know; I've never been there. Michaels implied it was on the same island."

"Of course they may have decided to camp on the beach. . . ." Heris looked over the rest of the data. "You said Bubbles had camped on one of the other islands. Odd — the flight path of that flitter doesn't look right. You'd think they'd have gone by Bandon to pick up supplies, at least. Did they take off with full camping equipment? Or would Michaels know?"

"I could ask," Cecelia said. "You think they meant to land at Bandon and didn't? They crashed?"

"Could be." Heris felt frustration boiling through her mind. Once she would have had the information she needed; once she would have had trusted subordinates to find out anything she lacked. People she could trust . . . she would not let herself remember more than the trust. At least they were safe, she told herself fiercely. At least they still had each other. She had bought them that much.

And she might have the chance to see Lepescu again. Without Fleet interference. Without witnesses.

"Lepescu," she murmured, hardly aware of saying anything. "You bastard — what are you doing here?"

"I remember," Cecelia said. "He was the admiral who

got you in trouble." Heris looked up, startled out of her train of memories.

"He was the admiral who nearly got us all *killed*," Heris said. "The trouble was negligible, really. . . ." Now she could say that. "The question is, why is he here? To cause me more grief? It would have been easy for him to find out who hired me, and where we were going, but I can't see why — or what he can do worse than he's done. Aside from that —"

"Bunny didn't invite him," Cecelia said smugly. She had the authorization codes for Bunny's personal guestlist database, and had run them on the deskcomp. "Never has, according to this. Let's see . . . no, nor any of Bunny's relatives. He's another crasher."

"Here? No, because Sirkin said that transmission went to a shuttle landing at Bandon."

"Where nobody's supposed to be," Cecelia reminded her. "Where I didn't know there was a landing zone equipped for shuttles."

"Whose ship did he come on?" Heris asked. Cecelia couldn't know, she realized, and asked Sirkin, who had stayed online.

"All I know is it's a charter yacht out of Dismis, the *Prairie Rose*. I'd have to have authorization to find out more. . . ."

"We'll do that," Heris said. "But post the orders to monitor that flitter beacon, and any and all traffic on that island or the ones next to it. I'll want flitter IDs, com transcripts, everything."

"Yes, Captain. Right away."

"And be prepared to patch my signal from a flitter or other light craft. Lady Cecelia and I will be checking on that beacon ourselves." As she said it, she raised her brows at Cecelia, who nodded. It was crazy, really. At the least they ought to tell their host and let him assign his own security forces to it. But the thought that she might come face to face with Lepescu, unwitnessed, slid sweet and poisonous into her mind. With Cecelia's authorization, she could confront him — an uninvited gate-crasher — and demand the answers that had eluded her before.

She closed her eyes a moment, imagining his surprise, feeling her hands close around his throat. . . . Her mouth flooded with the imagined taste of victory, and she had to swallow.

"Heris?" Cecelia was looking at her strangely. It was that expression, on the faces of her classmates at the Academy, that had first given her an inkling that she had inherited her parents' gift of command, the essential ruthlessness of decision.

"Just thinking," Heris said, pulling her mind back onto the designated track. It was crazy, she thought again, almost as crazy as the orders she had refused to obey. She and Cecelia had no idea what was going on over there, she knew Lepescu was dangerous in any context, and yet they were preparing to fly off as if it were an afternoon picnic. As if they were safe, protected by the social conventions of Bunny's crowd. But Lepescu wasn't part of Bunny's crowd. Why was he here? What was he doing, and what would he do when he saw her? How many unauthorized visitors were on this island, and why hadn't Ronnie and Bubbles called in?

"At worst," Cecelia said, interrupting her thoughts again, "I suppose we'll find the crashed flitter and they'll all be dead. Otherwise they'd have called in, if they needed help." She didn't sound certain of that.

"Um." Heris dug through her daypouch for the notepad and stylus she carried out of habit. "We need to do a little planning here. Worst case — all dead. Next worst — injured, needing evacuation. We really should bring some help. The local security force, a medic or two —"

Cecelia looked stubborn. "I don't want to. It's my nephew, after all. If I can get him out of this without Bunny's knowledge, keep it in the family —"

"Have you considered violence?" asked Heris. At Cecelia's bewildered expression, she explained. "I told you about Lepescu. If he's here, uninvited, I would expect some kind of nastiness going on. There are stories about him and his cronies —" She could feel her lip curling.

"But what could he be doing?" asked Cecelia. "He doesn't have any troops to command here — wait — you

don't think he's trying to *invade* or something? Take over
Bunny's holdings?" She looked frightened.

"No . . . I don't think so." It did not make sense that a
mid-list admiral would alienate so powerful a family;
besides, he could not invade without troops, and one
shuttle load would hardly be enough. Heris thought for a
moment. "Wait — remember that Kettlegrave woman?"

"The one blathering on about blood sports?"

"Yes. She said something — about fox hunting leading
to other things, those who would hunt innocent animals
being just as willing to hunt people —"

"Ridiculous!" Cecelia sniffed. "Bunny's as gentle as his
nickname —"

"Bunny is. But Lepescu is most definitely not. What if
there's some kind of illicit hunting — no, not people of
course, but something *else*, that Bunny wouldn't like, with
the fox hunting season as cover —" Even as she said it,
she remembered that Lepescu belonged to a semi-secret
officers' club. She had not been invited to join, but Perin
Sothanous had. He'd refused, and kept his oath not to
talk of what he'd learned . . . but she had heard him say it
was "— really sick — they think the only true blood-sport
is war."

"You have a wicked mind," Cecelia said.

"I know. But it makes sense. You told me that Bunny
has some rare and valuable animals that are practically
pets. What if they're being hunted? We'll go armed, and
expect trouble: it's the only sensible way."

"Armed?"

"Of course. Lepescu is dangerous, and he's not alone.
We don't know what those youngsters have gotten into,
and we have to be able to get them and ourselves out."
Even as she said it, she knew they couldn't possibly do
this alone. It was stupid. Militarily, it was suicide. A flitter
held eight easily, ten if cramped — could they squeeze in
some muscle on the way out? No — she could not command any of Bunny's staff, and she wouldn't trust them
anyway. She ached for her lost crew, for Oblo and Petris
who would have stood behind her in anything. *Except the
trial*, her mind reminded her. She argued back to her

memory: They would have, but I wouldn't put them through it.

She shook herself physically, as well as mentally, and signed off with Sirkin, giving the few final orders. She would have to do this alone, because there was no other way. At least she could prepare Cecelia for what they might face.

"Rifles," she said. "At a minimum, and if you can use a bow —"

"Of course," Cecelia said, still looking shocked. "But why —"

"It's quieter." Heris had pulled out her notepad again, and was figuring on it. Supplies: they'd have to assume they couldn't use Bandon, so they'd need food, medical supplies, ammunition for the weapons she intended to take, protective gear, whatever communications and electronic gear she could lay her hands on — she looked at the wall chronometer — in half a standard hour. They'd need to leave before the day's hunt gathered. It was crazy. They should tell Bunny; they should use his staff for this.

"Should we take something larger than a standard flitter?" Cecelia asked.

"Hmm? What else?" Heris computed cubage and mass on her notepad and entered the total. They would have to change from hunting clothes, too, or take along something more suitable and change en route.

"A supply flitter, I was thinking. We could take more supplies, and if one of them is injured . . ."

"Good idea. Will they sign one out to you?"

Cecelia looked affronted. "I've been a family friend for years — of course they will. Michaels will be glad someone's checking on the young people."

"Fine. Then get this list" — Heris handed it to her — "loaded as soon as you can. I'll pack my kit, and what else we need.""

"The weapons." Cecelia scowled.

"Yes. The weapons." The weapons were going to be a problem, any way she went at it. Personal weapons were common enough, but Cecelia, as a dedicated fox hunter, had brought none with her, and Heris's own small handgun would not be enough.

That morning the green hunt gathered at Stone Lodge, so the house staff at the Main House seemed less rushed. The housekeeper's eyebrows went up slightly when Heris mentioned weapons, but the brief explanation that Lady Cecelia wanted to find her nephew brought them back down, as if Lady Cecelia could be expected to take after her relatives with firepower.

"Senedor and Clio have a shop here during the season," the housekeeper said, mentioning a firm of weapons dealers as famous in their way as the great fashion houses. "I imagine they would have anything Lady Cecelia might want."

"Thank you," Heris said; once she'd heard the name, she remembered seeing the S&C logo outside one of the little stone buildings that made up the commercial row: saddlers, bootmakers, tailors and bloodstock agents.

Senedor & Clio's local representative welcomed her with a wink and a smile. "Lady Cecelia, eh? What's she doing now, deciding to turn elphoose hunter? You're her captain. . . . You look like regular military."

"I was." Heris did not elaborate. She had thought of a good story on the way over. "Look — I'm buying two lots — they'll need separate accounting. Lady Cecelia's yacht is woefully undergunned; the crew's arms are pitiful." In fact, the crew had no weapons at all. "I finally convinced her that in some of the places she wants to travel, she needs to arm the crew with something more advanced than muzzle-loaders from the family museum."

The man chuckled. "A lot of these aristocrats are like that — they don't expect to need real protection."

"And most of them probably don't," Heris conceded. "The ones who make a safe round from hunting here to deep-sea fishing on Fandro and back to court for the season . . . but you know Lady Cecelia isn't like that." The man nodded. "So . . . I'm going to do my job and see that she isn't hijacked somewhere."

"Umm. We don't carry many of that sort of thing down here," he said. "But let's see . . . here." The holo catalog showed something that looked like the landing troops' rifles and submachine guns. Exactly what Heris had been hoping for. "These are made by Zechard, who as you know supply the fleet marines. Ours, of course, go through additional testing from the factory. We have a gross of each model up at Home Station, and we could deliver anything up to that quantity direct to Lady Cecelia's yacht. The *Sweet Delight*, isn't it?"

Heris wondered if Lepescu knew that somewhere on Home Station were a gross each of military quality rifles and the stubby-barrelled weapons which had been called OOZ for time out of mind. Heris remembered that one instructor at the Academy had said they were supposed to be 007's, but through a computer glitch they'd been renamed. The landing force's gory jest was that they were called OOZ because that's what they made of anyone foolish enough to get in the way. And how many were on the other Stations? She did not ask, but smiled ruefully at the salesman instead. "That would cause problems," she said. "At least now. You've probably heard that we've a standing watch aboard —?"

"Yes — that's why I thought —"

She shook her head at him. "The Stationmaster was none too pleased about that; Lady Cecelia is sure he will not like having that crew armed with modern weapons. Of course they're harmless — it's only a handful, and most of them don't yet know how to use these —" She tapped the holo catalog and the image shivered. "But she said to gather the weapons here and transport them under her personal seal and responsibility when we leave. She is concerned as well that such weapons look too . . ." Heris's lips pursed and she gave the salesman a look of complicity. "Too real. You know — it would ruin her decorating scheme or something. I wondered if you had a small number of those which could be customized to look more like hunting weapons."

The man's eyes brightened. "Ah . . . yes. Here." The catalog image flicked to something with a stock of burnished wood instead of extruded carbon-fiber/alloy and a civilian-style sighting system and computer socket. "It's the same, exactly, but with add-on about two hundred grams heavier. It does cost more. . . ."

"Perfect," said Heris firmly. "Twenty of the rifles, and five subs. . . ." The OOZ had been prettified with wood and inlay, but less successfully. They would pass, however, for the weapon many explorers carried on pioneer worlds.

"I don't have that many set up," the man said. At her frown, he added quickly, "But it doesn't take long. The hunt's away today, and my techs are both free. A few hours only. . . ."

They didn't have a few hours. "How many do you have ready?" Heris asked. "I wanted to show milady what they would look like."

"If brasilwood and corriwood are acceptable, I've got a couple of beauties already made up." He vanished behind a mesh grill and returned with two of the rifles and a single submachine gun. The rifle stocks had the curly green and blue grain of brasilwood, probably from a plantation on this very planet; the OOZ's wood decoration was in the pale yellow and gray grain of Devian corriwood. Heris ran her fingers over both; the rifles felt silky and the sub a bit tacky, giving a grip that would always hold no matter what. She picked up each weapon to check its balance.

"You'll want to fire them," the man said with certainty. "Our range is back here —"

"Just a moment," Heris said. "This is not all, remember? On Lady Cecelia's personal account, not the yacht account, I will need to select personal weapons for her." She paged through the catalog, and allowed the salesman to lead her towards the items she already knew she wanted. Light hunting rifles with day-and-night optics, IR range finding, and computer links for special purposes, a narrow-beam optical weapon that could also be used to operate ship controls, personal protective gear. . . . The salesman seemed to consider it natural that she ordered for herself as well, but she dared not put vests and helmets for the young people on the list.

Then it was done, and he led her through another mesh grill to the indoor firing range without waiting for her opinion. She forced herself to follow with no sign of hurry. Surely Cecelia wouldn't get the flitter loaded in the time limit she'd given her. And despite her need to hurry, her training held — you could not trust a weapon you had not personally tested.

When all the weapons had checked out, as she had been sure they would, she came back to the main show-room and glanced around. "I'll contact you when Lady Cecelia approves the choice of wood for the stocks, and I'm hoping to convince her to buy appropriate armor for the crew as well. We'll be using these in the next few days; I'll need ammunition. . . ."

"Here," he said, stacking boxes of clips. "And I pre-sume a weaponscart?"

Heris nodded, glad that she would not have to pay for this. Cecelia's credit cube went into the reader, and the assembled weaponry stacked neatly into a covered cache on a cart that looked like a miniature flitter and hummed at her.

"Palm-print it," the man said. Heris laid her palm on the membrane set in one side of the thing's bow, and it bleeped. "It won't open the cache to anyone else," he said. "It'll follow you; if you want it to stay somewhere, palm-print and say, 'Stay.' But I'd keep it with you; if it's stolen someone could break in. Local law says those weapons are your responsibility now."

"Thank you," said Heris, and retrieved Cecelia's cube. She hadn't even looked at the total; it was like going into Fleet refitting.

On the way back to the flitter bays, Heris's mind caught up with her again. What she was about to do, with Lady Cecelia and a supply flitter, was exactly what Admiral Lepescu had demanded that she do with her crew and ship . . . what she had refused to do, in fact. Why was she so willing *now* to charge into an obvious trap? If she wouldn't risk a crew of professionals, why would she risk one rich old lady? And what did that say about her loyalty to her employer?

If she tried this, and failed, Lepescu would have beaten her twice — he would have made her play *his*

game, something she couldn't avoid as a military officer.
. . . But now she had options.

If she could think of them. If she had time. If she could
convince her employer who was even more stubborn, if
less vicious, than Admiral Lepescu.

Of course, she could try another end play and tell
Bunny herself. Let Lady Cecelia fire her, if that's what it
came to. That's what she'd done last time, and it hadn't
worked. . . . She did *not* have to make the same mistake
twice.

This time, if what she suspected was true, Lepescu was
in the trap — not her. She could win, using her own strategy, and prove she'd been right.

But she had to convince Cecelia.

✧ Chapter Thirteen

"This is the island we're on," Petris said, outlining it on the chart. They had survived their first night on the island; Ronnie felt much better, and ignored the dull pain in his head. He had kept that first ration bar down, and another this morning; he was sure he was over his concussion. "About eight kilometers by five," Petris went on, "but most of it's narrower. Relief's about two hundred meters — this hill's given as two-twenty. It's steeper on the west, but nowhere difficult, except for this little ravine here —" He pointed. "Now — the cover is mixed: open forest, on these slopes, and down near the water scrub undergrowth. It's full of trails as a kid's playground in some park —"

"That's what it was," Bubbles said. "I told you; we all camped over here. My cousins, too. About — oh — five years ago was the last time I remember. We'd stay here while the grown-ups were on Bandon. We'd sail over in little boats. My father thought it up — it was out of some old books from England on Old Earth. Kids went camping on an island —"

"Yes, well, this isn't camping." Petris dismissed her memories abruptly. Oblo spoke up.

"Do you remember seeing anything that indicated someone else used the island that way?"

"No." Bubbles wrinkled her nose. "No — in fact, we always had to clear the trails every year. I wanted to have someone do it, but my father insisted we 'have the fun' as he put it."

"So this kind of hunting was either somewhere else, or not going on then," Oblo pointed out. "It would be interesting to know when it started, if your father hired someone new, who could have set it up. It would take connections — someone who knew likely clients —"

Bubbles frowned. "I'm trying to think. Daddy mentioned he'd hired a new outrange supervisor when Vittorio Zelztin retired, but I don't remember what he said. It didn't seem important."

"Not as important as staying alive," Petris said. "And we need to break this up and get moving. Let me finish the briefing." He waited until Ronnie wanted to ask why, then went on, sure of their attention. "They introduce new prey when they have confirmed killing all but two of the old ones. Those are the preeves, the previous survivors. That's how we know some of the things we do, and that's where our few weapons come from. New prey's given two days free, then hunting resumes. They supply basic rations every four days at a single site on the west side of the island, during a non-hunting period. They hunt no more than fourteen Standard hours a day. The problem is, we're not sure *which* fourteen hours. Sometimes they do a split shift. If we don't keep a constant watch, they're over here before we know it.

"What the preeves told us is that the first week they hunt only in daylight. That weeds out the really stupid and incapable, they think. Then they start night-hunting. They have dark gear; we don't. If they hunt all night, they'll leave us alone the following day, but they usually hunt only half a night shift. From sundown to midnight, or midnight to sunrise, say. We've been here a couple weeks, so they're night-hunting almost every night. Last night they didn't — I expect they were waiting to see if you were followed."

"If they have Barstow sensors, why don't they just find us and wipe us out?" asked George.

"They don't use Barstows," Petris said. "Again, that's not 'sporting' in their books. The preeves say if someone eludes them the full month, they'll use a Barstow to find and capture him — but that almost never happens."

"But if they know *we're* here — and they want to eliminate witnesses — won't they use Barstows sooner this time?"

"I was hoping you wouldn't ask that. They might. And if they do, we're out of luck. We can't build a shelter that will shield us from Barstow scans *and* escape notice in flyovers. The island's not deep enough, and the woods aren't thick enough."

"That other flyover," Raffa said. "That could've been a rescue attempt, but we weren't there." Ronnie had missed the flyover, but they'd told him about the flitter that came, hovered above the wreck, and then departed.

"They'd only want to rescue us if they could do it before we made contact with the prey," Bubbles said. Looking at her now, Ronnie could hardly believe that was her name. None of the fluffhead left, none at all. "They'll think — if we met them — the secret's out. Either they have to kill us all, and fake an accident somehow, or they have to escape. And even if they do escape, there's the evidence. . . ."

"So the only logical thing for them to do is add our names to the list and go on." Raffa shivered. "I don't like this. Yet — if they kill us, there'll be the evidence then, too. When someone comes to look."

"Unless they try to capture you four," Petris said. "And then kill you in some way that can be explained. They might well try a chemical weapon. Knock you unconscious, take you up in a flitter — even your own — and drop you into the rocks. If we're all dead and gone — or if they can create that accident on another island — it might well pass. Ordinarily, the preeves say, they don't use chemicals, but now they might."

Ronnie lifted his head. Had he really heard something, or . . . Petris was alert too. Something — but he couldn't define it. "Flitter," said Oblo. "I'll see about it."

"We make a plan every day," Petris said, as if nothing had happened. "You have to . . . else it's just running and waiting to be killed. That's what happens to most. Or they make a plan, and run the same one every day. That won't work either. The only hope is to make the hunters work . . . get back at them."

"Attack them?" George asked. "You do have more men, don't you? How many hunters are there?"

"More, but not more firepower. Not more resources. We can't attack in force, but we do feint. We scare them sometimes. They like that, the preeves tell us; I hate to give them the satisfaction, but it does make them slow down and be careful. As for how many, it seems to vary. I'm sure we're not seeing the same ones each day; if it's anything like big game hunting, there's a larger party of hunters over on Bandon, and they take turns. I'd like to kill them but so far we haven't."

"Has anyone ever?" Raffa asked.

"So I hear," Petris said. "But you don't know how much to believe. The preeves they send with us are not exactly reliable. They've been known to turn a group that was doing too well. We found a locator on Sid, for instance."

"But you didn't kill him," George said. "Why not?"

"Do you kill everyone who just might hurt you someday?" Petris looked disgusted. "Get some sense, boy. Everyone who's been through this has knowledge we need; we can't afford to lose anyone. He knows we know he might turn; he knows his best chance at survival is with us — at least now."

"So how many do you have, altogether?"

"Never you mind. What you don't know, you can't tell. But we've lost only two, in the time we've been here; the preeves say that's much better than usual. Now — what we're going to do is this. . . ." Petris leaned over the map. "We've got to separate you four, because they need you worst. Can't let them get you in a lump. The longer it takes, the more chance one of you'll be alive to report all this. At the same time, I can't protect you all. My people wouldn't go for it, and I don't have the ability anyway. So you ladies will have to go here" — he pointed to the ravine on the map — "unless you can find those hiding places you think you remember . . . ?" He looked at Bubbles.

"I wish Kell hadn't been so secretive," Bubbles said. "I'm sure there is a cave somewhere —" Petris ignored this; he had not been impressed with a possible cave she had never seen for herself.

"You want me to go somewhere *alone*?" Raffa asked. She looked pale.

"It would be best," Petris said, almost gently. "That ravine's hard to climb; they avoid it except at the ends, and there's a lot of cover — big rocks and so on. They go along the edges, and watch both ends, but they can't see everything. If you tuck yourself under a boulder, that's as safe a place as I can offer."

"I want to *do* something," Raffa said. "Not sit under a rock and shiver."

"We don't have any training," Bubbles said to her. "Not even as much as Ronnie and George. The best we can do is stay out of the way."

"No." Raffa glanced at Ronnie and away; he felt his heart contract. She was thinking about him, he knew it.

"You two," Petris said, with a nod to Ronnie and George, "are another problem. You might be useful, or not — I can't tell until I see you in action. What we're going to do is try to make them think you wandered into the forest north of the stream, maybe heading for the point up there. It's more rugged country. I want you to go up there now, and make some trail. Scuff and scrape as if you're dragging something or someone. Drop something unimportant that might have fallen off your packs. There's no way to disguise what happened to your flitter, but they may not have realized we've met. If you headed that way, and we were keeping watch to the south and east, you could have gotten away from us. Not really, but they might believe it."

In other circumstances, it would have been a pleasant afternoon's hike up the ravine. Bubbles found it hard to remember the danger; the lower forest smelled as fresh as she remembered, and then the scramble up the rocks took her breath away. A clear rivulet still splashed from pool to pool, and red and gold amphibians still hurled themselves into the water as she came near, with agitated squeaks. A few rocks had moved in seasonal floods — she recognized one boulder by an odd inclusion, now upside down from where it had been — but most of the trail was familiar.

Higher on the slope, a breeze stirred, lifting the hair

on the back of her head as it rose from the forest canopy below. She could see more of the sky, now, and smell the sea as well as the rock and flowers. Raffa, behind her, scuffed her feet in the dirt but said nothing. Bubbles was glad. She wanted to combine the old memories, once thrust away as too childish, with the present experience. Finally she stopped, winded, on a broad flat outcrop where the ravine angled south, away from the shore. Looking back she could see nothing but billows of green concealing the shape of the land itself. Raffa, panting, dropped to the rock and lifted the hair from her neck.

"You did this every year?" she asked, after a moment.

"Most years, for awhile. When my Uncle Gene would come, and bring the cousins. . . . I suppose, really, Mother wanted us out of the main house, away from more important visitors. All of us together could be noisy." She grinned down at Raffa. "When we camped over here, we'd divide in two groups, at least, and play hunting games. Stuff we'd read about or seen on the old cubes —"

"We used to go to my Aunt Katy's house and ride up in the hills," Raffa said. "On Negaire — no pretty islands there."

Bubbles shivered. "Ugh. Cold and wet all year round, isn't it? You didn't camp out, surely?"

Raffa nodded. "Better than in this heat. We pretended to be steppe nomads and so forth, but mostly we lived in caves. There was a big one, very handy, about a day's ride away, and another smaller one on the other side of the hill. We painted monsters on the walls; one of my cousins tried to paint us, but he couldn't draw."

"Cave." Bubbles glowered at the water. "I wish I knew if Kell told the truth. He said it was big enough for all of us, but he wouldn't share it, the pig. He's like that still, loves secrets and won't share. There's no place else as good, if it's real."

"You're sure you have no idea where it is?"

"Only where it isn't. We did look, but we never found it in the likely places — up here, or in the valley between this hill and the next. And knowing where not to look still leaves a lot of island. Why — you think we should look?"

"If we found it, we'd be a lot safer than hiding under a rock," Raffa pointed out. "And we'd better be going; we certainly aren't safe sitting here chatting."

"We'll climb straight over the spine," Bubbles said, leading the way up the narrowing ravine. "I hope the old trail along the crest is still there. It has a few hidey-holes I know about."

Along the spine of the island, the rock outcrops formed stout pillars, two to three meters tall, in ragged rows that wobbled along parallel to the crest like rotting teeth. Between the rows, the hollows were unevenly filled with soil and overgrown with thorny vines and bushes. A winding thread of trail had been hacked clear at the very crest; Bubbles could not tell if it had been cut by hunters or hunted. It didn't really matter. They would have to get off it quickly, because the hunters certainly knew about it.

She counted the pillars. If only she could remember the pattern . . . three tall ones, a short, two talls and then two — three? — short ones . . . there. She squeezed between two of the shorter rocks — had she been that much thinner five years ago, or had the rocks shifted? — and then crouched to wiggle beneath the huge briar that lay over what had always been her own special hiding place. The hooked thorns scraped on her knapsack as she slithered further in, her nose hardly off the dark, dank-smelling soil. It hadn't felt this small the last time. . . . She called back to Raffa. "You have to go under this thing — you can't go through it with anything short of power tools."

"Give me a steppe pony any day," Raffa said, but she gave only one muffled yelp when the thorns caught her hair, and slithered very efficiently for someone who often pretended disdain for physical exertion. "Do you want me to do anything about the way we came in?"

"Nope." Bubbles edged past the cluster of woody stems and felt around the far side of it. She had had a little hole there, once, with a box in it, but she couldn't see. It was dark under the briar's canopy after the brilliant sunlight on the trail, a warm brown gloom lightened by freckles of sun.

"As much as we've shaken it, the outer branches will go back down. I used to do this all the time, and the guys never found me." The little hole in which she'd tucked a boxful of handy items years before had grown into something a handspan across and deeper than her fingers. Burrow. Something was living here. She tried to remember just what did live on this island. Nothing venomous, nothing particularly large or dangerous. Except the hunters. She realized she'd forgotten them for a few minutes, here where her safe childhood was so real, and the hunters hardly believable.

On the far side of the briary tangle, lodged in fallen leaves against another standing stone, Bubbles found her box. She blessed her younger self for insisting she wanted a *real* expedition box, the kind that was supposed to last through anything. She dragged it out of the leaves and scrunched sideways so that Raffa could come up beside her.

"I forgot this the last time we were here," she said. "We were in a hurry to leave — I was going to St. Eleanor's for the first time — and by the time I remembered I'd left it, there was no time to go back." The box had no lock, only an L-shaped catch, now crusted with dirt and time. Bubbles broke a fingernail on it and muttered. Probably nothing in it — a decayed sandwich, some childish bauble — but something drove her to open it.

"Let me try," said Raffa. Bubbles slid the box over to her, and sucked her bruised fingertip. Raffa had picked up a twig, and used that to prod out the caked dirt around the latch, then spit on it. When she pushed, the latch moved with a minute squeak. "Here," she said, handing the box back. "You open it — it's yours."

Bubbles felt a curious reluctance to open it, as odd as the determination a moment ago to make that latch move. Silly, she thought. There could be nothing really useful in this box — not as useful as the things in the survival packs on the flitter. Just junk that would remind her what a silly child she had been. She struggled for a moment, having forgotten the exact movement it took to pry the lid up — the box had a good seal on it. Then it lay open, a time capsule from her childhood, her forgotten treasures rattling a little from the movement of her hand.

A seashell, one of the purple cone-shaped ones. A bracelet woven of dune-grass — she blushed, remembering who had woven it, and why. A little black blob, smooth all over . . . raked from the fire the time Kell had melted the handle from the frying pan. A single sheet of photocells, ready to be spread in the sunlight again . . . if she had anything to recharge. A bit of faded ribbon . . . she remembered clearly the shade of purple it had been. A whistle, a foil-wrapped ration bar, a tube of first-aid ointment and a packet of bandages, a length of fine fish-line, neatly coiled, with two hooks and a handful of differently shaped sinkers. And the compact silvery locator beacon, with the lanyard still looped through the ring on top.

"Isn't that a —?" Raffa started to ask.

"Yes. And it will work." She looked at the charge level on the side; as she'd expected, it had held its charge. . . . The good ones did, and her dad had always provided them with good ones. Besides, she had the photocells to top it up with. "We can get help," she said, and sat up cheerfully only to ram her head into the nest of thorns close above. Her eyes watered, and she held very still. It was the only way with these island briars: jerk away and she'd lose half her hair and part of her scalp. In the time it took Raffa to work her free, she was able to think why they couldn't use the locator yet. There would be no easy rescue, any more than easy extrication from the briar.

"But if we could get to Bandon," she said. "If we could steal their flitter, maybe, while they're hunting the others . . . this will override anything."

"There's more of them on Bandon," Raffa reminded her. "Hold still, yet. You've got a thorn right in your scalp. Do these things leave the husk in?"

"Sometimes, and it festers if they do. Get it all if you can." She was a little surprised at how deft Raffa's fingers were, and how calm she was staying. Was this the same Raffa who had seemed an obsessive worrier?

"There," Raffa said finally. "I don't think there are any husks, but if you'll hand me that tube of gunk — thanks

— I can put a dab on a few places . . . yes . . . they were bleeding a bit. Keep the flies off, eh?"

"How long has it been?" Bubbles asked, putting everything back in the box and latching it. They had left Petris and the others before noon, and she realized they had better think about where to spend the night. Light came to them between the stones, sideways; the slope below, on the west side of the island, would still be in daylight for awhile, but where would the hunters go? Up here, along the high trail? Along the slopes?

"Should we stay here?" Raffa asked, as if she were seeing the thoughts in Bubbles's head. "We're out of sight, but if they have any kind of sensors —"

"I don't know a better place, not without time to look for it." Bubbles peeked out the west side of the tangle; they were high enough that she could see out over the lower forest to the sea. The few clouds drifted past, their shadows sliding up the slope like vast hands caressing the trees. "The main thing is to keep well away from Petris and the others. . . . Someone has to get back. . . ."

"Oh . . ." Raffa's breath came just as Bubbles realized one shadow wasn't sliding upslope. . . . Small, regular, it moved swiftly against the wind, downslope to the south of them, and then ran along parallel to the ridge.

"Eyes down," Bubbles said, taking her own advice. Now that it was upwind, they could hear the faint whine of the flitter. Surely the briar was thick enough — old, tangled, too dense for anyone to see through. But every freckle of light suggested it was as porous as a fishing net. She felt sure she had something shiny on her back, something that would glitter — she should take it off. But her arms had no strength; she lay, hardly breathing, trembling.

The flitter's shadow passed over them, as if a cold hand lay on her back, and went somewhere else. She could hear the whine moving north, she thought, toward the tip of the island, but she dared not move.

"So," Raffa said, hardly louder than a breath. "They're here. And it's not a game."

"No." Immediately below them, on the west slope, the

rock nubbins were only sparsely covered. . . . They couldn't count on reaching the cover below without being seen. They would have to stay here until the flitter landed somewhere. What if it didn't? It had not occurred to her that the hunters might well keep someone aloft, especially in this emergency.

"How come people in entertainment cubes never need a bathroom?" asked Raffa.

"Mmm. You're right." Now that Raffa had brought it up, she felt the same desperate need. "We can't leave cover now," she said. She wriggled toward the north side of the briar, where its canopy lay along a lower stub of gray stone. Just beyond that was another hollow; she could see into it by risking another hair-pulling match with the briar's canopy. This one had no handy roof; a small tree had died and collapsed, and the vines that covered it matted the ground.

"We should've found a place before we came in here," Raffa said.

"You're right," Bubbles said, squeezing onward around the briar's central stem and root complex. In the northeast corner of their thorny shelter, she found what she remembered, a niche in the big stone between them and the trail. Here the briar, reaching for light, lifted enough to allow someone to sit upright. And below was the other refinement of her childhood hiding place, a standard expedition one-man composting latrine unit, carefully dug into the soil. Her parents had been, she'd thought then, ridiculously fussy about pollution; one summer they'd all been yanked back to all-day lessons at the Big House for two weeks just because one set of cousins had dug a real latrine in a spurt of enthusiasm for historical authenticity. They had all had to memorize the list of diseases they could have given themselves, and the life cycles of innumerable disgusting parasites, before they could come back. They could have all the prefab units they wanted, her father had said, but they must use them. She scrabbled at the lid, said a brief prayer to some nameless deity that none of the more agile crawlers had gotten into it, and pulled it open. "But here," she said triumphantly. "All the comforts of home, more or less. Deodorizing, too." Since she was in place, she took the first turn, and felt much better. Raffa followed her, gave a sigh of relief, and latched the lid back down.

"Now if you could just excavate us a cave right here . . ."

"Nope. I tried hard enough, but it's solid stone below a few inches of leaf-drift. And I think we'd better get what rest we can. Just at dusk we could move downslope, if we're careful."

Bubbles had not really expected to sleep, cramped under the briar in the hot, sweaty dimness, but she woke at the crunch of footsteps somewhere nearby. It was completely dark, and for a moment she could not think where she was. Then she remembered. The hand on her ankle, a grip hard enough to pinch, must be Raffa's hand. She reached back and touched it, and Raffa gripped her hand instead. Her breath seemed trapped in her lungs. The footsteps came nearer, not hurrying. Panic clogged her ears with her own heartbeat; she could not tell how far away the sound was. A voice murmured something she could not distinguish. A faint crackle followed; her mind raced, suggesting that the crackle was a comunit, which meant the footsteps were a hunter's. *I knew that already*, she argued back at her mind. Raffa's fingers in hers were cold; she shivered, but forced herself to lie still. Another crunch, a boot on the rough path beyond the stone. She heard a scrape and a soft curse as someone found the space between the stones too narrow. Something shook that side of the briar, as if the hunter had taken a stick to it; the branches squeaked overhead. Raffa's fingers tightened suddenly. Could she see something from her side of the briar? But the footsteps went away, the faint scrunching growing fainter. Raffa's fingers relaxed but did not pull away.

Her breath came out all at once; she felt dizzy and faint even lying down. What if she'd been asleep . . . and dreaming . . . and had snored? Her first school room-mates said she snored. Just when she thought it might be safe to murmur something to Raffa, she heard another sound. Not nearly so loud as the first, as if the feet wore something softer than boots. Three steps, a pause. Four, and another pause. Two . . . whoever it was was now just outside the cleft they'd come through. Bubbles held herself rigidly still, trying not to breathe.

Then the crack of a weapon echoed along the stones, and the person nearest them gave a soft cry. Bubbles heard the slither and thump as he fell, and the ragged breathing louder than the stifled moans. The other footsteps came back at a run and paused; even from behind the rock, Bubbles could see the glow of light as the hunter turned on a torch.

"Got one," he said, this time loud enough for Bubbles to hear; she assumed he was talking into his comunit. "By the tattoo, it's one of the preeves." The comunit crackled and muttered back to him. "Right," he said. "I'll bring the IDs. No sign of the others." Bubbles heard the click as he shut the comunit cover, and then a grunt and thump as if he bent to set down his weapon and lean over the body.

Then — "Got one too," said the other man, in a harsh voice thick with pain. The hunter squealed, then gasped, and Bubbles heard the fall of another heavy body, the thrashing of limbs, the rattle and clatter of equipment banging on the rocks. The light went out. Then silence, but for a final few noisy gasps.

For the first time in her life, Bubbles envied those of her friends who had a religion: they would have had some deity to swear to, or at, or on. "We can't stay here," she said quietly. Her voice surprised her; it sounded as calm as if she were in her mother's drawing room discussing the weather.

"He touched me," Raffa said. Her voice, too, was quiet. "With a stick or something, when he prodded the briar."

"We have to go," Bubbles said. "They'll send someone." Through the gap in the stones, the smell of blood and something worse rolled as if on a stream of water. Her stomach churned.

"How can we? We can't see anything. . . ."

"We have to. It won't be so dark out from under this briar. Turn around and let me get past."

"You're not going *that* way?" The calm seeped out of Raffa's voice, leaving honest fear behind.

"I want his weapons," Bubbles said. "And his comunit, and his night goggles."

"But then they'll know someone came after," Raffles said. Bubbles paused. She hadn't thought of that. As it was, they might assume that what it looked like was indeed what happened — a victim not quite dead who killed his careless killer. If she took anything, they'd know someone else had been there. But it didn't matter.

"They know we're here," she said. "They're going to hunt until they find us. His things will give us a better chance. You stay here — we'll go downhill afterwards."

Out from under the briar, starlight gave a faint glow to the standing stones; in the distance, the sea glittered. Bubbles paused in the gap between the stones, listening. She could hear nothing. When she peeked out, she could see the tangle of dark forms that must be the two men's bodies. Quickly, before fear could overwhelm her again, she forced herself to move out onto the path. Her foot slipped, and when she put her hand down it was into warm, wet, stinking slime. She choked down her nausea, and wiped her hand on the nearest body. They were dead; it didn't matter now. She fumbled at the bodies, expecting every moment the shot that would kill her, the hiss of gas that would paralyze her.

The bodies were still warm; she hated the feel of the skin, the stiffening texture of it, as she felt around for the hunter's night gear. Goggles around his neck, on a thong — he would have dropped them before lighting his torch. They felt wet — blood? She cut the thong with her knife, and felt around for the torch. She risked a quick flash of it. The goggles were covered with blood, which she cleaned off with the dead hunter's shirt-tail. There was the comunit which she scooped up, and there the man's rifle with its targeting beam. Her own hands were covered with blood, and one foot would leave bloody footprints until it dried. She flicked off the torch, and called softly to Raffa.

"Come on out — if I go back through, I'll leave a trail.

. . . We'll leave the main trail farther down, and have this hidey-hole again later if we need it. Bring my box." She put the comunit in her shirt pocket.

A cautious rustle, and Raffa came out with both knapsacks. Bubbles handed her the rifle, and put on the night goggles. Now she could see well enough without the torch to finish rummaging in the dead hunter's pack. He had carried a backup weapon with a removable stock in his pack; she took that and his needler, and the dead preeve's knife. Unfortunately the hunter had not carried an extra set of night goggles. Finally, she did her best to clean her bloodiest hand and foot, so they'd leave no more traces than necessary.

Then she led Raffa southward down the trail. Neither of them questioned who should lead; it was her island, and her duty to protect Raffa if she could. There had been a series of parallel trails down the west side of the ridge, long ago; as she recalled, you could go down almost anywhere. She ducked between another pair of standing stones, and fought through a tangle of vines, and then found the next gap downhill. To her enhanced vision, the broken slope below was empty of anything but crumbling rock and low scrub; Raffa, behind her, said, "How is it?"

For answer, Bubbles passed her the goggles; she felt suddenly blind when she took them off. "See for yourself. Pick a route, stay low, and don't hurry. We've got to be quiet."

"You need these." Raffa passed the goggles back; Bubbles pushed them away.

"It's your turn, and I'm supposed to know this place. I'll go first; then you can find me. Not too close." Her eyes were adjusting; she squeezed them tightly a moment or two, and when she opened them found she could just make out the larger rocks. Slowly, carefully, she edged downward, placing each foot with precision so that she could test the ground before putting her weight on it. She remembered reading her brother's service manual on this sort of thing; she had found it funny. She had imagined the dapper George crawling about in the dark counting his steps on zigzags and getting dust on his impeccable

trousers, or slithering on his stomach. And here she was
. . . wishing she knew if crouching was enough, if she
should be down flat, crawling, if the zigging and zagging
from one rock to another was actually doing any good, or
only taking longer. A pebble rolled out from under her
foot with a faint clatter. She froze. She could hear nothing
now but her own pulse beating. She took another step
down, and another. The black line of trees rose toward
her, welcoming.

✧ Chapter Fourteen

"Well, well . . . hello, darlin'." It was not a voice she wanted to hear, that confident male purr. "A gal could get hurt, wanderin' around in the dark like you are. . . . You better let me give you a hand." A blot of nearer darkness rose from the trees and moved toward her, boots scraping on the rock; she could see a narrow gleam that might be starlight on the barrel of his weapon.

"No . . ." She hadn't meant to say anything, but fear left no room for the breath in her lungs.

"C'mon, hon," he said. She couldn't tell quite how far away he was — two meters? Three? "Wasn't that your flitter crashed on the other side of the island? Your dad sent us out to find you. . . ." For a moment relief washed over her, but she couldn't believe in it. Still, if he thought she didn't know, he might not kill her right away. And if he thought she was alone, if he hadn't seen Raffa, perhaps Raffa could still get away.

"You're . . . one of the outrange patrols?" she asked. A confident chuckle came from him.

"That's right, hon. And you're gonna be fine, now. Just come along with me. . . ."

For the third time that night, Bubbles heard death close by. This time she heard the bullet smack into him an instant before the loud crack from upslope, where Raffa was. The impact threw him back, to land with a crash in the low vegetation of the slope. A few loose rocks clattered on downhill. Bubbles doubled up, retching. It was too much. She had little in her stomach to lose, but wanted none of it. She could hear Raffa coming down, much faster than she had, with the aid of the goggles.

"Are you all right?" Raffa's voice, from near the fallen hunter.

"Y-yes." Her body gave a final convulsive heave, then allowed her to lift her head. "I . . . didn't know you knew how to shoot."

"My Aunt Katy. She made us learn. Gave prizes." From the sound of it, Raffa was fighting her own nausea. Bubbles felt shaky and ashamed of herself. She was supposed to be the leader here, and she'd fallen apart. She forced herself to stand, to stumble the few strides in the dark to where Raffa bent over the dying man.

"I thought they died quicker," she said, trying for the calm tone of earlier. "They do on the action cubes." The man's breathing sounded horrible, bubbly and uneven. She was glad she couldn't see his face.

"Here." Raffa pushed a set of goggles into her hands. "Now we can both see. And we'll take his weapons and comunit." She spoke hurriedly and roughly, her voice slightly shaky. "I saw him, after you started down. I didn't dare call. . . ."

"Right," Bubbles said.

"I kept wanting you to go more to the right. Give me space. I was so *scared* —" For a moment they clung to each other, shaking, wanting to cry but knowing they had no time. "Got to go," Raffa said finally, pushing away. "They'll be coming."

Bubbles stood, staggering a little from the weight added to her original pack. They each had two rifles now, and a needler, and a comunit, and more knives than they could possibly use. If they could get some of this back to Petris . . . but they couldn't. Quickly, careless for the moment of the noise, they got themselves into the forest below.

Once or twice, in childhood, they had tried skulking around in the woods at night. With torches, of course. They'd given it up, except for raids along the beach, after someone — she couldn't remember who — had broken an ankle while trying to climb the ridge in a cross-island overnight race. They'd had to call for help, and the adults had been scathing about children who didn't have enough sense to stay off slippery rocks in the dark. Buttons, the acknowledged boss of the campsites, had forbidden night wandering, and they'd mostly obeyed. Bubbles hadn't minded, because she preferred to sleep at night rather than nap in the daytime.

Now, with the night goggles on, she was glad of the covering darkness. She could see well enough to avoid hanging creepers, thornbushes, and other hazards; she knew from her time on the open slope that no one without night goggles could see her. Of course the others had them . . . but so did she.

Soon she slowed, and began listening again. She stopped completely for a moment. Her stomach growled loudly, reminding her it was empty. She heard Raffa scrabbling in her knapsack, then a faint metallic rasp and a gurgle. Water. She realized how thirsty she herself was, and took off her own knapsack, trying for silence. Where was the noisy wind when you needed it? The water eased her throat and washed away the foul taste of her nausea. Now she was hungry. She tapped Raffa's arm, and when she leaned closer murmured to her. "Eat now — while walking." She could see Raffa's nod as clearly as if it were daylight.

They had the survival rations from the flitter, tubes of thick goo that tasted of fat, sugar, and salt. Bubbles swallowed half of hers at once, and tucked the rest into her pocket. She started off again more slowly, trying to remember how the land went on this side of the island. How far south were they, and how near was the swamp? Should they start back north, and hope to work into the more rugged terrain along the north shore?

Nothing moved in the woods around them. She remembered, from those childhood visits, flocks of birds and many small animals — lizards, some nonvenomous snakes, land crabs. Once she'd been frightened by a tortoise big enough to sit on; she'd thought it was a shiny brown rock. There was less undergrowth than she remembered, and she found it easy to walk between the trees. The slope flattened beneath her feet; the forest rose higher overhead, and even with night goggles she couldn't see that much. Whenever she stopped to listen, her legs trembled; she knew they needed to rest.

Raffa tapped her shoulder. Bubbles leaned close to her, and Raffa said, "I think I hear water."

Bubbles tried to filter out the sigh of the breeze in the leaves . . . yes. A rhythmic rush and silence . . . waves breaking, but gently, in this little wind. "You're right," she said quietly. "And they might have someone on the beach — it's narrow here." Now which way, south or north? Her mind was clogged by exhaustion and fear. She had started out hoping to find her old hiding place, and then thought of Kell's cave, wherever that was . . . but now . . . she wished she knew just where they were, and how far it was to someplace else.

"I'd vote north," Raffa said, as if she'd asked. "Away from their camp." For a moment Bubbles wanted to protest; they had weapons themselves, now, and night gear. They were as dangerous as the hunters. But they weren't, really: they were untrained girls, and very tired. Staying as far from the hunters' camp as possible made sense.

"Good idea," Bubbles said, and turned right, away from the beach. They walked slowly, as quietly as they could manage, stopping every few minutes to look around them. The walk took on a dreamlike character — the eerie landscape in the night goggles, that looked like something meant to be scary but done on a low budget, the silence, their exhaustion that forced concentration on the simplest movements. When a great tree loomed up that Bubbles remembered from her childhood trips, she moved into the dense shadow of its massive bole and stopped.

"We've got to rest," she said, "while one of us can stay awake to watch. You sleep first."

"Right." Raffa's vague shape folded up to sit against the tree. Bubbles leaned, but did not sit. If she sat, she *would* sleep. She could not be scared enough to stay awake, not now. She fished the rest of the ration stick out of her pocket and ate it, and drank more water. Her legs ached; the pack straps seemed to burn along her shoulders, but she was afraid to take the pack off. What if they had to run for it?

She realized then that she hadn't even checked to see if the rifle she carried was loaded. She fumbled at it. It wasn't exactly like the one she'd been taught to use, and she couldn't find the little doohickey — it had a name, but she'd never learned it — to release the clip. She found something sticking out of the stock, and pushed it, and a line of red sprang across the space under the tree to another tree trunk. The rifle hummed; desperately she pushed the knob this way and that until it moved and the light disappeared and the hum ceased. She stared around, sure that someone must have seen that red light, but nothing moved and no sound disturbed her. After awhile, her heart quit trying to climb out her mouth, and she tried to think what that had been. Firearms were not her hobby; she had learned to shoot only because of the elphoose hunts. Her father had insisted she must learn.

Red light. A hum. Red light made her think of the vidcams in the drama department . . . range finders . . . so it might be a range finder. And the hum . . . like the hum of the automatic focus adjustments. She felt carefully along the entire stock. A tiny flap covered a socket — pins inside — a connection for some computer attachment? She found three more buttons or knobs, and left them alone. The scope . . . she lifted the rifle to her shoulder and tried to peer through it, but the goggles interfered. After a quick look around, she slipped them off and looked through the scope. It gave a brighter image than the goggles, in crisp grays rather than smudged greenish yellow. Her finger found knobs on the scope, too. . . . She left them alone, and put her goggles back on.

Something flared in her pocket, a small blinking light that the goggles made into a white beacon. Without goggles — through her pocket — it was hardly visible. The comunit she'd taken from the first hunter . . . blinking a two-three sequence. When she looked at Raffa, asleep against the tree, her pocket too winked, this one in a two-two sequence. She had not thought they might be locators, but now it seemed obvious. If she didn't reply, with some code she could not know, the hunters would know where to look. . . . They might know anyway.

"Raffa!" She kept her voice low, but Raffa woke instantly.

"What?" she asked.

"We have to get rid of them — if we leave them here, that's too close — we don't know how long it will take —" She felt like crying . . . she was so tired, *she* hadn't had any sleep, and it was too much. Raffa hugged her.

"We'll throw them in the water. Let 'em think we tried to swim for it."

"But they might be on the beach!" She could hear the incipient hysteria in her own voice. Raffa's hand tightened on her arm.

"We're alive and two of them are dead. Two unarmed, untrained society girls, against trained hunters with night gear, and who has the weapons now? We're going to stay alive, and they're ALL going to be dead, and no you're not going to have hysterics now. Take a deep breath."

Bubbles took a deep breath; her ribs ached. "Right. Sorry."

"No problem — I got some sleep, and you didn't. Now . . . let's get to the shore, and if someone's there we'll blow him away."

"I can't even tell if this thing is loaded," Bubbles said softly. "I tried to find out and got something that made a red light and hummed at me."

"Really? Sounds like a Maseter range finder to me. Here — let me check your status." Raffa took the rifle, did something Bubbles couldn't follow in the dimness, and handed it back. "Full clip, round in the chamber. When you pull that trigger, you'll shoot something."

"Let's go, then." Bubbles angled left, toward the shore. As she remembered, the big tree had been only a couple of hundred meters from the water. She noticed, after a few minutes, that the blinking lights on the comunits had died. It gave her no comfort. . . . A missed signal would rouse them to search, she was sure. At least they had thick cover to the very edge of the beach.

As they neared the water, the night goggles had more light to work with, and brightened once more. At the same time, the undergrowth increased, as it always had near the forest edge, though it was not so thick that they needed to go out of their way. By the time Bubbles peered through the last screen of bushes and vines, she could see up and down the narrow beach at least a hundred meters in each direction. She saw no one . . . although someone could have been hidden in the undergrowth, as they were. A gentle swell out to sea produced small lapping waves that slipped up and back like the strokes of a massage, rolling the little pebbles that made up the beach here so that they clicked and whispered.

"How deep is it?" Raffa asked. "Any chance the things will be too deep for them to find?"

"It's a steep drop-off," Bubbles said. "We used to beach the sailboats on this side of the island sometimes. Give me that one —" Raffa handed over the comunit and Bubbles took another look up and down the beach. Nothing. She shrugged out of her knapsack and left it with Raffa, then moved slowly out of the cover, expecting any moment to hear another shot. The pebbles crunched under her shoes; she thought of wading in a little way, but remembered the times she'd slipped and fallen here. She didn't need to be sopping wet, not on top of everything else.

"Throw it!" muttered Raffa from behind her. Right. As if she were good at throwing. She felt like an idiot as she cocked her arm and threw the first comunit as far into the sea as she could. It wasn't, she thought, all that far; it landed with a juicy splash. With the next she tried harder, and achieved an even noisier splash — it must have been spinning — and no more distance. She found the two uphill steps back to the treeline almost impossible . . . but the impossible, she was discovering, didn't even take longer. It was just harder.

"A little farther," Raffa said, "and it's your turn to rest. Just get back from the edge."

But they actually walked another half hour, by Raffa's watch, before finding another place Bubbles remembered, where a rib of the central ridge ran all the way to the water. From there around the northern end, the island had no beach, but a vertical wall of stone.

When they lay down — this time neither could stand — Bubbles fell asleep at once. She had expected to have frightening dreams, but she woke with no memory of them. When she opened her eyes, she could see Raffa curled into a tidy ball, catlike; her rifle lay across her sleeping hand. Bubbles yawned, stretched, and rubbed the hipbone that had been on the bottom. Her back never hurt after sleeping on the ground, but a hipbone always complained. She had tried all the tricks she'd read about, back in her camping days, and none of them worked. She sat up; Raffa opened one eye and said, "Don't tell me it's morning."

"It's morning." Unless they'd slept all day, and she didn't feel that rested. Besides, the light was brighter; the leaves overhead began to look green, not black. She stretched again, arching her back, then rolled to her feet. Nothing stirred but the leaves overhead, as the dawn breeze strengthened. Her shoulders were stiff and sore from the pack straps. Raffa yawned, and groaned a little, stretching.

"I hate morning," Raffa said. Then her eyes came open all the way, and she sat up. "It's real."

"What?" Bubbles knew what, but she wasn't sure she believed it yet.

"Us. Here. Last night." Raffa was staring at her own hands. "Blood."

"Yeah." Bubbles had already seen the disgusting mess on her own hands. And she'd eaten something held in them. "I guess we should've washed off when we got to the beach." Her slacks were filthy too, and she could smell her own sour smell. Raffa looked as bad, her dark hair in lank dirty strings and the knees of her slacks black with dried blood and dirt.

"They won't have to see us," Raffa said. "They could track us by smell. Without dogs."

"Then we'll get clean." Bubbles had no idea how they would get clean. They certainly could not light a fire and boil a pot of water for washing. For that matter, she needed to think where the nearest drinking water might be. She picked up her knapsack and got it on, wincing as her shoulders complained. "Come on," she said. "It won't help us to sit here and wish."

Raffa stood, shook herself, brushed at the stains, and finally picked up her knapsack and weapons. "I know, I know. What's the boys' regimental motto? 'Onward to glory' or something equally unreasonable?" She got the knapsack onto one shoulder and grunted. "This thing weighs twice what it did yesterday. And don't scold me; I'm getting my complaints out of the way all at once, early, before they can bother you. You notice I didn't complain last night."

"Right. You complain in the morning, and I'll complain at midnight or whenever it was I went bonkers, and between us that'll cover the whole day."

"And leave us time to survive, evade the hunters, kill them all, and save everyone. Tally-ho." Raffa started off, then looked back. "By the way, where are we going now?"

"Water, I thought," Bubbles said. "Water first, then someplace to hide."

"Like last time," Raffa said, but with a grin. "A hiding place convenient to a trail so that we can get weapons and supplies from dead hunters."

For all the banter, they went warily enough once they started. Without talking about it, they began to move apart, so they could just see each other, and take alternate pauses for listening and looking backwards. Nothing disturbed them but the silence, which the wind in the leaves overhead seemed to emphasize. The sky lightened; Bubbles knew that it was now full day, though they were walking in the shadow of the ridge. The slope began to fall away under their feet, and Bubbles turned right, inland; she remembered that there was another, smaller stream in a ravine between the last hill on the main ridge, and the outlier hill at the north end of the island. It rose from a spring on the ridge, and over the years the children had made a series of wading and splashing pools along its path to the sea. Between them, the stream was no more than ankle-deep except after a rainstorm, but they might find enough water in one of the pools to wash their clothes. Even if all the dams had fallen apart since the last campers, there should be enough loose handy stones to let them build one up again. It wouldn't take long.

When she finally saw water, it was one of the larger pools. Someone had repaired the dam — she assumed it was the prisoners — and raised it enough so that the pool looked to be waist-deep. Its surface was littered with fallen leaves and twigs. She started towards it, then waved Raffa back to cover. It looked safe and deserted, but . . . she noticed something glinting at the upper end of the pool. Warily, she worked her way towards it, trying to keep to thicker growth. A foil packet with one end torn off, that's all, discarded by some careless hunter. It could have held rations, candy, a damp wipe to clean with. She relaxed, then saw the first dead amphib, turning slowly in the pool, its legs extended. Another lay by the stream; with a growing sense of horror she realized that the "floating leaves" were in fact a mass of dead amphibs, insects, fish. She backed away, her hands to her mouth.

"What?" said Raffa, from behind her.

"Poison. They've poisoned the stream." And if this stream, then all the streams — and if the streams, probably the springs as well. After horror, anger. This was *her* place, her childhood, and she had spent hours lying belly-down beside one stream or another, watching the brilliant red-and-gold amphibs, the speckled fish, the brilliant blue and green butterflies that came to drink. "The . . . I can't even find words bad enough. . . ." She had used all the bad words she knew for common things like escorts who got drunk and threw up on her, or girlfriends who told someone else her secrets — she hadn't known there was something worse to save curses for. "How could they —?" How could anyone destroy so carelessly . . . anyone past childhood, that is.

"It would be hard to hide, in an autopsy," Raffa said thoughtfully. Bubbles almost hated her at that moment. Of course it wasn't her island. She had never seen it as Bubbles remembered it. "What I mean is," Raffa went on, "it's probably meant to put us to sleep or something. The . . . the other things are accidents."

"That's what's worst," Bubbles said. "They have a

reason to kill us. A bad one, but a reason. To kill all these, just by accident, as a sort of by-product —"

"We shouldn't stay here. They'd check this pretty often, I'd guess."

"Right. Upstream, then." They might have someone stationed upstream, too, but she had to know if they'd poisoned it all. She had to. She wondered when they'd done it — the day before, dropping packets from the flitter? Landing at each small stream? Or had someone been walking the forest that night, someone who might have walked past them as they slept, not seeing them? She shivered; it would do no good to think of that. As she walked, what Raffa said began to make sense. The same things had different effects on humans and animals — she knew that. A drug to make them sleepy might have killed the amphibs by accident, or . . . didn't the fish need to swim for their gills to work? So if they drowsed and didn't swim, they'd die just from that . . . but she was still angry. She felt decades older than the day before, than even the night before.

Upstream, as anywhere, grew steeper and narrower. They came to another pool, with its scum of dead amphibs and fish; she had seen nothing alive along the banks of the rivulet. Beyond that, the stream forked. To the left, poisoned water gurgled pleasantly in its narrow bed. To the right was the waist-high ledge that formed a miniature waterfall in the wet season. A damp patch of mud in the hollow above it was the only sign that a creek had ever flowed there.

"That way," Bubbles said, heaving herself up and over the rock ledge. "We can't take any water from that stream, and there might be a spring up here they didn't notice."

"You don't know for sure?" Raffa asked, as she sat on the ledge and swung her legs up.

"No . . . my favorite places were the eastern ravine, where I could watch the sunrise, and my bramble. And our camp was on the eastern shore, south of where we crashed. Sometimes we had three or four main camps, depending on how many cousins showed up. Kev and Burlin used to set traps and things up at this end of the ridge — then they'd sit there and snigger."

"Urgh. I wouldn't have wanted to have them along."

"Well . . . Silvia finally told on Burlin, and that was the end of them. But somehow he always made Buttons and me feel like it was our fault. If we'd had a more exciting island, he wouldn't have gotten into mischief."

"Like Stanley, my cousin that always blamed his pony for everything. But he brought it back with whip welts once, and my Aunt Katy wouldn't put up with that."

They followed the dry creekbed upstream, careful not to step in any drying mud. Bubbles looked for any sign that the hunters had been there, but the few scuffmarks could as well have been those of desperate prisoners. Her breath came short; it was hard to climb the steepening slope, and she realized they were close under the ridge. The creekbed turned suddenly, leading them into a narrow cleft roofed with trees; it closed around them, and Raffa exclaimed over the ferns draping the walls. Ahead, the cleft ended in a sheer wall hung with shaggy ferns and vines. At the foot of it, the ground seemed damp, but there was no spring.

"Well," Bubbles said, a little blankly. "That's it. No water here." She sat down; her legs had suddenly given out, and her eyes burned, though she could not cry.

Raffa crouched beside her. "We're hidden, at least. If we stay quiet, and they don't find our trail. They can't come on us from behind."

Bubbles nodded, but could not speak past the lump of misery in her throat. She set her rifle carefully to one side, away from the damp spot, and pushed the knapsack straps off her shoulder.

"We should eat something," Raffa said. "We never did have breakfast."

"Not without water," Bubbles said. "At least, that's what the books say." But at the mention of food, her stomach cramped and rumbled. She felt she could eat three meals at once.

"We have some water," Raffa said. "And what about tropical fruits and things? They have water in them."

"I . . . haven't seen any. It's the wrong season, or the prisoners have eaten them, or something. . . ." Bubbles leaned back against the ferny rock, careless of insects. Her eyes sagged shut.

"Come *on* — you can't give up!"

"I can rest," Bubbles said, not opening her eyes. "Just a little while." She wasn't sure what she felt, except exhaustion and hunger, and right now she didn't care if a whole troop of hunters came up the creek.

"All right," Raffa said, "but I'm not giving up." Bubbles heard Raffa move around her, and the scrape of Raffa's pack on the pebbles. "Although a soft place to rest my aching back may be a good idea. Aahhh —" That relaxed sigh ended in a yelp, quickly muffled. Bubbles opened her eyes. Raffa lay on her back, covered with ferns to the waist; she seemed to have fallen *into* the rock. The mass of ferns and vines had hung over some opening like a shaggy curtain. From the muffled splutters, she was trying to say something. Bubbles grabbed her feet and pulled.

"Are you all right? Need help?"

Raffa undulated, snakelike, and slithered out on her back, spitting dirt out of her mouth. "It's a wonder I didn't crack my skull."

"What is it, a hollow or something?"

"A hollow, yes. A cave!"

"Cave?"

"Yes. And I heard water dripping. Come on. . . ." Raffa grabbed her knapsack and started to shove it through the curtain of ferns.

"Wait — they'd know we went in." Bubbles looked at the broken fronds of fern where she had been resting, the bruised moss. If someone came this way — and they probably would — they'd start looking harder. And they wouldn't miss a cave, she was sure.

"We'll make it look like we rested here, and then went somewhere else," Raffa said. "Come on — shove your pack in, and the rifles. It's the best chance we've seen yet."

Bubbles shrugged and complied. She didn't have any better idea, and if Raffa had found water inside the cave, surely it hadn't been poisoned. She hoped. Raffa went in with their things, and reported that she'd found plenty of room; they could both hide there, with their gear. She crawled back out, as Bubbles lifted the vines cautiously.

"Now for disguise," Raffa said. "A few footprints going in both directions, just in here where we got careless because we figured no one would have tracked us further back. We sat here and rested — that's the squashed ferns on your side. Actually they may not know there *are* two of us, so why don't I make all the footprints?"

"Because we might both have left them somewhere else," Bubbles said. "If we were going to leave here, which way would we go? Back up the ridge, I think — we came here looking for water, didn't find any, and started up to find a spring. . . ." Together, they edged back out of the narrow cleft, and cautiously made a few scuffmarks up a steeper slope. Since they had been careful not to make prints on the way in (and didn't see any) they walked back normally.

The hanging ferns and vines looked undisturbed, Bubbles noticed, even after Raffa had been through twice. Raffa went first, and then Bubbles slid in backwards. They had left marks, sliding in; it looked like someone had dragged bodies over the ground. She was trying to think what to do about it when she heard a shot, from high overhead, and then another. She didn't try to see who it was, or if they'd seen. . . . She jerked backwards under the matted vines and tried not to breathe. Raffa's hand closed on her arm, almost as tightly as the night before. Had it been only one night?

Although it was near midday, inside the cave she could see very little. The thick vines shut out nearly all the light, and it was cool and damp. She lay on level stone thinly coated with damp mud. She could hear the musical plink and plonk of water dripping into deep water, somewhere behind her in the dark. A cold drop hit the back of her neck, and she jumped.

"We should get back from the opening," Raffa said quietly. "Just in case they find it."

"Let's try the night goggles." Bubbles fished hers out and put them on. The nearer part of the cave appeared in shadowy blurs, with stabbing brilliance coming from the entrance. Several meters behind them, a black level surface had to be the water they'd heard. To the left, the cave's inner wall dove directly into the water, but on the right, their flat ledge extended around a buttress and out of sight. Overhead, even the night goggles could not define the roof; when Bubbles reached up, she felt nothing.

Slowly, Raffa got to her knees and crawled away to the right. Bubbles followed, backing up at first so that she could watch the entrance. She had never been one for caves; she had not expected that the light would fade so fast. She slipped the goggles up; the blackness pressed on her face, as if it would invade her skull. Shuddering, she put the goggles back on, and stared at the faint glow from the entrance as if to remember it forever.

"They shot somebody!" George grabbed Ronnie's arm. Ronnie shook it off.

"They shot *at* somebody," he said. "You don't know they hit anyone."

"But the girls are up there — you know that."

He knew that; he could close his eyes and see Raffa's face, smell her hair. "They're in the ravine. They're in cover somewhere. And the hunters wouldn't shoot the girls right off. . . ." He wished he hadn't said it; that thought was no better.

"If Bubbles tried to fight — she's kind of wild sometimes."

"Petris sent one of the preeves up to the high trail, he said. Could have been that. And the hunter might've missed. And we can't even be sure where the shot came from." Although he was sure enough: high on the ridge, south of them. That put it too close to the girls, entirely too close. The hunters were supposed to come this way, and fall into the trap he and George had spent the afternoon constructing. They were just off one of the larger trails, that angled up and over the gap between the main ridge and the outlying northern hill.

Time had gone rubbery; he did not want to trust

George's watch. His had not survived the crash. George's could have been damaged. He was aware that not trusting a watch was as silly and dangerous as not trusting the instruments in an aircraft; he knew he'd had a concussion. But time felt wrong; the glowing digits seemed to hang forever or race past. A vague irritation seized him: *he* had had the concussion, he shouldn't be having to calm George.

Another shot, more distant. His shoulders twitched. He had thought during Petris's briefing that he understood exactly where everyone would be, at least to start with. Now he found he could not remember who might be southward on the ridge, or on the west side. . . . He felt sick and sleepy both, and kept wanting to yawn.

"We ought to go find out," George said. "That's got to be somewhere near them. . . ."

"And if we go crashing up there we'll just lead the hunters to them." Ronnie tried to sound soothing, but even to him his voice seemed lusterless and whiny. "Petris said stay here, and we should stay here."

"He's not even an officer," George said, but he didn't move.

Ronnie stiffened in the midst of a yawn. A rhythmic noise flicked the edge of his hearing. Like someone walking, but walking with an intentionally odd gait. A few steps, a pause: a few more steps, a pause. The sound of steps — the swish of leaves, the soft pad of foot — varied in number but not duration. Despite his fear, Ronnie grinned to himself. They'd been warned about that mistake. . . . He'd done it himself, counting to himself as he tried to move stealthily, he'd put four or five or three steps into the same interval, thus making the sound as periodic as a pendulum. This person varied his pause intervals, but not the walking ones. Ronnie reached out to touch George in case he hadn't heard. The walker might come within reach, if they were lucky.

Ronnie's mind drifted. It had been, he thought, an impossibly bad day, and it had started far too early. Yet he didn't feel as bad as he should; he knew that, and knew, in some distant corner of his mind, that it had something to do with the bump on his head. He wasn't tracking right; he wasn't feeling what he should feel, whatever that was. The long, hot afternoon after the girls left, when Petris tried to figure out what to do with them, where to put them, when the others tested Petris's command, wanting to kill them, wanting to leave them anywhere and get away safely themselves. . . . It had been hell, but a hell from which he felt somewhat remote. As long as he didn't have to talk, as long as he didn't have to do anything, the others could do what they wanted.

✦ Chapter Fifteen

"We cannot do this alone." Heris put into that all the command voice she'd ever had. Cecelia merely looked exasperated.

"We've been over that. I don't want to bother Bunny."

"Lady Cecelia." The formality got through; Cecelia actually focussed on her. "Do you remember why I lost my commission?"

"Yes, but what's that —"

"This is exactly the same thing. If we go off, the two of us — you with no military experience whatever — with no proper intelligence, no backup, no plan — that is exactly as stupid, in the same way, as what Lepescu proposed. It is frankly suicidal, and I will not cooperate."

Cecelia stared at her. "I thought we settled it; I thought you agreed."

"In anger, yes. At the thought of getting Lepescu's neck between my hands, yes. But I have no right to risk you and your nephew and the others to serve my vengeance. We don't know what we're facing; we don't know what shape they're in; we won't have backup or medical assistance — and if we get killed, what about the youngsters?"

For a moment, Heris thought Cecelia would explode; she turned red, then pale, then stood rigidly still. And finally shook herself slightly and let out a sharp *huff* of air. "I suppose you're right. That's why I came to you; you have the military background. So — you want me to tell Bunny?"

"I think we should both go. He may want confirmation from Sirkin up in *Sweet Delight* — and besides, I still want to be part of the row."

"Fine." With no more argument, Cecelia called Michaels over. "Michaels, Captain Serrano feels that we should not go alone on this." Heris noticed that Michaels relaxed slightly; he had had more sense than either of them, but not the courage to say so.

"Yes, milady?"

"I'm going to tell Lord Thornbuckle; this will mean telling him that you knew Bubbles took the flitter." Heris had not thought about that — how much trouble would he be in? Not much, she hoped.

"I don't think you should tell anyone else about this," Lady Cecelia went on, as if Michaels were a child to be lectured. "I'm sure you'll be hearing from his lordship very shortly."

"Yes, milady."

"All right," Cecelia said. "Now we have to find Bunny before that damned hunt starts. We're lucky Stone Lodge is at this end of the settlement."

The others were mounted, ready to set out, the hounds swirling around the horses' legs. Heris was sure that only Cecelia could have gotten Bunny off his horse and into the hall of Stone Lodge so quietly and quickly.

"What is it?" he asked, the moment the door had shut out the sound of milling hooves and human chatter. Cecelia explained, giving as clear an account as Heris herself could have done: her discovery that the young people were missing, Michaels's report of where they had gone, and the beacon data and data from *Sweet Delight* which indicated that they were on an island near Bandon. Then she mentioned the uninvited guests, the intruders that Heris suspected might be hunting illegally. Lord Thornbuckle looked at Heris.

"You know this person?" Heris thought she had not heard anyone pronounce "person" with that intonation before; just so did seniors at the Academy refer to incoming cadets.

"Yes, I do," she said. "He cost me my commission; he has a bad reputation — but the relevant point is that he is here without your invitation."

"Yes . . . I see that. Just a moment." He went out the

door, leaving Heris and Cecelia staring at one another. In moments, he was back inside. "I told Clem to take over the hunt today; no sense in having them hounding us, as it were. Buttons has already ridden out with the blue hunt; I'll have him brought back —" As he spoke, his fingers tapped on his personal comunit. Heris had seen him only at the hunt, or at leisure after dinner; he had always seemed friendly enough, but not particularly decisive except when some fool rode too close to the hounds. The nickname Bunny had fit him well enough, the long slightly foolish face, the quick movements of his head at dinner, on the lookout for unpleasantness. Now, though, she saw someone used to command responding to an emergency, someone for whom a title made more sense than a nickname.

"Sir, the other thing —" She interrupted him cautiously; he raised an eyebrow but nodded for her to speak. "There must be someone in this household working with them — whoever they are. Someone to give warning if you're headed that way, at least."

He nodded. "And it can't be Michaels, because he knew about Bubbles and whoever was there didn't."

"We hope." Lady Cecelia looked grim. "They haven't called in; their flitter's not at a regular field —"

"Which island?" Lord Thornbuckle asked. "Could your ship make that out?" He called up a map which displayed on the hall wall as thin green lines.

"That one," Heris said, pointing.

"Bubbles's favorite," he said. "The children camped there many summers; she knows every meter of that island. I wonder if she's just camping and hiding out."

"If it weren't for the unauthorized shuttle, and the fact that Lepescu is on Bandon —" Cecelia began.

"We hope on Bandon, and not on this island," Heris put in, tapping the map again.

"Yes. We must assume he is, and that he's up to no good." His focus shifted to her, completely. "You were formerly an officer in the Regular Space Service, isn't that right, Captain Serrano?"

"Yes, sir."

"Then please give me the advantage of your professional assessment. What are we facing here, and what is your recommendation?"

Heris felt like a junior officer caught out at an admiralty briefing. "We are presently lacking important information," she began. "We know, or rather strongly suspect, that Admiral Lepescu is on Bandon. The shuttlecraft that landed him could have held as many as fifty individuals, but since it came from a chartered yacht, it is reasonable to suppose that it did not. That it was configured for luxury work, with a maximum of perhaps ten. We do not know how many such shuttle flights have been made to and from Bandon, or the number of people on each. However, it's reasonable to assume that an actual invasion force is unlikely."

"Why, Captain?"

"Both practical reasons and the character of Admiral Lepescu, sir. Practically, invading an inhabited planet is difficult, and one like this would require complicity of too many of your employees. You have four orbiting Stations, additional navigation and communications satellites, and a high-tech population scattered around the planet. An invader would have to gain control of communications to prevent an alarm being sent. Your own militia would have to be suborned or defeated in battle, and from what I've heard of your militia, they're loyal and tough, and very well equipped. Right now, you have thousands of legitimate guests, and their crews and servants — and it might be easier to sneak onplanet in the confusion, but it certainly would not be easier to deal with so many . . ." She struggled for a word that expressed what she meant without rudeness.

"Difficult individuals?" suggested Lord Thornbuckle, with a smile.

"Yes, sir. And as well as practicality, there's the matter of Lepescu. He's not a man to involve himself in something that blatant; his tastes run otherwise."

"Ummm. You said he cost you your commission?"

"Yes, he did." When Lord Thornbuckle's expression did not change, Heris realized she was going to have to say more. Anger roughened her voice.

"He considers war a noble sport, sir. He considers that putting troops in impossible situations is sporting; his expression is 'see what they're made of.' Until recently, the only way he could do this was by risking his own ship, but two years ago he attained flag rank and was given command of a battle group. You are no doubt aware of the Cavinatto action. In that conflict, he ordered my ship, and the ground forces under my command, to make a frontal attack on a strongly defended lunar complex. The defense could have been breached another way — in fact, several other ways, which I and other captains presented as alternatives. But he insisted that it must be done the one way likely to fail — even the battlecomps said so — and certain to cost the most lives."

"Is that legal?" asked Lord Thornbuckle.

"Perfectly," Heris said. "An admiral's fitness for command is judged afterwards, by results. He is not obliged to take advice from anyone but his own commander, and our group was operating far from anyone more senior. It was something Lepescu had worked towards for years."

"Did his order to you risk the whole operation?"

"No. Most of the group would attack the main objective, and while his orders for that were not what I'd have given, they weren't as reckless. Our diversionary action was important, but it need not have been suicidal."

"Did this admiral have a grudge against you before? It seems he must have. . . ."

"I'm not sure." In her own mind she was sure, but she would not condemn even Lepescu on the basis of her personal belief. "I had not anticipated anything like this. But the point is, that in the event I did not obey his very plain orders. My ship and forces attacked the lunar complex, and gained control of it, but I didn't do it his way." At the change in his expression, Heris nodded grimly. "That's right: I deliberately disobeyed the order of a lawful superior, in combat status. Grounds for court-martial; in fact, that's what I expected. I knew exactly how serious it was; my family's been Service for generations, after all. I had evidence, I thought, that would protect my crew at least, and that seemed better to me than losing several thousand of them because Admiral Lepescu enjoyed 'a good fight.' There was even a chance that a court might see it my way — small, but there it was."

"And then what?"

"Then I was offered the chance to resign my commission, in exchange for immunity for my officers and crew, or a court-martial for all. The scan data had disappeared; accidents happen in combat. I had some junior officers whose careers would be cut short forever by a court-martial now, even if they won . . . the stigma never really goes away. And some hotheads in the crew would, I knew, convict themselves if they got before a court; there are always people who can't keep quiet even to save themselves. So I resigned."

"You didn't tell me all that," Cecelia said. "Not about what he wanted you to do."

"It didn't seem relevant," Heris said. The rest of it boiled up in her mind — what Lepescu had said to her and about her: *Coward. Stupid bitch. Typical woman, only good to lay and lie.* And more, that she would never tell anyone. Who could understand?

"So I judge from your report," Lord Thornbuckle said, "that Admiral Lepescu is more likely to put someone else in danger than to risk his own hide?"

Heris struggled to be fair. "He's not a coward, sir; he had a name for boldness when he commanded his own ship. But he's also ambitious in politics and society. He would enjoy hunting here under your nose, but he would not chance making such a powerful enemy by attempting open invasion."

"What about taking hostages?"

"Possibly. Especially if he found himself in a trap."

"Do you think he's the head of whatever is going on?"

"I don't know. He has other hunting friends —" Quickly, she told him about the club she'd heard of, and the rumors about it.

"And you would recommend?"

"Taking in enough force to make resistance futile — and there's the problem of surprise and collusion. If they find out you're coming in, they might get the shuttle off, and the yacht —"

"Not if their crew's in the Bay," Lord Thornbuckle said. "That'll be easy enough to find out; it's on a routine report." All this time, he had been tapping out orders on his personal comunit. "There's a Crown Minister here — Pathin Divisti — but I hate to involve the Crown if we can avoid it. And he's here for hunting; he brought no staff."

Heris hoped her face didn't reveal her reaction. She thought of Crown Ministers as a particularly bloated form of bureaucratic incompetence, whose internal struggles for power resulted in unexpected budget changes for the Services.

The door chimed; a servant Heris had hardly noticed opened it to a militia squad, uniformed and armed. Lord Thornbuckle smiled at Heris.

"Captain Serrano, if you'd brief my Captain Sigind while I get some more information —"

Heris stepped outside; the hunt had ridden off some time before, and she could just hear the hounds giving tongue somewhere in the distance. Captain Sigind was a lean, tough man a decade younger than she, whose expression hardly wavered when he saw he was to be briefed by an older woman in hunting attire. Heris laid out the situation as far as she knew it, and he nodded.

"I know Bandon, of course, and something of the other islands. Haven't been there in a couple of years, but here's the layout." He pulled out a map display and flicked through the file. Bandon came up in a standard military format, with topo lines and color-codings for vegetation types. "The landing field's here — with shuttle extension into these woods. When they expanded the field, they cleared a little place at the lodge itself for small flitters — right here. It's grass, not paving. It'd be real handy if we knew how many were at the lodge, and how many on this other island —"

"All I know about is one shuttle load, and I don't even know if it was troop-fitted or civilian," Heris said.

"Ah. You're military?" His pale eyes were shrewd, wary.

"I was. Regular Space Service."

"Any ground combat experience?"

"No, not myself. That's —"

"Why you didn't rush into this like a damn fool. Smart." His brisk nod approved. "But you see our problem. . . ."

"Of course. You need to know how many they are, what their resources are, and which of Lord Thornbuckle's employees are on their side."

"The outrange supervisor, for one," he said. "I'm sure of that, because it's his responsibility to know who's on which settlement, and when. They'd have needed his codes to get the Bandon beacon functioning for the shuttle."

"And someone at that Station," Heris said. "Where the charter yacht that launched the shuttle came from, because I understand that the use of private shuttles isn't permitted."

"Right. But back to you — you say this man Lepescu is part of some sporting club? Most sportsmen have self-imposed limits on the weaponry they'll use — or is he a trophy hunter type?"

"I don't know," Heris said. The door opened, and Lord Thornbuckle came out. The bony face she had once considered amiable but weak now looked anything but amiable.

"Complete shuttle records for the past thirty days," he said. "The same station where that charter's berthed has launched twice its normal quota of shuttles. Cargo and supplies, most of them were said to be, for Bandon lodge. We don't land supplies for Bandon there very often, not offworld supplies. Certainly not at this season. One of my comsats recorded the same conversation your officer picked up, Captain Serrano — as well as these —" He handed over strips of hard copy, which Heris glanced at. She could not read that fast, and he was still talking.

"I've relieved the Stationmaster there, and put old Haugan in charge — I know he's loyal, at least. Suspended all shuttle flights, and all communications, with the explanation of power problems on the Station. If I understand correctly, there are fewer than twenty people who've taken shuttles like the one Lepescu was on. All but one have returned to the Station. You were right,

Captain Serrano, that they were fitted for civilian luxury use, with a total capacity of ten passengers — and carried less. Here are the latest satellite images of Bandon and the adjacent islands — there's some cloud interference, apparently a storm overnight —"

Heris and the militia captain leaned over them. Three Shots of Bandon, five minutes apart, and two of each adjacent island. They looked at the Bandon pictures first. One atmospheric shuttle stood on the end of the runway; no other vehicles were near it. Three flitters were parked on an apron off to one side in two pictures, and only two in the third and last. A tiny blob the captain identified as an electric groundcar moved along the narrow driveway between the landing field and the lodge. Comparing the three pictures, they could tell that it had left the lodge for the field — and then a flitter had taken off.

On the islands to the east, south, and west — four in all — the captain found nothing remarkable, though heavy clouds still clung to the peaks of the eastern island. But the island to the north — "where the children camped" — Lord Thornbuckle put in — they saw what they were looking for. A flitter on the east beach, hatch open. A flitter parked on the south end of the island another a few hundred meters offshore, as if approaching. They could see nothing on the visual of the island's center; it, too, was cloaked in cloud.

"We have continuous loops, of course," Lord Thornbuckle said. "And we can get infrared and radar images. But it seems to me that's enough to go on."

"Right, sir." The militia captain closed his eyes a moment, and then said, "We'll need all the Homestead militia, and those at the Neck. Day 'n night gear both, full armor, and riot weapons —" He paused, as the clatter of hooves broke upon them. Heris looked up to see Buttons riding breakneck up the avenue on a lathered horse. Servants ran out to take the horse; he flung himself off and ran up the steps to the portico.

"What happened? Is Bubbles all right?"

His father glared at him. "What do you know about Bubbles?"

"She took a flitter with the others to Whitewings for a few days — she asked me to cover for her — what's happened?"

"We don't know. We know the flitter's down on that small island north of Bandon, the one you youngsters camped on. We haven't been able to contact her, and Cece's Captain Serrano has reason to believe she's in great danger."

"And you want me to do what?"

"Be my representative with the rescue force. We expect some opposition. . . ."

"Opposition?"

"Captain Sigind will brief you fully. You'll need your personal gear —"

"Liftoff in thirty minutes, sir," the militia captain put in.

"Right." Buttons dashed into the hall, as changed as his father from the amiable and rather foolish young man Heris had thought him. Captain Sigind eyed her thoughtfully.

"You want to come along?"

"Of course we're coming —" began Lady Cecelia, but the militia captain's eyes never wavered from Heris's. Heris shrugged.

"It's your operation; I don't know the terrain, the entire situation, or your troops. If you can find a corner where I won't be in your way, yes — but I'm not going to step on your toes."

"Heris!" Lady Cecelia's bony finger poked her in the back. "We have weapons —!"

"We have weapons, milady," said Heris formally, "but you have no training and I have not been on a groundside operation in years. We are superfluous, and we might even be in the way. Captain Sigind must decide."

His earlier indecision came down on the side of respect; she had won that much. "Thank you, Captain Serrano. I'm glad you understand. Now, if you and the lady will agree to act under orders, I'm sure we can fit you in."

"We had a supply shuttle almost loaded," Heris said. "Including personal armor for Lady Cecelia and me, and decent weapons."

"Good. Then I can send a squad with you — expand

the standard medical unit — and now if you'll excuse me, I'll be off. Twenty-five minutes, now."

Heris set off for the flitter hangars again, Cecelia in tow. They'd have to change there into whatever clothes Cecelia had packed earlier, or go in hunting attire and look like idiots. It shouldn't bother her, she told herself, after that purple uniform. She knew it wasn't really the clothes that made her feel incompetent. She had never been on a mission as an observer; she had always had a place, a duty. Now her duty was to keep out of the way, stay out of trouble, keep Cecelia out of trouble. It felt wrong.

"I wish we could take the horses," Cecelia grumbled. Heris looked over at her. Cecelia was not used to being rushed; the bustle and scurry of the militia's preparation, the need to scramble out of her clothes and into others in the cramped restroom at the flitter hangars, had ruffled her composure, and she had reacted with a string of complaints. The personal armor Heris had insisted she wear under her jacket made her look, Cecelia had said, ridiculous.

Heris didn't agree; nothing looked as ridiculous as holes in one's body. She hadn't said that, since it hadn't been necessary. Heris's own armor felt odd, shaped differently than military issue, but she hoped it would be effective. She hoped even more that they wouldn't need it. The supply flitter's cargo compartment held food, weapons, tools, ammunition, clothes, medical supplies, and flexible plastic tanks of water. With them were four trained medics, two of them full-time militia. A saddle wouldn't have fit aboard, let alone a horse.

"Horses? To this island? What good would that do?"

"I've always said war wouldn't be as bad if I could ride into it." Cecelia twitched her shoulders. "Not that I could ride with this thing on — another advantage of riding."

"You'd be dead before the first stride," Heris said. She could feel her own breathing tighten. . . . It always did, until the action began, and here she had no way to work it off. The supply flitter, needing no pilot, stayed in position well behind the troop carriers. The medics talked softly among themselves, eyeing her as if checking her for stress levels. She made herself open her hands, let them rest lightly on her lap as if she were relaxed.

"It's on an island, with a forest," Cecelia said. "Horses are faster over the ground than people."

"Bigger target," Heris said. She didn't want to talk; she never wanted to talk ahead of time. She wanted to pace, to check over the plans she had not made, to see the faces that were not her people look at her the way her people had.

"You're nervous," Cecelia said more quietly. Heris glared at her.

"I am *not* nervous." It came out with more bite than she intended; Cecelia did not flinch, but nodded as if it confirmed her opinion. Heris stretched her hands and shrugged. "Not nervous, exactly . . . just unsettled. It's not the way I'm used to."

"Did it bother you when you had command?"

"Bother me? Yes, and no." She knew what Cecelia was doing, trying to keep her focussed intellectually, but she did not mind. It might help both of them. "I worried — one always does — about the plan. Was it good enough, had I missed something, would people die because of my stupidity? And that includes preparation — had I trained them well enough, often enough? Would they make stupid mistakes because I'd been too lenient? But beyond that, it didn't bother me. There's a . . . a sort of quiet place, between the commitment and the combat itself. In a way you probably felt it, from what you've said of starting a cross-country. Once you're on the course, once the horse is galloping, the time for worry is over. From then on you just deal with it, one fence at a time."

Cecelia nodded slowly. "I hadn't thought of it that way — but that is what I said, and that's what I did. One fence at a time, but remembering all the ones ahead, too."

"Oh, yes." Heris sat still a moment, remembering. "You don't quit riding the course until it's over — the last fence, or the last opponent, can kill you if you're careless at the end. But the commitment is there. The difference here — I can't begin to explain it."

"I was surprised that you backed away from it," Cecelia said, even more quietly. "Bunny would have let you —"

Heris shook her head vigorously. "It wouldn't work. These aren't my people; they don't know me, and I don't know the local situation well enough. The person who doesn't fit in, who doesn't know the people or the terrain, is going to get someone killed. Other people killed. I'm old enough to let someone else do the job for which they're trained, and simply chew my nails until it's over."

"Umm." Cecelia looked out the canopy, and then back. "A point where riders differ from soldiers, I suppose. I've taken on someone else's mount if they were injured. If you're a good enough —"

"That's different. But I'll bet you didn't drag some first-timer off her horse just because you thought you could ride it better." Cecelia turned red. Heris looked at her. "You did?"

"I didn't think of it that way, but —" She shifted in her seat, and looked away. "Money and influence are another way of dragging someone off a horse — with the coach convinced Ivan would never do for that horse what I could, and the All-Union Challenge coming up in six months —"

Heris knew her expression had said what she thought before she could hide it. Cecelia, still red, did not try to excuse her younger self.

"I shouldn't have done it — and even at the time, I felt a bit guilty. It wasn't until much later that I realized how much even the best riders — even I — depended on finding an outstanding horse; I thought Ivan's failure to stay in the senior circuit after that reflected his ability. Justified the coach's decision, and my . . . influence."

"Was that your . . . your best horse?" Heris hoped not. She wanted to think better of Cecelia.

"No. It was a horse I thought might replace my best horse. A big piebald from Luminaire, that Ivan found on a farm, and bought literally out of harness. Ivan had done all his early work, but I thought — we all thought — the horse was such a natural anyone could have made an eventer out of him. What he needed was a better rider, we thought. After I got him, he slammed his stupid hoof into a stall partition while being shipped to the Challenge, and ripped his leg up. Never jumped sound again. I had another mount qualified, and you'll probably think it justice that she dumped me headfirst in the water — along with the minicam on my helmet."

Heris struggled not to laugh. "A cube they never made, eh?"

"Oh, they made it. You can buy my dive into the water along with a number of other embarrassing incidents, and since it was full-sim pickup, you can program your own simulator to take the same bounce and see if you can stay on. Sometimes I can." She sighed. "It was a stupid mistake — and to be honest, I've never quite forgiven myself for it. It was just the sort of thing I hated to see, and never meant to do. Yet I could never go back and apologize to Ivan — and a few years later, he was killed in a slideway accident, nothing to do with horses at all."

Ahead, Heris saw the lead carriers spread out. She knew — they had been kind enough to tell her — that they planned to land two on Bandon proper, to secure the island, and two on the island where the flitter had crashed. The supply flitter would land on Bandon behind the others. She could see the smudges of islands ahead, distorted by the curve of the canopy, but she couldn't recognize them. Cecelia prodded her side, and pointed. Sunlight glinted off something large and shiny on one of the islands.

"Shuttle on the field," said one of the medics. Their squad leader spoke into his com, then turned to glance at Heris.

"Shuttle's not primed for takeoff; there's nothing on the field with a hot signature. Captain's got the satellite data, and thinks there's fewer than a dozen people on Bandon proper, maybe less."

"Thanks." Heris managed that much before her throat closed. She didn't want to sit back here with Cecelia; she wanted to be up there — not even in this flitter, but the lead one. The flitter droned on; the medics, after a long glance out the canopy, went back to checking their gear, over and over. The squad leader stared ahead, not speaking. Ahead, the islands rose out of the sea, by ones and twos, their forest-clad flanks showing dark against glistening beaches and the glowing blue sea.

✦ Chapter Sixteen

"We're in luck," Raffa murmured. Even that soft voice woke complex echoes from the water surface, the stone spaces in the cave. Bubbles inched backwards around the corner, fighting her terror of the blackness.

"Light," said Raffa. It flared too brightly in the dark goggles; Bubbles tore them away and stared. Raffa had found an old-fashioned candle lantern, and the striker to light it. Without the goggles, it lit the space around them only dimly, yet it felt so much better . . . that warm flame the color of afternoon sunlight. Bubbles tried to breathe slowly and calmly, and felt her body gradually relax. They were hidden . . . they had light . . . they were, after all, alive.

"D'you think it's safe?" she asked, hoping for reassurance.

"In daylight, certainly — they can't see a little light like this around the corner, not after being out in real daylight. At night — they'd still have to put their heads through that vine curtain, and maybe see sparkles on the water." Raffa put the lantern back on the stone shelf it had come from. Bubbles saw there the other evidence of Kell's occupation: his initials, carved into the stone above the ledge, a row of seashells and colored stones, a tangle of wire leaders, coils of fishing line, and some fish hooks, and a pile of wooden blocks, all daubed with white painted numbers, and lengths of twine with lead weights attached.

"I wonder what that's all about," Bubbles said. "They look like bobbers, for fishing, but why so many? And why numbered?" Raffa meanwhile was exploring the space below.

"Look at this — a sleeping bag or something — soft, anyway. My aching bones will appreciate that."

"I wish I knew if the water was safe," Bubbles said. "We still have some, but —"

"We could look for dead fish." Raffa picked up the candle lantern again, and carried it to the water's edge. When she held it low, Bubbles could see how clear the water was, how pale and unappealing the bottom. Something almost colorless fled through the edge of the light. "Fish," said Raffa, as if she were sure. "My aunt's caves had some pools with fish like this. No color, shy of light."

"So it's probably not poisoned. If these fish are susceptible to the same poison."

Raffa laughed, softly. "So you *do* pay attention in class sometimes. Maris claimed she had to spoon-feed you all your answers to the exams."

Bubbles snorted. "Maris couldn't tell the truth if she were being interrogated under truth serum by the Imperium. I didn't mind learning things but you know how it is —"

Raffa nodded. "Never show how smart you are, dears, or someone will envy you. And then we're supposed to show how rich and prominent our families are, as if no one would envy *that*." In the faint glow of the lantern, Bubbles could not quite read the expression that Raffa turned to her. "D'you mind if I ask something?"

"No . . . while we're hiding in a cave from people who want to kill us, I think your questions are not going to be that threatening." Nonetheless, Bubbles felt a twinge of anxiety. Surely Raffa wouldn't ask about Cecely's infamous birthday party. . . . She didn't want any more lies between her and death.

"Why *do* you let them call you Bubbles?" The very unexpectedness of it made Bubbles laugh aloud; the cave's echoes laughed back, hollowly. She choked the laughter down.

"That — I'm sorry — that's a long story, well suited to this place, I guess. You have brothers and cousins, though — you'll understand." Raffa gave a soothing murmur that might have been anything. "The fashion for Old-Earth,

North-European great names was at its height. . . . You know we're all stuck with things like Cicely and Marilys and Gwenivere — your Raffaele is actually pretty, but some of them —"

"My cousin Boethea Evangeline," said Raffa. "My brother Archibald Ferdinand."

"Right. Well, Mother had finally come over to fashion, after reasonably naming Gari and Tighe; Buttons got stuck with Bertram Harold Scaevola. I really think they made a mistake there: Scaevola doesn't sound British to me, but Mother said it was an important name in history somewhere. Then I came along. You promise you won't tell?"

"Tell whom? The hunters? Don't be ridiculous."

"All right. Brunnhilde Charlotte."

Raffa smothered an obvious bleat of laughter. "What!" Bubbles felt her face go hot.

"Brunnhilde Charlotte. You don't have to make a production out of it. Anyway," she hurried on, "Buttons is only two years older, and when they told him he had a baby sister named Brunnhilde, he could only say 'Buh-buh.' My mother thought it was cute. . . . She liked the idea of a little girl called Bubbles. Then I turned out blonde, and 'Champagne Bubbles' became the family form of Brunnhilde Charlotte. They all thought it was cute. . . . I was only a baby, Raffa. I didn't know what they were setting me up for."

"So you sort of lived out the Bubbles persona, hmmm? Like Dr. Fisher-Wong in psych class says happens."

That cut too near the bone. "Some children are naturally cheerful and . . . and . . ."

"Bubbly. I know. But you're not the fluffhead you act like sometimes." Raffa softened that with a grin. "And you haven't been acting like a pile of bubbles on this little jaunt."

"No. Well . . . to be honest . . . I've been getting tired of Bubbles myself. But look at the alternative. Brunnhilde? What kind of name is that?"

"Brunn isn't bad, as a short form. Wonder what it meant."

"For all I know, Brunnhilde is the Old Earth equivalent of bubblehead. But it sounds better and better the more people snicker at Bubbles. I should've changed years ago, but my cousin Kell — the one who had this cave — was just the sort to make nasty jokes. He gave me so much grief about Bubbles I pretended to like it, just to blunt the point."

"You could use Charlotte. Chara . . . that's not bad. Or Brun."

"Well." Bubbles shrugged. "That decision won't matter if we don't survive, and we won't survive without water, so I think the next step is to check it out."

"With your portable chemistry kit, of course," said Raffa.

"With Kell's portable chemistry kit," Bubbles said sweetly. "The one on the shelf that you didn't recognize." But the little bottles and tubes were all empty, their contents no more than a few dried grains of unrecognizable grit. "With our brains," Bubbles said, when she discovered that. "We can think it out. It's safe for the cave fish; they're alive."

"Alive now."

"Yes. And that's all we can go on. They're swimming normally, not gasping or floating. And that means —"

"We still don't know. Look — whatever it was had to be pretty quick — not more than a day — because Petris told us they'd never bothered the water. That flyover could've dropped the poison, or set someone down to do it afoot. So if one of us drinks here . . . and nothing happens in a day . . . then this water is safe."

"I'll drink. It's my island." Bubbles scooped up a handful of water and sucked it quickly. It tasted of nothing but water. "I won't drink much," she went on, "just in case. Maybe if it's only a little, it'll put me to sleep or something."

"Or only make you throw up once. You *are* a gutsy wench, and you shouldn't be stuck with Bubbles one day longer. Take your pick: Brun or Chara."

Bubbles sat back on her heels. "I'm used to the B. . . . Let's try Brun. If I hate it tomorrow, no one ever needs to

know." If she died of poison no one ever would know. . . .
She shoved that thought away.

"Good for you, Brun. Now . . . how can we do the
hunters the most harm?"

Ronnie could not tell whether the pounding in his
head was from the concussion or excitement. The too-
regular uneven footsteps came nearer, and he could just
hear George trying to breathe quietly. Then the footsteps
turned back toward the little creek; he heard a rock turn,
and splash noisily, and a muffled curse. One of the red-
and-yellow amphibians gave a tiny bark, and several more
answered. George's breath came hot and wet against his
ear.

"I *told* you," George murmured. "We should've put
our trap on the creek itself."

He wanted to say "Shut up" but the person at the creek
might hear. Instead, he touched George's wrist, a sharp
tap. He could hear the walker, moving upstream, occa-
sionally tipping a rock, and then the squelch of wet boots
on mud.

"Let's follow," George said, tickling his ear again.
"Maybe we can take him."

Maybe we can get killed very easily, Ronnie thought. If
the hunter had night goggles, if he had a fully equipped
night-hunting rifle, they would be easy prey. "Wait," he
breathed, as quietly as he could. "The spring's not that far
away. . . . He may come back and spring the trap."

Another splash, some ways upstream, and the sound of
something large moving through brittle brush. "He ought
to be more careful," George said.

"We too," Ronnie said pointedly. George subsided,
though his sigh was louder than Ronnie approved. After
an interminable period, they heard sounds returning. The
same hunter? Another whose planned route had crossed
his? One of Petris's men? Ronnie didn't know. His neck
prickled; he felt that someone was looking at him, that he
was outlined by a spotlight. He blinked, hard. . . . No
spotlight, nothing but darkness. Whoever it was coming
downslope stayed in the water, for the most part. . . . They

could hear the rocks grinding and turning under his boots, and occasional splashes. He moved faster, as most people do going downhill, and as if he could see his way.

He passed their position, still moving downstream, and did not turn aside along his former path. Apparently he was going to follow the stream all the way down.

"This is stupid," George said in Ronnie's ear, all hissing s's. "If we stay here . . ."

Ronnie's control broke; he grabbed George's mouth and dug his fingernails into his lips. "The idea is to stay alive," he muttered. "Be quiet." He let go as quickly as he'd grabbed, and they spent the remaining hours of darkness in icy silence, both furious. An occasional shot rang out at a distance; they heard no cries, nor anything that let them know what was happening.

In the first faint light of dawn, when Ronnie realized he could see his hand in front of his face again, the peaceful gurgle of the creek off to their left seemed to mock their fears. Not even the amphibians were making their usual racket . . . no sound but the faint sigh of a breeze in the leaves far overhead, and the water in the creek, and the sound of waves below, borne on the wind. He had heard no shots for a long time. His head ached dully, an ache he was almost used to now. His eyes burned. He felt stiff, dirty, sore . . . but alive. He looked at George, who had fallen asleep leaning against a tree. Perhaps he should let George sleep a little longer? But as he thought it, George produced a faint noise that ripened into a snore, and woke up, almost falling.

"We survived," Ronnie said, trying for cheerfulness. The sound of his own voice woke painful echoes in his head.

"Survived!" George rubbed his eyes, looking disgusted but still dapper. When he brushed at a smudge on his sleeve, it actually vanished. "We should have gone after that fellow. . . . We haven't done anything useful yet." He gave their trap an angry glance. Even in that early light, the leaves they had cut to conceal it drooped and no longer matched the greenery around them. Ronnie hadn't realized that they'd wilt in only twelve hours or so.

"It was a stupid idea, just the sort of thing you might expect from someone like Petris."

"All he said was stay up in this area, and perhaps we could trap someone. You're the one who had the idea for the trap itself."

George glared, but silently. Ronnie wondered if they should take the now obvious trap apart, or leave it. Moment by moment the light increased, and the trap's outline became clearer. It would take, he thought, a very stupid hunter to step into it now.

George stretched. "We'll have to clear that mess up," he said. "It certainly won't fool anyone."

"I suppose not." Ronnie wanted to lie down and sleep, preferably for two days straight, and wake up in a clean, comfortable bed. He did not look forward to undoing the trap, particularly when he couldn't remember exactly how the lines ran on this side. "Although . . . suppose we left it, and they saw it and sniggered, and then we had another trap they didn't see?"

"Like what?" George asked. It was a reasonable question for which Ronnie had no answer. "Dig a pit trap with our fingernails and disguise it with more wilting greenery?" Ronnie resented the inherited knack for clever phrasing.

"Perhaps a snare sort of thing — you know, where a rock drops on them." Somewhere, in some class, Ronnie remembered seeing something . . . a leaning stick or limb, with something heavy balanced above, and when someone went through —

"A rock . . . and where are we supposed to find more rope and a rock?" Evidently George didn't have the same illustration in mind. Ronnie didn't think his had rope in it.

"I've . . . got to sit down," he said, as his head and stomach renewed yesterday's quarrel. George, after all, had slept standing up. George grabbed his arm as he went down, more a fall than a controlled descent.

"You look awful," he said. Ronnie felt slightly less sick, lying on his back, but his head pounded just the same. George's thumb appeared in front of his face. "Focus on this — can you?" He could, but he didn't really want to let

George assess his eyes' ability to focus — George wasn't even a medic, let alone a doctor. He let his eyes close. "I'll get water," George said, and Ronnie heard his footsteps heading toward the creek.

Silence. Aside from the untalented drummer in his head, lovely dark silence lay around him. No buzzing insects, no barking amphibians — he remembered how startled he'd been to find how loud a sound those tiny wet bodies could make. The sea sounds lay at the threshold of hearing, below the headache's contribution most of the time. He wiggled his shoulders in the soft leaves, hoping no biting insects would get him, and felt his stiff muscles relax.

He did not know he was falling asleep until he woke; the sun had speared through a break in the forest canopy, directly into his eyelid. He squinted, twisted, and bit back a groan. He still hurt, though not as badly. He had slept some hours — too many hours; it must be near midday. George should not have let him sleep so long. He forced himself up on one arm and looked around. He couldn't see George.

Silence lay on the forest, heavy and dangerous. It wouldn't be that still if nothing was wrong. Slowly, carefully, Ronnie sat up, then levered himself to one knee, then to his feet. Nothing stirred. No birds, no insects — nothing. His own breath sounded loud to him. His mouth tasted foul, and his lips were dry. Where was George?

He had gone for water. Ronnie remembered that much, and after a short panic remembered which way the stream was. He glanced at the trap — the leaves covering it were now a sickly brown — and eased his way toward the creek, as quietly as possible.

It lay in a steep-sided bed, just here; he could see the glint of water trickling down from a pool above before he could see it right below him. Then he saw George. George sprawled gracelessly, as if he'd simply slumped to the ground while climbing back toward Ronnie. Ronnie looked around for the enemy he assumed had shot him . . . but saw and heard nothing. When he looked again, he saw no blood, no burn mark, no injury at all.

Ronnie sank to his heels and tried to think this out. George down, without a cry, but — he could now see his back move — breathing. Had he just fallen asleep? And why there? He glanced at the creek, and frowned. From here, he could see something floating, a bit of scum or something. He stood, and moved closer to George. George was definitely breathing, and from the new angle he could see that his eyes were closed.

"George," Ronnie said softly. Nothing happened. He reached out and touched George's shoulder. No response. He glanced around again, sure someone was watching, but saw and heard nothing at all. George's slack hand lay atop the water bottle he'd carried to the creek; its cap had come off in the fall, and it held only a scant swallow or two. Ronnie poured it on George's face, hoping to wake him, but aside from a grimace, George did not rouse. Perhaps more would work. With another look around, Ronnie took the bottle to the creek to refill it.

The scum he had seen lay in drifts against the rock. At first he didn't recognize it . . . but when he swished it away to put the bottle in, there were the limp legs and tails of the red and gold amphibians, the motionless fins of tiny fish. Dead . . . beginning to stink. . . . He stared at them, his hand frozen in place, not quite touching the water, the bottle half immersed. Then he moved his arm back, and let the bottle drip on the ground. Thoughts whirled through his mind in odd fragments. The man they'd heard last night. The silence — nothing croaking or barking after he came back downstream. George asleep. The dead things. The water he hadn't touched. . . . He hoped the dizziness he felt suddenly came from his concussion, or even from fear, and not from the touch of that contaminated water.

That unseen hunter had somehow poisoned the water . . . killed everything in it . . . and whatever it was put George to sleep. Or was he dying? Ronnie staggered back to George and felt the pulse at his neck. It beat slowly, but regularly, against his sweaty fingers. He shook George's shoulder. Again no response. A frantic look upstream and down . . . tree trunks, vines, bushes, rocks. No moving figures, no sounds that shouldn't be there.

But if the poison was supposed to put anyone who drank the water to sleep, that meant someone might come to collect them. He couldn't leave George so near the water, out in the open. He grabbed George firmly under the arms and heaved. His headache escalated from dull throbbing to loud rhythmic pounding, and his stiff ribs felt as if someone had dragged sharp knives across them. George, meanwhile, had moved hardly a centimeter, but he did begin to snore, a loud unmistakable snore that Ronnie was sure could be heard a long way.

"A . . . whatchamacallit," Ronnie muttered to himself. "Something to drag him on . . ." He looked around. An older cousin had gone through a period of enthusiastic camping, but Ronnie spent that long vacation at a music school, honing what his mother fondly believed to be superlative talent. After hearing his cousin's stories, most of them involving borderline criminal assaults on the younger campers, he milked the talent he himself knew to be minor, and managed another session of music school. By then, his older cousin had moved on to other amusements, and Ronnie had escaped even one six-week session at his brother's camp. Right now, he would have accepted a few buffets, tosses into ice-cold ponds, burr-pricked mounts, or stinging crawlers in bunks, for some of the practical knowledge Knut had claimed. Ways to drag heavy loads when you didn't have lifters or flitters, ways to make traps that actually worked.

His first version of the travois bound with vines cost Ronnie three blisters, an itchy rash from the vine sap, and most of the hours of afternoon. When he finally rolled George onto the vines and lifted the handles, George's limp body worked quickly through the vines to the ground before Ronnie had, with great difficulty, pulled it ten meters. Cursing softly, Ronnie untangled George and tried to weave the vines into a more stable configuration. That was when he noticed the itching rash. He had never woven so much as a potholder; he knew in theory how weaving worked, but nothing about fishnets or hammocks or anything else that would hold a sixty kilo body safely between two poles as someone dragged them along.

He did not let himself notice hunger or thirst, but the darkness creeping out from under the trees finally blurred his vision before he had anything that would support George. He had tried dragging three times, and all he had to show for it were the obvious scars in the forest soil.

And now it was almost too dark to see. . . . His hands were itching, burning, shaking; when he tried to stand, cramps seized his legs and arms; he staggered. Now he was thirsty; his mouth burned. He took several steps toward the creek before he remembered.

Don't panic, he told himself. Think. But he could not remember when he had thought last . . . days ago, it seemed. For a moment it was hard to think where he was, or why. . . . Then it came clear. They had had supplies, of course they had. Back where the trap was. He could get water there, and food. He started back, in the near dark, hoping he could recognize which dark blur was the right tree.

The worst thing about being in a cave, Bubbles thought, was how you could lose track of time. They had drunk some of that cool, clean water, eaten a little food, and then, while trying to figure out all the things Kell left, day had turned to night. Even with night goggles on, she could see nothing. If they left the candle burning, anyone who looked in the entrance might see it sparkle on the water . . . and she didn't want to go outside and make sure no gleam showed through the leaves.

Sleep came to them slowly, with many starts and twitches, but they were both still tired from the night before, and finally slept. I'm not Bubbles any more, was her last conscious thought. I'm grown up now — I'm someone else, named Brun.

What woke them was the sound of rock falling someplace. In the echoing darkness, they could not tell how far off it fell, only that it was inside and not outside. Bubbles had slept with the goggles on, and when she woke could just make out a paler smudge beyond the rock buttress. Raffa's hand reaching for hers almost made her squeak, but she managed to stay silent. She squeezed Raffa's hand and then put it aside. She would have to crawl to the edge of the buttress, and look around, to see how near daylight it was.

The pool of water tinkled pleasantly, as if it were being rained on, and when she got to the corner of the buttress, she could see light seeping in from the entrance. Not as bright as the day before (if it was the day before — had they slept the clock around?) but enough to show that no one was in the visible part of the cave. If someone had caused the rockfall, they were now out of sight. She started to creep around the buttress, and realized suddenly that her knees were wet — the pool was rising. Yesterday there'd been at least two meters between the buttress and the pool, and a meter between the pool and the entrance. Now the gleam of light reflecting from water extended to the entrance . . . perhaps even outside. She backed up until her feet bumped into Raffa.

"I think it's raining," Bubbles said softly. The cave felt slightly less resonant, or perhaps the tinkle and chime of dripping water, and its echoes, covered her voice. "The pool's up."

"Can we get out?" Raffa asked.

"For now, yes. . . . It's probably not more than a couple of centimeters at the entrance. And I doubt it goes much higher for long — that's never a large creek out there."

"The creekbed — yes." Raffa sounded pleased. "If it actually flows, it'll take care of our tracks coming in."

"What about our tracks going out? And with water coming out there, it'll be obvious something's inside."

"Maybe we won't have to go out. . . . Let's look." Raffa lighted the candle-lantern again, and they peered at the water, then the cave walls. A pale streak topped by a dark one ran along the wall perhaps knee-high. Farther up, a blurrier mark showed.

"That's common — probably a seasonal flood. And the other is older, and rare. Didn't you say there were seasonal rains?"

"Yes — and this is supposed to be the dry season."

"Well, then: I'll bet it won't get that high." Raffa

pointed to the lower mark. Bubbles thought she sounded entirely too cheerful.

"That's our lives you're betting," Bubbles said.

"That sounds like Bubbles and not Brun. It's our lives either way — if we go out now, they'll have nice muddy footsteps to show where we were. How long do the off-season rainstorms last?"

"Only a few hours, usually, but they can drop a lot of rain when they hit." Bubbles sighed. "I'm not used to being Brun, you know. It's going to take some getting used to. You're right — it's not likely to come up even as high as the wet-season floodmark. And even if it does, we can climb — there are ledges. . . ." They looked big and high enough. In the meantime. "We can use Kell's floaters and weights to mark the pool's edge and see how fast it's rising." She took down the pile of floats, and poked the weight tied to one at the edge of the water. Luckily they had a supply of candles for the lantern, and need not sit in the faint light that came from around the buttress.

Several hours passed with only the musical tinkling of water falling into the large pool. A bar of concentrate eased the hunger pangs, but Bubbles would have been very glad of a hot breakfast. The cave's damp coolness no longer seemed a comfortable refuge from the heat outside. Slowly, in tiny lapping ripples, the water rose. Each hour, Bubbles put another weight at the edge of the water. The first one now lay two centimeters under; the last, as the third hour came to an end, was hardly covered by a skim of water.

"Made it," Raffa said, giving Bubbles an affectionate shove. Then they both heard the voices. Raffa reached out and snuffed the candle in the lantern; darkness closed around them. They dared not move, lest they trip on something and make a noise. Bubbles slipped the dark goggles back on, to find her vision just as black.

Then a ray of light flared across. . . . Someone had flashed a light inside. A man's voice, magnified and distorted by the cave's echoes, boomed from the entrance. "Nothing. There's water right up to the entrance; if anyone had come inside, we'd see the marks."

Another voice. "— got here before the rain?"

"Not likely. Nothing — no sounds, no movement — nothing on IR scan." Bubbles blessed the thick rock that lay between them and the entrance, and the cold cave water that had covered any mark they'd left. She had thought of the hunters having dark goggles; she'd forgotten the special equipment on the rifles.

"— those weapons?"

"Nah. They'll be basic by now — they don't have any way to revalidate them. C'mon." The light vanished, and the voices faded. Bubbles realized she was shaking, and tried to take deep slow breaths. What had they meant, the weapons would be "basic" by now? She reached out and found Raffa's shoulder; Raffa grabbed her back and they hugged, both of them still trembling. For an unmeasured time they clung together, until they were both breathing normally.

"We were stupid," Raffa murmured in Bubbles's ear. "We didn't even have our weapons within reach."

"It's so hard to believe," Bubbles said. "I keep remembering the old camping trips: we played at chase and smuggling and capture . . . but it was just play, though we took it seriously then. Now — it's real, but it's hard to keep remembering that."

"I'm going to check that rifle." Raffa stood up and reached for it. "It can't have a locator, or they'd have known it. Must have been something else." Bubbles heard soft noises, Raffa handling the weapon, and then a grunt. "Ah. I see. That socket in the side must be for a computer link — probably an ID chip. That's what they meant by validation. None of the good stuff works now — the range finder, IR scope, all that — but it'll still fire."

"Which means?"

"It can't see in the dark. We have to be better. But if we avoid them completely, we won't need them anyway."

Bubbles had forgotten the earlier alarm, the sound of falling rocks, but when it came again, an echoing clatter and roar, she remembered. *Something* was in the cave with them. Her mind pictured all the large predators on the planet, even though she knew none were on the island.

"What was that?" asked Raffa. Her voice sounded shaky and breathless.

"Rocks," Bubbles said. "I guess." She lifted the rifle, although she had no target at all. "Maybe the water loosened something, and it just fell."

Ronnie had found the meager cache of food and water, and a couple of swallows restored some of his wits. He couldn't move George alone. Even if he got the vines woven the right way, dragging the travois alone would leave obvious tracks. He would have to find Petris and the others, even though that had been against his orders. He sucked at a ration bar, letting the surface coating of salt and sugar revive him, then took another swig from the safe bottle. He shouldn't eat much, he remembered, if he was short of water.

A gust of wind stirred the trees overhead, and its warm moist hand brushed his face. If only it weren't dark — if only his head didn't hurt — if only he had someone to help him . . . but reality settled on his shoulders like a cloak of misery. Dark, hurt, alone; either he figured it out, or no one would.

He made his way back to George's unconscious body in the dark, tripping more than once on unseen roots and stones. How long would the drug or poison keep George unconscious? He wished he knew more about drugs. He tried to redo the vines, in the dark, by feel, but his heart wasn't in it. A drop of cold water flicked his hot neck, and he jumped. Then another. Now he could hear the spatter of rain, as well as the rush of wind gusts in the trees.

If it rains, he thought, if I can pull George along, the rain will wash out our tracks. He didn't let himself think how much harder it would be to pull the travois through mud. Instead he yanked at the poles, straining, staggering uphill, away from the creek. Suddenly it was easy; he lurched forward, almost jogging, then realized that must mean George had fallen off, or through, the vine webbing. He was almost sobbing as he turned back. It was too much, the pain in his head, the rain, the danger, the uncooperative vines.

He had just found George's body when he saw the lights in the sky. A flitter, its searchlight directed into the forest. . . . He threw himself back, away from George. They had IR sensors, of course, and night-vision goggles. They could see George. They could see him. He crouched, shaking from fear and exertion both, dithering. Above the wind and thickening rain, he could just hear the flitter's drone. Its searchlight flicked among the trees, probing, but the canopy was thick here near the stream, and the light never touched him. It did flick across George, and that garish beltpack he'd refused to bury . . . and it came back, and centered there. Ronnie bit back the groan he wanted to utter. Why hadn't he taken the thing off? He'd known it was stupid . . . too late now.

The flitter sank into the canopy, its searchlight illuminating slanting lines of rain above, and drips below. He heard the squeal and clunk of a hatch opening. They would have a ladder or line, he realized, for dropping hunters directly into the forest. If he stayed here . . .

He took a deep breath and plunged away, into darkness. Upslope, upstream, into the thicker forest and more broken country. If he could get rock between him and the IR scans, they couldn't see him. He picked his way from tree to tree in the dim radiance of the flitter's light. It would do no good to hurry; he must not fall and make a noise. He had a few seconds perhaps, as someone came down the line from the flitter, someone who surely must be concentrating on a safe descent rather than a possible fugitive.

He heard the metallic clatter of someone landing, a weapon (he was sure) rattling against something else, the cable or a ladder. Light brightened behind him; he dared a peek and saw a lightsource at head level. A helmet light, feebler than the flitter's searchlight, but perfectly adequate for close work. It lowered, as if its bearer crouched. Over George, Ronnie was sure; he struggled against the desire to go back and protect his friend. He heard the peculiar squawk of a badly tuned comunit, then another clatter as if someone else had come down. Now two helmet lights glowed back there. The flitter's engine whined

— retracting its cable? — and then moved off, to the east. He heard voices, muted by wind and rain.

He had to leave. He had to go now, while they did whatever they were doing to George, because they must not catch all four of them. That was the only chance. But he had never imagined that he might have to leave a friend behind. He made himself move, one slow step after another, away from the lights. *I'm sorry*, he let himself say to George in his mind. *I'm sorry*.

He had covered perhaps fifty meters when he heard the shout behind him. Reflex threw him forward, into a wild panicky run. The shout came again, then a shot smacked into a nearby rock. Ronnie fell over another rock, banging both shins, and scrambled up. Too late for silence, for subtlety; only speed would help him now. Lightning flashed overhead, blinding him momentarily. He tried to move faster through his memory of what it revealed and fell again. He was in the creek, now only a meter wide; rain lashed at him as he climbed, stumbled, climbed again. Another shot rang out, but he never heard it hit anything. Surely, the one rational corner of his mind thought, surely the lightning will blind those in night goggles even worse. . . .

Ronnie struggled on, uphill, ignoring everything but the need to get away. His feet slipped on wet rocks, in mud; rain beat in his face, plastering his hair down, dragging at his shirt and trousers. Flash after flash of lightning revealed a grotesque landscape of wind-whipped foliage, ragged rocks, wind-tossed rain. He followed the creek, no longer worried about the poison in its water, until he reached its source. Behind him, he could see flickering lights . . . the hunters, following what must be an obvious trail. He licked his lips, grateful for the pure rainwater that drenched him. Where now?

The next flash of lightning showed him a narrow black cleft, above and to his right. He clambered over the wet rocks, hoping it was deep enough to hide in, hoping it wasn't just a trick of lightning. Thunder shook the ground, trembled in his breath. Behind him, a shout and a stab of light; his shoulder burned. He plunged to the ground, behind a rock, and tried to see where the cleft had been. Lightning again; there, only a jump and stretch. It still looked deep, a black gash in the rocky slope. Rain poured down, even harder now. He forced himself to stand, to take those few steps, to reach up and haul himself into darker darkness.

When the next lightning came, he saw it as a blue-white flash against dark walls. Limping, staggering, he tried to work his way further in. Water trickled along between his feet, getting deeper; pebbles rolled and he lurched against the rocks, biting his tongue at the pain in his shoulder. Then the ground fell out from under his feet, and he slid down a crumbling slope into black oblivion.

✧ Chapter Seventeen

George awoke with a stiff neck and aching head. It was dark. Night, he thought. He tried to stretch, and discovered that his wrists were bound behind his back. This, he thought, will never do. He blinked several times, and drew in a breath that stank of cleaning solution, old wood, and sour water. When he let the breath out in a gusty sigh, the sound seemed small and confined, as if he were in a closet. He felt around with his legs, glad to find that his captors had not tied his ankles. He could sit up, though he felt dizzy.

The mind his father always doubted he had began to work. He couldn't remember how he'd gotten into this, but his friends never pulled tricks this unpleasant. He forced his mind back to the last clear memory, then tried to go forward. The flight to the island — the crash — Ronnie pale and sick — the ragged islanders who claimed to be the victims of a manhunt. He and Ronnie, building a trap of leaves and branches — a sound in the night — dawn — then nothing.

He had not liked capture the first time, with Petris and Oblo; this time, when he was sure it was their enemies, he liked it less. He had been captured somehow — that he could not yet remember — and he was confined in something that sounded and smelled like a closet for cleaning supplies. The others must still be free — or some of them — or he would be dead.

He brushed that thought aside. He, George Starbridge Mahoney, was not going to die. That would not happen; sordid deaths happened to others, not to young men of good family whose trousers never lost their crease. He was going to escape, and warn Lord Thornbuckle, and then go rescue Ronnie and the others. And the first thing to do was find out more about his prison.

With difficulty, he levered himself up to his feet. It was remarkably hard to find his balance in the dark. He backed up slowly, until his hands bumped a wall. His fingers recognized wood, then something papery, then more wood. He edged along, feeling for a corner, and bumped into a shelf that caught him painfully above the elbows. Something rattled on the shelf, and he felt a small bump against his back as whatever it was fell over and rolled.

It occurred to him then that he should not let that object fall off the shelf. It would make noise, and noise might bring his captors, and his captors might think he knew where the others were hiding. His captors might even be unpleasant. He had not enjoyed the classes on interrogation resistance which even the Royals found necessary; he wanted nothing to do with the real thing.

He leaned a little on the shelf, trying to encourage the small item to roll backwards, and the entire shelf fell off its supports. Hard, sharp-edged cans banged against his arms, the backs of his legs, and clattered on the floor; something breakable smashed. Stinging fumes rose, and he choked, then coughed helplessly. His eyes burned, tears rolled down his face; he staggered away from the shelf, tripping over unseen rolling hazards on the floor, and hit his shin on a bucket with a loud clang. He gave a most ungentlemanly curse.

Light stabbed his eyes, and the door opened. He lunged toward it, but the shadowy figures there shoved him back so hard that he could not keep his feet. He fell against the bucket — it hurt just as much on the backs of his legs — and sat down hard in a puddle of whatever it was with the strong smell. He could feel it oozing through his expensive Guilsanme trousers.

"Shut up!" said one off the shadows, before he knew his mouth was open. "Or get another dose."

Another dose. That meant he'd been drugged or poisoned — he had a tiny, shrinking vision of a creek, of a full waterflask coming to his lips. With that memory came thirst, worse even than his headache.

"I'm thirsty," he said, surprised by the rough weakness of his voice.

Someone laughed, unpleasantly. It reminded George of the senior bully, the year he'd started school. "Too bad," someone said; the voice sounded as if it belonged to the laugh. "But not for long."

"No, wait . . . if they autopsy, they'll look for dehydration." The other voice had an undertone of anxiety.

"So?" George tried to squint past the lights aimed at him, but still could not see either figure — or if there were more than two. "Seawater might do that —"

"Nah. The old man said take care of 'em until we got the whole bunch —"

"He didn't say tell 'em the whole plan!" The door slammed; George could hear raised voices, but not the words. He glanced around the closet. In the light of its single fixture, it was as cramped and unpleasant as his experience in the dark suggested. It was about two by three meters, with the door on the middle of one long side, and shelves on either side of the door. Above the shelf he'd broken, two more supported a collection of brushes, cans, and jugs; on the other side of the door, the shelves held bathroom supplies in neatly labelled boxes. Behind him mops and brooms hung from a rack; he had been lucky not to dislodge any of them when he fell over the mop bucket.

It had to be a large house or building, probably on the neighboring island. Bandon, its name was. Bandon where the landing field had signalled that they were unwelcome. Where the hunters, according to Petris, were living in comfort in the lodge, while the victims struggled to survive on the island.

George shook his head at the state of his trousers, which the bright light revealed to have suffered from the island even before the noxious green liquid that still filled his nose with stinging vapor. Never in his life had he been this disheveled. . . . He noticed a rip in one sleeve, and a long greasy stain, as if he'd been thrown in a dirty cargo compartment for the trip here. He probably had. And without the use of his hands, he could not even tidy himself up.

But he could get out of the puddle of smelly green stuff, which he was sure would do his trousers more harm than simple grime. For all he knew it would eat its way through his skin, as well. He braced his back against the wall of mops, and stood. There. He could just grasp the handle of a mop. . . . There ought to be some way of using it as a weapon the next time those persons opened the door. But he couldn't think of one, and the door opened again.

"You weren't supposed to get up," said the voice he associated with the nasty laugh. With the two spotlights trained on his face, he still could see nothing of the men holding them.

"I couldn't breathe," George said. "That stuff chokes me."

He had been right; it was the same laugh. "I wouldn't worry about that," the voice said. "But you said you were thirsty — come on, then."

Was it safe to go out? It wasn't safe to stay here, he knew that much. He tried to step forward with assurance, as if he weren't even worried, but the green liquid was slippery as oil. He staggered, and fell into the door frame. Ungentle hands caught him under the armpits. "What a comedy act you are, aren't you?" He had no time to catch his breath before it was slammed out of him at the end of a hard fist, and he fell back against a wall. Thick cloth muffled his head, blinding him, and he felt hands — large, strong, and gloved, he thought — yank him along.

He tried to judge from the sounds — the scrape of shod feet, the sound of breathing — what sort of space they were in, how far they'd come. A corridor, he thought, but he could not judge distance, not with the hard hands shoving him this way and that, breaking his concentration with slams against the wall or yanks on his bound arms.

Finally he heard a door open — a swing door, he thought — and a final shove sent him forward through it just as the cloth was pulled away from his face. He staggered, and fell onto a hard, cold floor in the dark, and heard the snick of a lock on the door behind him.

For a time he lay there, nursing his new bruises, and wondering what to do now. But thirst drove him to explore. This smelled different, cleaner, colder. Like a bathroom, he decided. He got to his knees, and considered shuffling around like that, but the hard floor hurt his knees after only a few awkward moves, and he realized he would have to stand up. Again.

This exploration, however, ended in success. He found the door through which he'd been shoved, and beside it the predictable panel of switches to control light and ventilation. Cool white light showed him a bathroom — certainly a staff facility, for it had none of the amenities the family rooms would have had. A row of sinks set into a counter, with mirrors above — he winced away from his image — and a row of plumbing fixtures. The stack of clean glasses on the counter mocked him. How was he supposed to turn the water on? Or get it in the glass?

That struggle occupied him some time. The sinks had watersaving faucets, so that they would not run long without a finger on the control — and the control was mounted at a convenient height for someone with free hands. George had to hitch himself up onto a sink, almost sitting in it, to reach the control. . . . He was sure the entire counter-and-sinks arrangement was going to fall off the wall and cause a flood. He could turn the water on, but he could not drink, not while facing away from the sink. And the sinks had no plugs, so he could not fill one and drink from it. Finally he realized that he would have to take a glass from the stack and position it in a sink — all out of his sight — and then climb up to start the water and hope the glass was in the right position. Then take the glass out of the sink and set it on the counter, close enough to the edge that he could tip it with his mouth, and finally drink.

It took a very long time; he broke two glasses, cut his fingers, and almost decided that thirst was better than this struggle. But his stubbornness forced him on. And the lukewarm water, the half glass of it he managed to drink before the glass tipped over and spilled the rest down his chin and neck, tasted amazingly good. He could almost feel his brain cells soaking it up and going back to work. Now he would think of what to do; now he would get back to his own script for this miserable outing, and come out as he always did: clean, pressed, and in control.

It was not so bad, being locked in a bathroom. Basic bodily functions accounted for . . . he stopped, halfway to the fixture he had planned to use, and realized another problem. How was he supposed to open his trousers with his hands tied behind him? It wouldn't do any good to yank on the waistband from behind, not with these; they were designed to withstand incredible force.

He would think about it later; it was not that big a problem. Yet. On the other hand, he would make do with that one half glass of water, and not waste energy trying to get another.

"You really should consider the legal aspect," George said. His stomach growled; the food the two men were stuffing into their mouths with such indecent haste smelled delicious. He had been given no food, though it was promised for "just before you go swimming." He had, instead, been given the novel experience of cleaning all the plumbing fixtures in the building with a toothbrush held in his teeth. He had not been willing, but the two men had not offered him any alternatives. His bruises throbbed, and his shoulders ached abominably from the strain of his bound arms.

"Like what?" asked the slender one. "You think this will come up in court or something?" He was the bully, George had discovered, when after some hours of jeering and shoving, they had finally helped him lower his trousers to use the toilet; the stocky one who looked meaner, with that scar across his chin, was only rough, not cruel. In the hours since, the slender man had taken every opportunity to cause pain in ways that would not show on an autopsy.

"Probably," said George. It was most inconvenient, having one's hands tied. He had not realized how

dependent he was on gesture, a habit learned from his
father. "My father gets most things to court, and he will
certainly sue someone when I'm dead." He was proud of
himself; he said that without a quaver.

The men laughed, and looked at each other. "Poor
Lord Thornbuckle," the slender one said. "I'm sure he'll
be worried."

George stared into space above them, the closest
he could come to the pose he usually achieved at
these moments. "Oh — I expect my father will represent
him, too. A class action suit, I imagine. Damages,
negligence —"

"Nonsense," the slender man said, and took a bite of
toast. Through it, he said, "And don't think you can scare
us with your father. I've known better lawyers than your
father, in my life."

George managed a casual chuckle. "I doubt that. You
don't even know who my father is."

"He's not in the same class with . . . oh . . . Kevil Starbridge Mahoney. Now is he?"

George laughed aloud, this time with genuine pleasure. "My dear lads, he *is* Kevil Starbridge Mahoney, and if
you know him, you know how surely he will pursue anyone who harms his family. I'm George Starbridge
Mahoney."

A pause, during which the slender man chewed steadily, and the stocky one cast nervous glances from George
to his companion. Finally the slender man swallowed, and
pushed himself away from the table. George felt his heart
begin to pound. "I don't believe you," the slender man
said. "And I don't like liars." He spoke quietly, but with a
studied viciousness that promised pain. George hoped his
face didn't show how frightened he was, a sudden burst of
fear that made him glad he was in the chair, and not trying to stand up.

"Now wait," the stocky man said. "We aren't supposed
to mark 'em up, remember?"

"I won't." The slender man smiled at George. "Now
. . . what did you say your name was?"

"George Starbridge Mahoney," George said. He was

going to be hurt anyway, just as the bully at school had twisted ears or arms no matter what you said, but one might as well tell the truth. And if they concentrated on asking him about himself and his past, perhaps they wouldn't ask where the others might be hiding on the island. He braced himself for whatever the slender man might do, but he did nothing. Then he slipped a hand into a pocket, and came out with a glove.

"You're sure of that," the man said, putting the glove on, and tapping its fingers on George's head, just hard enough to sting and demonstrate that the fingers were tipped with something hard. "Then I suppose you know all about Viilgas versus Robertson Colony."

"It's against ethics to talk about cases outside professional venues," George quoted. A gloved finger probed behind his ear, and he squirmed away. "But . . . sometimes at home, of course, it did happen." The whole case was over, appeals and all, long ago; what harm could it do to admit that? And, now that he thought about it, there'd been a threat against the family; his father had insisted that none of them go out without an escort. "I remember the threat," he said, as the finger jabbed behind his other ear. "But I was only eight."

"Ah. Which would make you now . . . ?"

"Twenty-three." Had it really been fifteen years? He would never forget the bomb in the vegetable shipment that had destroyed the old kitchen and scared the cook so that she went into early retirement. Of course she hadn't been in danger; none of the servants were even in the house for the duration of the threat. His father had insisted on that.

"And was the threat ever carried out?" The finger prodded beneath his chin, only slightly painful so far.

"A bomb in the vegetables," George said. "It blew all the tiles off the wall." It occurred to him that this man might have been involved, for all that he didn't look old enough. How old did you have to be to send bombs through the food system? Perhaps he'd started young. Perhaps he wanted revenge. . . .

"And what was the outcome — the real outcome?"

That, too, he would not forget, because he had been just old enough to recognize the discrepancy between the public news and what his father said to a colleague in the study. "How did you know about the real outcome?" he asked, and was rewarded by a sharp jab in the neck. It hurt more than he'd have expected.

"Answer the question," the slender man said.

"The Robertson Colony paid an indemnity," George said sulkily. "Enough to keep them working hard for the next fifty years, my father said, with no offplanet travel until it was paid. Slocumb and DeVries got mindwiped. Viilgas died, but they hushed it up, so his heirs could get the profits."

"Mmm. You do know more about it than the average young sprout. Tell me this, then: when your father, assuming he is your father, approaches the bench, what does he do with his hands?"

George's arms strained, trying to reproduce the familiar gesture; he could not say it without doing it. And was it the left hand or the right —? Finally he got it out. "His left hand's in his vest pocket, as if he felt a pain, and his right hand is holding down the tail of the frill."

The slender man turned away a moment, to look at his companion, then turned back to George. "So . . . if you're Mahoney's son, why should we care?"

"You said already — you know what he's like. He'll see money somewhere, and go after it."

"I'm not rich," the man said, and went back to the table. He served himself another plateful of eggs and sausage, and George's stomach growled again. "Why should I worry? He'll go after the deep pockets."

"He'll go after anyone involved," George said. Some tone in the other's voice let him think he'd made an impression. "Deep pockets hire their own lawyers. . . . Will they hire one for you?"

"Don't try to scare me," the slender man said. "It won't work." But he said it without full conviction, and he glanced at his stocky partner a moment too long. George knew what his father must feel, in the courtroom, when some change in his opponent's body or face let him know he had scored. He had always assumed law was dull — all those racks of data cubes, all those hours under the helmet — but he had never felt anything like the rush of excitement that now roared through him.

Then the slender man's eyes came back to his face, and the triumph chilled. . . . This man enjoyed pain too much to give it up, even for safety.

"If I escaped," George said, quickly, against the lust in those eyes, "I could call Lord Thornbuckle. You'd have time to get away, if you wanted, although I would testify that you helped me. The people who thought this up are the real criminals. My father would be on your side then."

"It's a thought," the stocky one said. "I'd rather have Mahoney on my side than cross-examining me."

"If it came to that —" The slender man stared at George in a way that made his insides twitch. "If we can't get it out of this 'un . . ."

George hoped his shrug was casual enough. "I don't know where the others are. You can get me to tell you where I last saw them, but if they were still there they'd have been captured. And I've been here at least a day —" He was sure it was two; why else would they have shoved him back into the closet for a time, and kept him below ground level except for that one foray of bathroom cleaning in the upstairs suites? He tried very hard not to think about the cave Bubbles had mentioned. He didn't know where it was; he was very glad he didn't know where it was . . . and they might not be in it anyway.

"More," said the stocky one, and hushed at the other's gesture.

"Time's going to run out," George said. "Someone will notice that we're gone, and start hunting for us. They can get Michaels to say we went to Whitewings, easily enough, but we aren't at Whitewings, and it'll be obvious we weren't. Besides, that flitter beacon still operates. If anyone checks the satellite logs —"

"He's right," the stocky one said, this time with complete conviction. "They should've pulled out as soon as the flitter crashed there. Someone was bound to come looking; it's a wonder they haven't before now. There wasn't really a chance of catching the passengers —"

"A sporting chance," the slender man said. "That's what our admiral likes, remember? The more chance, the more challenge. But if we can get out from under, while he takes the blame . . . then that's a chance I like." He gave George a smile that was anything but benign. "You do understand that we want to be free and clear?"

"Of course," George said. His father's son could not miss the undertones. But it was a chance. The slender man nodded at the stocky one.

"Go check upstairs," he said. "We don't want to run into the admiral, though he said he wouldn't be back until it was over, or we got something out of this one."

George had hoped for a glimpse of the outside world on his way to the communications setup, but the com shack at Bandon Lodge was in the basement. Two long light-gray corridors and a windowed door . . . he didn't even know if it was day or night outside. The slender men tapped the main board's controls; screens lit and the soft hum of the audio units sharpened.

"Satellite bounce to the Main House?" the slender man asked. "Or up to Home Station?"

"I'd try for Main House," George said. "That'd be quickest; there're people who know me."

"Here, then. You're ready."

George had a moment of panic when he couldn't remember the flitter's number, but it came to him. He pressed the button and spoke.

Heris, in the supply flitter with the medical squad only a few minutes from landing, recognized George's voice at once. So did Cecelia.

"Why, then there's nothing —" Cecelia said; Heris grabbed her arm and Cecelia hushed.

"— Captive and in danger," George was saying. "Armed men are hunting them, the condemned criminals and us both. The hunters have poisoned the water. We need assistance; I am at Bandon Lodge; the flitter crashed on . . . on the island north of Bandon. Be

prepared for —" His voice stopped, suddenly. Heris
found she was holding her breath, and let it out. How had
that young fool, of all of them, escaped to Bandon? When
he spoke again, his voice sounded different: still clearly
George, but a George who had changed in the space of a
few moments. "And please recognize the assistance of
two men formerly in the employ of the hunters . . . Svaa-
gart Iklind" — Heris stiffened. Another Iklind? A
relative? — "and Kursa Dahon. Without them, I could
not have made this call."

A moment's silence. Heris could not tell, over the
sound of the flitter itself and the stirs of those around her,
if the com stayed live or dropped the signal. She closed
her eyes. She wondered what the militia captain —
Sigind — would do. She knew what she would think of so
convenient a signal. Which, of course, Lepescu and his
cronies would have heard — if they hadn't arranged it.
Her mind began to replay the words she'd heard, even
the ones overlain by Cecelia's voice. "Hunters." What had
George meant by hunters, by "condemned criminals"?

Hunters . . . she had expected to find Lepescu hunting
some rare animal illegally, with a band of cronies; she had
expected him to be dangerous to innocent youngsters out
for a spree. But . . . criminals? People? She shivered suddenly, and Cecelia laid a hand on her arm.

"Heris? What is it?"

She could not see her own face, but Cecelia's reaction
told her what she must look like. The older woman drew
back, as if frightened. Heris saw others glance at her; one
stared.

"That —!" Words literally failed her; the worst words
she knew were not bad enough. She fought to breathe
past the knot in her throat, and finally said, "He *is* hunting
people. It's a manhunt; he's not hunting animals at all!"

"Who?"

"Lepescu." Her mind raced, fitting it all together. "He's
gotten convicts from somewhere —" Could they be
R.S.S. convicts? She shivered again, at the thought of
shipmates — not her crew, of course, but someone's shipmates — being hunted by Lepescu as if they were only

wild beasts. Though it was no better if he had raided
other prisons; at least military prisoners would know how
to defend themselves, might have a chance. She heard
others muttering, the same tones of shock and outrage
that she heard in her own voice. "It can't be!" someone
said, and someone else said, "Must be crazy — Lord
Thornbuckle'll tack his hide up in the kennels." She
would have said more, but the flitter swerved, and she
lurched against Cecelia's arm. She turned to peer out the
forward canopy. Ahead, the first attacking ships had
dropped to their final approach.

"I can't believe it," Cecelia said. "Hunting people — he
wouldn't do that. I know you hate what he did to you —
what he tried to do to your crew in battle — but he
couldn't be crazy enough to think he'd get away with . . .
with this. Not right under Bunny's nose."

Staring ahead, trying to see what she knew she could
not see — how the assault was going — she did her best
to answer. "He would think that made it better. More . . .
sporting. A risk for him, other than the risk from the people he hunted." Had he given them weapons? Had the
young people had weapons? "I told you, he once commented that he considered most hunting demeaning,
because it wasn't dangerous enough — that the proper
game for a real man was man."

Cecelia considered this silently as their flitter dropped
steadily towards the Bandon field, now occupied by the
two militia flitters. Heris appreciated the silence, but
knew it wouldn't last. She knew her employer too well. "I
don't think," Cecelia said at last, in the remote and formal
tone Heris had not heard for weeks, "that I want to know
this person. A disgrace to his uniform."

"Yes." Heris braced herself for landing. The militia
squads already down had vanished except for a single soul
waving them in. Then they were down safely, onto a quiet
field with no sign of conflict. Heris did not need the
squad leader's warning; she knew that silence was decep-
tive.

The medical squad went through a low-voiced routine
of some sort; she supposed they were reminding each

other what equipment was in whose pack or something. The air smelled fresh and wet, heavy with fragrances completely different from the woods and fields near the Main House. A comunit squawked, and Heris jumped. She didn't understand; she hated not knowing the local codes, not knowing anything, not having a place in this. The medical squad scrambled back into the supply flitter, and the squad leader said, "They've found the kid; he's hurt" just as the flitter lurched into the air again. Cecelia gasped; Heris grabbed her hand and squeezed until the older woman's color returned.

"George," she reminded her. "It has to be George they mean. He's the one on this island."

At the lodge proper, the supply flitter crowded the parking area; the medics poured out and Heris and Cecelia followed. No one stopped them; Heris saw no sign of trouble until they came to the room where George lay with a medic already working on him. One dead body sprawled across the control board of the communications shack; someone else gasped noisily from another clump of medics. Cecelia leaned against the wall, but pushed Heris forward. "Find out," she said. "For his father."

Heris had no interest in George's father. She picked her way across the floor, blood-spattered and already littered with the detritus of emergency medical care, to a point where she could see George without interfering. He was alive, breathing on his own, with one IV line in. He looked dirty, and pale, and both older and younger than she remembered him. She knew that look, from the youngsters she'd seen in her own ship's sickbay; being flat on their backs in clean pajamas made them look like children, but what they had been through aged them.

"What happened to him?" she asked quietly.

"Caught in crossfire," one of the medics said, without looking up. "Small caliber in the abdomen, missed the big stuff." Which didn't mean it felt good, or even that he would recover, just that he was likely to make it back to a hospital without dying on the way. Caught in crossfire . . . maybe, she thought, and maybe not. Perhaps someone wanted to get rid of witnesses. There must be more than one traitor in Bunny's pay. Heris watched the medics, who seemed to go about their business as quickly and competently as any she'd seen, then met George's gaze.

"Captain . . . where's Ronnie?"

"On the other island, I presume. Militia went there; he'll be fine." He might not be, but George needed to hear the best chance, not the worst.

"Don't talk," said a medic, and put a warning hand on George's shoulder. "You need to lie still."

"Cave," said George, struggling now, his eyes locked on Heris's. "Might be in the cave . . . Bubbles said . . ." and then a groan he tried to bite back, as the medics did something that hurt even more.

"I understand," Heris said, as much to reassure him as because she did. "Bubbles knew about a cave, and they might be in it. All of them?"

"No — Ronnie — hurt —"

The medic's angry face looked up at Heris. "He shouldn't talk; don't bother him. He's got other injuries, too." Heris glanced down and saw that they'd cut George's shirt away now, revealing the deep bruises along his side; broken ribs, maybe.

"He — shot me," George said, struggling against the medic's hands. "He —"

"It's all right, George," she said again. Time enough later to find out which *he* George meant. From the glazed look in his eyes, they had given him some drug, and he wouldn't be thinking clearly now. She hoped he had been right about the cave. "Everything will be fine." The medics lifted George onto a stretcher, and rolled him away. He lay quiet, eyes already closed. Her mind raced. A cave — a cave Bubbles knew about. Did Lepescu? Ronnie hurt, and not in the cave. What kind of hurt? If Ronnie was hurt, why hadn't he been captured? And again: did Lepescu know about the cave? Did the others being hunted? Did the militia captain know about that cave, and if so —

She went back to Cecelia, who looked less pale than when she'd come in. "George has a gunshot wound he should survive, assuming Bunny's got a good trauma center in his hospital."

"Very good," Cecelia said. "Riding horses at speed is hardly a safe hobby." Her voice was a shade brittle, but under control.

"He hasn't lost anything vital yet," Heris said. "Could you hear what he said?"

"No — not really."

"There's a cave on the island where the others are; Bubbles knew about it, and George thinks the others might be hiding in it." She waited to make sure Cecelia understood that. Then she went on, "Would the militia captain know about it? Did you ever hear of it?"

"A cave . . . no. I didn't. I don't know if anyone else would, besides the children who camped there. A big cave?"

"George didn't know, I suspect. But the militia captain needs to. If there's a cave, anyone might be in it: the youngsters, or the hunters, or whoever they're hunting." Heris looked around. Someone had dragged the corpse away, and the other wounded man, whoever he was, and one medic was stuffing medical trash in a sack. "We can't just comcall the militia commander; Lepescu would overhear it. If that's where the youngsters are hiding —"

"We'll go tell him," Cecelia said, and pushed away from the wall.

"Yes, but —" Heris stifled her doubts. They'd been told to stay here, safely out of trouble, and she'd agreed to that. She looked around for the person in charge.

The person in charge, busily arranging transport to a hospital for George and the other wounded man, was in no mood to listen. Heris had no idea what the insignia on his collar meant but he was acting like a harried sergeant.

"The captain said you were to stay here," he said. "And here you'll stay. You don't even know where this cave is, or if the kids are in it, or if anyone else knows about it."

"That's why —" Heris began, but he flapped a hand at her.

"The captain's got good maps of the island; if there's a cave worth worrying about, he'll know. He's got a bloody mess over there —" Then the man shut his mouth and glared at her, as if she had extracted that information

unfairly. "Just because you used to be a spaceship commander doesn't give you the right to throw your weight
around here. Captain Sigind said to keep you safe here,
and that's exactly what I'll do. Now if you'll get out of my
way so I can do my job —"

Heris swallowed more years of experience than this
person had age, and said, "Excuse me," very quietly. No
use arguing with this sort; she had seen them before. The
problem now was working around him, and that was most
easily done out of his sight.

✧ Chapter Eighteen

It had amused the prince to come hunting with the older men, political cronies of his father. He knew they invited him to curry favor, but still — it was thrilling. Illegal, but thrilling. He had been on this planet before, of course, at the invitation of Lord Thornbuckle. Everyone who was anyone had, at one time or another, spent interminable hours riding large stinking vicious beasts chasing after small stinking vicious beasts. Silly work, on the whole, and he had heard others — including this group — snicker about it privately. Lord Thornbuckle didn't care; he could afford to not care.

But this — this was different. What can be the thrill of chasing a harmless small creature bioengineered to be chased and killed? So the admiral had said, and so he had agreed. Other game — even other animals, large and dangerous in themselves — offer more sporting chances. No, my boy, the admiral had said (he had hated the admiral's arm on his shoulder, but he knew he must endure it), there's only one game worth the trouble. Show your stuff, prove yourself, and in the process finish off some useless criminals. And besides, after that . . . we'll have a party. With lots of girls.

He hadn't expected to feel queasy about it. He had felt queasy when he read the reports on the prison colonies, things his tutor had thought he ought to know. That was cruelty, if you liked, confining someone to dirty, dangerous work and mean, ugly surroundings, for years on end. Killing someone cleanly with a bullet in the head was merciful by comparison. He had agreed, in more than one not-so-casual conversation, that this was so; imagining himself a prisoner, he would rather have died in the open like that than slowly of boredom and overwork. And hence, the invitation to this hunt, which had thrilled him as much with its illicit nature as with its prestige. He was born to prestige; he didn't need it . . . but he found himself craving the respect of Admiral Lepescu and Senator-at-Large Bodin.

Still, the first one he killed himself — that had startled him with his own reaction to it, the nausea and guilt, the feeling of shame for being ashamed, the reluctance of his fingers to touch the tattooed ear which he must hack off and turn in to get credit for his trophy. He had done it, but he had made a private pact with himself to be content with one. That was surely enough to prove his ability, to prove he wasn't just a spoiled wastrel who got into quarrels over opera singers (his father's words).

So after that first kill, he found reasons to hang around Bandon lodge the rest of that day. It was easy to play cards too late, drink too much, and sleep heavily when someone knocked on his door. He roused late on the morning after his "blood party" as they called it . . . and found the lodge quiet and nearly empty. Fine with him; his head ached and the ear, proof of his trophy, looked disgusting in its jar of preservative. He stared at it morosely and rang for medicine and breakfast. After that he went back to bed and slept heavily, having promised himself he would find some way of avoiding more hunting.

But now something had gone wrong. He didn't know what. Lepescu had yanked him out of bed in late afternoon, and insisted that he had to come hunt again, right now, whether he wanted to or not. The habit of obedience to older men got him into the flitter before he could organize his mind to protest, and then it was too late. They were on the island, and Lepescu was telling him where to go and what to do in the rough voice he probably used on his subordinates in the Regular Fleet. Before he could argue, Lepescu was gone.

The prince stumbled around that night, angry and tired, and found nothing but mudholes in the swamp. He measured his length in one, and only his custom hunting suit kept him dry. He heard some shots in the distance, but nothing close enough to startle him. At dawn, Lepescu reappeared, and handed him a mealpack. "Eat this here," he said. "We have to get them all, fast. None of us are going back until we do."

"Why?" the prince asked. The mealpack had a picture of helicberry tarts on it, and he hated helicberries. He wanted puffcakes with sarmony honey, fat sausages, a bone-melon.

"Just do it," Lepescu said. He strode off, looking more military, in the dangerous sense, than the prince had seen before. And the prince, tired and hungry, sat down and ate his excellent breakfast. He did not follow Lepescu afterwards; he did not patrol his alloted section of island. It had ceased to be fun, or exciting, or anything but a deadly bore, and he would insist on returning to his comfortable bed on Bandon as soon as someone else showed up. Long after noon, someone else appeared — one of the servants with vaguely military bearing — and brought him two more mealpacks, coldpacks of water, and warnings. He was to stay on the island; he was not to drink any local water; he was not to call anyone on his comunit; he was to shoot anything that didn't identify itself instantly.

The prince was more than somewhat annoyed. One did not do this to princes. Even powerful political figures — even admirals — did not do this to princes. It was supposed to have been an adventure, with girls to follow, and the chance to reminisce for years to come, and the camaraderie of men who had proved themselves real men. It was not an adventure anymore, and no one had said anything about the promised girls for days. He said nothing to the servant, who strode away almost as purposefully as Lepescu, and ate his excellent lunch, then his excellent supper, and finally lay down where he was (protected by his excellent weatherpack) to sleep as long as he liked. If the criminals got him, so much the better: Lepescu would find his head in a noose.

He woke to hard rain drumming on the shelter and the smell of wet leaves. Good. No one would be skulking around in *this*, and Lepescu would have to let him sleep.

Lightning crackled, thunder boomed, but the prince slept on, unconcerned.

The Admiral Lepescu who woke him in the dark dripping aftermath of the storm was someone he had never met. He could now credit the more vivid rumors about the admiral's career, faced with that cold, angry countenance, those still gray eyes with so much hunger in them. The tongue-lashing he got for not having followed orders actually frightened him; the scorn in Lepescu's face shamed him all over again. He wanted to please this man, and only the habits drilled into him from early childhood kept him from cringing apology.

"I don't understand the problem," he said stiffly, when Lepescu paused in his tirade. "These are just criminals. . . ."

"You don't have to understand," the admiral said. "You have to obey." Then, as if suddenly remembering who the prince was, he added, "Your highness."

"But what's the hurry?" the prince asked. "You said we'd be here four or five weeks, and it's only been —"

"Someone knows about the hunt," the admiral said. "You wouldn't want to be compromised. . . . You know what this could do to your future career. And we can't get them all without your help before we're discovered. Someone is bound to recognize Ser Smith."

"But surely —" the prince began, but the expression on Lepescu's face stopped him. "All right," he said, trying to sound decisive rather than scared. "I'll be glad to help out." The moment it was out of his mouth, he realized how silly that sounded; he could feel his ears burn. He still didn't understand why they couldn't just flitter back to Bandon, take the shuttle up to the Station, and find some compliant girls there, but he knew he couldn't ask Lepescu. Not now.

Morning had brought an end to the rain, though clouds still clung to the ridge and mist rose from the sodden ground to meet them. Somewhere on the other side of the ridge, the sun might be spearing through that mist, but not here. The prince sighed, punched the button on his breakfast mealpack, and waited for it to heat. He would get his boots muddy again, and they would drag at his feet. . . . He hated mud. This whole expedition looked more and more like a mistake, rather than high adventure. The invitation had specified that they would be here in the dry season, that it could not possibly be compromised . . . and now he was going to be wet, muddy, and in trouble with his father. Not so much for blowing away a few criminals (or rather, one criminal) as for getting caught doing it.

Nonetheless, he set out to do what he was told, and worked his way up the west side of the island. He left his comunit off; he didn't want to be distracted by whatever might come over it. Twice, he saw something move that wasn't ID'd as hunter, and shot at it. Once, whoever it was shot back. He found two bodies, both criminals, with the ears clipped. Lepescu's plan didn't make sense to him — herding the criminals into the interior ridge and its rough terrain would make a final cleanup harder — but he went along. He couldn't think of anything else to do. He followed the stream uphill because it was easier to walk that way.

The clatter of rocks falling echoed through the cave; Bubbles was sure it was loud enough to be heard outside. Had the hunters found another entrance? Was Petris trying to find them?

"We have to move," she said to Raffa. "We might find a better place to hide, and here we're trapped."

"Good idea," Raffa said. "We'll have to take the candles, and mark our way —"

"We can't mark it; someone could follow."

"How could they tell how long ago the marks were made? We can't just go into the cave and not know how to get out —"

"Right." Bubbles picked up her pack, and stuffed into it everything of Kev's that would fit; Raffa would have to carry the rest. The night goggles gave her a blurry picture of the inside of the cave, and she could see a ledge extending along the left wall. Black water lay still and smooth at its edge. She fumbled at the rifle she'd taken, making sure it had a round in the chamber, and slung it on her shoulder. This is an adventure, she told herself. Just do it like you used to, and it will come out all right.

Raffa followed her lead; Bubbles shuffled along wishing she dared light a candle as her vision dimmed. Even with the goggles, she could see very little by the time she came to the first angle of stone that blocked the entrance. She ducked around it, and leaned against the damp wall. Ahead, all was black, utterly black. Water dripped into the central pool in an unpredictable rhythm. Somewhere in the distance, another rock fell. Raffa touched her arm, and she jumped.

"I think it's safe to light the candles now," Raffa said. "We're out of sight of the entrance."

"But they could reflect on the water," Bubbles said. "And if we're the light source, then anyone hiding back here would see us first."

"Yes, but if we don't have a light, we'll step off a ledge somewhere — we can't just feel our way along."

"I know." She took a long breath. The darkness pressed on her eyes, her face; she could almost feel furry hands clasping her. Ridiculous. She'd never been afraid of the dark before. But then she'd never been in this cave before, either. She pushed the goggles up, so that the sudden flare wouldn't blind her, and scraped the lighter until a spark caught the candle. Dim yellow light flickered around them. She put the candle into its lantern, and four beams made clear the distinction between light and shadow. Raffa's face, underlit, looked strange and dangerous and oddly exciting. Bubbles pushed that thought away — she had no time for anything but the present crisis. She looked around. They had turned a corner into a rough corridor, low, narrow, and twisting. On the opposite wall, a blurred mark showed, one of Kell's she had no doubt. It looked like a cartoon sailboat; she had no idea why. She moved the lantern about, looking on all the rock surfaces nearby. Another mark, this one somewhat sresembling a tree, near what might be a niche or another corridor, a black gash in the rock. The central cavern's water extended into all the dark entrances she could see, as if all drained into or from it.

"Boat equals water," Bubbles said finally. "Water flows downhill, meets the sea —"

"A way out?" asked Raffa.

"We know where the trees are," Bubbles said. "On top of this cave, and full of hunters." She turned to continue downward, the way she hoped the boat indicated.

A clatter of rock, clearer now, from the tree-marked gash, and then a splash. And a scream.

"The light!" Raffa said, but Bubbles had snuffed it already. In the darkness, they clung together again, hearts pounding. Bubbles saw red and yellow blotches floating on the darkness, and told herself they were the after-image of the candle. Irregular splashes continued, coming nearer; Bubbles thought she could hear rough breathing, something that might be boots scraping on stone. She felt Raffa's warm breath tickling her ear, and Raffa said, "He must have seen the light somehow."

They must not move. In the dark, they would make the kind of noise he was making; he would surely hear them; he would have one of the weapons with night-sensing equipment. Bubbles realized she'd left the night-vision goggles hanging around her neck while carrying the candle lantern, and pushed them into place, but there was no ambient light to amplify. Thick darkness pressed in on her again. I hate caves, she thought.

"I *hate* caves!" came a male voice from somewhere in the echoing distance, to the accompaniment of a clatter and splash.

She was never sure which word, which intonation, made recognition sure.

"Ronnie!" said Raffa, not quite aloud. "It's Ronnie!"

Bubbles concentrated on relighting the candle in its lantern.

He looked like someone who had been at the tail end of a hunt on a muddy day, Bubbles thought. Wet, his clothes streaked heavily with clay, his face haggard with exhaustion, he stared at them, swaying slightly, in the feeble light of the candle lantern.

"You're not hunters," he said hoarsely. Stupidly.

"Raffa . . . Bubbles," said Raffa, her voice warming to a gentle hum that left Bubbles in no doubt of *her* feelings. "Don't you remember?" She had rushed to him; she hovered now as though he were a fragile ornament she might break with her gaze.

"Yes . . ." His voice trailed away; he stood there, his hands trembling, and seemed to be near collapse. One of his eyes had a dark stain around it. Bubbles saw raw scratches and scrapes on his hands and face.

"You need to be dry, and you need food," Bubbles said. "Come on, Raffa — get him to dry ground." He stood in ankle-deep water, with a dry ledge not a stride away — but of course he'd been in the dark the whole time.

It was harder than she had imagined to dry a large, very wet and dirty young man in a damp cave. Once out of the water, he dripped water and mud onto the ledge; she had no dry clothes for him, and nothing to dry him with. Food — the food she had brought along from the first cache — he held in his hand as if he couldn't remember its purpose.

Finally she and Raffa had to undress him, struggling with the wet fasteners, the uncooperative cloth, and use every scrap of spare clothes to dry him. His skin was cold, as disgusting to touch as a meat from a cold locker. He sat huddled, shivering, hardly seeming aware of them. Bubbles heated the food bar over the candle lantern until it sizzled and gave off an oily, heavy smell, then pinched off a bit with her fingers.

"Here," she said firmly. "Eat this." His mouth gaped; she pushed the food in. His jaw moved a little, and he swallowed.

"I'll do that," Raffa said. "You keep watch." She pulled off her shirt and laid it around Ronnie's shoulders. He didn't even glance at her slender nakedness; Bubbles looked away as she stood up.

Keep watch. Fine idea, but how? They needed the candle lantern; it made them visible. They had to talk; it made them audible. Bubbles moved back to the margin of the main cavern, and peeked around. She could just see, with her goggles on, the smudge of light from the entrance, across the water.

An impossible situation. And yet, in the near-silence, with the murmur of Raffa's voice coaxing Ronnie to eat, with the random tinkle and splash of water drops into the lake, in the almost-darkness, she felt secure. Cupped in some great hand, a feeling she remembered from those camping trips, when she had felt the land under her as a benign presence. Silly, her schoolmates would have said. She had said it herself, of younger girls' illusions.

Here she felt like herself again. Her real self. Not the mosaic of consensus she was in public, in society. Here she felt connected to the little girl who learned to swim in the waves with the cetes, who learned to scramble up steep rocks, dig holes. The little girl who had been called Bubbles, and had thought of herself as a great hero out of some tale. . . . She felt her face shifting to a grin, felt the pressure of the goggles change with that grin. Such a tomboy, her mother had said . . . her brothers had said. But tomboys grow up.

Not always, she thought. At least not if it meant changing completely. Ronnie's aunt hadn't.

"Bubbles — he's better. Come —"

It had been long enough that she was stiff, but she thought at once that Raffa had forgotten to use her new name, the name she now felt was really hers. This was no time to worry about that — but she wouldn't forget. She shook herself and retreated to the lantern light, pushing the goggles down. Raffa nestled close to Ronnie; Bubbles thought to herself that he was undoubtedly warm on that side, and suspected that Raffa had done more than lean against him. Ronnie had expression on his face now: misery and worry.

"They got George," he said. "He was alive then, but —"

"How?"

"They poisoned the water — I don't suppose you know —"

"Yes," Bubbles said. "We did. That's how we found the cave, going upstream to look for safe water." Ronnie's voice was still unsteady; she didn't know if they should press him to talk. Whatever had happened to George must be over now. But he pushed aside Raffa's arm, and made himself explain what had happened. . . . She wasn't at all sure he had it straight. How many times had he lost consciousness or fallen asleep? Where had they been, exactly? He had no idea where he had fallen into the cave, except "upstream" from where he'd left George.

"Never mind," Raffa was saying, trying to soothe him. "You couldn't help it, and it'll be all right."

It wouldn't, of course. If Raffa thought about it, she'd know. Ronnie surely knew, though he might let himself be comforted by Raffa. Certainly she, Bubbles, knew that everything would not be all right. The hunters might keep George alive, trying to catch the rest, but too many had died already. Too much had happened. However this turned out, things would not be all right, not the way they had been before.

"We have to help George," Ronnie said, more loudly. He sounded hoarse, as if he were catching cold. "We have to get out of this cave." He tried to stand up, and Raffa pulled him back down.

"Not until the hunters give up," Bubbles said. She knew they wouldn't, but she didn't want Ronnie yelling and charging around making it obvious where they were.

"They probably took him to Bandon," Raffa said. "If they didn't kill him right away." From her tone, she could no more imagine George dead on the ground than Bubbles could. George would be at Bandon, tied up like someone from an adventure cube, to be rescued later and reunited with his friends. In the cube, she would be the designated girlfriend, the blonde who gave him a passionate kiss as the end music came up.

The problem was that she didn't want George to die, but she didn't want to be the designated blonde, either. She was Brun, not Bubbles, and so far Brun wasn't a designated anything. She put that thought aside to think about later, and with a glance at Raffa set to work to cheer Ronnie up and keep him from doing something rash.

Muddy footprints led to a sheer cliff with water seeping

out from under a thick mat of ferns. The prince felt safe, enclosed by the rocky, fern-covered walls, although he realized it could be a trap, too. Someone overhead who happened to see him could shoot him easily. He peered up into the overlapping layers of green, and shivered. He was tired, hungry, and confused. What could have happened? Where were the promised girls?

Wet leaves dripped on his head and neck. It made him feel stupid, as well as tired. In the solitude and silence, he had time to track the feeling back and analyze it. Long ago — it seemed long, anyway — he had been at school with boys who had known each other for years while he'd been isolated at court. Someone had thought it would be fun to play a joke on the prince, to make him late for roll-call and incidentally make him look stupid. Ethar Krinesl, that had been. He had been lured from his bed on a dark, rainy night by the promise of a rendezvous with girls from the neighboring school. . . . He had trekked across the campus to crouch in a muddy ditch, while (he learned later) the other boys had sewn his clothes together so that he couldn't possibly dress in the morning. And the shadowy figure that had come in the dark, and with giggles had agreed to kiss him, had been Ethar's older brother Potim. Ethar had had the cube recorder.

Painful as the memory was, it made him feel better. Now he understood what was going on. All the other men were older, and they formed a tight clique. This was a joke; they were testing him. After a time, when they thought he had been sufficiently humiliated, they would come out and take him into the group, as Ethar and his crowd had done. It was annoying, but understandable. The prince was proud of having figured it out, and felt a little superior to the childishness of the older men. They should have realized he would not panic; he had already killed someone and proved himself. They would have swept the criminals from in front of him; they weren't really risking his death. Perhaps the criminals had never been armed with anything lethal. Not very sporting, perhaps, but prudent.

The girl's voice completed his understanding. Soft,

hardly audible, it could still be nothing but a girl — a girl some distance away chuckling softly at something. That had to mean the original promise held; girls *were* part of the entertainment here. He looked around carefully. She might be hiding anywhere.

The voice came again, from the rock wall in front of him. He stared, then saw that two big, cleated bootprints lay half under the ferns. He felt himself tingling with excitement. A cave. It must be a cave, full of the girls he'd been promised, hidden away in safety until the dangerous part of the hunt was over. And he'd found them without being shown — perhaps before the other hunters, even. Carefully, he stooped and lifted the mat of ferns, peering into the darkness beyond. Water lapped at his boots; he could see that he stood on the edge of a large pool. He pulled his night goggles out of his pocket and put them on, squinting until he got his head inside where it was darker. A large domed chamber, with smudged reflections off the surface of water as far as he could see. But clearly someone was inside. He smelled cooking food, and again he heard what had to be human voices, distorted by the shape of the cave and the water.

Had they marooned the girls in a lake? No, all that rain had probably made the water rise. They were somewhere inside, dry and safe. He imagined nooks and crannies cushioned with colorful pillows and rugs, rock-walled chambers where naked nymphs bathed in clear subterranean pools or streams. In all likelihood there was a way in that wasn't very deep. With his goggles on, he should be able to find his way safely around — ankle-deep water wouldn't bother him, not in his boots.

Now that the hunt was over, or mostly over, he saw no reason to crawl under the hanging mat of ferns; he was dirty enough already. He kicked at it until most of it fell, revealing a hole large enough to get through if he stooped. That let more light into the entrance; even without goggles he could now see the shape of the first chamber . . . and hear more clearly the distorted murmur of girls' voices. The other hunters would be surprised, he thought, to discover he had found the place himself, ahead of whatever time they planned to start the party. He might even be the first; he could see, now, that the bootprints he'd noticed stopped there, and backed out again. Of course anyone coming after him would know someone had gone in, but he wasn't hiding from anyone — certainly not unarmed criminals.

The light coming from behind him made it hard to see, even with the goggles. Some things were too bright, and others hazed into murky reflections. He had to feel his way along the edge of the cave, so he chose to move to his left, where his right arm was still free to hold his weapon. Not that he'd need it, he was sure. The girls might be startled, but he had the patch that identified him as a hunter, and afterwards . . . He stumbled over something and bit back a curse. It would be much more fun to sneak up on them. The smell of cooked food grew stronger.

The first flicker of light blazed into his vision, and he pulled the goggles off, blinking. Now he could see nothing. Standing still, silent, he heard murmuring voices that might have been nothing more than a trickling stream — but not that smell. After a few moments, his eyes adjusted, and he saw a faint sparkle ahead, where some light source reflected from moving water. He crept through the darkness, smugly certain of what he would find. The light strengthened; he felt his way around a corner of the rock, and saw them at last.

His first thought was disappointment; he wasn't the first to find the girls after all. The dark-haired girl had her arm around the lucky first-comer; the prince wondered why he'd preferred her to the more curvaceous blonde. His second thought stumbled over the first in a wave of righteous rage. Ronnie!

"You unspeakable cad!" he said. "What are you . . ." His voice trailed away as he realized that the two black circles were the bores of hunting rifles like his own. Both girls, blonde and dark, held them steadily. "You're hunters, too?" he asked, with a half-nervous laugh.

Ronnie's head came around, and he saw the dark stain of a black eye and bruised face. "My sainted aunt,"

Ronnie said, in a voice that didn't sound much like his own. "It's the prince."

"Gerel?" the blonde girl asked. She peered at him, but the rifle did not waver. Her nod, too, came without a move in the weapon's aim. "It is. And you know what? He's not on the list either."

The prince took a deep breath. Whatever was going on here, it had to be irregular. "I demand to know what you're doing here," he said firmly. "I am here at the invitation of —" But that, he suddenly realized, he couldn't finish. Ronnie might mention it; it could be embarrassing. He interrupted himself with an alternate line of reasoning. "You might introduce me to your — uh — young women."

Ronnie gave a harsh bark that might have been intended for laughter but sounded more like pain, and the dark young woman touched him with her shoulder, not removing her hand from her rifle. The blonde one laughed louder.

"Introduce me? Heavens, Gerel, you've been dancing with me since boarding school." He couldn't think of anyone like this at any dance he'd been to. She was blonde, yes, but hardly stylish in rumpled pants and shirt, with her hair yanked back behind her ears. She looked older by five or ten years than he was, someone serious and even dangerous. "Bubbles," she said finally. "Lord Thornbuckle's daughter — surely you remember now."

Bubbles. Ronnie. None of it made sense. If this was Bubbles — and he supposed it was, though he did not recognize her in these clothes, with her hair pulled back — then she could not be one of the girls Lepescu meant. Those girls would be . . . another kind of girl, from another kind of family. Not Bubbles the wild sister of Buttons, and Ronnie the wild son of a cabinet minister, and . . ."Raffaele?" he asked uncertainly.

"Of course," she said. It sounded like her voice. The prince swallowed, and wished very much to sit down.

"I don't understand," he said.

"You're wearing an ID tag," Bubbles said. "What is it?"
He had forgotten the bright-colored tag on his collar,

which transmitted a signal to other hunters. "This? It identifies me to other hunters."

"Other . . . hunters." That was Raffaele again. She sounded grim, nothing like the witty girl with the silvery laugh he remembered from the parties last season. "You'd better put your rifle down," she said, using neither name nor title. That made him nervous, and he couldn't think why.

"But if you're one of us . . ." That didn't make sense either. He knew the others; they had all been at the lodge. No women, certainly not these girls, and no Ronnie. He turned to Ronnie. "I thought you'd been shipped off somewhere for punishment."

"Put your rifle down," Bubbles said. When he looked at her, he felt almost assaulted by the anger that radiated from her. "Now," she said, and he felt his arm moving before he thought about it.

"But this is ridiculous," he said, not quite obeying. "I'm the prince. You're friends. Why should I —"

"Because I have the drop on you," Raffaele said. "And so does Bubbles. And you're standing there with the same ID patch as men who tried to kill us."

"Kill *you*? Why?"

"Drop it!" Bubbles yelled suddenly. Her voice rang in the cave, echoing off odd corners and coming back as a confused rumble. Rocks clattered somewhere, as if her voice alone had riven the stone. His hand was empty; he could hear the afterimage of the rifle's thud on the damp floor of the cave. "You idiot, Gerel," she said more quietly. "And I'll bet you've led the rest of them straight here, too."

✧ Chapter Nineteen

Heris seethed inwardly. Of course she had no right of command, but it should have been obvious that knowing where the young people might be was important enough. She led Cecelia outside the room. There had to be some way — perhaps she could get hold of a flitter —

"Excuse me, ma'am." A young, earnest-faced militiaman had followed them out. Heris nodded at him.

"Yes?" she said through gritted teeth.

"You said you might know where the young miss is?"

It took her a moment to untangle that: young miss? Bubbles, of course. "I'm not sure," she said. "Why?"

"I'd take you over there to tell the captain," the man said. "If you wanted. . . ."

Of course that's what she wanted, but why was he being so helpful? "What about your boss?" she asked. He reddened and grinned.

"Well, ma'am . . . that Bortu, he just got promoted, you know. Never been on anything like this before."

That could indeed explain it. On the other hand . . . Heris looked at Cecelia. "What about it? This — what's your name?"

"Dussahral, ma'am."

"This man says he'll fly us over to meet the captain — want to come along?"

"Of course," Cecelia said, looking determined.

"Thanks," Heris said, smiling at him. "Go find us a flitter — we'll need to stop into the . . ." She nodded at a door down the hall.

"Don't be long," he said. "In case that Bortu figures it out."

"Just a moment, promise." Heris watched him go, then led Cecelia to the bathroom.

"What's that about? I don't need to —"

"Yes, you do. We need a couple of minutes to make plans, and you never go into combat with a full bladder."

"We're not going into combat; we're just going over to tell the militia captain where to look for Ronnie."

Heris caught her employer by a shoulder and turned her around. "Listen. We're going into an unsecured zone where people are shooting at each other — possibly three different sets of people *all* shooting at each other — and if you can think of a better definition of combat, tell me when we're safely back in our hot tubs. Now. I am taking a very dangerous chance here, because there's no reason to trust Dussahral —"

"But he wants to help us."

"So he said. Didn't it occur to you that Lepescu might want to know about that cave just as badly as the captain? And if he had an agent in this batch of militia, that person would be eager to tell him?"

Cecelia frowned. "Why would he be stupid enough to stick with what is obviously a losing side? Any smart agent would clam up and wait to see what happens."

"Not all agents are smart. And Dussahral may be innocent and completely loyal to Bunny. But —" Heris ducked into a cubicle and continued talking through the closed door. "But if he's not, we need a plan. We take our weapons. He will think I'm the dangerous one; I'll let him jump me, and you shoot him if he does."

Cecelia, too, had gone into a cubicle. Heris heard the seat squeak. "Me? I've never shot anyone. Just game —"

"New experiences keep you young. You have to; he won't expect it from you. Just have a round in the chamber, in case, and don't shoot me by mistake." Heris came out and washed her hands. Cecelia, when she emerged, had a strange expression on her face.

"You're trusting me with your life."

Heris shrugged. "You trust me with yours in the ship. Besides, what I'm really doing is taking you into danger. You could get killed too. Remember that, when you're tempted to wonder if you really should shoot." Then she grinned at the older woman. "Now — cheer up. I'm wearing body armor under my clothes; he doesn't know that, and it will help. And don't stare at him as if you suspect him. He's thinking of you as a helpless old woman in a flutter about her nephew."

Cecelia snorted, and the color came back to her cheeks. "I can see," she said, "how you commanded a ship." They walked out side by side, as if they had nothing better to do than sightsee, and the guards now posted in the corridors smiled and nodded at them.

Dussahral, when they reached the parking area, had one of the flitters rolled out where the supply flitter had been. He looked tense and excited, but that was reasonable. Heris smiled, and accepted his hand up into the flitter.

"Lady Cecelia should be in back," she said. "In case of stray rounds." He nodded, and looked at Heris.

"You want to copilot?" There wasn't much copiloting to be done in a flitter, but Heris nodded.

"I'll keep a lookout," she said. "Maybe I can spot the captain." Little chance of that, but he relaxed a bit, as if this evidence of her inexperience in ground operations eased his mind.

The hop across to the other island took only minutes; it looked short enough to swim. Heris noted its narrow spine, higher than Bandon's low rounded hills, the beach along the south and east — and two flitters parked at the south end. A squad of militia there worked on something — she could see what looked like bodies. She hoped Cecelia hadn't spotted them.

"Is that the captain's flitter?" she asked Dussahral, who shook his head. "Should we land there?"

"No . . . that's the number two . . . captain must've gone somewhere else. I'll fly up along the beach." They flew north slowly; Heris tried to see into the thick canopy with no success. Then Dussahral touched her arm and pointed, and Heris saw a flitter sitting lopsided on the beach. Not the command flitter: it had the serial number they'd been told was on the one Bubbles checked out.

Heris saw the gaping hole along one flank, something else she hoped Cecelia missed. The flitter hadn't landed, or simply crashed — someone had shot it down. She felt cold.

Dussahral swung the flitter inland, and they rose over the central rocky spine, where tufts and wisps of fog still swirled. Down the other side — and the man waved suddenly. "There — I see something — I'll put us down in that clearing."

That clearing, to Heris, looked entirely too convenient a place for a trap, but she said nothing. She had seen nothing of the captain's flitter, either. But if there were a cave, surely it had to be in the hills somewhere.

Dussahral made a steep approach, dropping the flitter so rapidly that Heris caught her breath. They landed hard; she felt the jolt out the top of her head . . . and let herself act more stunned than she was. Dussahral, she saw through nearly closed eyes, changed the setting of the flitter's comunit and pushed the transmission switch all the way over. With his other hand, he had shoved the canopy back.

"Come on," he urged. "I'm sure I saw the captain's signal over there —" A wave toward the higher ground. "I'll help you. Do you have any idea where the cave might be?" All this in a voice easily loud enough to carry over the comunit.

Heris pushed away his hand, but slowly, as if she almost needed it, and clambered out, intentionally clumsy. She held her rifle loosely. Dussahral waited for Cecelia to clamber out — Heris hoped the jolting landing hadn't jarred Cecelia's reflexes. She also hoped Dussahral was as stupid as he seemed so far. They could get rid of him quickly, and still have a chance to block Lepescu, now that the cave was no longer a secret.

Dussahral led them into the forest, away from the flitter. Upslope, Heris noted, across a streambed with a trickle of water in it. Heris wished she dared jump him now, but there was a chance he was leading her to Lepescu — perhaps he had a real signal to home on — and in that case it would be stupid to strike too soon. He

halted soon enough, and pointed to a rocky bluff. "There
— the captain's probably up there. I'll go back and keep
an eye on the flitter."

"I can't see," Heris said, trying to sound querulous. She
felt querulous; it had just occurred to her that he might
have wanted an excuse to bring the flitter for Lepescu's
escape. Even now the admiral might be flying away to
safety, however temporary. "Where?" She pushed past
him, giving him every chance. His sudden grasp on her
arm was vindication, even as the feel of his weapon prodding her side made her face the next likely outcome. She
wondered if her armor would hold against a point-blank
shot, but he slid the muzzle of the weapon up, as if he
knew she wore it. Of course — he had seen Lady
Cecelia's, and guessed that she had armor too. Her mind
insisted on showing her, in vivid detail, what would happen if he fired now, with the muzzle where it was at the
back of her neck.

"Stop here, ladies," he said, this time in a voice unlike
the deferential, pleasant tone he'd used so far. "I think
Admiral Lepescu might have something to say to Captain
Serrano."

Cecelia let out a terrified squeak, and Heris's heart
sank. So much for civilians. Dussahral smirked.

"You're not going to give me any trouble, are you?" he
asked. "I know you ladies don't go around with loaded
weapons, so don't try to pretend you'll shoot me."

"I won't," said Cecelia, eyes wide. "I — I — don't hurt
her."

"Drop the gun," Dussahral said. Heris wondered
whether she could reach her bootknife and decided she
couldn't. Cecelia stood there, gawky and gray-haired,
clinging to the rifle as if it were a child. She probably
hadn't chambered a round, Heris thought, so it wasn't
really dangerous to be standing here with the bore pointing at her. . . . It shifted a little, and Dussahral sighed. She
could feel his disgust; she felt it herself. "Listen, lady," the
man said, "you can't shoot me with an unloaded rifle, and
I'm not going to be fooled. Either drop it, now, or I'll
shoot you, not just your friend." Cecelia said nothing, and

looked as if she couldn't; Heris had never seen a better picture of frozen panic. Dussahral shifted his weight; Heris tried to shift her own to take advantage, but his blow to her head came too fast. She didn't quite lose consciousness, but she stumbled, unable to move fast when he let go of her and swung his weapon toward Cecelia.

Then the crack of Cecelia's rifle and the ugly sound of a round hitting bone came together, and Dussahral was flung away from her. Heris stared. Her employer stared back. "You said to pick the right moment," Cecelia said. Bright color patched her cheeks. "I think I did." She held the rifle steady, as if she were perfectly calm.

"Damn." Heris felt her head. It hurt, but she was alive, not a scratch, and Dussahral lay dead, the back of his skull and its contents splattered for a meter or more on the forest floor. "Yes — you did. But I thought for a moment —"

"I wanted him away from you — at least his weapon." Cecelia shivered suddenly. "I never — did that before. Not a person."

"You did it perfectly." Heris picked up her own rifle, and walked back to Cecelia. "You saved my life, is what you did." It occurred to her now just how stupid it had been to give Dussahral a chance. If she made the same mistake with Lepescu . . . well, she wouldn't.

"That's what I meant to do — but he's so . . . so ugly."

"They are." Heris turned Cecelia away from it, but Cecelia twisted back.

"No. If I do it, I should see what I did." She walked deliberately up to the body; already a few tiny flies buzzed near it. "So little time between life and death. We think we have years . . ." Heris did not tell her how long it often took men to die of wounds. Not now. Now they had other prey.

"It's amazing," Cecelia went on, "how young men like this think we old people are frail, emotional, likely to fall apart at any emergency." When her eyes met Heris's, it gave Heris a chill; they were the cold gray of frozen oysters. "Because of course," Cecelia continued, "we've done everything they imagine they might do. One time or another."

❖   ❖   ❖

"But that's crazy," the prince said. He had said it before, and Ronnie thought he would go on saying it until he died. "No one would kill *you* — not like this. Let me call Admiral Lepescu and get you back to civilization." After he'd dropped the rifle, the girls had grudgingly lowered theirs, and let him sit down. He had refused to believe they were really in danger, and continued to defend the hunters.

Had he listened at all? Ronnie thought not. "What about the others?" he asked. "Serrano's crew."

"There's some kind of mistake," the prince said firmly. "Those men are criminals, condemned to life at hard labor; they have this option, risking death against a chance for a lesser sentence on a colony world. This is easier, for some people, than life in prison."

It occurred to Ronnie that he himself would have made that argument not long before. The topic of life sentences versus the death penalty had been a favorite debate in the mess. Of course, none of those debating ever expected to face either alternative.

"They're not criminals," Raffa said hotly. "They're decent people your admiral has a grudge against."

"I know it's fashionable for some people to argue against the justice system," the prince said. "But these people have all been tried and convicted and sentenced; do you think I'd be here if they weren't?"

A long silence. Finally Bubbles said, "I am frankly surprised that you're here even though they are. Does your father condone hunting people for sport? The last time I heard, he was scolding my father for hunting foxes."

Another long silence. "Well . . . he doesn't exactly know," the prince said, staring at his boots. He looked younger than Ronnie remembered, more the schoolboy he had known. "I'm supposed to be at the Royal Aero-Space depot on Naverrn. Admiral Lepescu fixed that for me."

"Mmm. And do you think he'll approve, even if they are convicted criminals? Which they aren't, but just to argue the point." Bubbles, on the other hand, looked older, tougher. She had laid aside her weapon, as if the prince were no longer a threat. Except for his stubbornness, Ronnie thought, he wasn't.

The prince scuffed his boot along the wall. "Probably not. But he doesn't need to know everything I do, and he certainly approved of my association with people like the other men in the club. Men of stature, men with . . . with . . ."

"Influence," Bubbles said. She made the word sound like something with little legs scuttling along the floor.

"The thing is," Ronnie said, "we've got to get out of here and rescue George."

"George? The odious George Starbridge Mahoney is here too? How fitting." The prince chuckled, leaning back against the stone. "Don't worry — no one will hurt George once they realize who his father is."

"They know who my father is, and they've tried to shoot me," Bubbles said. Ronnie glanced at her. She had changed as much as any of them, he realized, and in a way he could not have predicted. She looked like someone it would be dangerous to cross.

"Of course," the prince went on, ignoring that, "as soon as we *do* get back to civilization, I've a bone to pick with you, Ronnie. We simply can't ignore it; we must duel."

Ronnie stared at him. "A duel? You mean — formally?"

"Yes, of course, formally. It wouldn't have been necessary had we not met, but we did. And I had told them, if I saw you again anytime in the next twelve months, I would insist on it. It's a matter of honor." The prince drew himself up, glanced around at the two girls, and posed. Bubbles burst into giggles; Raffa merely looked scornful. Ronnie could not decide whether to laugh or scream.

"Look," he said, trying for reasonableness, "that whole thing is over. Past. Gone. She's all yours, and I'm sorry I said anything, and I'll never bother you again, but —"

"You're not going to back out of a duel, are you? That's —"

Ronnie felt anger roll up from his gut to the top of his head in one refreshing wave. "I am not going to pretend to stick holes in you with a holographic sword because of a stupid quarrel over a stupid opera singer who is probably sleeping with both our younger brothers right this moment! Can you get it through your skull that we are being *hunted*, by people with *real* weapons who want to kill us *really* dead? We are — Bubbles and Raffa and George and I — and I am not playing your silly games any more."

"Honor," the prince said, "is not a game."

"No," said Ronnie more quietly. "You're right; it's not a game. But my honor doesn't depend any more on the kind of things we got into in the regiment. I have other claims on it now."

"But what will I tell them when I get home?" the prince asked.

"If you get home," Bubbles said, "tell them you grew up. If you did."

The prince shook that off and stroked his moustaches. "Well — if we're to rescue George, we'd better get on our way. If you're convinced Lepescu is dangerous to you, how do you propose to get to Bandon?"

"Now what?" Cecelia asked. "We don't know where the captain is, we don't know where the cave is, and we don't have a flitter any more."

"Now . . . we think." Heris rubbed the knot on her head. She felt stupid, and she didn't like feeling stupid. "We can be reasonably sure Dussahral didn't put us down near the captain, but he might have put us down near Lepescu, if Lepescu needed a flitter to escape in."

"Fine." Cecelia looked thoroughly annoyed. "So now we've provided the villain a *machina* for his *deus* to come out of."

"Not if we get back to it and use it ourselves," Heris said. "Of course, explaining how all this happened might be tricky later — but we can worry about that when the time comes. Nemesis, as well as helpful gods, arrived by air."

She led the way back downslope. The streambed, she noted this time, had a lot of boot tracks in it or alongside.

Some went upstream, and some — not as many, she thought — went down. She wasn't enough of a tracker to know when they had been made, though they looked fresh.

Cecelia stopped, and looked more closely. "Expensive boots," she commented. "Look — that pair's Y and R." That meant nothing to Heris, who let her expression speak for her. "Custom, high quality, and even higher prices," Cecelia said. "These won't be the designated victims, nor even Ronnie's. I saw most of his things, and his boots are Pierce-Simons. Also expensive, but not quite as exclusive. Might be George's, but the tracks are too fresh."

"You can tell?" Heris asked.

"I hunt," Cecelia said, not looking up. Her fingers hovered above first one print, then another. "Not the girls' boots, and not Ronnie's — that means a hunter's up there somewhere."

"The way Dussahral was leading us," Heris said. "Lepescu, I would bet."

"You've noticed that two matching sets go that way and back —" Cecelia pointed. Heris hadn't noticed that, exactly, but she didn't explain her own ignorance. "Expensive, from hunting outfitters, but not as unusual as the Y and R pair. One pair of Y and Rs going up, and not coming back, and an even fresher set of Dolstims going up . . . two hunters, but not together. Not long ago, either — within an hour."

"So we go upstream?"

Cecelia pursed her lips. "I'd say so. Assuming that the men who went downstream wanted our flitter, they'd have it before we could get back. And upstream . . . I'm really curious. I thought Y and R put this symbol" — she pointed at what looked to Heris like a squashed bug — "only on boots they made for the royal family. Does your Admiral Lepescu have a habit of stealing shoes from princes? Or does he pretend to be one?"

"It wouldn't surprise me," Heris said. She was past being surprised, she thought; who would have expected someone like Lady Cecelia to know much about tracking? "Let's go find out."

She led the way upstream, weapon ready, all senses alert. Was this another stupid idea, following the tracks so openly? What they should be finding was the cave Ronnie and Bubbles might be in, or the militia captain. But she went on, because after all the hunters were the danger here. Anticipation shivered in her stomach. Hunters all, she thought. We're all dangerous.

All the hunters but two were safely dead: no threat. He touched the canisters in his pocket lightly, careful not to depress the switches. One only still menaced him, and that the most difficult to kill without reprisal. But it had to be done, unless the man could somehow be made to kill the others; after that, blackmail would be easy. It would be easiest to kill, and not attempt that — but he had always found the most difficult hunts the greatest pleasure. Worth a try, anyway, and if he had to kill even that one, he would have no witnesses.

That broadcast from Bandon had startled him — shaken him, he would even admit to himself. He wondered if the guards he'd left with the boy had turned against him. One of them could be difficult. At least his name had not been mentioned. Perhaps the prisoner didn't know about him. Soon no one would.

The prince led the way back to the cave entrance. They hadn't been able to talk him out of it, although they had tried. The argument had gone on longer than he'd expected. The girls seemed to think their opinion should weigh equally with his own. Bubbles had even threatened to shoot him, but when he pointed out that shooting a member of the royal family could be a serious offense, she had looked at Raffa and shrugged. Of course she would not shoot him, now that she knew who he was, any more than he would have shot her. One did not prey on one's own class. And he was the right one to decide what to do; he was the prince, after all. He felt only slightly nervous with the girls behind him carrying their weapons; he had insisted that they not carry loaded weapons, in case they stumbled. He didn't want them to get in trouble for shooting him by accident, either. Once they were outside, in the light, they could reload — though he hoped to dissuade them. If Ronnie hadn't been so shaken (he felt sure that he, in a similar situation, would not have been a wet, shivering mess) he'd have had Ronnie carry one of the rifles, but as it was the girls were actually less dangerous than Ronnie. As for any danger — he was sure there wouldn't be any real danger, not once he told Lepescu who they were — he could protect them himself.

Light shimmered and bounced from the surface of the pool; already it had gone down a few centimeters. He squinted against what now seemed like glare, and never saw the figure that waited until it stepped out of the shadows to confront him. He stared. Who could that be, in a protective suit almost like a spacesuit, with a hunting rifle in the crook of the right arm, and something clasped in the gloved left hand?

"Ah . . ." a voice said. The prince shivered. Lepescu? "You found them. Congratulations. Very good . . . now shoot them."

"What?" He had misunderstood. He could not have heard the words his memory now replayed to him. Behind him, he heard the girls' indrawn breath, Ronnie's muttered curse.

"Shoot them, I said." When he hesitated, Lepescu gestured with his rifle. "Either you shoot them," Lepescu said, his voice only slightly distorted by his suit's filters, "or I will have to kill you, too. Surely you see the necessity."

"But they're *ours*," the prince said. His voice trembled slightly. "Can't you see? This is Lord Thornbuckle's daughter — you can't kill *her*. And Raffaele, and Ronnie Carruthers —"

"I thought you hated Ronnie," Lepescu said. "Isn't he the one who dishonored you with your —"

"I do, of course, but — but I can't kill them. Not just . . . just shoot them." Silently, he begged someone to shoot Lepescu . . . but he had insisted on unloaded weapons. The girls could not reload now. If they tried, Lepescu would shoot . . . and he was in the middle. Sweat rolled down his sides, sudden and cold.

"We should never have let him talk us into this —"
Bubbles muttered. "We *knew* better. He can see me —
can you —?"

"Too late smart, too soon dead," Raffa said. Neither of
them had sounded as frightened as the prince felt. He
wished he could see them. He wished he could see any
help at all.

Lepescu's hand turned, showing a slick gray canister.
"It would be a more merciful death," he said. "If you care
about that." The prince realized that fear had layers he
had never imagined. . . . That had to be a gas canister.
Riot gas? Nerve gas? He struggled to stay calm; he had to
convince Lepescu.

"But they're my *friends*," the prince said. "You can't
expect me to do it; there has to be another way." This
could not be happening; it must be some kind of joke or
test. He had to find the right thing to say. "We could agree
to keep your secret."

"I doubt it," Lepescu said. Even through the gleaming
curve of his face mask, his eyes looked distinctly from face
to face. "Lord Thornbuckle's daughter is not likely to
keep such secrets from her father."

"You're right about that," came Bubbles's voice from
behind the prince. "Not that killing us will do any good in
the long run. He'll find out, and then he'll find you."

Lepescu lifted the canister in a mock salute. "To your
courage, my dear. You may stop that shuffling you're doing;
you cannot screen your friend as she reloads; I can shoot
the prince, and you, before you shoot me . . . and I'm
wearing protection." With a change in tone, he addressed
the prince again. "As for your friend Ronnie, a young man
who cannot keep from boasting about his amatorial
conquests is hardly likely to hold his tongue about this, the
next time he gets drunk. The dark girl — well, it's a pity,
but many have died already, and so it goes. You choose: kill
them, and I know you will not talk. It would not be in your
own best interests. I have a flitter; we can escape somehow.
I always do. But if you cannot kill them . . . then I'm afraid
you, too, must die." After a moment he went on, "Go ahead
— it won't be easier for waiting."

❖   ❖   ❖

Heris followed the bootprints up the narrowing cleft.
Suddenly one pair stopped; whoever it was had shifted
around, trampling his own prints, and then completely new
prints — larger, with a different tread — set off again. She
frowned at them, trying to remember where she'd seen
that tread pattern, then shrugged. It really didn't matter.

"He put on overshoes," Cecelia murmured, from
behind her. "Why?" Heris waved a hand to hush her.
They had to be close; she could tell the slope was closing
in ahead of them.

If she hadn't been following the tracks, she might have
missed the angle to the cave entrance . . . but the tracks
led directly to it. A mat of wilting ferns and moss, a gaping
hole into darkness, and a voice — no, more than one
voice. She was sure one of the voices was Lepescu's.

She pulled Cecelia close and murmured into her ear.
"He's there — ahead of us — and I think it's the youngsters. Stay back; be ready to shoot if I go down. And
watch for anyone behind us." Cecelia nodded, eyes hard
again. Heris crept nearer to the cave entrance, fighting
down a surge of excitement that threatened to send her
charging straight at Lepescu, no matter what.

Now she could hear his voice clearly. She knelt in the
mud, and peered around the edge of the hole into the
dimness. Nothing but water, a pool almost lapping the
entrance. She would have to go in. Voices came from her
left, around an angle of stone. She gave Cecelia a last look
and ducked inside.

Her eyes adjusted quickly; more light came in the
entrance than she'd have thought from outside. She flattened herself against the damp stone to her left and
edged around it. There. A big, bulky shape in a protective
suit, its back to her, and four faces beyond, pale against
the black behind them. The suit had to be Lepescu.
Could she get him without hitting them? Was he wearing
armor under the suit? And why the suit, in this weather?
What contamination did he fear? Then she saw the
clenched left hand, and caught her breath. If that was a
gas grenade —

She edged nearer, hoping none of the youngsters would notice her, although she knew she must be a very visible dark blot against the bright entrance. Lepescu was still talking. . . .

"Go ahead," he was saying. "It won't be easier for waiting."

What did he mean? And why *four* people? Heris stared, just able to make out Ronnie, Bubbles, and Raffa . . . but who was that fourth young man with the extravagant moustache and a gleam of earring? A friend of Lepescu's? She bit her lip; she could not possibly get both of them before someone else got shot. She wondered if Lepescu was wearing armor under the suit; she reset her weapon for the alternate clip of ammunition. This should penetrate personal armor. More danger to bystanders, but not as much danger as a live Lepescu.

But as her eyes adjusted to the dim light, she saw the mysterious young man shift his weight, his expression changing from bewilderment and disbelief to mulish stubbornness. "I won't do it," he said, and dropped his weapon. "And I think you'll find it impossible to explain *my* disappearance." Heris aligned her sights, and shifted a little to clear Ronnie. It was at best a tricky shot. . . . The ricochets would be wicked. . . .

"Not really," Lepescu said. "An inconvenience, yes — but not nearly an impossibility. It's a pity, and I'm sorry — this is not a sporting proposition, but —" He rocked forward, blood spraying out the front of his protective suit. Echoes of the shot and the impacts on him and on stone roared through the cave, deafening, confusing. Lepescu dropped his rifle; the canister dropped from his left hand, bounced, and rolled along the stone toward the water. Heris flinched; she was too far away to do anything more. If its seal broke, they were all dead. Ronnie and the prince leaped together and landed on it like two eager players trying to recover a fumbled ball.

"Run!" Ronnie yelled to Raffa and Bubbles; Heris knew it would have been useless. The girls didn't run; after their first startled jerk, both of them seemed to be calmly reloading their weapons. Heris stared at them.

They must have known they were in danger; why hadn't they had a round in the chamber? Then the echoes died away . . . and the canister had not fired. . . . It lay under the young men, inert and deadly only in anticipation. They were alive; they were going to stay alive.

Heris rose from her careful crouch, and walked light-footed across the cave to Lepescu's body . . . not body yet, for he was alive though mortally wounded. She looked down at him warily. He might have other weapons.

"You . . ." he began, but pain caught at him, and he could not go on. His breathing sounded loud, now that the echoes of the shot had faded; she could hear the ominous snoring rattle that meant his lungs were filling.

She could not think what to say. All the clever retorts she remembered from history crumbled and blew away in the wind of her anger. "Yes," she said, and it came to her that she did not need to say much, under the circumstances. "Commander Serrano, with all due respect."

Even dying, even in pain, he had a courage she could not deny. Scorn dragged his face into a mask of contempt. "Wait —" he breathed. "Haven't won — yet —"

She wanted to throttle him, finish it with her fingers on his throat, but she could not do that. Instead, she removed, with such control that she felt herself almost a machine, his other weapons; she paid no attention to the bubbling breaths that faded to nothing.

Cecelia could not have stayed out of the cave after the gunshot if someone had chained her to the rock. She scrambled into the darkness, stumbled into the pool and back out, and came up, panting, against the stone buttress that had blocked Heris's vision. Now, shocked and fascinated by her captain's behavior, she had let her attention wander from the cave entrance. When she thought to look around, there was another stranger, this one dirty and ragged, as well as armed. Another stood behind him. He glared at her, his weapon aimed where it could menace all of them.

"What . . . are *you* doing here?" The pause, Cecelia was sure, held a dozen suppressed curses. The man looked dangerous and probably was. He must be one of those the hunters had chased.

"I'm Lady Cecelia —" she began. Then she realized he wasn't even looking at her. He was looking past her, at Heris.

"Petris . . ." Heris said. Her voice wavered.

"Captain Serrano. Heris." His didn't, nor did the muzzle of his weapon.

"*You're* with Admiral Lepescu?" Quiet though it was, that question held a vast pain; it got through to Cecelia, who stared at her captain.

"You know this man? Who is he?"

Heris shook her head; for that instant she could not speak. Petris with Lepescu? Had he always been Lepescu's agent? Was this what Lepescu's dying words had meant?

Cecelia started to reach for her ID packet, but the shift of his weapon stopped her hand. Not her tongue. "I'm Lady Cecelia de Marktos, as I said; we came looking for my nephew Ronnie and his friends. With the militia."

"Ah." Petris still looked past her, to Heris. "The rescue arrives." He glanced briefly at Cecelia. "Tell me what you know about Admiral Lepescu."

Cecelia thought of objecting, but the weapon suggested caution, even cooperation. She had not realized before just how large the bore could look, seen from this angle. "I don't know him," she said.

"She didn't tell you?" he asked, jerking his chin at Heris.

Cecelia's patience snapped. "Whatever she told me is no concern of yours, young man." He laughed, a short ugly sound with little humor in it.

"You're not the best judge of that," he said. Then, to Heris, "And *you* think I'm working with the admiral?"

Cecelia glanced at her, and recognized Heris's expression for what it was, sorrow and despair, a great wound. Even when telling the story of her resignation, she had never looked this shattered.

"I know he organized the hunt, here," Heris said. Her voice had no vigor, as if the words lay dead in her mouth.

"And why else would military personnel be here with him —?"

"*With* him." Petris's voice was no louder, but the passion in it would have fuelled a scream. "You — of all people — can believe I might work with that — that — and does it look like I'm *with* him? Is this a uniform?" His voice had risen then, chopped off by a gesture from the other man. "No," he said savagely. "I am not with Lepescu." He turned away, still pale around the mouth. Cecelia stopped him.

"Excuse me, young man, but although you and my captain may be perfectly clear about what is going on, I am not. Heris has told me the admiral is an old enemy she would rather not meet save over a weapon. When my nephew and his friends disappeared, and we found that Lepescu was expected, she became convinced he had something to do with it."

Finally, the man seemed to focus, really focus, on Cecelia. "*Your* captain? You're her . . . uh . . . employer?"

"That's right. Captain Serrano signed a contract with me only two days after resigning her commission."

"And then?" He matched her gaze, as if he could pull answers out through her eyes.

"And then she took command of my yacht, and we came here. Now —"

"Directly?"

Cecelia drew herself up, annoyed. She had questions of her own, and he kept interrupting her. "No," she said, not caring if he realized she was miffed. "No — although I don't quite see what business it is of yours. My former captain had been negligent, if not actually criminal, in maintaining systems, and we had to detour for emergency repair of the environmental system."

The man turned to Heris, the corner of his mouth twitching. "*You* didn't check things yourself before you started?"

"The inspection sheets had been faked," Heris said dully. "Lady Cecelia's schedule had already been set back; she wanted a quick departure, and I —" Her voice trailed off.

"You couldn't wait to escape," Petris said. Sarcasm edged his voice. "You took your bribe and ran off —"

"Bribe!" This time it was Heris's voice that got the silencing gesture from the other man. At least, Cecelia thought, the insult had broken through and forced a live reaction. "Is that what he told you?"

"He told us nothing, except the list of charges."

"Charges? But I resigned so they wouldn't prosecute any of you —"

"Wait." Petris lowered his weapon suddenly. "Then it's true what this youngster heard?" He nodded at Ronnie. "Will you tell *me* you resigned? To save us, without any . . . any reward?"

"Yes. That was the choice. Resignation, and no trouble for you, or courts for all. It wasn't fair to put all of you through that; it had been my decision. What do you mean about charges?"

"That . . . motherless son," Petris said. Cecelia remembered hearing once that on some planets that was still an insult, although most people were now decanted and not birthed. "He got you out of the way, brought us to trial, and then had us here, to play his little games with."

Heris stared, the whites of her eyes showing clearly in the dimness. "You — it was *you* he was hunting?" Petris nodded. Heris shook her head, like someone who has just taken a hard blow, and turned to Lepescu's body with such violence that Cecelia was afraid she would attack it bare-handed. "Damn you! I killed you too soon! If only I could —" She was shaking now, starting to cry. Cecelia gaped; she had never imagined Heris losing control.

Petris strode past Cecelia and grabbed Heris by the shoulders, dragging her away. "He's dead — don't . . . you can't change it now —"

"I'd have — have done *something* — it's not fair —!" She turned a tear-streaked face back to Cecelia. "He took my ship — my career — and then to *kill* them this way —" And then to Petris, suddenly dry-eyed again, a sorrow too deep for tears. "I'm sorry, Petris. I didn't — imagine this. I couldn't. I believed they'd hold to the agreement."

"No," he said soberly. "You couldn't. I'm sorry I misunderstood what you'd done."

"How many — how many died?" Heris asked. Cecelia

could hear the fragile control, the tremor in her voice.

"Too many," Petris said. "But it's over now."

"It's not over," Heris said. "It will never be over." But she stood straight, motionless, and Cecelia watched her usual control return, layer by layer.

"Well, it's mostly over," said a cheerful voice from the cave entrance. Petris and the other men whirled, startled, but relaxed when they saw the distinctive uniform of Bunny's militia. The militia captain was grinning at them. "Unless one of you is the wicked Admiral Lepescu?"

"Admiral Lepescu is dead," Heris said. Her voice seemed to hold no emotion at all; it was the simple statement of fact.

Captain Sigind came nearer, glanced at Lepescu's body, and nodded. "You shot him?"

"Yes; he was threatening them —" Heris nodded at the young people. Ronnie and the prince had untangled themselves from each other, the floor, and the quiescent grenade, and now stood more or less at attention. Raffa had gone to Ronnie, Cecelia noticed, as if he were her responsibility. Bubbles stood a little apart from the group, rifle in hand, watching Heris intently. Cecelia had time to wonder why, when both girls were armed, neither had shot the admiral.

Captain Sigind looked them over.

"And here's Lord Thornbuckle's daughter, and I presume that's your nephew, ma'am, and the other young lady, and who's this —?" The militia captain looked at the prince, and the prince looked confused.

"Mr. Smith," said Ronnie firmly. "A friend of the family."

"Ah." Captain Sigind allowed a dubious expression on his face, and then shrugged it away. "Mr. Smith, indeed. An invited guest? Pardon, but I'm required to ask."

Bubbles spoke up. "Mr. Smith has often been an invited guest here; my father will confirm it."

"I . . . see." The captain looked as if he would like to pursue that, but again chose discretion. Well trained, Cecelia thought; a quick glance at Heris's face, and she caught another well trained expression. Heris, however, would certainly pursue the matter later. The captain did not quite shrug before going on. "Well, if everyone will come along, we can get you back to Bandon this evening, and fly you back to the Main House by morning — or you could spend the night on Bandon, and fly back tomorrow, whichever you prefer." He spoke into his comunit; Cecelia heard something about "retrieve the bodies" and "forensics" and then realized she was very, very tired indeed and wanted to sit down.

"What about George?" she heard Ronnie ask. Then she heard nothing.

✦ Chapter Twenty

Cecelia awoke only moments later, thoroughly ashamed of herself, to find Ronnie kneeling beside her. He looked, she thought, far worse than she possibly could, with that colorful pattern of bruises on his head and face, his muddy, still-wet clothes, and the pallor of exhaustion and hunger. She glanced around for Heris. Her captain was talking to the militia captain, who nodded as he keyed information into a wristcomp. Other militia had appeared; Lepescu's body had already been put into a black bag and lifted onto a stretcher. . . . She saw it being carried out.

"Are you all right, Aunt Cecelia?" He sounded genuinely concerned, not annoyed by an aunt who had fainted.

"I'm fine," she said, and pushed herself up on her elbows. She was too old to faint; at her age people took it seriously and talked about medical causes. "Just hungry," she said, which was now true. She was ravenous, and remembered that she had not had breakfast or lunch. Ronnie looked around frantically, as if he thought she expected him to pull a good meal from the rock. "Don't worry," she said, more tartly than she intended. "I forgot to eat, that's all." When she glanced around again, she saw that the two young women were sitting together, doing something to each other's faces, and the other young man stood awkwardly alone. "What's the —"

"Mr. Smith," Ronnie said softly but firmly. "He's Mr. Smith — I don't know if you've met."

"Oh, we've met." She eyed him, then glanced at the prince. "Mr. Smith, is it? Did you two arrange to meet here and continue your disagreement?"

"No!" Ronnie hushed himself with a shrug. "He was here on . . . other business. Finished business, now."

Cecelia looked at the prince, who seemed to feel her gaze and returned it. In the cave's uncertain light, she could not be sure of his expression, but he approached them.

"Excuse me," he said. "Ronnie, I really do need to talk to you. About the duel —"

"Mr. Smith," said Cecelia, in the voice that had not failed her in forty years or more. "You do not need to talk to anyone. Under the circumstances, Mr. Smith" — she emphasized the name slightly — "the less you talk to anyone the better. I very much doubt your father knows where you are."

"Well, no, he doesn't, but still —"

"You would be wise, Mr. Smith, to wait until your father explains your situation more fully. There is no question of a duel. Is that quite clear?" Cecelia put her eye upon him, the eye that had quelled many a brash young man even when she herself was young. He subsided; even the stubborn knot along his jaw went away, and the jaunty curl at the tips of his moustache seemed to droop. His voice lowered to a hesitant growl.

"What I was going to say, ma'am, was that your nephew's courage in landing on the gas grenade cancelled out any previous disagreement we might have had."

"You did, too," Ronnie said quickly.

"Wise of both of you," Cecelia said, allowing them to see her smile. "Now if someone can find me something to eat —"

Cecelia had never thought about how long it could take to move a few people across a short stretch of ocean. She had always been, she realized, the one who didn't have to wait. This time, she waited, and heard from both militia and the young people what had happened. Even with her wits restored by hot broth and half a survival bar from Bubbles's pack, it didn't make sense to her.

"Lepescu killed the other hunters? Why?"

Heris rubbed her nose. "My guess would be that he

thought he could get away alone. No witnesses on his side, convicted criminals — if any survived — on the other. . . . If he'd killed the young people, gotten into that flitter, and made it away —"

"But he couldn't possibly —"

"I'm not sure. Suppose we had still been on the mainland when George's transmission went out. He'd have had hours, not minutes, to complete his plans. Kill the witnesses, gas the remaining victims from the flitter. Fly back to Bandon, take the shuttle up. A wild gamble, but he liked wild gambles. Better than surrendering tamely to be tried himself."

"But why not get the others to help him?"

"Likely they wouldn't. That Mr. Smith — and by the way, are you and the others going to tell me who Mr. Smith is?"

"Someone who shouldn't be here," Cecelia said. "Later, perhaps —" She glanced around at the militia who might be within earshot.

"Ah. Like someone's son, perhaps? Yes." Heris's eyes twinkled. "Anyway, Mr. Smith explained that there had been a lot of confusion after the flitter crashed here, and the admiral had insisted on continuing the hunt. He might well fear that his allies would turn on him. If he had gotten away — well away — we would have found an island full of dead people and no witnesses to convict him. He would not necessarily know that I was here at all, or that I knew he was onplanet." Heris cocked her head. "A bold plan, typical of him, but as usual wasteful of resources."

"And Raffa told me about what happened after they crashed — although she doesn't know all of Ronnie's story, or George's, or the others'. Were they all your crew?"

"Apparently not. This wasn't the first such hunt, and Petris said some who survived a few weeks of a hunt were kept to seed the next, to keep it 'interesting.' " Her voice flattened on the word. "Too many were, though. I never thought — I *swear* I never imagined any such thing —"

"Of course not." Cecelia leaned against the rock, and

smiled at the younger woman. So much older than the younglings, Ronnie and his friends, but still so vulnerable. . . . She clearly needed someone to reassure her. Yet, in Cecelia's experience, no reassurance made up for bad results . . . and this had to be a bad result, no matter how selfless the original decision. She looked away from Heris, and thought about what she could do. Did she know anyone in the admiralty?

By the time Heris and Cecelia landed on Bandon again, the young people — except for Buttons, who remained the family's representative on Bandon — had been taken to the mainland along with two wounded militia and three wounded victims. Ronnie needed medical observation; the girls had wanted to check on George themselves, and Bubbles had an appointment with her father. Cecelia relaxed in the luxury of Bandon Lodge — a full set of servants had been flown out as soon as the island was secured — and left Heris to her own devices. Heris, after a bath and change of clothes, gathered her courage and went to see if her former crew would even speak to her. They were scattered through the guest rooms, according to the information in the deskcomp. She found door after door with its privacy locks engaged, and didn't try to intrude. Finally she found one door ajar, and tapped lightly.

Petris looked out at her. "Ah. Captain Serrano." The formality went to her heart. "I was just about to bathe."

"I'm sorry. I'll —" Wait, she would have said, but she had no right to force him to speak to her if he didn't want to.

"I'm sorry I yelled at you, back there," he said. "It was just hard to believe —"

"I'm sorry I thought you could have been with . . . with Lepescu."

"Look — I'm still stinking filthy — I was checking on Oblo, and he's fine. Let me get clean, and why don't we go walk somewhere?"

At least he was willing to talk to her. Heris nodded, silently, and turned away. Back in her room she tried to relax, but her eyes kept moving to the window, with its striking view of the beach and the other island across the water. The sun slid lower; the colors of sea and sky changed minute by minute. Flitters came and went; they were, she supposed, picking up the bodies and taking them away, bringing more investigators to look for more clues. . . . Her head ached. She had fallen into a restless doze in her chair when the tap on her door woke her.

Bathed and dressed in clean clothes, Petris looked more like the man she remembered — and less. He was not in uniform, the only clothes she'd seen him wear except for the rags of the island. He was not in the mental uniform that had kept them both from acknowledging what they could feel if they allowed it. His eyes challenged her. "If you need a rest, we could hold this until morning."

A night with issues unsettled would be no rest. "No. I'm ready."

To her surprise, he smiled at her. "My favorite captain. Always ready." He held up a basket. "I've had my first free meal, but thought we should bring something. There are enough cooks here to feed two cruisers. And the young lord, whats-his-name —"

"Buttons," Heris said. "They call him Buttons."

"The staff don't. Anyway, he gave me a map, and suggested something called the 'seabreeze trail.' "

She started to object — she had no idea where such a place might be — but didn't. After what had happened, she had no right to quibble. "How is . . . everyone?"

Petris shrugged. "Most of 'em are asleep, I think. Oblo said to tell you thumbs-up on coming to the rescue, and I said I would. He said there's a nurse in the clinic, there on the mainland, that almost makes the whole thing worthwhile. Remember the time we had to get him out of that rathole on Sekkis?"

Heris grinned, genuinely amused for the first time. "Oh, yes. Purple dyed skin and all."

Petris led the way down the carpeted hall, hung with soft-toned pictures of flowers and birds, and out to the parking area. "The young man said we could take a flitter or walk — which would you rather?"

It was nearly dark — though why that should matter, she couldn't think. "Let's walk," she said. "If it's not too far."

"Nope. Just down this way." In the gathering dusk, he led the way to a trail edged with white stones. It wound around one wing of the Lodge, skirted a clump of very tall trees, then dipped to the shore. Far off the sun hung in a glowing net of haze; the sea held the light and threw it back at them. The island across the strait showed a pale edge of beach, and a dark hump, but no details.

They walked on, along the beach, to an outcrop of gray rock very like the rock on the other island. It lay across the end of the beach, and beyond it Heris could see a rougher, stony shore where the sea nibbled and sucked hungrily. Here they stopped, as if the rock were a real barrier, although its blunt steps could have been climbed by a child.

Petris set down his basket. "While we still have light, we should see what the cooks came up with. Ah . . . *real* food." He spread the serving containers out. Heris sat down abruptly. It couldn't be this easy. Something had to happen, some further punishment for her mistake. It would be fair, she thought dismally, if he had put poison in the food, if he leapt on her and strangled her. She hadn't meant bad to come of it, but it had — and when had intention ever been justification for causing the deaths of innocents?

He looked at her and shook his head. "Captain — Heris —" It was the first time he had used her first name except to yell at her. "You're about as relaxed as a novice gunner before the first battle. What do you think, I'm going to scold you?"

"You'd have a right," she said.

"Well . . . yes. In one way, I do. In another, I don't." He looked into her eyes. "I think you *want* your scolding, is that it?"

Tears burned her eyes. "I — don't know. I want — what happened to be different. For it to have worked the way it was supposed to. You safe —"

Anger roughened his voice. "By the gods, Heris, do you think we'd have joined the Regs if we'd wanted to be *safe?* And safe at the cost of the best commander we ever had? Keep us from being butchered by that fool and his stupid tactics, yes — but not ruin yourself, and us, into the bargain."

"You're right," she said. No use denying it. "I was wrong." The rest of the pain she had put off feeling stabbed her, the thought of her crew, from that scrawny new kid in Power Systems, who had burst into tears with the first mail from home, to the wizened old senior medical mate, finishing out her last tour before retirement. What had happened to them? Tears spilled over; she could feel the wind chilling them as they ran down her cheeks; she struggled to control her breathing.

Petris moved close, and put his arm around her, a firm but gentle hold.

"You should have trusted us," he said, his breath stirring her hair. "Did you think we'd fail you?" She could hear in that the pain she had dealt them — worse for some than the pain of court-martial and public dishonor.

"I had failed *you*," Heris said. "The scan data were all lost — they told me you'd all be court-martialed along with me, risk discharge at least and probably time in prison."

"So you resigned. Walked out."

"Yes." It all came back, the nightmare she'd relived so often these past months. The Board behind their polished table, the familiar faces as strange as masks, the feel of her dress uniform collar tabs on her throat, a blade no less dangerous for being fabric and not steel. "I was told," she went on, careful to withhold all emotion, "that if I resigned immediately, they would take no action against you — the crew. They would hush it up; it would not have happened. Sorkangh — my father's friend, one I'd counted on to help me argue my case — he said that. And if Sorkangh was against me —" She shook her head. She had said this already; it made no difference. She had had her reasons, she had fought herself to make that decision, and none of her reasons mattered. It had been wrong, as wrong as not anticipating any enemy's position and fire-power.

"Well," he said, squeezing her shoulders, "if it helps, not all your crew was as loyal as they should have been. Lepescu had a ringer in, and that's what happened to the scan data."

"How'd you find that out?" She had wondered, but could not have proven her suspicions.

"First transit brig. Friend of a friend of a friend — couldn't do much for us, but did tell us who did it and on whose orders. We took care of *him*."

Heris shuddered; she didn't want to understand, although she did. "How many . . . ?"

"I'm not sure. They split us up, early on — we were tried in different groups, supposedly determined by our level of responsibility. Some weren't formally charged, I heard — but I couldn't tell you what happened to them. Of those brought to court, the scuttlebutt is that all but three were convicted. Some were discharged, and some had the usual loss of rank, or pay, but no brig time. They decided to make an example of about fifty of us, the senior NCOs and officers, and from that about thirty were brought here. The others are in the prison system somewhere."

"I'll have to do something about that," Heris muttered.

Petris shifted beside her. "I don't see how you can, now," he said. "Maybe if this comes out, their cases can be reevaluated, but whatever Lepescu was up to, the original charges are still there."

"I'll think of something," she said. "Maybe Lady Cecelia —"

"Maybe." He didn't sound convinced. "But I had something else to say to you." She braced herself, but he didn't go on for a long time. Then he sighed. "I wish it was darker. Thing is . . . you're not my commander now, right?"

"Right." Heris picked up something — it was dark enough she could hardly see the food — and stuffed it in her mouth. Cheese and pastry and something; she nearly choked.

"You were always professional . . . you know . . . but I used to wonder if you felt something . . . something like I did." He wasn't looking at her, but at the last fading purple glow in the west. Then up at the stars. Heris had time to remember times she had not wanted to be professional; she choked down the food in her mouth.

"Mmm. Yes. Something . . ." How could she have known it was a mutual feeling? They had both understood professional etiquette; nothing must come of any feelings, and thus better to leave them unfelt — or at least unsaid.

"So?" The flat, gray light, all that was left of sunset, caught in his eyes. Heris opened her mouth to say how impossible it was, then realized it wasn't. Not any more.

"So . . ." She still could not say it. She moved, instead, into the arc of his arm.

"You should have trusted *me*," he said again, but without heat. "It hurt, when you went away like that, without a word."

"Yes. It did." She leaned against him; his arm felt good against her back. Better than good. "It hurt a lot. But I'm here now, and I'm trusting you."

"About time." Then his grip tightened. She had never allowed herself to imagine — really imagine — what embracing him would be like. It would have been too difficult to go through everyday shipboard life, if she had. Now she was glad of her former discipline. She had no nagging comparisons to make, just the experience to savor.

"I fixed it," Cecelia said. She sounded smug. Bright morning light gilded her hair, and she looked crisp and refreshed by ample sleep and good food.

"Fixed what?" Heris had bathed and changed, when she and Petris got back to the Lodge shortly before dawn, but inside her clothes her body felt lush and relaxed. She wondered if Cecelia could tell. She had her own list of things for Cecelia to fix, and hoped her employer hadn't used up her energy on something minor.

"Your resignation," Cecelia said, as if continuing a conversation in progress. "I hate to lose you, but I know how you've grieved. And the evidence is clear. So I just argued my way along, and they've agreed to take you back. Quite willingly, in fact. Everyone knows that George's father will sue Lepescu and his cronies, and the Regular Space Service is anxious to dissociate themselves from any of that."

Heris stared, her brain racing. Cecelia had fixed *that*, in a few hours, from an obscure planet with no real-time communications beyond its own system? Then: Go back? Retrieve her command, her career? She felt her heart begin to hammer, the racing pulse pounding her body, making her hands shake. Exultation flooded her; she could see the look on her father's face, on her mother's. . . . She could imagine how her younger brother, still in the Academy, would react. *Yes*, she thought. *Yes*.

"How?" got out of her mouth first.

Cecelia beamed, clearly glad to be asked. "I'd been afraid it would take weeks, but you remember Bunny said a Crown Minister was here hunting? Bunny asked me to speak to him about Mr. Smith, and of course I told him about you. I pointed out that going through the usual channels would require your complete explanation, and you, as an honest person, could hardly fail to mention Mr. Smith when you justified the killing of Admiral Lepescu."

"Mr. Smith," said Heris blankly. She had almost forgotten that mysterious young man. Then her brain snapped back into focus. "A . . . royal, you said, about the boots." Which, given his age, meant . . . *"Not* the one Ronnie was in trouble for —"

Cecelia grinned. "Quite so. The Minister saw my point, of course, and assured me that no statement from you would be required, under the circumstances. Enough evidence of Lepescu's unfitness existed to overturn the judgment without recalling whatever court or board it was. You can trust him," Cecelia went on, as if anticipating Heris's doubts. "With Mr. Smith's reputation at stake, he would do more than this. Luckily for us, the Minister requires a special communications link — I don't know what you call it, but it's almost instantaneous through some kind of relay back to Court. He was able to contact the necessary officials, and —"

"And the surviving crew?" Heris asked. She felt already

like a Spacefleet officer, the purple uniform forgotten along with the past several hours.

Cecelia nodded briskly. "Oh, yes. All rehabilitated, as they called it. I knew you would want that, so I insisted. Wherever they are, if some of them were not on that abominable island." When Heris didn't answer at once she went on. "I *do* understand, you know. We are both aristocrats, even if we aren't in the same aristocracy."

"I — thank you, milady." Only that formality would serve, could possibly express her gratitude.

"I will hate losing you," Cecelia said, more softly. "Not only as a captain, and student of equitation, but as a friend. I like you, and I don't like many people." Then her voice firmed again. "Will it be difficult, for you and Petris?"

Heris stared at her, disoriented by the double-change of direction. "Petris . . . ? Oh." So Cecelia had noticed. At once the exaltation left her, as quickly as if someone had pulled a plug in her heart. She could go back, and he could go back, and they might serve on the same ship . . . but they could not go back to the past hours. Not ever. She tried to imagine him as a civilian . . . husband . . . but that would destroy him. "Oh, my," she said, hardly hearing her own voice. "I didn't think."

"Most people don't, in your position," Cecelia said. "That's why I mentioned it, before you go and tell the others. You can go back . . . but you don't have to."

Didn't she? She could hardly breathe for a moment, in the alternation of possibility and impossibility. She could not give up her chance in the R.S.S. again — she could not give up Petris. She could not ask him to give up his career, as miraculously restored as her own, but if either of them . . .

"Damn," she said. It was all she could say. She sat down suddenly, and Cecelia made a show of turning away, preparing something to drink, offering her a steaming cup of some brown liquid. . . . She should know what it was, but she couldn't recognize anything.

"As a classical maiden aunt," Cecelia said, not looking at her, "I am qualified to give useless advice, which you are free to ignore. You love that man, and he loves you; that was obvious when I first saw you two together. You can't be together in the Service, and neither of you will be happy as a civilian partnering the one who stays in. If you do go back, Heris, be sure you're never on the same ship. . . . You know that."

"I know that." Her lips felt numb — was it the drink? Was she going to faint? She never fainted; it was ridiculous. But her skin remembered his touch; her ears remembered his voice, the sound of his breathing, the beat of his heart when her head lay on his chest. She wanted that, wanted it more than anything . . . except her commission, her ship, her crew . . . which she couldn't have, if it meant him.

"I still need a captain," Cecelia went on. "I need new crew members — you told me that. If you chose not to reenter the Service, you would have a place with me."

And Petris would become just a crew member on a rich old lady's yacht — she could not see him being happy with that. He had taken as much pride in his career as she in hers. He would not settle for less.

"You ought to ask him," Cecelia said, as if reading her face. "You didn't ask before, and look where that got you. Give him the chance, now, while you have the chance . . . while you are, for the moment, free."

It was true. She had not thought she had a chance, before; she had taken the commander's way, the solitary way, and had not asked anyone, and because of that Lepescu had been able to ruin her *and* her crew. This time she could ask him. She stood up, nodding to Cecelia without saying a word — she could not have said a word — and went to find Petris.

He was staring out to sea, staring at the island on which he had been hunted. "Looks pretty from here," he said as she came up.

"Yes," she said. Her throat closed on more. He looked at her closely.

"What's happened?"

She couldn't answer; tears flooded her eyes. He reached for her, hugged her close, his lips in her hair. "Heris . . . Heris . . ." he breathed. She gulped, tried to calm herself, and finally choked the lump down.

"Lady Cecelia has intervened," she said finally. Her

voice came out thin, unlike herself. "With the Service."

"You're getting your commission? Good." His arms loosened, and she heard the effort in his voice. "I hoped you would — they ought to have that much sense."

"They're reversing all the disciplinary actions," she said. "All the survivors will be reinstated, with all records cleared. It would probably have happened anyway, but Lady Cecelia —"

"Has connections. I'm glad she cares that much — you must have impressed her." His arms dropped from her shoulders, and he stretched. "Well. Back into harness for us, eh? And —"

Heris stared at the sand. "We don't *have* to go."

"Eh? Of course you'll go — you're not meant to be a yacht captain."

"She said I should give you the chance. The chance I didn't give you before."

He stared at her; when she looked up, his gaze was fixed on her face. "What do you mean? Are you saying —?"

"Petris —" She used his first name deliberately. "Petris, there is a choice. If we go back, you know — you know it would be best if we never serve together. But if we don't go back —"

"You love it," he said. "Your family — the Serrano Admiralty —" She had heard that phrase before; it was inevitable for a family that had produced admiral after admiral through many generations. She had never considered how they might look from underneath — from out to sea, like a great cliff wall made of stars and flags, with no safe beach to land on. She felt herself a rock loosed from that cliff, now rolling in the surf, being broken into fragments the cliff would no longer recognize.

"My family," she said slowly, "have already endured the worst: a Serrano resigning under a cloud rather than face a court. They will abide my decision, one way or the other . . . or they will not, and I will abide their decision. I don't know what they'll do, but I don't fear it. Your family?"

"Mine." He stared past her now, at the island again. "Farmers and small merchants on Vonnegar's World; I was the outlaw there, too. Ran off to join the military, like kids have always done. . . . Wouldn't walk behind a plow or pull onions if I could see stars. They wouldn't mind — they gave me up for lost when I told my uncle Eth what I thought of farming. I couldn't go back and ask for land, that's sure. But away — I can do what I want." A quick glance to her, then away again. "I liked my work."

"I know that. You can have it back; that's what Cecelia told me. She's got you all cleared."

"Ah . . . yes, but it can't be the same. Not just us, the whole thing. Some of 'em died, through this; I can't forget that."

Heris felt cold. They had died because of her, because she had left; she already knew that. If he couldn't forget, he probably couldn't forgive either, and last night had been . . . last night.

But he was looking at her again, this time steadily, eye to eye. "But what did you offer as an alternative? You said if we don't go back —"

"We could both work for Lady Cecelia. On her yacht." Of course he had already said *she* wasn't meant to be a yacht captain, and of course he wasn't meant to be on a yacht's crew either, but she had to ask.

"You must like her a lot," he said, "even to consider it. What do you . . . do?"

She could tell he was avoiding the familiar terms, like "mission." "Lady Cecelia travels," she said. "From the existing records of past voyages, she travels widely, and from the events of the first weeks I worked for her, her yacht has harbored smugglers . . . without her knowledge, of course."

"You're sure of that." It was not quite a question.

"Yes. She's stubborn, opinionated, and all the other things you expect from a rich old lady, but she's honest."

"Like you," Petris said, without a smile. "No wonder you get along. So — you'll continue?"

"It depends." Even as she said it, she wondered if it did depend on his decision. Oddly, she now thought of going back to the Service as a kind of defeat. Someone else had fought her battle for her; someone else had bought her commission back. She hated that. Bad as Lepescu was, some would always mistrust her loyalty; she would never be the unflawed Serrano in clear line of succession to an

admiralty. Even her family would have reservations. She
did not realize she had said some of this aloud until the
end. . . . "— and I would rather take an honest salary from
her than a commission restored with her influence. So . . .
it's either stay with her, or look for something else, and I
have no reason now to leave her. At least not until I've
straightened out that crew."

Petris chuckled. "I know that tone. All right, then — I
think all of us will have the same problems. Those who
don't think so are welcome to go back, but as for me . . .
no. D'you think your Lady Cecelia will hire more than
one of us, and will we have to bow as she sweeps by?"

"Are you saying yes?"

"No . . . I'm saying yes, *ma'am* . . . since I believe that's
the correct civilian usage." The end of that was smothered in a hug, out of which he said finally, "I gather the
restriction on fraternization doesn't apply either?"

"No," Heris said firmly. "Not off the bridge." Her
thoughts raced, crashing into each other like fox hunters
of two hunts in collision. What came out, at last, was the
professional ship's officer. "I've got to check in with Sirkin
— the standing watch — and let her know there's a sealed
weapons cargo coming up to the ship. It's a good thing we
had a complete refitting at Takomin Roads. Did you know
the sulfur cycle was off by two sigs?"

He released her with a roar of laughter. "Dear heart
— Heris — Captain — your owner had better pull up her
bloomers or whatever they call them on aristocrats.
Weapons? Does she know?"

"Of course she knows; I used her credit line." That had
been — how long ago? And would Cecelia still authorize
those weapons? Better get them aboard before she
changed her mind. Somewhere the smugglers that had
put that contraband aboard had to be wondering what
had happened to it. The rich were no safer, if they didn't
bother to defend themselves, than someone on the docks.
In the depths of her mind, the final door to her past shut,
and she faced the future as a civilian without the old pain.
It would return, she knew, as old pains always did, in the
dark hours everyone faced . . . but the worst was over.

✧ Chapter Twenty-one

Discretion must be served. Two by two, the former prey, Heris's former crew members, left for the mainland hospital, where (Heris was assured) Bunny's excellent medical staff would check them out, and where they would live in privacy and luxury until they decided what they wanted to do. She had spoken to each one, but they were too dazed to talk much. She understood; she felt that way herself. Too many emotions, too much turmoil. Finally, with the lodge empty, it was her turn. She and Cecelia and Petris had a luxurious flitter, with Michaels himself at the controls, for the flight back. No more clouds. . . . The wrinkled ocean lay blank and blue under a clear sky until they reached the mainland. Heris stared at it until she felt the pattern was imprinted forever on her retinas. She wondered why Petris was travelling with them, then wondered why she wondered. And why couldn't they talk? After that first night, she had not expected the awkwardness of the days and nights since, when they could cling together . . . but not complete a sentence.

The flitter delivered them to the wide courtyard before the Main House rather than the flitter hangars. Here it was cold, with low clouds racing across the sky before a sharp wind. Heris sealed the jacket she had not needed on the island and shivered. She was glad she wouldn't have to walk up the hill from the other end of the village. Inside, Petris looked up the great staircase that first time with an odd expression that mingled delight and apprehension.

"This is exactly how I thought a great lord's house would look, and I don't trust it," he said finally. "It's too perfectly what it is, like an entertainment-cube version of a fleet cruiser."

"It's intimidating," said Heris. Now she could admit that. "I couldn't believe anyone actually lived in it. But they do." She wondered where the servants were; usually two or three at least were in the hall at this hour. But the one who had opened the door had vanished, leaving it to Cecelia to lead the way upstairs.

Petris, she found, had the room next to hers, where she remembered someone else having been, but she did not raise her brows to Cecelia, who already looked entirely too smug. How had Cecelia known that?

"Don't forget," Cecelia said, "that Petris will need to check in with Neil. I'll let him know you're coming, shall I?"

Heris looked at Petris. He had not had the benefit of Cecelia's riding simulator. But he grinned. "I can hardly wait to see Heris on horseback, chasing a fox," he said. "Although I'm not looking forward to those early starts."

"Nonetheless. And of course I needn't warn either of you about discussing all this —"

"Not at all." Petris raised and lowered his brows at her, a clear dismissal.

"Dinner at eight," Cecelia said. She strode off down the corridor.

"Your employer —" Petris began.

"Our employer," Heris said. "Unless you change your mind."

"I never change my mind," Petris said. "Come in here —" He led her into his room, a twin of her own. "I don't believe this, either!" He was staring at the furniture, the gleaming expanse of the bathroom and its glittering toys. He walked around the room, opening and closing the doors of wardrobes, looking into drawers in tall polished chests. Heris could see the racks of clothes, and wondered. "I'm sure these all fit — Lady Cecelia would have seen to it. I always knew there was a good reason to leave the onion farm." Then he looked into the bathroom again. "Plenty of room, and warm towels. Shall I scrub your back, my love, or will you scrub mine?"

❖ ❖ ❖

Ronnie was sure they were all making too much fuss about his condition. George had been shot; George might die. He still had that nagging headache, and a collection of bruises and scrapes, but after a night in the hospital he was ready to go back to hunting. Or at least, back to living in the far more comfortable quarters he had enjoyed before.

"Time enough," the nurse said. "You're not leaving until the doctor agrees, and your scans aren't normal yet." It wasn't the same nurse as before, he thought, and wondered how often their shifts changed.

"Nothing's broken," Ronnie said. "You let that fellow in the other bed leave just twenty-four hours after a broken leg —"

"Bones aren't brains," the nurse said. Ronnie closed his eyes, feigning sleep, and was surprised to find dark outside his windows when he opened them again. The next morning (which morning?) he woke without a trace of the headache, and the awareness that he had not been clearheaded before.

"And you're not yet," the doctor said, when she arrived to talk to him before he left. "You think you are, but it's like climbing out of a hole: it's lighter where you are, but you're still in shadow. I know this will disappoint you, but I've already notified Lord Thornbuckle's head groom: you are not to ride for at least ten days, and you'll have to be reevaluated then."

"But I didn't —" Ronnie began, but the doctor smiled and patted his knee as if he were a child. Considering her white hair and wrinkles, she probably thought of him that way. *I didn't want to ride*, he said silently. *And now I don't have to.* "What about George?" he asked. They had told him nothing so far except soothing murmurs. He braced himself to hear that George had died.

"*That* young man," the doctor said. "Do I understand that everyone calls him the odious George?"

"Yes," Ronnie said.

"I can see why," she said. "He can have visitors — in fact, he has visitors all day, now. So if you want to know, just take the lift up one, and it's the third door on the left.

He's still on the surgical floor, though really —" She shook her head without finishing that and left. Ronnie pulled on his clothes, hardly wondering where they'd come from, and went to see George.

George lay propped up in bed, looking like an advertisement for a hospital company: dark hair perfectly in place, fading bruises on his face suggesting courage without diminishing his good looks. Ronnie knew that on anyone else the yellow and green and dull purple would have looked hideous, but George's luck seemed to hold.

"Ronnie!" His voice sounded the same, if not quite as loud as usual. "I wondered when you'd make it up here. You missed all the excitement."

Ronnie stared at him. Missed all the excitement? Had no one told George about the admiral and the gas grenade, or the prince, or —

"My father's on the way," George said. He looked exactly as he had always looked, smug. Odious. Ronnie wanted to hit him, but you couldn't hit someone in bed with a gunshot wound. He went in, nonetheless, holding a vague grudge but not sure how to let it go. Should he tell George about the prince? He thought he remembered it was supposed to be a secret.

George's face changed, and his voice softened. "I — was really scared. You passed out on me, then they caught me, and those two —"

"Who?"

"The guards back on Bandon. I never saw the hunters at all, just these two men."

"They're the ones who shot you?"

"Oh, no. One of Bunny's militia shot me, and it wasn't an accident, either. I tried to tell Captain Serrano, but couldn't get it across. . . . He was standing there, eyeing your aunt as if he'd like to kill her right then."

"Did you tell Bunny? When you got back here?" Ronnie had an urge to leap up himself, right then, and go find his aunt.

"It's all right. That's part of what you missed. That's the same man who tried to kill your aunt and Captain Serrano when they went to find you in the cave."

"Oh." Ronnie tried to remember if he'd heard about that man before. He remembered some things vividly: finding George unconscious, trying to build a litter, the storm, Raffa's warmth against him in the cold, dark cave, that moment of sheer terror when he jumped for the gas grenade. But he had no clear mental map of the time . . . how long they'd been on the island, or whether they'd stayed on Bandon overnight or flown straight back.

"Your aunt plugged him," George said, with relish. "He had the captain covered."

"She would," Ronnie said vaguely. He hated not remembering; it was like being very old, he thought. He had probably said things, and done things, without really knowing it. What if he had said something stupid? What if he had said something stupid to Raffa? Was that why he couldn't remember seeing her in the hospital?

George sobered again. "It's not that easy, being a hero. At least, it wasn't for me. You —"

"Not for me, either. There's a lot I can't remember."

"There's a lot I wish I couldn't remember." George scowled. "I have never been so scared, so humiliated, in my life — not even that first term at school." He sounded far more human than usual. "At least you didn't have to scrub any toilets."

"Not that again!" Raffa's voice; Ronnie turned to look. She might never have been off the mainland; she looked like all the other polished young women who had come for the hunting party, and she looked like no one else in the universe. Bubbles, beside her, leaned against the door and grinned broadly.

"Now I can quit holding Raffa's hand every night. You had us all scared, Ronnie."

"Me? George is the one who got shot."

"All George needed was a good surgeon, a day in the regen tank, and a personality transplant; my father could supply the first two, but not the last."

"You'll regret that, Bubbles —" George said, but it had no bite. "My reputation depends on being odious. And wrinkle-free."

"Your reputation depends on your father," Bubbles

said. "Or someone would have beaten the odiousness out of you long before."

"Unfair," George said. Then he grinned. "Well — partly unfair. And I do resent the damage to my good trousers."

"I assure you," Bubbles said, in the same dry tone, "that you'll be wrinkle-free and out of here in time for the Hunt Ball. *If* you promise to keep your mouth shut and cause no trouble about Mr. Smith."

George made an innocent face that would not have fooled anyone. It certainly did not fool Ronnie or the girls.

"If you don't promise — and keep that promise," Bubbles went on, "I'll make sure that someone slips the wrong stuff in the regen tank for your next treatment, and you'll have wrinkles in places you don't think wrinkles can form. *Permanent* wrinkles. Then you can stay in this room until you die of genuine old age."

"And I," Raffa said, coming over to take Ronnie's hand, "will personally ruin every garment you own *and* send your tailor a certified letter giving your new measurements. *Interesting* new measurements." She mimed the anguish of someone in trousers with a short rise, the problems of skimpy sleeves and a baggy, short jacket.

George rolled his eyes dramatically. "You might have trusted me. Lawyers' sons learn *some* discretion." The others snorted. He went on. "All right. I promise. No leading questions, no suggestive remarks, nothing about Mr. Smith or his . . . mmm . . . other identity. But how am I supposed to explain my disappearance from the noble sport of fox hunting?"

"We took the flitter to go picnicking, and we crashed, and you and Ronnie were hurt saving us. Very simple, very —"

"What about Lady Cecelia and Captain Serrano?"

"Unrelated, except that Lady Cecelia is the one who let Bunny know we were missing — just as it happened. We're hoping to get past the Hunt Ball without the whole story coming out."

❖   ❖   ❖

Neil had pronounced Petris's seat "untidy but effective," and passed him into the blue hunt at once. Heris had little interest in riding to hounds any more, but also little choice; if she stayed home, it would be noticed, and tongues were already wagging. Cecelia, pleading age, could go out only twice a week; Heris had to ride five days out of seven. She knew Cecelia was up to something again — or still — because the Crown Minister stayed in the same days as Cecelia.

"I might just as well go back to the ship," she argued with Cecelia one afternoon. Her horse had stumbled on landing from a wall, fallen heavily, and come up lame; Heris herself had bruised her shoulder. The fox — if there was a fox — had got clean away. She wanted to be back on a decent ship, where large heavy animals didn't dump her off and then roll on her. Her leg wasn't broken, but it felt reshaped.

"You should go by the hospital and spend a few hours in the tank," Cecelia said. "You've had a hard fall, and you're sore. It'll heal."

"We'll have crew changes —"

"You can't go until after the Hunt Dinner and Ball. We have to finish out this much of the season, or it will be suspicious. You notice that no one comments on what happened?"

"But —"

"But Mr. Smith is safely contained; I've offered to take him home since we already officially know. We'll stay until the Hunt Dinner, and leave the next day. I *always* stay for the first Hunt Dinner." Heris found this confusing, since in the books she'd read there was only one official Hunt Dinner per hunt club, but presumably Bunny did things his own way. And with such a long season, perhaps most people didn't stay for the whole thing. Cecelia patted her shoulder; Heris tried not to wince. "Now go spend a few hours in the tank, and ask Sari to give you a good rubdown. Petris will be in the green hunt, Neil says, by the day after tomorrow, and you'll feel much better by then."

Heris didn't want a rubdown from Sari; she wanted a pleasant night with Petris. But with her bruises, it wouldn't be pleasant. "When is this Hunt Dinner?" she asked, resigned to a trip to the hospital. She would remember to look in on everyone.

"End of next week." Cecelia took a few twirling steps that startled Heris. She flushed. "I may be old, and plain, but there's no law that says I can't dance."

Dance. Heris thought of dancing with Petris, and felt her bones begin to melt. She would manage not to hunt in the next week; she didn't want to risk missing that. It might even be worth the hours in the regen tank. She was in the tank, trying to relax as the technicians fussed over her bruised arm and leg, when one of the things Cecelia had said brought her bolt upright, splashing.

"Sorry," she said, to the technician who had contained his own curse but not the expression on his face. "Bad memory." The prince. Cecelia had said they were going to transport the prince home. That meant . . . she squeezed her eyes shut, and thought about it. Would Ronnie stay here? Surely she wouldn't have that pair on her ship at the same time!

The last week passed in a flurry . . . cold blue days, icy nights, glorious rides across the open land the green hunt favored. Heris had come out of the tank with more than her bruises healed, and suspected Cecelia of telling someone to load her IV with mood elevators. Either that, or the old books were right when they described the glow of lovers riding stirrup to stirrup at a gallop.

"Gallop by day, and . . . other gaits by night," Petris said, his arm under her head again. Heris didn't answer, as the gait in question required concentration. They could talk again, she had discovered, but this was not the time. Later, he asked, "And what are you wearing to the ball tomorrow?"

"A dress," Heris said. She could feel herself starting to chuckle in anticipation, a quiver that Petris must surely recognize. He tapped her nose with his finger.

"A dress. Amazing. I thought fox hunters wore skins and furs to a ball. Or horse hides or something equally barbaric. What are you laughing about? Are you wearing a fur dress?"

"No . . . but I won't tell you. You'll have to see it." An extravagance, which she had not intended, but it had made an excuse to miss one day's hunt. It made a sizeable hole in the salary Cecelia had yet to pay her. She could hardly wait to see Petris's face when he saw her in it.

Heris had not meant to wait until the day of the Hunt Dinner to tackle Cecelia about the changes needed in the ship, but there never seemed to be time. But she had made promises to Petris and the others; she had to make sure Cecelia understood before they actually boarded. The argument (she was sure it would be an argument) must be private. She slithered into her own gown, and shook her head at the image in the mirror. The beaded bodice shifted color with every movement, shimmering; the soft pleats of the midnight-blue skirt were spangled with random beads, as if the bodice had dripped fire onto it. And she looked . . . very unmilitary, she decided. *Very* unmilitary.

She found Cecelia almost dressed, and fiddling with the amber necklace she favored. A flounce of ivory lace refused to lie properly beneath it.

"I need to talk to you about the ship," Heris said.

"What's wrong?"

"Nothing's wrong. . . ."

"So what is it now?"

"Some changes will have to be made." Heris watched Cecelia as she said it. The older woman had looked tired for the last week, and claimed it had nothing to do with the ship. The Minister? Mr. Smith? The Service?

"Such as?" Cecelia's voice was tart. "Oh — I suppose we'll have to have another environmental system, to take care of the extra people?"

"Not really." Heris ignored the tartness, and went on. "You have four crew who have asked for separation. Three want to stay here, and have applied for employment with Lord Thornbuckle's personnel. The other wants to leave at the next major Roads. Then there's a member of your house staff who got pregnant in Hospitality Bay — Bates says he is sure of intent, in this case, because she had pursued even him. And one of your undergardeners — so you see, we won't be overloaded."

"What changes then?"

Heris met the problem head-on. "Weapons," she said. And as Cecelia stared, her mouth opening, she talked on. "You are a very wealthy woman in a very luxurious and capable ship. Remember that you've already been used by smugglers. What if they want their cargo? What if they want the whole ship? What if they want *you*? The places you like to travel are not exactly the safest corners of the universe. We need proper armament —"

"Now that you have gunners, you have to have guns." So, Cecelia had understood — or found someone to translate — the military specialty codes her new crew members carried. Heris cocked her head; Cecelia could hardly claim to be a philosophical pacifist, not after having shot someone herself.

"What's the matter, milady? Do you think I'll deliberately lead you into danger?" Of course, she had done just that, but it was for a good reason.

"No. I don't know." Cecelia moved restlessly, her long fingers tangled together. "Things have changed. Before, I knew what I was doing — yes, I was just cruising around having fun, but I knew that was it. Now . . . when I think of leaving here and going off to Roledre for the qualifying trials, or on to Kabrice for the finals, it's — it's not that interesting."

Heris smothered a grin. Better than she'd hoped for. "If it's bothering you, milady, I'm sure we can find *something* to do with this ship."

Cecelia's eyes narrowed. "Something? You mean you still consider me an idle old lady?"

"You said it; I didn't. But think; you are healthy and tough, and yet you had smugglers using your ship. Don't you have friends, equally old and wealthy —"

"Not really," muttered Cecelia. Heris ignored that.

"— who might have worse parasites aboard than even your Captain Olin? There are," Heris said, thinking of it in that moment, "other things to hunt besides foxes, and other mounts besides horses."

"Which prey is beneath the notice of the Regular Fleet?"

"Or too elusive for the less agile. Consider —"

"How many guns, Heris? What size? And do I get to mention cost?"

"No more than we need, no bigger than we need, and I will respect your resources only less than your life." She didn't remind Cecelia about the weapons already purchased.

"As you did at Takomin Roads — no, don't defend yourself; I knew what you were doing and agreed. But from now on, I want to be a member of the hunt staff, not just the owner who pays the fees. You'll have to keep teaching me about my ship, and let me be part of your plans."

"You have earned that, and more," Heris said, and meant it. Cecelia grinned back at her.

"Then let us go down and dazzle the Hunt Dinner, and dance the night away," she said. "And as for the future . . . a hunting we shall go. . . ." And she grabbed Heris's arm and led her down the corridor to the main staircase, where Petris, correct in formal dinner attire, waited below. Heris saw his expression shift from surprise through amusement to admiration as she and Cecelia came down arm in arm, singing. "Tan-tivvy, tan-tivvy, tan-tivvy — a hunting we shall go . . ."

"Ladies, ladies! Such unseemly levity!" But his lips twitched. He offered an arm to each, and cocked an eyebrow at Heris. "You settled it, I gather?"

"She was never a military officer, Petris," Cecelia said with a sweet smile. "She was born to be a pirate. Look at her."

"I'll do more than look," Petris said into Heris's ear. "Later . . ."

But the tumult of the others interrupted whatever Heris might have said. Already the tall rooms rang with many voices, and more and more men and women in their formal best came down the stairs. Bunny, looking as foolish tonight as he had at first, chatted with one group after another. Then he caught sight of Cecelia, and came over without obvious haste.

"So glad you could stay for the Ball," he said, including Petris in the greeting with a nod. "We may have a slight inconvenience. . . ."

"Oh?" Cecelia's brows raised.

"Mr. Smith. He's eluded the Minister's manservant again."

Again? Heris stared; she hadn't realized Mr. Smith had been loose before.

"Declared he wasn't going to be sent home like a naughty schoolboy, in an old lady's yacht with a battleaxe for a captain." Bunny's mouth smiled, as if they discussed the day's run, but his eyes were cold and angry. "As you know, the Minister had refused to let me place him under a proper guard . . . but as the Minister does not know, I put a tracer-tag on him. He dashed off to the woods, silly twit. Captain Sigind will bring him in, but I'd like to sedate him and send him up in a shuttle right away, if you don't mind. I can isolate him in the Station sickbay —"

Cecelia's expression hardened. "You've got every right to lock him in your local jail. On bread and water. Stupid boy!"

"Since there's a standing watch aboard, milady," Heris said, "we can have him aboard your yacht straight from the shuttle. Fewer eyes to see, fewer mouths to talk."

"Fine. Do it." Cecelia looked angrier than before; Heris couldn't understand why. Then she changed expression, to astonishment and relief. Heris looked over and saw Ronnie, George, Bubbles, and Raffa. With them was a heavier man whose resemblance to George lay more in manner than in feature. Bunny turned, and waved them over.

"Good to see you up and about," he said. And to the older man, "And you, of course, Ser Mahoney."

"I have no quarrel with you, Bunny," the older man said. "Don't go formal on me, or I'll have to start wondering if I should."

"All right, Kevil. Just so you know I took this very seriously indeed."

"I can see George, and I know what happened; that tells me you took it seriously. Your lovely daughter was in

it too, I understand." He patted Bubbles on the shoulder;
Heris was surprised at the expression on the girl's face.
She had changed, Heris thought, in some way that none
of them yet knew — perhaps not even the girl herself.
"And of course Cece's nephew. Those two have never
been in trouble alone, or out of it together." Kevil
Mahoney had a trained voice that could carry conflicting
messages with ease; Heris watched both George and
Ronnie flush, then subside without saying a word. He
leaned closer to Bunny, and let that voice carry another
weight of meaning with little volume. "And Mr. Smith?
How is that estimable young man?"

"He will go home shortly," Bunny said. His eyelids lowered. "Transportation has already been arranged."

"Ah. Well, to be honest, Mr. Smith's travel arrangements
do not concern me, at least not this evening. I'm simply
delighted to be here for the festive occasion, with both lads
out of the hospital and able to enjoy it." Kevil Mahoney
smiled, bowed slightly, and walked off, leaving the young
people behind. They heard him call out to someone he
knew, and then he had disappeared in the crowd.

"I promised," George said, looking anxious, "but did
my father?"

"Enough," Bunny said. "It's almost time for the dinner,
and I will not have it ruined by speculation. Captain Serrano, if I might have the honor of your company?"

Heris had not expected this. She glanced at Cecelia,
who after all ranked her in every conceivable way these
people calculated rank, but Cecelia now looked more
relaxed, and simply smiled and nodded. Petris, after one
startled look, offered his arm to Cecelia, who accepted it
with another smile.

Heris took Bunny's arm and hoped she did not look as
confused as she felt. He led her through the crowd, and
she could hear the subdued murmurs that must be comments on this unusual occurrence. Just as they reached
the entrance to the dining room, a fanfare rang out. Heris
jumped, and Bunny chuckled. Under cover of the music,
he murmured, "Didn't mean to alarm you, Captain, but
this is traditional."

His wife, Heris noted, was standing with Buttons. As they made their way into the dining room, she realized that the participants in the recent adventures had been provided with partners that justified their being seated at the head table. Bunny's wife with Buttons, and George with Bubbles, and Ronnie with an elderly lady, and Raffa with an elderly man of the same vintage.

"That's my aunt Trema," Bunny said, "and my wife's uncle. They're both quite deaf," Bunny said, "and they've refused implants. They love coming to a couple of Hunt Dinners a year; they sit together at the ball afterwards and write each other saucy notes on their compads. Eccentric, but harmless." Petris, with Lady Cecelia, certainly had a place at the family table. George's father sat at the far end, with another elderly relation on one side, and one of the gawky cousins on the other.

"You see the advantages," Bunny went on, with a slight smile, "of a reputation for eccentricity and archaicisms?"

"Indeed yes," Heris said. She looked down the long dining hall, to the trumpeters in their beribboned tunics who were ready to lead in the feast. Most of the guests had found their places, but Bunny waited until even the clumsy soul who overturned his chair had safely reseated himself. Then he nodded at the trumpeters, who lifted their instruments once more.

To the blare of trumpets and the shrill wailing of pipes, the feast came in. Cecelia reached around Petris to say, "It's about as authentic as the foxes, but it's fun." Bunny winked at her, and Heris began to relax. It could be worse . . . would have been worse, if Cecelia hadn't told her, if they hadn't told Bunny, if she and Cecelia both had not been good shots. They could all have been dead.

She pulled her mind away from that with an effort, and made herself enjoy the spectacle. Serving trays loaded with exotic foods whose origin she couldn't even guess. Servants in colorful livery. And the music. The food, when she tasted it, drove the last grim thought from her mind.

"I hadn't had a chance to thank you," Bunny said, somewhere between the soup and fish. "It's been hectic since you got back."

"I didn't realize Mr. Smith had been giving trouble," Heris said.

"Mmm. Although that's not the reason I asked you to come in with me, it may prove convenient to have you here when he's found. If you're sure the transfer to Lady Cecelia's yacht poses no problem."

"Not if I have a direct line up."

"Of course. My debt to you continues to grow. I don't know if you actually enjoyed the sport, but please consider yourself welcome here anytime." Under the pleasant tone, the calm expression, Heris sensed tension and even savagery. They ate in silence for some minutes, as the fish course came and went, and slices of roast appeared. Bunny sighed, and resumed as if he had not paused. "Bubbles — says she wants to talk to you."

"To me?"

"An experience like that would change anyone; I understand. But she's been the youngest, the wildest — so of course her change had to be greater."

Heris eyed her host. "Did she tell you about it?"

"Some. Not all. She thinks you — because you were military — will understand her better."

Heris could think of nothing socially acceptable to say. She could imagine the sort of thing Bubbles would think she could understand — and she did understand, but not in the way Bubbles would want. Nor did she wish to interfere in this family, especially not now. "She's almost certainly wrong about that," Heris said. "But of course I'll listen to her."

"I must admit," he went on, cutting a slice of roast into matching slivers, "that before I knew you better, you would not have been my choice of confidante for my daughter."

"The military woman?" Heris asked, lightly.

"Not exactly. The Serrano Admiralty is well known . . ." His voice trailed away, and his gaze slid sideways to meet hers. Heris was surprised, and probably looked it.

"My family? They think *I'm* the disgrace — why should you object to them?"

"I prefer you," Bunny said, and did not answer the rest

of the question. He pushed the slivers of meat aside. Something bleeped, beside his plate, and he picked up a silvery button and clipped it to his ear. Moments later, his jaw bunched. Heris tried not to stare, and made inroads on her dinner. Beside her, Petris was chatting with Cecelia, almost pointedly ignoring her. Cecelia winked past him — so she had explained. Or so Heris hoped.

Bunny touched her wrist lightly, and she turned back to him. "We may have a problem," he said. "Mr. Smith divested himself of the tagger. Captain Sigind found it, but not the . . . Mr. Smith. He's already sealed the flitter hangars and other sources of transport, but Mr. Smith is a skilled rider."

Heris spoke before her tact caught up with her tongue: "We are not going out looking for that scamp on horseback in the dark!"

"No. You're right, we aren't. The militia are, and if he founders that mare he stole, I will have his hide on my wall. I don't know how a Registered Embryo could end up this stupid."

"He'll come here," Heris said softly, thinking it through. "He wants in on the fun, that's all. There's a party; he wants to play. He's like Ronnie was before. He'll think of a disguise, or something from —"

A crash from outside the hall interrupted, followed by the obvious clattering of hoofs on a hard floor. Before anyone could get up to investigate, someone outside flung the doors open. There stood a masked man in a costume more bizarre than any in the room. Puffed breeches under a loud tartan kilt, white hose, buckled shoes, a doublet, a wide-sleeved shirt, a short cape, and a curious pile of velvet and feathers on his head: it looked as if he had ransacked a costume shop. He held the reins of a skittish horse, and brandished a sword. Someone whooped nervously; Bunny sat rigid. From the far end of the table, the elderly lady Ronnie had partnered stood up abruptly.

"Now this is ridiculous. Disgraceful mixing of periods. Not one of these young people has any respect for historical reproduction. Imagine wearing a kilt over breeches! Just what century does he think he is, anyway?" She had the loud, off-pitch voice of someone who has not heard herself speak for years. She glared at Bunny. "If this is your surprise, young Branthcome, it is singularly unamusing."

For once Bunny had nothing to say. Heris stared at the masked man with instant certainty. No one else on the planet would do something like this. Were those moustaches sticking out from behind the mask? And what should she do? They had to capture him, but also conceal him. Some of the people here must have met the prince face to face. Could she and Petris subdue him without displacing his mask? She caught a glimpse of a servant behind the horse, trying to edge nearer, but the frightened animal plunged and kicked, and the servant retreated.

"It is traditional, I believe, to have a masked stranger make away with a beautiful woman at affairs like this. . . ." The man's voice certainly matched that of Mr. Smith. Heris looked around the room. The Crown Minister had turned white, but most people were amused, interested . . . already the hum of conversation had returned. The servant Heris had first seen came in sight again; the masked man turned and handed him the reins. "Here — hold my mount, please." Wide-eyed, the servant did so. Then the masked man strode into the dining hall, up the length to the family's table, and grabbed Raffaele firmly by one wrist. With a bow to Ronnie, he said, "You stole a singer from me; I but return the compliment —"

"Imposter!" Ronnie leapt to his feet and yanked the mask from the man's face and the sword from his hand. Heris heard the startled gasps. Mr. Smith, without a doubt. But Ronnie's furious stare down the table denied it. "You would have us *think* you're the prince, because everyone knows I quarrelled with the prince . . . but you're only a common mechanic."

"Let go of my arm," Raffaele said, in the tone she would have used to a social inferior. Mr. Smith complied, looking confused.

"But I *am* the prince —"

"You're a . . . a *mole*," Ronnie said. Raffaele rubbed her

wrist and looked away, pointedly ignoring the intruder. Heris suddenly realized where Ronnie was going with this, and could hardly believe he had thought so fast. She waited for the cue she was sure he would give. "Don't think I didn't see you ogling Raffa on my aunt's yacht. Just because you're fair-haired and tall, just because you know how to use makeup, you thought you could pass yourself off as the prince." He shook the man's shoulder. "Look at you! You're in a roomful of people who know the prince — didn't you think of that? Did you really expect to fool people by covering your face? Did you hear what Lord Thornbuckle's aunt said? We know how to dress in period costumes — this mess you have on is a — a travesty. Pitiful." He looked down the table at Heris. "I must complain, Captain Serrano, about the actions of your crewman."

Heris stood smoothly. "You're quite right. I regret that I didn't recognize him in his disguise, but he is only the junior environmental tech, and I've never seen him in anything but a shipsuit. I take full responsibility. Petris —" Petris stood, as well. "We'll make sure this — individual —" She could not think of a name to give him. Mr. Smith was too dangerous now. "— doesn't intrude again, and I daresay his working papers will be cancelled permanently."

"But I *am* — and this was all I could find —"

"Silence." Bunny had found his voice at last; when he chose to be loud, he could be heard across an open field in a blowing wind. Here it silenced everyone, even the furtive whisperers in the corners. "I insist that my militia escort this individual to the shuttleport, and all the way into the custody of your yacht, Lady Cecelia. I believe I am correct in saying there may be charges beyond my jurisdiction, involving impersonation of a member of the Royal Family —?" He inclined his head to Kevil Mahoney, who nodded. "Then I would not have him on this planet one hour longer than necessary. Captain Serrano, if you will inform your standing watch?"

"With pleasure."

Still protesting, but uselessly, Mr. Smith found himself overpowered and dragged away by militia, while Heris called the yacht and arranged for his confinement.

Ronnie still stood at the end of the table, and when the room quieted, he looked to Bunny for permission to speak. Bunny nodded.

Ronnie rubbed his nose a moment, until he had everyone's attention. "Most of you know that I was exiled for a year after the prince and I had a dispute. Some of you know more. But what you may not know is how I could be so sure the prince had not come here in some disguise or other. When I knew where my aunt was bringing me, I worried about that myself, and looked it up. The prince was posted to the Royal Aero-Space Service depot on Naverrn —" Ronnie was looking at the Crown Minister, who, Heris noted, suddenly looked very alert. "I'm sure any of you can check that posting, and confirm it. And this man — I don't even know his name — caught my eye on the yacht because he did somewhat resemble the prince, and he was sneaking around Raffaele."

"But are you sure it wasn't the prince *pretending* to be an environmental tech?" asked a woman near one corner.

"Of course it wasn't," Ronnie said. "We had both sworn an oath to duel if we saw each other within the next year — do you think *both* of us would be coward enough to ignore that? That — that *person* didn't even know how to use a sword." He looked angry; Raffa patted his hand, and he sat down again.

Heris could almost hear the collective lurch with which everyone tried to return to the mood of a Hunt Dinner and Ball and ignore the interruption, as Bunny signalled and the servants brought in another course.

George leaned against the mirrored wall of the ballroom feeling sulky again. Ronnie and Raffa hardly seemed to notice the music, but flowed with it like leaves on a stream. Captain Serrano and Petris . . . he would like to have made a jest of them, but could not. They had gone through so much; they deserved their obvious happiness. If only Bubbles had not turned against him . . . they could have made another good match, he was sure. He liked her well enough, now that Raffa had turned to Ronnie. Blondes set off his own dark handsomeness.

It was unfair. He and the prince alone, out of all that crowd, could not enjoy the party. And while he was luckier than the prince, in being here and not under guard somewhere, he had no one to share his evening. He watched the whirling dancers idly for awhile, then stared. His father. His father and Ronnie's aunt. Talking, laughing, obviously enjoying each other. . . . They danced by, and Lady Cecelia winked at him. His father, and that old . . . although she wasn't all that bad, really. She danced remarkably well, in fact. He just didn't want her as a stepmother, or aunt, or whatever she and his father might have in mind. The two of them together were definitely too smart for him; he and Ronnie would never enjoy more pranks. He turned away, ready to take a long walk somewhere, and almost fell over the girl coming his way. Her eyes widened. "You're — you're George Starbridge Mahoney, aren't you? Kevil Mahoney's son?" He knew what to do with that kind of look, and drew himself up.

"Yes," he said. "I am."

"Somebody told me your nickname was Odious, but I don't believe it. I think you're nice." She had hazel eyes and fluffy hair of a red-brown shade he couldn't have put a name to. Something about her made him feel protective, something more than the slender wrists and hands, he was sure, or the somewhat pointy face. "You don't know me," she said, almost timidly. "I'm just one of the cousins; you've seen me out hunting, but usually covered with mud."

"I should have seen beneath it," he said gallantly. He liked being gallant. "Would you care to dance?" He led her onto the floor.

"I love Hunt Balls," the girl said. They whirled around; she danced as lightly as a fox over a fence on its way to take a chicken from the coop. George drew back a moment, wondering. Was he the hunter, or was she? It didn't matter, he decided; she couldn't be that certain herself.

"So do I," he said, and took her past his father and Ronnie's aunt, enjoying their reaction. "So do I."

THE END

SPORTING CHANCE

Elizabeth Moon

'Pure satisfaction from cover to cover'
Anne McCaffrey

Heris Serrano thought she would simply be marking
time captaining a rich old woman's interstellar yacht.
But Cecelia de Marktos is not the ageing dilettante
Heris expected. She's a leading member of one of the
galaxy's most influential families, and she takes her
responsibilities very seriously indeed.

In an attempt to avoid a royal scandal, Cecelia has
volunteered herself and her yacht to return her nephew
Prince Gerel – first in line to the throne – home to his
worried parents. Cecelia remembers her nephew as a
rather bright young man. But as the voyage proceeds,
the Prince becomes less and less like himself, and
Cecelia begins to suspect foul play. Someone is
poisoning the heir to the throne, and once again Heris
finds herself in the midst of a deadly mystery.

Join the cast of *Hunting Party* for another fast-paced
science fiction adventure from the author of the
acclaimed Deed of Paksenarrion fantasy sequence.

<u>WINNING COLOURS</u>

Elizabeth Moon

'Once again Elizabeth Moon has crafted a fine, rousing piece of space opera . . . *Winning Colours* is a prize worth taking home' *Starlog*

Heris Serrano thought her life was over when a treacherous superior officer forced her to resign from the Regular Space Service. But captaining a rich old woman's interstellar yacht has proved more exciting – and fulfilling – than she could ever have imagined.

Heris has at last been offered a chance for vindication and reinstatement in her beloved Fleet – and reconciliation with the family she thought had abandoned her. But it means standing alone against the military might of the Benignity, an interstellar criminal cartel more colloquially known as the Compassionate Hand. With only a few small ships and the space yacht *Sweet Delight*, she must become the galaxy's first line of defence and stop a vastly superior invading fleet dead in its tracks . . .

Join the cast of *Hunting Party* and *Sporting Chance* on another action-packed space adventure from the author of the acclaimed Deed of Paksenarrion fantasy sequence.

SHEEPFARMER'S DAUGHTER

The Deed of Paksenarrion Book I

Elizabeth Moon

Paksenarrion – Paks for short – is somebody special.
She knows it, even if nobody else does yet. No way will
she follow her father's orders to marry the pig farmer
down the road. She's off to join the army, even if it
means she can never see her family again.

And so her adventure begins . . . the adventure that
transforms her into a hero remembered in songs,
chosen by the gods to restore a lost ruler to his throne.

This is her tale as she lived it.

'Brilliant. Superbly cast with protagonists and
supporting characters that will enchant the reader'
Bookwatch

And don't miss:
Divided Allegiance, The Deed of Paksenarrion Book 2
Oath of Gold, The Deed of Paksenarrion Book 3
Available from Orbit

SASSINAK

Anne McCaffrey and Elizabeth Moon

Volume One of THE PLANET PIRATES

Sassinak was twelve when the raiders came. Old
enough to be used, young enough to be broken – or so
they thought. But they reckoned without the girl's will,
forged into a steely resolve to avenge herself on the
pirates who had killed her parents and friends.

When the chance comes to escape, Sassinak grabs it,
thanks to the help of a captured Fleet crewman.
Returned to the Federation of Sentient Planets, she
initiates her revenge by joining Fleet as a raw recruit
and surprising everyone by her rapid rise to senior rank.
Then her vengeance begins in earnest.

Anne McCaffrey and Elizabeth Moon have woven
a story worthy of Robert A. Heinlein in its
tough-mindedness, reminiscent of Larry Niven and
David Brin in its description of human and alien
races coming together both as friends and enemies.

Also by Anne McCaffrey in
THE PLANET PIRATES SERIES

Volume Two:
THE DEATH OF SLEEP (with Jody Lynn Nye)

Volume Three:
GENERATION WARRIORS (with Elizabeth Moon)

Available from Orbit

DINOSAUR PLANET

Anne McCaffrey

On Earth they had died out seventy million years ago.
But on Ireta they ruled in all their bizarre splendour.
Relics from a forgotten age, the dinosaurs roamed a
planet as strange as any in the galaxy.

The members of the expedition sent to explore this new
world soon find themselves trapped, and when their
relief ship disappears the situation goes from
bad to worse.

For the heavyworlders – half the expedition's personnel
– have reverted to type, and systematically begin to
hunt down their colleagues. Only the frozen sleep of
cryogenics offers an escape. But for how long?

DINOSAUR PLANET
A magnificent feat of the imagination from the Hugo
and Nebula award-winning author of the Pern books.

SURVIVORS

Dinosaur Planet II

Anne McCaffrey

To escape extermination by their heavyworld
colleagues, Kai, Varian and their companions sought
refuge in the suspended animation of cryogenic sleep.
Now it is time for the survivors to emerge from
their hibernation.

Ireta, the Dinosaur Planet, is much changed. The
heavyworlders have regressed to primitive barbarity.
Most of the necessary life-support equipment has
malfunctioned or disappeared. And the very face
of Ireta has altered.

But help is at hand: a rescue ship is on its way. Even as
hope begins to spring, however, new problems arise.
What are the motives of the mysterious Theks?
Why are the intelligent Giffs – pterodactyls locked in
an evolutionary blind alley – acting so strangely?
Above all, what possibly could be the cause of the
mindless hostility of the heavyworlders?

MID-FLINX

Alan Dean Foster

Flinx: born in controversy as the product of illegal genetic experiments. Flinx: raised an orphan in the streets of Draller on the planet Moth. Flinx: the extraordinary young man with a rare flying snake for a companion, always the inadvertent centre of danger and galactic intrigue.

Even in the backwater worlds of the Commonwealth, Flinx finds himself in trouble, as a rich local bully takes an unwelcome interest in the minidrag Pip. Fleeing into space, Flinx arrives on the strange planet of Midworld, where an immense kilometre-deep jungle is home to an incredible array of plant and animal life, all of it unknown and all of it deadly. It soon becomes apparent that his hiding place is rather more perilous than he bargained for . . .

THE HOWLING STONES

Alan Dean Foster

The newly discovered planet of Senisran is a veritable paradise, its oceans dotted with thousands of lush islands containing vast deposits of rare-earths and minerals. But Senisran is also the Humanx Commonwealth's problem child, for each island is inhabited by a different tribe of aboriginal natives. Each has to be negotiated with separately for mining rights – and the Commonwealth is locked in a race against the vicious AAnn Empire to secure those rights.

The clans of the Parramat Archipelago on Senisran are resisting entreaties by the Commonwealth and AAnn alike. But Pulickel Tomochelor, xenologist and first-contact specialist, is confident of his ability to handle the negotiations.

What Pulickel hasn't counted on is the secret of Parramat: the strange green stones that the natives use to bless crops, ensure plentiful fishing, heal the injured and ill, and control the weather. For within those stones lies an awesome technology the origin of which is lost in time – a technology that has to be kept from the AAnn at any cost.

Set in the amazing world of the Humanx Commonwealth, *The Howling Stones* is an incredible adventure from one of the most exciting storytellers in science fiction.

THE SEAFORT SAGA

by David Feintuch

Look out for these magnificent adventures:

Midshipman's
HOPE

A hideous accident kills the senior officers of
UNS *Hibernia* – leaving a terrified young officer in command of a
damaged ship with no chance of rescue or reinforcement . . .

Challenger's
HOPE

An alien attack and an admiral's betrayal leave a wounded
Commander Nicholas Seafort stranded aboard a doomed ship of
arrogant colonists and violent street children . . .

Prisoner's
HOPE

To save the world, Nicholas Seafort must forsake his vows – and
commit an unthinkable, suicidal act of high treason . . .

Fisherman's
HOPE

Alone at the centre of a cosmic apocalypse, Nick Seafort
faces his final battle . . .

Voices of
HOPE

For Nicholas Seafort, the race to save mankind from destroying
itself has become personal – for to save his son, he must
save the world . . .

THE SEAFORT SAGA

The science fiction adventure of a lifetime.

Published by Orbit

ENDER'S GAME

Orson Scott Card

When humanity is under threat from an alien race, Ender Wiggin, at the age of six, leaves his family on Earth to journey to the Belt. There he enters Battle School, where his life is strictly disciplined by mind games and computer mock-battles fought in deadly earnest. Instinct, compassion and genius make Ender unequalled. But while he trains, the invasion approaches fast. And Ender will be pushed to the limits of endurance, for his is a unique destiny . . .

Orson Scott Card's Ender saga has changed the face of science fiction. *Ender's Game, Speaker for the Dead* and *Xenocide* are towering novels – classic science fiction of the highest order.

Orbit titles available by post:

☐ Sheepfarmer's Daughter	Elizabeth Moon	£5.99
☐ Divided Allegiance	Elizabeth Moon	£6.99
☐ Oath of Gold	Elizabeth Moon	£6.99
☐ Sassinak	Anne McCaffrey/Elizabeth Moon	£5.99
☐ Dinosaur Planet	Anne McCaffrey	£5.99
☐ Survivors	Anne McCaffrey	£5.99
☐ Mid-Flinx	Alan Dean Foster	£5.99
☐ The Howling Stones	Alan Dean Foster	£5.99
☐ Midshipman's Hope	David Feintuch	£5.99
☐ Ender's Game	Orson Scott Card	£5.99

The prices shown above are correct at time of going to press. However, the publishers reserve the right to increase prices on covers from those previously advertised, without further notice.

orbit

ORBIT BOOKS
Cash Sales Department, P.O. Box 11, Falmouth, Cornwall, TR10 9EN
Tel: +44(0) 1326 569777. Fax +44 (0) 1326 569555
Email: books@barni.avel.co.uk

POST and PACKAGING:
Payments can be made as follows: cheque, postal order (payable to Orbit Books) or by credit cards. Do not send cash or currency.

U.K. Orders under £10	£1.50
U.K. Orders over £10	FREE OF CHARGE
E.E.C. & Overseas	25% of order value

Name (Block Letters) _____

Address _____

_____

Post/zip code: _____

☐ Please keep me in touch with future Orbit publications

☐ I enclose my remittance £_____

☐ I wish to pay by Visa/Access/Mastercard/Eurocard

☐☐☐☐☐☐☐☐☐☐☐☐☐☐☐☐☐☐   Card Expiry Date

_____